10/3/12

To Jonh

Enjoy the story

Regards,

Dave Jauller

The Oyster Navy

A Novel

By

David Faulkner

Edited by: Paul Bendel-Simso

Map Art by: Nicole Wright & Carolyn Faulkner

Cover Art by: Todd Engel

Published by: Pipe Creek Press
www.pipecreekpress.com

Distributed by: BookLocker.com, Inc.

The Oyster Navy

For my family with love.

Acknowledgements:

My thanks to Lt. Gregory L. Bartles—Maryland Department of Natural Resources Police.

Preface

At the end of the American Civil War, the world's growing appetite for oysters attracted hordes of rapacious oystermen to the Chesapeake Bay. By that time, the state of Maryland had enacted laws that limited oyster harvesting in the Bay to state residents; required oystermen to be licensed, and delineated restricted harvesting areas.

Competition for the oyster, or "white gold", grew intense inciting deadly confrontations between watermen, and fostering a reckless disregard for these laws. Poaching of shallow water oyster beds reserved by law for tongers, (independent watermen usually operating one and two man crews) was common. Larger oyster dredge boats, often manned by ruthless captains and unsavory crews, (known colloquially as drudgers) waged a relentless offensive against the tongers in an effort to drive them from the rich shallow water "oyster rocks."

In 1868, Maryland created a state naval enforcement arm designed to quell the lawlessness and bring law and order to the Chesapeake Bay. This force, dubbed The Oyster Navy, often clashed with legitimate oystermen angered by the intrusion of the state into their livelihood, and frequently engaged in violent encounters with fleets of well-armed drudgers.

Honga River
Eastern Shore of Maryland
December 8, 1868

BOOM!

BOOM!

BOOM!

"Is that them, Mister Jacoby?"

"Aye, Captain. Marrok Blanchard and his boys with their morning salute. Sort of a warning to announce they are headin' out for a day of plunderin'. Telling everyone to get out of their way."

Haynie McKenna commanded the *Emma Dunn*, a screw steamer leased to the fledgling Maryland Oyster Navy. He peered across the ship's rail into a fog stacked thick as sodden cotton over the foredeck.

"They must be damn fools to be under sail in this weather."

"Aye. That'd be them, sir."

"Our orders are very clear: Find the Blanchards and arrest 'em, or sink 'em. They'd have to ram us before we could find them in this fog. We can't see our own rigging."

Haynie turned to the mate. "We need a plan."

"Aye, Captain, we'll need a good one. The Blanchards ain't ones to give up. They got cannon and we ain't gonna sink 'em with them old muskets and pistols stored below."

Haynie nodded. "We'll worry about that after we catch them poaching a rock."

Haynie McKenna, the deputy commander of the Maryland Oyster Navy, was being thrust into a battle not to his liking.

In August, he had accepted an appointment as second in command of Maryland's incipient seagoing law enforcement agency and moved his family from Crisfield, on Maryland's Eastern Shore, to Annapolis the state capital.

The Proceedings and Acts of The Maryland General Assembly for 1868 detailed powers of the State Oyster Police popularly called the

Oyster Navy. To the men of this naval police force, knowledge of the laws regulating watermen on the Chesapeake Bay was fundamental.

Haynie and Hunter Davidson, the Oyster Navy's newly appointed commander, spent their first weeks together laboring to understand the enforcement powers they were to assume. Huddled for endless hours in an ill-lit, cramped room in the lower reaches of a state office building, they struggled to understand the wording of the legislative acts.

Haynie looked across the stack of bound documents and grunted.

"They gave us the power to shoot poachers when we have to," he said. "But they didn't give us much to shoot with."

Hunter Davidson removed his spectacles and rubbed his eyes.

"We'll keep that in mind when we hire officers," he said. "A man with a side-arm is more valuable than a man without one and a man with a musket or rifle is the most valuable."

Haynie laughed, "Maybe we'll get lucky and find somebody who brought a cannon home from the war."

Davidson got up, shook out the cramps, and edged his way between the desk and the wall. Both men were forced to a stooped posture when moving about the windowless room.

"That's not too far-fetched," Davidson said. "No doubt there are hundreds, maybe thousands, of cannon abandoned over the countryside, just rusting away. I have folks scouring both sides of the Potomac looking for any farmer who'd be happy to have such an eyesore toted off his land."

Davidson grew pensive, his tone grim.

"Sufficient arms will be hard to come by because some in the assembly are worried they have created a force of seagoing vigilantes. I'm issuing a strict protocol covering the use of firearms aboard our ships. For one thing, all weapons will be stored under lock and key. The captain is the sole authority to issue arms to the ship's crew."

Haynie agreed. "We have to be careful that we don't get a name for shooting without good cause. Some oystermen think nothing of shooting it out with each other over a rich bed. The question remains; will they be as quick to fire on law officers doing their duty? It's all uncharted waters; we'll have to sail among them before we know for certain."

"For now," Davidson replied, "all of our sailing has to be done aboard the *Kent* or the *Emma Dunn*." He stopped to make a quick note. "I'm going up to Baltimore Towne Thursday and see what's holding up delivery of the *Leila*. She was to be commissioned months ago. 'Spect I'll need to get coarse with that builder."

Haynie nodded. "Even when the Leila is commissioned, we'll still have trouble covering all the bay waters, rivers, coves and inlets. Drudge boats are going to be our biggest problem. It's not likely one or two tongers in a log canoe will fight us and they won't be able to outrun us. But when we run up against a big drudge boat with a crew of armed rascals..."

Davidson lifted a sheaf of bound papers, held it at arm's length before releasing it heavily onto the desk. "The legislation creating the Oyster Navy was passed by a narrow margin and some delegates would be happy to give our budget to their cronies in other departments. We have near as many enemies in Annapolis as we will have on the bay; and both are going to give us a fight."

Hunter Davidson sported a full head of black hair, parted on the left and heavily oiled. Bushy side-whiskers joined a full mustache at the corners of his mouth. Thick brows crowned dark, vigilant eyes.

He scratched at his facial hair. "One thing we have going for us," he said, "The Oyster Navy has the ability to turn a profit, which most other state agencies don't."

"You mean by bringing in more in fines than our budget."

Davidson nodded. "And seizures. The law says we can bring in a boat, the catch and gear, along with the crew. If the captain is found guilty, the court can sell his boat and gear; the money goes into the state Treasury along with the fine. It is only fitting the brigands should pay our keep. If we account for enough revenue the assembly will be hard-pressed not to increase our budget next year."

Haynie shook his head. "I never thought it would be so troublesome to do the right thing. We will make it work. I'll fight the sea battles, if you fight those on land. And," he grinned, "I'll have the best of it. It's been my experience that a waterman will let you know, right up front, where you stand with him. But, you can never be certain with a politician."

Davidson nodded. "Don't turn your back on either one."

During the weeks that the two men worked in close confinement, the fact that they fought on opposing sides during the recent war was never an issue.

Hunter Davidson graduated from the U.S. Naval Academy in 1847, resigning his commission in 1861 to accept the rank of lieutenant commander in the Confederate Navy. Following the war, he returned to Maryland and worked as a journal clerk for the Maryland Senate.

Haynie McKenna enlisted in the 1st East Virginia Loyal Volunteers and spent the war marching across Maryland and Virginia. Though well read, with intelligence equal to any of his peers, he failed to rise above the rank of corporal.

Following the war, he returned home, angst-driven and unsettled; still haunted by his father's murder on the bay, fourteen years earlier. His anger was focused on his father's unknown killers; and the state of Maryland, which in 1853 had no lawmen to pursue outlaws who menaced the bay waters and shore towns.

For years, Tench McKenna scraped out a living tonging oysters in the creek beds and shallow waters along Maryland's Eastern Shore. He worked the oyster beds alone in a log canoe he fashioned from a loblolly pine tree and named *Miss Letty* for Haynie's mother. The hours were long and the work arduous, but he chose working alone, to the whimsy and prattle that came with having someone else on board the small boat.

He had been shot and killed while tonging a bed in Tangier Sound at the Maryland-Virginia state line. Haynie was twelve years old and in his second year at the Chesapeake Academy, on the outskirts of Baltimore Towne, when he learned of his father's murder.

"Tench was a good man," some said, "likely cut down by some Virginia poachers, or a drudge boat crew ravaging the bed."

Others believed Tench McKenna may have drifted into Virginia waters, making him the poacher.

The death of a lone tonger was of little concern to anyone outside of the man's family. Tench's family consisted of his wife, Lettie, and two sons, Haynie and Caleb.

Haynie's older sister Mattie had married in haste and move to Baltimore Towne a few years before her father's killing.

"I am escaping this dreadful place," Mattie had confided to Haynie. "Get out if you can."

She had returned for Tench's funeral and then quickly boarded the next packet off the island.

"She fled," Lettie McKenna would say of her daughter.

Tench McKenna was a stubborn man, determined that his sons should not endure the perils of a waterman's existence. He understood that a good education was necessary if Haynie and Caleb were to have a better life. Schooling on Smith Island was sporadic at best, so Tench and Lettie sacrificed to send Haynie to a proper school at the edge of Baltimore Towne.

"What are we going to do about Caleb?" Lettie asked. "We're scrimping to send Haynie."

Tench had responded with a shrug. "Caleb's young. We have time. God will see to it, He always does."

Haynie knew that he could not return to the academy following his father's funeral. Even if money were not an issue, he was needed on the island. After all, he was the man of the house.

A chill breeze rose out of the northeast, stirring the fog bank, which began its retreat across the *Emma Dunn's* foredeck. Haynie shrugged deeper into his greatcoat and moved away from the railing.

"Let's see the charts, Mister Jacoby."

"Aye captain." The mate followed Haynie amidships and unfurled a map of the Chesapeake Bay across a hatch cover.

Haynie pressed a forefinger on a dot marked Lower Hooper Island at the mouth of the Honga River, then pushed it across the river toward the land mass marked Dorchester County; stopping just offshore at Fox Creek.

"We're told the Blanchards come out of Fox Creek."

Haynie drew his finger back to Lower Hooper's Island, the *Emma Dunn's* present position.

"It's impossible to guess where they're headed on a given day. Around Pack's Head into Fishing Bay, or south to Tangier Sound. Either way, it looks like they'd be sailing past us, here."

The mate leaned forward and removed a glove. "If I may, captain," he said, pointing a stubby finger at the map. Years before, that finger had been mashed to the first joint by an anchor chain. Now, the mangled tip quivered over the chart as Jacoby spoke.

"If you recollect sir, while it appears that the Honga is separated from the bay by a long point of land, this stretch is really three islands; Upper Hooper, Middle Hooper and Lower Hooper, where we are. They could head up river and duck out between islands. If they're headed out for a day of mischief, they could go in any direction."

Haynie peered at the fog bank, still dense as fresh-poured concrete beyond the starboard rail.

"If the fog lifted and we saw a boat, we'd have to make certain it was the Blanchards. Even using a glass, we'd be close enough they could just as easy see the *Emma Dunn*."

"We could strike the flag. There's a chance they wouldn't know it was us, 'til it was too late."

"It's likely *Emma Dunn's* the only screw steamer in these waters. We would have to trail their wake to catch 'em in an act. It is doubtful they'd lead us direct to where they were going to plunder."

Jacoby shrugged.

Haynie said, "They'd be damn brazen to plunder while we watched."

"That'd be them, sir. But from what I heard, it's likely that most times they don't have a set place. They sail along until they come upon easy pickin's."

Haynie shook his head. "It's one thing for us to cruise the bay until we come upon poachers or buccaneers. It is quite another matter to find and track a particular boat hoping to catch them in the act."

The mate, whose stocky frame was ideal for maneuvering along a deck in the roughest of seas, now shifted uneasily and looked up at his captain.

"What you expect we're to do about the Blanchards, sir?"

Haynie headed aft toward the galley. "First," he said over his shoulder, "we're going to be smart enough to sit inside drinking hot coffee while we talk about it."

The mate smiled and grabbed up the charts. "Sounds like the beginning of an excellent plan, sir."

Inside the cabin, Haynie shed his greatcoat, hung it on a wall peg and grabbed a tin cup.

Skillets, the ship's cook, shook his head resisting an impulse to snatch up the battered coffee pot and fill the captain's cup. Other captains with whom he sailed demanded to be served. Whether a cup of coffee or a full meal, such men seized every opportunity to set themselves apart from the crew. Many brought their own china and flatware aboard, insisting Skillets keep their service separate from the crew's tin ware. Certain captains became enraged if their dinnerware was washed in the same tepid water as that of the crew's.

The first day out of port Haynie had waved away the cook's attempt to serve him. "Thanks, Skillets," he said, "I'll dish my own, as will all the crew. You have enough to do without coddling me."

Haynie filled his cup, nodded to Skillets and sat at the table. While waiting for the mate, he reflected on how little he knew about the other men aboard the *Emma Dunn*. How would they behave under gunfire? Which of them could he rely on when bullets started hitting the deck around them? Was there a traitor in his crew? He resolved to find a billet for Gerhard and persuade him to come aboard.

For now, circumstances compelled him to place his trust in *some* members of this crew. His instincts told him that Jacoby and Skillets were logical choices for that trust.

The case for the first mate was uncomplicated. Nathan Jacoby had served with Hunter Davidson aboard the ironclad Confederate ship, the *CSS Virginia*. Haynie trusted Commander Davidson, therefore he trusted Jacoby. Moreover, he had taken a liking to the mate.

Life aboard an oyster boat or small freighter was grueling, dreary and, above all, dangerous. Unless ashore, drinking in a tavern, crewmen were invariably sullen and morose. Jacoby was an exception, ever cheerful with a wide smile atop his bandy-legged swagger.

As for the cook, Haynie judged his age at near 50. From accounts, Skillets had spent years in the galleys of passenger ships and freighters plying the world's seas. Unlikely such a man would be in league with local brigands.

Of the others, Haynie knew little more than their names. Though each one hailed from a different region of the state, they shared one thing: Each was there because of his relationship to some politician.

From the outset, Haynie and Commander Davidson agreed that sworn crewmen on ships of the Oyster Navy would be addressed as Peace Officers. It would serve as a reminder to each of them, and all within hearing, that this was a law-enforcement agency.

Smokey Noble, the ship's engineer, arrived with the *Emma Dunn* and was not a sworn peace officer. Haynie did not count on him for help when the shooting started.

Zachariah Bramble, in his early twenties, was sworn in within the past month. Though nominated for the job by his brother-in-law, a state senator from Talbot County, he seemed energetic and anxious for a fight. Likely, he would get one shortly.

Peace Officer Bryce Tydings, near Bramble's age, had worked on a small fishing boat, a bugeye out of Annapolis. Tydings kept to himself, saying little, and Haynie had no inclination how he would behave in a gun battle.

Stavros Dimitri, several years older than the others, came from Snake Hill on the edge of Baltimore Towne itself. When introduced to Haynie, Dimitri had mumbled that he preferred to be called Steve. That was the extent of their communication thus far.

Commander Davidson identified Dimitri as the nephew of a small time political boss. The politician had boasted that he would soon know everything the Oyster Navy did. When Haynie questioned Davidson about Dimitri, the commander shrugged.

"Nothing we can do; just be careful around him."

Devil Furniss, was a rugged waterman from Deal Island. In a brief meeting with his captain, Furniss said he was sick of being run off a good rock by drudgers and was ready to fight them. If the Oyster Navy did its job, he would be able to return to tonging, with only Mother Nature to worry about.

Furniss had cheerfully admitted that Devil was his given name.

"As you may know, sir, years ago Deal Island was called Devil's Island. Mainly 'cause it was the home of pirates and English criminals. When I was born, my pap believed I would measure up to the name. So far I have not disappointed."

Haynie was pleased to have him aboard.

Peace Officer Clyde Stainbrook was another matter. Discipline of the crew would be difficult due to each man's political connections, but that fact was especially troubling in Stainbrook's case. Haynie had asked Jacoby to pay particular attention to the man's performance of his duties.

2

Honga River
Eastern Shore of Maryland
December 8, 1868

First Mate Nathan Jacoby bustled into the cabin and spread the ship's charts across the table.

"Sorry for the delay, Captain," he said, and moved to pour himself a cup of coffee. "I had to get Peace Officer Bramble on deck to take the watch."

If Jacoby thought it foolish to refer to the ship's crew as Peace Officers, he did not betray it.

"Mate," Haynie, said, "If I recollect you're from Dorchester County."

"Aye," Jacoby answered as he settled in across the table.

"Can you tell me anything about this Blanchard clan?" Haynie asked.

"Well sir, before the war, I had a small place along Keene's Ditch. And while it was in Dorchester, it was a hike from Fox Creek, where the Blanchards are moored. Since the peace took over, I been aboard one ship or another most of the time. That's by way of sayin' I know *of*'em, but I don't *know* "em, if you get my meaning."

Haynie nodded. "Anything will help."

"Well, sir, the old man, Marrok, runs the show. Downright ruthless, as I hear it. The three boys are slivers from the same board, if you get my meaning. The oldest is Benoit, then Renard and Guy, the youngest. "

"They have any crew to help when they're out drudgin'?"

"No outsiders. Marrok captains a bugeye and the boys are all the crew he uses. They sail some smaller boats for raidin' and other mischief, but he's got cannon on the drudge boat. They spent the war years ducking the Union army recruiters and plundering."

"They after anything in particular?"

"They're not picky from what I hear. Talk is they sail around close to shore until they spot something to their liking that's not being watched to close. They'll stop in and help themselves to some tools or a boat."

"What about poaching?"

Jacoby nodded "It's known that Marrok has no regard for the law. They take oysters wherever it suits their fancy. I guess he figures why work in deep water when they's plenty to be had in close.

"Another thing. If they come in with a load, and Marrok doesn't like the market price, they got secret places they'll run to—some out of the way creek or inlet. They dump the load over the side and come back for 'em later, when the market's up."

Haynie nodded. "That's an old waterman's trick."

Jacoby said, "Here's something. I hear tell they got it rigged so a judge just up and gives them a boat." Jacoby laughed. "It takes some of the stink out of them stealing it."

"How does that work?"

"I don't know if this is the real law or what the Blanchards and their judge claim is the law; but it comes out the same. Well, you'd know Captain. They claim that if they come across anyone breakin' the law on the bay; like drudging in restricted waters, or being unlicensed, they can take 'em in. The Blanchards don't require actual law breaking; they make it up as they go along. As master of his own boat, Marrok can haul a lawbreaker into a justice of the peace. That sound right, to you?"

Haynie nodded. "White men, who are masters of vessels, can arrest violators and take them before a court of law. Ships masters can summon the posse comitatus to assist them if need be."

"If you mean like a sheriff's posse, the Blanchards don't need no help. Marrok's got his own posse."

"How do they get a boat out of it?"

"The story goes that they always bring their prisoners before the same justice, name of Orville T. Cromarte up to Cambridge. You know of him?"

Haynie shook his head.

"Can't prove none of this, mind ya. The talk is that anyone the Blanchard's bring in is always found guilty as charged, by Judge Orville T, after which he seizes their boat and gear. The Blanchards somehow wind up with the boat, which they either keep for themselves or sell off. I reckon the judge gets a share; either way they come out ahead."

"Does this happen a lot?"

Jacoby shrugged. "Don't know, sir."

"And, I'll bet they don't bring in anyone with a leaky boat."

"You're right there Captain. Only a boat they'd sail themselves, or would bring top dollar at sale."

Peace Officer Bramble stepped into the cabin. "Sorry to disturb you, Captain. Thought you'd want to know the fog's lifting."

"Thank you. Any other boats in the area?"

Bramble shook his head. "It's just now raising up. Still can't make out the other shoreline."

"Keep a glass handy and, if you see a boat of any description, keep it on her and fetch me."

"Aye sir."

Haynie and Jacoby turned their attention to the map.

"We're down here," Haynie said, "because some politician from Dorchester County cornered Commander Davidson and demanded action against the Blanchards. They said somebody needed to do something before that family takes over the whole county. Do you know the town of Tyaskin, Mister Jacoby?"

"It's a wide place in the road a ways up the Nanticoke River."

"They say the Blanchards deviled the town so much it formed up a militia to fight 'em off. The Blanchards sent word they would burn the town if they saw a militia man and the town threw down their guns.

"Tyaskin is across the Nanticoke. That'd be Wicomoco County."

"Vienna is just across on the Dorchester side. When those folks heard what happened in Tyaskin, they got scared. Must have figured they were next and came running to the politicians demanding protection."

Haynie put a forefinger at their present position on the map and made a swooping circle, from Holland Island, along the mouth of the Nanticoke River, across Fishing Bay and up the Honga River.

"We're told the Blanchards menace all this water and some of the villages."

Jacoby indicated Tangier Sound. "Some of the richest oyster beds in the whole bay are here, just below Dorchester."

"Commander Davidson didn't mention it. Course, Tangier Sound is mostly Somerset County's problem. The folks from Dorchester weren't there to plead anybody else's case."

"Somerset. That's your stompin' grounds, ain't it, Captain?"

Haynie nodded.

"The man who replaced me as the bailiff in Crisfield might know something about these fellas. If not, he needs to know what is going on. And there's an old friend down there I need to talk to."

"Sounds like we're making for Crisfield."

"Your story about the Blanchards, and that judge, changes our mission. We'll keep watch for them on our trip down, but I'm against steaming all over these waters looking for one particular boat. I need to send a wire to Commander Davidson, and the agent in Crisfield can be trusted."

3

"You boys must never forget: The name Blanchard means white and brave—in the French."

Marrok Blanchard's tone was crisp; as if this were the first time he had said those words. His sons, in turn, nodded intently, pretending they had not heard the same sentiment repeated as far back as they could remember.

The Blanchard men were seated at one end of a hewn oak dining table, which could comfortably seat sixteen diners. Marrok Blanchard sucked on a cigarette and dominated the room at the table's head. His chair, handcrafted of sturdy maple, boasted a high, ornate back, thick polished arms and a bulky brocade cushion to boost his small frame. Some years ago, the boys had named the chair, Papa's Throne, which pleased him.

As was their custom, the Blanchard men spoke in the French tongue and fumed as they waited for dinner to be served, by their women.

In some families, Edith Blanchard would be deemed the mistress of the house if not, indeed, the family matriarch. Being the wife of Marrok Blanchard and the mother of his three sons, offered no such distinction.

When Benoit, their first-born, was old enough to eat at the table, Edith asked her husband not to smoke during the meal. In a fury, Marrok struck her across the face and ground his cigarette into her food.

"As you wish," he snarled, and chewed noisily while she sobbed.

Edith Corkin was sixteen when Marrok Blanchard strode into her father's general store in Church Creek. Having left school years before, her days were filled by clerking in the store, while her father and brothers fished and hunted game. Edith was short, "tiny", some said, her stringy hair the color and texture of thirsty grass. Though she was as plain as one of the empty potato sacks lying in the corner behind her, Marrok Blanchard saw something he wanted. She wasted no motion while filling his order and an agile mind tallied the bill without use of pen and paper.

She's a worker, he thought. *Smart, too.*

Marrok Blanchard stood only five and a half feet tall and understood that dominating a wife, as was his intent, required that he be physically superior to her. His mate, though necessarily smaller, must be sturdy enough to bear his sons with a resilience that would return her quickly to her chores.

It was Blanchard's assessment that this girl would serve his needs as a wife. With her looks, it was unlikely she had a beau, or ever received much attention from any boy.

As he collected his goods, Blanchard said, "You're a pretty little thing. What's your name?"

Edith reddened and twisted furiously on her apron.

"Oh. My—its—I'm, Edith. Edith Corkin."

Blanchard, arms laden with his purchases, nodded.

"Edith Corkin," he said, "My name's Marrok Blanchard." He indicated the black beret cocked low, just over his left eye. "Marrok means—"of the sea"—in the French. I'll be back for you. Be ready."

He turned and marched out the door. Edith, red-faced and mouth agape, worked her apron with both hands as she watched him leave. She turned to madly straightening shelves while her mind raced over his words. When her initial giddiness subsided and reason returned, she shook her head.

"Likely he tells that fish tale to all the girls," she said aloud. Then, to herself, *He ain't very big, but ever inch is all man.*

Moving along the shelves, she giggled. *Even though he wears that floppy cap, it was nice to have a man pay some mind to Edith the woman, not just Edith, the Corkin family slave.*

She hurried to the door and looked up and down the street, hoping for a glimpse of this mysterious man. Disappointed, she shuffled back to the counter.

Likely, he's all talk. Still, I'd feel real foolish, and—just awful—if he was to come for me and me not being ready. Believe I'll wrap some things up and keep 'em 'neath my mattress.

Marrok Blanchard came for her three mornings later. When he appeared in the doorway, Edith was cutting dress cloth for Mrs. Pattison.

"Edith Corkin," he called out.

Startled, she looked up from the bolt of cloth and scissored a large chunk out of Mrs. Pattison's order.

"I got business at the hardware store," he said. "I'll be walking past your door in the next few minutes. If yer out here on the porch, you can fall in with me. If yer not there, I won't be by again."

When he was gone, Edith, hands shaking, laid the scissors on the counter next to the cloth.

Her voice quaked. "Mrs. Pattison, you'll have to finish cuttin' this cloth."

Edith took off her apron and folded it neatly on the counter. She started for the front door, then stopped and looked back.

Mrs. Pattison, arms folded across her breasts, followed Edith with her eyes.

Edith said, "I'm trusting you to leave the money on the counter. That's quality cloth and its 35 cents a yard."

"Look-a-here, young Miss Corkin, what's going on? What am I supposed to tell your father?" She stamped a foot. "What kind of man wears a funny-looking' cap like that?"

"What's goin' on here is Edith Corkin's startin' a new life. As for Daddy, the old bastard can figure it out for himself."

The morning after their first son was born, Marrok stood at the bedstead and scowled down at Edith.

"It's near 7 o'clock. You're not layin' around all the day. Get yourself out to that stove and fix my breakfast."

Marrok started for the door, "I told the midwife the boy's name is Benoit," he said over his shoulder. "Means 'Blessed' in the French."

He closed the door behind him.

Edith sobbed quietly into her pillow, and then did what she had done every morning since: got out of bed and endured another dreadful day as the wife of Marrok Blanchard.

Thirty-one years later, little had changed for Edith Blanchard, except now she had the wives of her two older sons to help with the chores. Though Benoit and their second son, Renard, had built houses on either side of the family home, they took their meals in the main house.

The Blanchard property stretched for 2,000 feet along the north bank of Fox Creek and deep into thick woods, covering 120 acres. Four baying bloodhounds roamed the grounds discouraging the occasional hunter from straying to close to the houses.

The family compound was secluded among forty-foot pawpaw trees and towering chestnuts. A wall of white pines anchored the north bank of Fox Creek and screened the compound from passing boats.

The three houses rimmed a large spring-fed pond sitting more than 100 feet back from the creek. The pond accessed Fox Creek through a channel, hand-dug by the Blanchard men and big enough to accommodate Marrok's bugeye, the largest boat in the family's expanding fleet. Dense stands of cattails grew along the bank, serving to mask the mouth of the channel.

Marrok's boat, a forty-two-foot, two-masted bugeye named *Ville de Paris*, was docked in front of the main house.

Tied to a pier at Renard's house was a sleek twenty-four-foot fore-and-aft rigged schooner, the *Souverain*.

Benoit's twenty-foot gaff rigged sloop, the *Saint-Esprit*, was moored in front of his house.

Marrok Blanchard celebrated each of his son's majority birthdays with the gift of a boat, and a ritual, naming the young man a captain in the Blanchard family fleet. These festivities included a banquet dinner, attended solely by the Blanchard men; followed by a detailed accounting of the role of the French Navy in America's struggle for independence, less than one hundred years before. After each dinner, over port and cigars, Marrok, speaking French, invariably began his speech the same way.

"*Mes fils*, it is to the shame of the United States that no one teaches the true history of its war for independence. *C'est vrai*, it is true that, if it were not for the heroics of the Royal French Navy, the King of England would still rule this nation. George Washington and Thomas Jefferson would have been quickly hung and long forgotten.

"*Oui*, these Americans are eager to make George Washington a hero for defeating the English at Yorktown, but," Marrok paused for effect and jabbed his cigar toward the Chesapeake Bay, "on September 5, 1781, Admiral Compte de Grasse, with twenty-four ships of the line, defeated the British Admiral, Sir Thomas Graves, in the Battle of the Chesapeake. The brave French Navy stopped the Redcoats from aiding Cornwallis, ensuring his defeat at Yorktown. Sadly, it is only the living men of the Blanchard family, who honor the memory of *les sacrifices* in this country. Each boat we sail will be named in honor of one of those twenty-four gallant vessels."

At the first such tribute, for his eldest, Benoit, Marrok proclaimed, "*Mes fils*, as you know, the flagship of our own fleet is named the *Ville de Paris*. In 1781, the *Ville de Paris*, A three-deck, 104-gun ship of the line, was Admiral Compte de Grasse's flagship. It imposed its will on the Chesapeake Bay and all who dared oppose her. It is again so."

Marrok lifted his glass and saluted his eldest. "Benoit, it is with great pride that I name you captain of the *Saint-Esprit*—the Holy Ghost. During the great sea battle, the *Saint-Esprit*, an 80-gun ship of the line, fought valiantly alongside the *Ville de Paris,* as will you, *Mon fils.*"

Marrok presented Benoit with a black beret. "Wear it with honor. You may cross."

Four years later, Renard Blanchard received a salute and his own beret. His father said, "Renard means 'wise and strong' in the French. Now, Captain Blanchard, I award to you the third ship in our family's fleet, *Souverain*—Sovereign in the English. The *Souverain* was a 74-gun ship of the line that served honorably in the fleet of Admiral Compte de Grasse. You will do no less for the Blanchard fleet."

With a wave of the hand, Marrok said, "You may cross."

Renard proudly set his new cap at the same jaunty angle sported by his father and brother, before moving to take his seat in the area Marrok had named: "The Captain's Table."

Guy, the youngest, sat alone across the table from his gloating brothers.

Marrok grew angrier at being denied his dinner and slammed the table with a fist. He winked at his sons and, in English, yelled, "How long does it take to cook a couple of sea bass?"

Benoit's wife, Marie, appeared in the doorway. "Sorry, Papa Blanchard. The stove wood was still wet and we're having trouble getting a hot fire."

Marrok cursed her in French and she ducked back into the kitchen.

The first time Benoit Blanchard brought Mary Lashier to Fox Creek, they were already married. When Marrok saw her, he knocked Benoit down in a rage.

"You bring me a cripple!" he screamed and stomped into the house.

Later, Edith told Benoit that his father was angered because Benoit had married a woman who was taller than was his own father.

Benoit moved Mary into the house next door and took to calling her Marie to please Marrok.

Marie Blanchard walked with a visible limp, the result of a broken leg suffered in a fall from an apple tree at age ten. Marrok delighted in ridiculing the girl's weakness, yelling out *"l'infirme,"* while laughing as she limped across the floor, or labored to cover the ground between the houses.

When Benoit and Marie produced a son, Marrok smiled broadly proclaiming, "He will be called Louie. It means 'famous warrior' in the French."

Louie, now age six, adored his grandfather. Marrok had fashioned a cushioned chair tall enough to allow his grandson to eat his meals at the big table. The boy's chair occupied a place of honor alongside his grandfather's throne.

When Marrok shouted, *"l'infirme",* as the boy's mother passed through the room, Louie echoed the taunt. *"L'infirme"* he squealed, and the Blanchard men chortled.

Louie's blonde hair grew long and curly; his body seemed to be all arms and legs. It was already apparent that he would quickly grow to be taller than his grandfather. This worried Edith, but seemed not to trouble Marrok, who had the boy at his side whenever possible.

They often sailed together aboard the *Ville de Paris.* Marrok dismissed any protests regarding the perils of having a small boy aboard an oyster dredger. "He is a Blanchard," was Marrok's reply.

Finally, Edith sat a platter of fried fish in front of the Blanchard men. The other women followed with steaming bowls of boiled potatoes and root vegetables.

Marrok filled his plate and fixed a portion for his grandson. As he passed the food along to his sons, he glared at the three women now seated at the far end of the long table.

"You womenfolk," he said, his voice rising to a shout, "need to keep in mind what would happen if you let us men starve to death.

The three of you together couldn't do the work of one scrawny boy like Louie here."

The women sat impassive, hands folded in their laps, as they waited their turn at the serving dishes. Marrok held his gaze on them and chewed noisily, while his sons filled their plates. When satisfied that the women had learned their lesson, he tilted his head slightly.

Renard's wife, Nellie, waited for Edith's nod before retrieving the serving dishes.

The women ate in silence, ignored by the men who spoke French.

Years earlier, Edith, angered at being excluded from his conversations, begged Marrok to speak English, or teach her the French tongue.

"The French is for business. I'll tell you what you need to know," he sneered. "And that won't be much."

As her sons grew, it became evident that Marrok was teaching them the language while at sea. Once, when a younger Renard tried to speak to his mother in halting French, Marrok stung his cheek with the back of a gnarled hand.

Edith pulled Renard to her.

"The French is only for men," Marrok snapped. "We must not let women have their noses in our business."

In his arrogance, Marrok Blanchard had failed to realize that the Edith Corkin he married would not accept his churlish behavior unchallenged.

Eating in silence, she was pleased that she understood everything being said by the Blanchard men.

4

Crab Point
Dorchester County, Maryland
December 11, 1868

Andrew and his father, Tubman, anchored off Crab Point where Fox Creek empties into the Honga River. Their log canoe, *Miss Beulah*, bobbed easily as they tonged oysters from a rock at a depth of eight feet.

In the early spring, Tubman and Andrew began to assemble the *Miss Beulah* from logs cut from a grove of tulip poplar trees behind their Taylors Island home. The boat would be a five-log canoe, twenty feet in length. Determined to have the craft ready for the coming oyster season, the two men squeezed every second of daylight from each summer day as they stripped the logs of bark and shaped them with broadax and adze. When shaped, the logs were fastened together and overlaid with sufficient pine planking to serve as the culling board.

A store-bought canvas sail was out of the question, so, while the men worked on the boat, Tubman's wife, Beulah, sewed a patchwork cloth sail to be hoisted on the single mast.

Over the summer, word spread about the artisans building a splendid log canoe on Taylors Island. By July, as the boat took on recognizable form, people began to show up of an evening to watch the two men work.

The first few nights Negroes from nearby homes wandered by, stopping to watch the work in silence before continuing on their way. Later, the crowd grew; white folks from nearby Slaughter Creek began showing up, expecting to be amused by the antics of a gathering of emancipated coloreds. These interlopers were often crowded out to the fringes of the gathering and forced to stand on tiptoes, or remain in their buggies for a better view.

"Hey, you, darky fella in the dirty straw hat, scrunch down so I can see what's going on," one said.

"She's gonna be a beaut," said another.

If one of the whites spoke too loud, someone up front would yell, "Hush!"

One evening, around the 1st of September, Tubman and Andrew proudly erected the mast, amid murmurs of approval from the onlookers. It was then that two white men pushed their way through the crowd and stood at the boat's bow. Andrew glared at the intruders while Tubman concentrated on sanding rough spots in the new wood.

The older of the two whites, though much shorter than Andrew, carried an air of menace. Andrew and the younger one exchanged hard looks. Though the boy stood taller than the man, they were clearly kin.

The older one spoke quietly.

"Nice little boat you're putting together. Looking to sell it?"

Tubman, intent on his work muttered, "Not for sale."

The man smiled, "You don't need this much boat to catch a few catfish."

He waited, hoping for a reaction.

When that failed, he added, "I believe that's too much boat for coloreds to handle. Different than fishing off a dock, ya know. That funny-looking thing tied to the mast supposed to be a sail? A good wind'll rip right through it, and roll ya on over. "

Andrew stepped forward with clenched fists. Tubman pulled him back and drawled, "I been sailing the bay for over forty years. We'll be all right."

The white man glared. "Likely we'll see you boys again," he said, then turned abruptly and shouldered a path through the crowd.

Aboard the *Miss Beulah*, Tubman hunched over the culling board, separating the clustered oysters with the pointed end of a culling hammer. The culls were tossed over the side; keepers went into a barrel secured next to the board.

Tubman's tattered straw hat sat atop a fringe of gray. Mice had chewed away much of the brim, and the crown was secured with a piece of cord tied under his chin. A ragged knit sweater offered little protection from the chill December air.

Andrew stood at the rail, powerful arms working the long handled tongs into the oyster bed. When satisfied that the metal basket was full, he hauled the tongs aboard and released the shells onto the culling board.

They worked this way throughout the day. Periodically, Tubman straightened, to the extent his stooped shoulders would allow.

"Let me take a turn with them tongs," he would say.

Both men knew that he was no longer able to handle the fifteen-foot wooden handles attached to the heavy iron basket. It was Tubman's way of telling his son he needed a rest.

Andrew always smiled at his father and said, "Why don't we both sit a spell."

Tubman was enjoying a chew of tobacco when Andrew spied two boats, under sail, closing on them from up-river. As the lead boat grew closer, the hawseholes on either side of the bow revealed a two-masted bugeye. An anchor hung from the starboard hawse; the muzzle of a small-bore Blakely Rifle protruded from the port hawse.

A dredge boat armed with cannon was uncommon in these waters and of great concern to Andrew.

The bugeye maneuvered precisely alongside the *Miss Beulah*, allowing the muzzle of the Blakely to protrude over the deck of the smaller boat.

Standing at the dredge boat rail, was the white man who had pushed his way through the onlookers at Taylors Island in September. Now, he sported a floppy black cap. Behind him, a younger man held a shotgun pointed directly at Andrew.

The older white man vaulted onto the *Miss Beulah's* deck. "Permission to come aboard," he said and laughed.

Ignoring Andrew's glare he gave the boat an appraising glance.

"Yes sir, turned out real nice. Don't much care for the color though. Was seasick green the only color of paint you boys could steal?"

Tubman eased off the culling board, spit tobacco juice over the side and faced the intruder.

"Who might you be? Sailin' around these waters a bristlin' with shotguns and cannon; boardin' my boat without any by-your-leave. You the law?"

"The name's Blanchard. Captain Blanchard of the *Ville de Paris*, ship of the line. That's my middle boy, Renard, holding the shotgun on your young buck there."

Blanchard pointed to the other boat, a twenty-foot sloop, now sitting at *Miss Beulah's* stern.

"That's another Captain Blanchard at the helm, my oldest, Benoit. You may recall having had the pleasure when we visited you in September. The one looking for an excuse to fire his musket, that'd be my youngest, Guy."

Tubman took in the armed men on each boat. The youngest, Guy, was the only bareheaded gunman; the others each wore a flat black cap cocked low over the left eye.

Tubman was, by nature, easygoing and slow to alarm. It occurred to him to wonder why the young one wore no floppy hat. He turned his attention to the leader. "I'd like to know," he said, "why it is you have all them guns pointed at me and my boy?"

"Likely neither one of you can read, so you mayn't know about the new laws we got for the Chesapeake Bay. Got us a thing called The Oyster Navy to see that fellas like you obeys them laws."

Tubman watched Blanchard closely, trying to understand what was occurring behind the white man's eyes. "You sayin' you're the law?"

"The thing is, this here Oyster Navy is kinda shorthanded—being new and all. They're real hard-pressed to cover the whole bay, so we're giving them a hand. The law says a white boat captain—that's me—can bring in any scoundrel he sees is breakin' the law of the sea—that's you boys. We're takin' you in, as is our duty."

Renard menaced Andrew with his shotgun.

Andrew's muscles tensed, his hands drew into fists as he stepped closer to his father.

Tubman's voice remained a flat drawl.

"We been tongin' this water for some years," he said. "May I ask what law we broke?"

"First, I'm sayin' that you better keep this young buck in hand, so's my boys don't think he's of a mind to fight us. I'm against killin' unless forced to it."

Blanchard pointed toward the heavily wooded shoreline. "There's just us out here. If we wasn't peaceful men, see how easy it would be to shoot both of you—leave you here for the crabs—and tow this tub in? Who's to say we didn't find it floating along by its lonesome?"

Tubman responded, "My son knows better than to take on white men; 'specially ones with guns. Still, to ease my mind, I'd like to hear one law we broke."

Blanchard snorted, "For one thing, you don't have a proper license."

Tubman dug into his sweater pocket. "I—"

"Even if you got one, it ain't posted or, it's out of date; expired, as they say in the law."

Marrok pointed to the bugeye, "We're wastin' time," he said, and motioned Guy to come aboard the *Miss Beulah*.

He looked at Tubman. "You and the buck come along aboard my boat. Guy here will follow along in this tub. We're takin' you to the judge in Cambridge. He'll tell ya all the things ya done wrong. Real legal like."

5

Cambridge, Maryland
December 11, 1868

Tubman and Andrew stood before a scarred wooden table, which served as the judge's bench, and waited for the gray-haired magistrate to look up. Bony hands covered with parchment-thin skin shook so that the papers rustled as he held them. A nameplate, hand-painted on a small piece of sawed oak, sat in front of him. It read:

Orville T. Cromarte
Justice of the Peace.

The Blanchard men, guns gripped in tense hands, crowded Tubman and Andrew to the table's edge.

Tubman had experienced a lot of abuse by white men over his seventy-odd years. It had imbued him with infinite patience in his dealings with them.

Many younger blacks fantasized about the happier days ahead following their emancipation. Tubman had known better. While others grew bitter and raged in the war's aftermath, he grew more stoical.

These men, especially the little one in charge, would like nothing better than to brag to their women how they had to shoot a couple of uppity niggers today.

Andrew's body stiffened and Tubman prayed that his son would hold together.

The justice of the peace released the papers and slowly worked his fingers until they laced together. He gripped them as tight as his strength would allow, which did little to slow the shaking.

Tubman wondered if the old man was responsible for tying the string tie showing beneath his starched collar and, if so, how long such an effort would take.

Justice Cromarte fixed them with a withering glare.

Age done nuthin' to soften them eyes, Tubman thought.

The judge's head shook, and Tubman hoped it was caused by the man's affliction and not his anger with them.

Cromarte spoke in a voice rather too loud for the tiny room.

"You boys have gone and got yourselves into a heap of trouble. What do you have to say about it?"

Tubman removed the ratty straw hat from his head and held it in both hands.

In a pliant voice he said, "Beggin' your pardon, suh, may I ask a couple of questions?"

The justice maintained his unyielding glare and said nothing, his clenched hands thumping rhythmically on the tabletop.

Tubman, unsure of what to say or do, dropped his gaze, shuffled his feet and cleared his throat.

Marrok Blanchard clearly enjoyed the moment. "The judge is a deaf as that table," he said. "You're gonna have to call out a whole lot louder if we're ever to get out of here."

Tubman straightened and shouted. "I'd like to ask a couple of questions, if I may—suh."

"Of course. Of course," Cromarte answered. "This here is a court of law and every man is entitled to his say. Even your kind."

Tubman nodded at the sacks of feed stacked around them and the farming implements hanging from wall pegs. He took a deep breath and yelled out, "Sir, why is this court being held in the back room of a feed store?"

Cromarte scowled and, after working his fingers apart, tapped on the oak nameplate.

"I'm a duly sworn justice of the peace and my courtroom is wherever I set down this here piece of wood. Now, what else ya got?"

"Well, suh, I'd take it kindly if you would tell us what we done wrong?"

The judge struggled to regain the papers from the table. Eventually, he took control of them and resumed glaring at Tubman.

"Well, there's several serious crimes listed here—"

Tubman held out a hand. "Pardon me, suh, but may I take a look at those papers?"

Cromarte snorted through his bony nose and looked to Marrok Blanchard.

"Hear that?"

Turning back to Tubman he said, "Can you even read, boy?"

The Blanchard men laughed aloud.

Before Tubman could summon a yes, the judge continued with a wave of his hand. "'At don't matter. The most serious crime you done, is poaching."

Tubman shook his head.

"Don't shake your damn head at me, boy. You're guilty of poachin', that's all there is to it."

Andrew trembled with rage and Tubman grabbed his shoulder.

"How can we be guilty," he asked, "when we had no trial?"

Cromarte threw his head back and joined the Blanchard men in roaring laughter. "Mister Blanchard and his boys, all honorable men, will swear that they found you boys tonging off Crab Point. You callin' all these honorable white men, liars?"

"No suh. That's where we was for sure, but we been tonging that rock since Andrew here was this high."

Tubman dropped his hand from his son's shoulder and held it flat just above his own knee.

Cromarte turned to Marrok.

"Well, sir this is much more serious than we thought."

Blanchard nodded solemnly.

Swinging his head back to Tubman, Cromarte said, "Well, you done it now."

"What you mean, suh?"

"Well, that rock belongs to Blanchard here, and you just admitted to poaching on it for years."

Anger tinged Tubman's tone.

"Don't make no sense. How's a body get to own a chunk of the bay for hisself? And, if he could own it, how we supposed to know about it? Damn sure ain't no propity lines, no signs tellin' us to stay away. How's a body to know?"

Marrok and Benoit Blanchard each opened his mouth to speak.

The judge waved them to silence. "See here, what you coloreds haven't figured out yet is your new freedom means you got to act responsible. Before, when you all was livin' on some white man's plantation, how you behaved was his worry.

"Now it's up to ya'll. Judges and lawmen can't be runnin' around makin' sure your kind knows every law on the books. No time for it. And it's the duty of upstanding folks like the Blanchards here to make it known when your kind goes and breaks our laws. As a judge, it's my duty to see that you learned your lesson.

"Mister Blanchard don't have to go to a lot of trouble and cost, to tell folks which property is his. It's his and its private; that's why we call it private property. See how that works?"

Cromarte glanced at Marrok Blanchard.

"It's like mindin' small children, don't you know."

Tubman believed he saw an opportunity. Dropping his gaze, he shuffled his feet again and in a lazy drawl said, "Yes, sir, Judge, I see where we was wrong. I surely do."

He included his son with a nod of his head. "Both of us does. We're real sorry and it sure won't happen again."

He finished with a nod and smile. "Plenty of bay for all of us."

Justice Cromarte looked at the elder Blanchard.

"Well sir, looks like these boys are quick to learn our ways. What do you say?"

Marrok shook his head. "That sounds good Judge, but in all my dealings with coloreds, I have found them, by and large, to be liars. Oh, they'll smile nice and say the right things; but soon as they leave here, they'll likely head right back to Crab Cove. I got to look out for what's mine."

Tubman tightened the grip on his son's arm.

Before either could speak, Cromarte said, "You do make a good point, sir. It's my duty as justice of the peace to protect the private property of citizens like you."

He paused, glancing from Tubman to Andrew. "Some punishment is called for. I'll have to make a proper ruling on these charges."

Tubman responded. "Sounds like we gonna need a lawyer, and we wants a public trial."

Cromarte joined the Blanchards in another round of laughter.

"Ain't no lawyer in these parts gonna help yer kind," he said. "It don't matter no way, 'cause we ain't havin' no trial. Be a waste of everbody's time."

Cromarte tapped the nameplate and said, "Remember me tellin' ya'll about this being a court of law. Well, right in this courtroom, I heard you own up to getting away with these crimes for years. It's what white folks call a confession. No—you boys is guilty, all right. Now, all I have to figure out it what to do with ya."

6

Haynie McKenna helped himself to another slice of the venison roast. At the opposite end of the dinner table, Young Tench, perched atop an upended wooden box, pushed his carrots and turnips to the edge of his plate. Seated next to her father, Ella May, the newest occupant of the family's highchair, flung handfuls of food at her brother.

Lila set a plate of warm rolls in front of her husband and took her place between the children. She often said that when they were in a fit of pique, which was frequent, she imagined it to be like being wedged between Generals Lee and Grant during one of their battles.

Turning to Haynie she said, "Did you consider stopping your daughter from hurling her food about?"

"She was trying for Young Tench. He's too far away. I feel that any daughter of mine should be smart enough to figure that out."

"I'm sure she would have; meanwhile she's wasted a peck of boiled turnips and left them for me to clean up."

Haynie shrugged. "Sorry," he said. "I wasn't paying attention."

Lila grabbed Ella May's hand and held it. "Stop it, young lady. Eat your food or you are going to bed without a story. You've been waiting for your father to come home and read to you, so behave."

She turned and glared at her son. "You, too. Eat, or no story."

Young Tench held up two fingers. "This many."

"If you don't eat, how are you going to grow big and strong like your father? Ella May is going to clean her plate and she'll grow up to be stronger than her big brother."

"No, her won't," the boy said and began pushing the piles of food to the center of his plate.

"See," Haynie said. "You're much better at this than I am."

"That's because I get all the practice. Now, I want to hear all about your boat ride to Crisfield."

"Boat ride? You make it sound like I was there on a holiday."

"You might as well still be aboard the *Emma Dunn*. I was trying to get you back home."

"You're right, of course. I'm here so little; I can certainly do my musing on the water." Haynie smiled, "If you're wondering, I didn't see my mother in Crisfield."

"Did you go out to our house?"

Haynie shook his head. "No time. I needed to see Gerhard. He has been checking on the place, as he promised. It's still standing."

Lila studied her husband's face. "He has to go right past the Manor House to get to our place. Has he seen Lettie?"

Haynie reached for a roll. "Gerhard's seen her in town. Passed her on the boardwalk, tipped his hat and said, 'Good morning,' but she looked straight through him. He offered to look in on her, but I told him it is no use. She still hates both of us for running that preacher of hers out of town."

"There must be some way to get her to see that if you hadn't stepped in, he was going to steal everything she had."

Haynie shrugged. "I've given up. I tried everything I can think of, but he was her Messiah. I think she expects him to return."

"Do you think he will?"

"Doubtful. Gerhard told him to never come back. He can be pretty persuasive."

Lila put down her fork and refilled the children's milk glasses. "Did you talk to him about joining up with you?"

"Briefly. You know Gerhard. He is easily bored and doesn't want to go to the same job every day. But, he's a true friend and will do what I ask. Now, I just have to plot a way to get him on board the *Emma Dunn* as a paid officer."

"That's odd."

"What is?"

"It's hard for me to imagine how chasing after someone who is likely to be shooting at you could be seen as boring, on land or sea."

"I guess it bothers Gerhard to wake up every morning knowing he'll be doing the same work, regardless of what it may be."

Young Tench kicked the wooden crate with the heels of his shoes. Ella May, eager to ape her older brother, began banging her heels against the wooden high chair. With knit booties offering little cushion, she screamed in pain while she battered the chair with both feet.

Lila rolled her eyes. "Never mind Gerhard, take *me* with you. I'd prefer facing a boatload of armed poachers to dealing with these two every day."

Haynie stood and nodded toward the children. "I'll read to them and meet you for coffee in the other room."

Lila found him dozing in front of the fire, lulled by the soothing motion of his rocker. The Boston rocker was hand-turned from New England maple and finished with a golden veneer. Soon after they had moved to Annapolis, Haynie brought the chair home, elated over his find.

Lila, though concerned about the cost said, "It's beautiful. It will look lovely by the fireplace."

Now, she sat a pot of coffee and china cups on the table between their chairs. She colored her coffee with a dash of milk and sat back.

Haynie roused himself and picked up his cup.

"What are we going to do about Christmas?" Lila asked.

"You mean, are we going to Crisfield, or staying here?"

Lila nodded.

"I can't think of any reason to go back." He gestured with one hand. "We've got more room here than we had in the other house; maybe we should think of asking Mattie and Levin to come down for a night or two."

"Doesn't it bother you that your mother will be alone, down there?"

"We were right next door, last Christmas, and she didn't bother to come over and see Young Tench open the gift she left for him. She has never seen Ella May. I see no reason to include her in our life until she makes it known that she wants to be. Do you?"

Lila sighed. "I suppose not."

"After Muse got her in his clutches she was a changed woman. Unless there's some evidence she is no longer under his spell, I'm not interested."

"Haynie smiled. "Now we are in the state capital, amidst all kinds of interesting folks. You'll soon find social doings to occupy you're time while I'm gone."

"I'm certain of it," she said.

7

Annapolis, Maryland
December 14, 1868

Haynie McKenna bid Commander Davidson goodnight and headed for the concrete steps leading up to ground level. Once out of doors, he made his way across the capitol grounds the packed snow crunching under his boots. At State House Circle, he paused to admire matching chestnut horses pulling a fringed surrey as they pranced in front of him. Keeping a brisk pace, he crossed Church Street and approached Walton's Hotel.

He found the walk from the state office building to his home on Charles Street invigorating following days confined to pacing the deck of the *Emma Dunn*. His mind raced over his earlier meeting with Commander Davidson, pausing to review his presentation of First Mate Jacoby's mission in Dorchester County. He was recalling how readily Davidson had approved their plan when the sound of his own name penetrated his reverie.

"McKenna! Haynie McKenna! Hold up a minute."

Haynie slowed and turned to see a frail man clad in a black woolen suit, matching vest and a fine beaver hat, waving with both arms from the hotel veranda. The man moved down the steps and, as he approached, Haynie recognized the shrunken form of Colonel Silas Wallis.

The colonel's visage was shocking. Haynie had last seen his friend months before, at funeral services for the colonel's wife, Abbie. In the interim, the person of Silas Wallis had become a shambles. His once-plump frame was shriveled inside the tailored suit now worn with indifference. The colonel's face was gaunt, barely recognizable beneath a tangled gray beard.

Colonel Wallis reached him and stood gasping for breath.

With great effort, Haynie hid his shock. "Colonel Wallis, I wasn't aware you were in the capital."

Wallis gripped Haynie's hand and held on before reluctantly releasing it.

"Good to see you, McKenna," he said. "It's been too long."

"How are you holding up, sir?"

Wallis shrugged. "Some days are better than others. None good." He looked up, his eyes tearing. "I miss her so damn much."

"I don't know how you keep going. I can't imagine what I would do if the unthinkable happened to Lila."

"I wouldn't wish it on anyone—not even a carpet bagger. The worst time is when I'm home; even with others around, I feel very alone."

Wallis hung his head another moment, before saying, "Sometimes I imagine her just in the next room. I find myself calling out as if in response to her voice. 'I'm in the drawing room dear,' or, 'I'll be right there.'"

He looked away and his voice trailed off. "My children have taken to avoiding me whenever possible."

Haynie laid a gentle hand on Wallis's shoulder.

"Why don't you come home with me—to dinner?" he asked.

Wallis shook himself back to the present.

"Thank you, my friend. However, I have a business dinner scheduled for eight o'clock."

He took Haynie's arm and stepped toward the hotel.

"It would be my great pleasure if you would share a glass of wine with me. I have matters of some urgency to discuss and Walton's has a very nice cellar."

"Of course, Colonel."

Once inside the hotel, Wallis guided Haynie into the dining room taking a small table in a far corner. They were alone in the cavernous room, except for three colored lads distributing white linen tablecloths overlaid with settings of patterned china, crystal glass and gleaming silver service.

Immediately, a well-dressed man with a stern countenance approached the table rubbing his hands.

"I'm terribly sorry gentlemen, but we will not be serving dinner for another ninety minutes."

"George, it's me, Silas Wallis. This is Commander McKenna of the Oyster Navy. All we require is a bottle of your excellent Chateau Lafite Medoc, '58, and two glasses."

George's hands stopped abruptly as he stared down at the wasted man.

"My apologies, Colonel Wallis. I must say, in my defense, that I failed to recognize you. It's so nice to have you with us again. Of course—the Medoc. Excellent choice. Two glasses".

George bowed slightly. "A moment only, sir", he said, and hurried through a swinging door.

Silas Wallis stroked his beard. "I had no intention of giving George such a start. I did not realize my appearance had changed so dramatically. Maybe I should write ahead to alert old acquaintances before I arrive."

Before Haynie could reply, the colonel gestured with a sweep of an arm.

"My boy", he said, "Are you familiar with the history of this fine old hotel?"

Haynie took in the grandeur of the magnificent dining room. Reflected light from four chandeliers glittered across the room. Plush maroon wall covering and thick matching carpeting muted even the suggestion of sound.

Following Haynie's gaze, the colonel said, "The chandeliers are Tiffany crystal. The elegant wall covering is damask silk."

George returned, placed two long-stemmed glasses on the table and presented the bottle to Wallis. After receiving the requisite approval, George removed the cork and splashed wine into the colonel's glass.

Haynie watched as his companion swirled, sniffed and then carefully sipped the wine. It occurred to him that it was highly unlikely he would adapt to the cultured life of the state capital.

When George had retreated, Wallis raised his glass in salute. Haynie assumed he was expected to return the gesture.

Wallis touched his glass to Haynie's and said, "A toast to the Oyster Navy and order on the Chesapeake Bay."

Haynie tasted his drink and found it much preferable to the dandelion wine fermented by Kenny Sipes, his neighbor in Crisfield.

The colonel, clearly savoring his wine, said, "Fine wines have been a tradition on these grounds for almost a hundred years. General Washington traveled to Annapolis in 1783 to resign his commission as commander-in-chief of the Continental Army. While this building was not erected until a few years later, these grounds were home to Mann's Tavern. Thomas Jefferson came to Mann's to arrange for the event. He took special care in selecting the wines for the thirteen toasts Washington would receive—one from each colony you see—spending more than six hundred dollars in the process."

Haynie nodded at his drink. "It's very smooth. I haven't had much experience with wines—none at all with fine wines such as this. It would not do for me to develop a taste for it."

"I believe every home should have at least one bottle of a good vintage, for special occasions. As for me, having little appetite for food, a glass of good wine is my only pleasure these days."

Wallis took another drink and said, "How fortuitous that we should meet. I was going to inform you that I was coming, but," he pointed to his head, "in my addled state I have difficulty staying focused. My apologies."

"No—"

Wallis dismissed the issue with a wave of the hand. "No matter," he said. "We have some unfinished business. I presume you are still interested in the whereabouts of those scoundrels Hollins and Mooney, along with the woman we knew as Grace Stringfellow."

Carefully, Haynie placed his wine glass on the table linen.

"Of course, sir. Though, neither fired the shot that killed my brother, I hold them equally responsible as the man who did. Indeed, they will be a fixture in my thoughts as long as they are free."

"I, too, shall never forget them—nor can I forgive them. It was rounders in their employee who shanghaied our son, putting my sweet Abbie into a decline from which she would never recover. Moreover, that blackguard Major Hollins helped them steal 75,000 of my dollars. It is highly likely that where Mooney and the woman are, Hollins will be close by.

"Ironically, when I have been at my darkest over Abbie's death, my pique at his betrayal restored me. I will not rest until I see them dead or standing before the bar of justice, quavering as they await their punishment."

"That is my wish too, Colonel. Have you heard something?"

Wallis glanced quickly about. "This must remain between the two of us."

"Of course."

"I would be ashamed to have anyone else know what I'm about to relate. After what those, well, murderers—for that is what they are—did to both of our families, I know you will not judge me harshly."

Haynie nodded, impatient for the rest.

"The last we heard, they had scurried back to their hole in Virginia. Of course, you will recall the fellow Hopkins—Hoppy, I believe you called him—the caretaker of Mooney's house at Popes Creek. I am always amused when I recollect how he mistook you and your man Stein for Pinkerton operatives. Your account of how eager he was to assist you stuck with me."

Wallis paused and breathed deeply before admitting, "I sent someone to Popes Creek to offer this caretaker a sum of money to report on their activities, should they ever return to Maryland."

"Is that what you are ashamed of?"

Wallis nodded. "I certainly wouldn't want it known that I paid someone to spy on others; particularly citizens of another state. I arranged it so it won't be linked to me."

Haynie glanced around the room and then leaned closer. "I was afraid you were going to confess that you found them and had hired someone to have them killed."

Colonel Wallis studied his friend as he sipped his wine.

"That was always a possibility—a fantasy really—when I didn't know their whereabouts. But when I have dreamed that dream, I would soon hear my Abbie's stern words and vividly recall her look of disgust that always cowed me when I was its object."

"Are they back in Popes Creek?"

"They were there for one night. Not the woman—Mooney and another man. This Hoppy fellow doesn't know Hollins, but I'm certain it is him."

Wallis refilled his own wine glass, glanced at Haynie who shook his head, and returned the bottle to the table.

"What are you thinking?" he asked.

Haynie replied, "It's hard to see a way to get this done, legally. I believe their hired killer, Rat, told me all he knew about the gang before he died. Sheriff Gastineau was right in the thick of it, but Rat killed him. Doubt he would have talked anyhow.

"It doesn't figure that Mooney and Grace Stringfellow would tell on each other. Last I heard she is prone to fits of madness. Likely the only other one who knows all their dirty dealings is Hollins. I reckon he's the one Rat knew as Mister Brown. You have any ideas about getting Hollins to talk?"

Wallis shrugged. "Over these months, I've thought about what would happen if I ever laid eyes on him again. His being alive long enough to talk was never part of it.

"So, let me do some thinking out loud. You learned that Mooney fancied himself a dashing Confederate cavalry officer, though he was never more than a low-down spy during the war. He and the Stringfellow woman were really husband and wife in Virginia. They were sent up here by the Rebs, as spies, pretending to be brother and sister. Grace Mooney would be her real name. That about right so far?"

Haynie nodded.

"Grace sweet-talks old Isaiah Stringfellow into marrying her and bringing her up to his mansion in Baltimore. All the while, she tells anyone who will listen this story about Horace J. being her brother and sick with malaria. How sweet and wonderful her new husband is to let her sick brother recover at their place on the Potomac. Doubt anyone ever asked why a man stricken with malaria would spend his summers on the banks of the Potomac River. It is damn certain Isaiah never did. He was so besotted with her that he saw nothing wrong when she was forever leaving Baltimore to rush off to Popes Creek and tend to her ailing brother.

"Those two thanked the old goat by pitching him overboard from one of his own steamers while they are out sailing around the Chesapeake. Thereafter, they were free to use the house at Popes Creek for running spies back and forth across the Potomac along with guns and money for the Rebs. Have I left anything out?"

Haynie shook his head. "No. But do you know for certain that they killed old man Stringfellow?"

Wallis nodded. "I'm as certain as one can be without seeing it done. No doubt, they were Reb spies; you saw the evidence in the Popes Creek house. Likely, their orders were to take control of Isaiah's summerhouse for their smuggling. Killing him would have been part of the war to them. Nevertheless, I have a feeling they enjoyed it. Especially her."

Haynie said, "It's another heinous crime to add to the list of things they've gotten away with."

"And another dead end for us." Wallis added. "Isaiah's body turned up tangled in a patch of sedge grass. The law decided he was drunk and toppled overboard in a rough sea."

Haynie produced a folded sheet of paper and a pencil from a coat pocket.

"I'm going to make some notes on what we know and what we need to learn if we're going to have any chance of catching them."

Writing as he spoke, Haynie continued, "Besides that murder, we have kidnapping. They're the ones had the Drumm brothers shanghai men, like Landon, then turn around and sell them to the drudge boats, like they were a block of ice."

He paused to finish a thought in writing, and then went on.

"There were three Drumm brothers. Jake and Rodney drowned trying to board the *Water Mule*; the other one, Roy, ran off in their boat. Jake was the leader of that crowd, so nobody bothered looking for Roy. I doubt he's worried much about the law."

"But, can he tell us what we need to know?"

"Don't know. It is doubtful, but I'll put him on the list. Next is murder. Isaiah Stringfellow is the only murder we know of where Mooney and his wife did the actual killing, but those two are responsible for everyone killed by Rat while he was in their pay."

Lost in thought, Haynie gazed beyond his companion, tapping his teeth with the pencil. Colonel Wallis drank his wine and waited.

Haynie returned his pencil to paper, "It seems to me," he said, "that Major Hollins is the rock we have to turn over if we're to have a chance at catching those other two snakes."

Wallis nodded.

"He's the one has to tell on the others. We have to convince him that, unless he tells, he'll be the only one going to jail."

"But—"

Haynie, head down, scribbled intently. "We know," he said, "that Hollins took your $75,000 for Landon's ransom. Do you still have the money satchel I found in Mooney's house?"

"Yes."

"And the ransom note you received?"

Colonel Wallis leaned across the table, "Yes, of course," he said.

Suddenly, his shoulders sagged. "The city police said, because I handed over the money to him, and he was now very likely in Virginia, there was nothing they could do. Sounds absurd, I know, but..."

"We'll just have to do the job for them. What can you tell me about Hollins?"

Wallis's gaze drifted to the bay window and he studied two carriages passing on Church Street.

"I'm trying to be objective in my recollection, but it's difficult. We met here, in Annapolis, at some political function. It was right after the war. We shared some drinks and a couple of dinners, he seemed an affable fellow."

Wallis's eyes darted from table to table.

"We dined right in this very room. We hit it off, and I invited him to call on us in Fell's Point. Had him to dinner at the house on more than one occasion."

Wallis looked away. "Abbie saw through him," he said. "She didn't like him. Thought him a little too slick." Wallis sighed. "But I dismissed her concerns and I paid dearly, as was often the case when I failed to heed her counsel."

"Try to recall anything he said about his past. How did he earn a living during the months you knew him?"

"I gave this a lot of thought in the weeks after he made off with the ransom money. Of course, I am terribly embarrassed at being so gullible. I will try to put that aside for now.

"Hollins claimed to represent several business interests in their dealings with the governments of Maryland and Virginia. That accounted for his frequent visits here."

Wallis paused, drank some wine and dabbed his lips with a napkin. "He apologized for not being at liberty to divulge his other business interests, saying his line of work required the utmost discretion. Naturally this was reassuring, and eventually I put him on a retainer as an adviser to Wallis & Sons."

"If I may ask, sir, what sort of matters did he advise you on?"

"Yes, of course. Wallis & Sons merchant fleet does business at any port of consequence along the eastern seaboard. Problems inevitably arise, and, at the time, we had no one to represent us when difficulties occurred in Virginia. As Virginia has not been re-admitted to the Union, doing business there presents unique challenges. He claimed to have excellent contacts in Virginia ports as well as the commonwealth government."

"Do you recall the names of any of his contacts here in Annapolis?"

"No. And this didn't occur to me until too late, but I never saw him in anyone's company, man or woman. During our drinking sessions and dinners, no one ever stopped by to shake his hand or say hello."

"What about his personal likes, or dislikes?"

Wallis shrugged. "Not much there, either. He refused to talk about his duties during the war. Said it was too horrible to remember and he considered himself reborn in April of 1865.

"The only other thing I recall is that he is partial to Tennessee whiskey. Oh, and he is quite taken with the game of base ball. Talked endlessly about the Cincinnati Red Stockings."

Wallis sighed. "I'm afraid that's it. Precious little to help us."

Haynie finished writing and resumed tapping his teeth with the pencil. "This all happened more than a year ago," he said. "It's doubtful they are real concerned that anybody is still after them. And, it's equally unlikely they have gone straight. They might use the house at Popes Creek in some sort of mischief. We need to find out what they're up to."

"How are we to do that, besides using Hopkins?"

"We need to make some connections in Virginia."

Colonel Wallis nodded.

"It could be a problem," Haynie continued. "Watermen from both states are always fighting over which one is poaching. The Virginia Oyster Navy has been known to cross into Maryland waters to arrest our watermen. Naturally, Maryland watermen don't believe they were wrong and fight like hell to keep from being taken. I can see us showing up in the middle of a fight between our watermen and Virginia's oyster force."

Haynie paused to take some wine before continuing. "It should help that Commander Davidson was a respected Confederate naval officer. I won't tell him about Mooney and Hollins, but I will try and come up with a reason to talk to someone in the Virginia service. I'm sure Davidson can give me a name."

8

The *Emma Dunn* was making just over four knots in choppy seas as she passed the Holland Point Bar, bound for the Potomac River.

Captain McKenna had charted a course, taking the Oyster Navy's only steam-powered boat along the Western Shore of the Chesapeake Bay from the Severn River to the Potomac. They would pass the oyster bars of Thomas Point, Holland Point and Plum Point, while patrolling the coastline of Charles and St. Mary's counties. At Point Lookout, they would proceed up the boulder-strewn Potomac River as far as the Port Tobacco River.

After returning to the bay, the *Emma Dunn* would steam across to Tangier Sound before heading north along Maryland's Eastern Shore to Dorchester County.

Haynie saw no reason to trouble Commander Davidson with the details of their brief stop at the village of Popes Creek.

Peace Officer Furniss ducked his head as he entered the ship's galley. "Captain," he said, "the watch has his glass on two tongers working a rock. Do you want to check their catch and license?"

Haynie set his coffee mug on the table. "Yes, I would. Tell Mister Noble to set a course."

Haynie's muscles tightened; the coffee soured in his mouth. He swallowed hard and pushed the mug away.

"This is going to be a tough one."

Skillets stood nearby scouring the breakfast utensils.

"Aye," the cook replied. "The first time is the most worrisome."

"Drudgers poaching a rock would be one thing. I'd be eager to chase after such as them. But, a couple of tongers, facing foul weather for hours, working for a few bushels..."

Haynie shook his head.

"It's as if I were challenging my own father. Likely, they are men who have been doing the same work at the same place for years. Now we come along...I pray they've got their license and a legal catch."

Haynie shrugged into his great coat, picked up his fur cap and sealskin gloves, and stepped out on deck. A cold wind stung his cheeks and Haynie turned up his collar as he crossed to the rail.

Peace Officer Steve Dimitri lowered his glass as the *Emma Dunn* closed on the two small oyster boats.

"I don't see any name or numbers on either of 'em, sir."

Ahead, two men worked in each canoe. One leaned over the side working the long handled oyster tongs, the other hunched over the culling board wielding a hammer. The tonger in the nearest canoe turned to release a load onto the culling board and spied the *Emma Dunn* closing.

"We got trouble, boys," he yelled.

The culler in each boat dropped his hammer and grabbed a shotgun stashed nearby.

"Ahoy, captains," Haynie called. "Oyster Police, stand easy now."

The tonger in the first canoe spoke up. "Be best if you showed somethin' that says who you are."

Haynie held his hands away from his body, palms up.

"This is the *Emma Dunn*, a ship of the Maryland Oyster Police. As you can see, we are flying the state flag. I'm the captain, Haynie McKenna of Crisfield."

He paused to let his words register, before adding, "I have papers, including a letter from the governor, authorizing us to enforce Maryland's laws on the bay, and all of the state's waterways. One of you can come aboard and read them."

The tonger in the second boat spoke out.

"Any rascal can hoist up a state flag; don't mean nuthin'. As for the governor, he don't send letters to the likes of us, and if he did," the man swept an arm to the open water, "the postal don't come by here real often. How we gonna know that letter you got is gen-u-ine?"

The wind picked up, rocking both canoes. The armed man in each boat braced himself keeping a tight grip on his shotgun.

Haynie, his eyes fixed on the two canoes, called out, "Peace Officer Furniss go below and break out the muskets and ammunition. Arm each man and have them report to me."

"Aye, sir."

"Now, captains," Haynie said, "I can do no more to satisfy you that we are sworn peace officers, engaged in our lawful duty. We are required to determine that you are licensed, and are taking only a legal catch. I see you got men working culling hammers, so I'd guess that you are. If you follow the law, we can be on our way in just a few minutes with no harm to anyone. If not, it will take considerable longer and, likely, somebody is going to get hurt. Either way, we will do our duty."

The tongers exchanged looks, and then each one motioned to the armed man in the canoe beside him. As the cullers lowered their shotguns, the first tonger spoke out.

"We're gonna do as you say, but we ain't likin' it. Not one bit."

He turned and pointed toward the shoreline looming beyond the *Emma Dunn's* starboard rail.

"Captain, I am Chester Mulholland from right over there in Charles County. You can call me captain if you like, but to ever' one who knows me I'm just Chester. Walter Wye there, my neighbor, the same. I can't count the years I've worked these rocks. It's like my own back yard, no different than a farmer workin' his field. Farmer's got a horse and plow; I got a canoe and tongs."

Chester withstood the rolling waves effortlessly and clutched the front of his mackinaw. Nodding to the other canoe he said, "Walter, he's done the same."

"I understand, sir," Haynie replied. "But the farmer's been working in a private field." He swept the horizon with one arm. "While you and Chester, here, have had many good years on public land, so to speak. Now the citizens of Maryland have said they want the Oyster Navy to make certain you and Walter are taking good care of their property. That's what we're about."

"That farmer don't have to pray of a mornin' that he's gonna get home to supper that night. Ever'day we come out here God tests us with biting cold, icy decks and lines, thunderstorms and nor'easters. Of late, He's added poachers comin' out of Virginia, and drudgers who'd drown us without a second thought, while they plunder our rock. Now, it seems, one of them scalawags up to Annapolis has said, 'I don't believe Chester and Walter have enough troubles down there in Calvert County.' So they send you boys along to help out with that."

Walter, his head bobbing as he listened, spoke out. "I thought the Oyster Navy was supposed to help us," he said. "Why ain't you chasing after them poachers and other depredators, instead of worrying over a couple of poor watermen in old canoes? If you heard we was getting' rich off the public's bay here, you were misled, sir."

The crew of the *Emma Dunn* trotted across the deck and posted along the rail on either side of their captain, muskets at the ready, revolvers holstered on each hip.

Haynie indicated the armed crew at his side. "These men are sworn peace officers, law enforcers; not poachers, not vigilantes or bounty hunters. You men are citizens of Maryland and subject to the laws of this state, same as any other citizen. You do not have the freedom to ignore these laws, because you happen to work on the water, any more than your neighbor, the farmer can ignore them on dry land.

"I know it's going to take some getting used to. For too long, watermen have paid no heed to the law, precisely because there was no one to tell them different. My own father, an oysterman from Smith Island, was murdered on Tangier Sound. His killers were never caught, mostly because there was nobody to look for them. That's all in the past; we're here now."

Haynie shifted his gaze from one to the next; each waterman hung his head in turn. Satisfied that they would offer no further resistance, he said, "Three peace officers of the state of Maryland are coming aboard your boats to inspect your catch. Have your licenses out for them."

Haynie had appointed Devil Furniss acting first mate, during Nathan Jacoby's absence, and he viewed this encounter as a training exercise. It was an opportunity to see how this crew some of whom were new to the sea and all of them new to enforcing the law would perform.

He ordered Furniss to have the men leave their long guns on board the *Emma Dunn* and proceed to board the canoes.

Haynie studied Furniss as the man and his two comrades boarded the first canoe. The acting mate ordered one peace officer to check the catch for cullers; the other officer kept watch on the men nearest the shotguns while he spoke with the captain.

After both canoes were inspected Furniss called out, "Captain, there's no culls in either catch, but none of these men has a license. Shall we take 'em in?"

Haynie studied the tongers. "Captain Mulholland, Captain Wye," he said, "do you understand that you are required to be licensed by the state of Maryland to harvest oysters in these waters?"

After a moment Mulholland grumbled, "I've heard of such."

Wye nodded his head.

"Since your catch is all legal, we're not going to take you before the judge, this time. I am giving you five days, and then we will check with the county to see if you have bought a license. If not, your names will be added to our delinquent list and every boat of the Oyster Navy will have that list. We're in these waters frequently."

Haynie stepped away from the rail. "Peace Officer Furniss bring your men back," he ordered.

With all hands on board, the *Emma Dunn* resumed its course for Point Lookout and the Potomac River. Haynie left a man on watch and gathered the remainder around the small table in the galley.

"I want to say that you all performed well in this, our first enforcement situation. Well done. Any questions?"

Zack Bramble hesitated before saying, "If I may, sir, why was it that you wouldn't let us take our muskets aboard those canoes?" He looked at the others for support. "I'm sayin', what with them boys having shotguns and all."

Haynie nodded. "Reasonable question Peace Officer Bramble. In my judgment, our show of force had taken all the fight out of them. They are local tongers, not drudgers anxious for a fight. Those canoes were rocking pretty good and I was guarding against a musket going off accidentally. We come upon a couple of drudge crews with long guns it will be quite different. Peace Officer Tydings, you have a question?"

"Yes sir. It's about the delinquent list you mentioned." Tydings looked around. "Am I the only one who doesn't know what that is?"

Haynie laughed. "It's an imaginary list, to be distributed to our imaginary ships. However, it sounded so good when I said it, that I am going to recommend to Commander Davidson that we start one. It could come in handy—if we ever have more ships."

9

Popes Creek, Maryland
December 17, 1868

A crowd gathered to watch the *Emma Dunn* tie up to the dock at Popes Creek. At 93 ½ feet in length, the steamship was a novelty for the villagers, who pointed and nodded as the crew finished their work.

As Haynie came down the gangplank, the crowd grew quiet.

"Folks, I'm Captain McKenna, deputy commander of the Maryland Oyster Police Force and this is the *Emma Dunn*."

He turned and pointed to the deck. "Up there is Peace Officer Bramble. Any of you who would like to come aboard may do so. Officer Bramble will show you around and answer any questions you have."

Haynie stepped aside as the crowd surged to the gangplank and clamored aboard.

Unnoticed now, he left the pier and made his way up the road edging the river. At the crest of the hill, he turned inland down a dirt lane toward a two-story manor house, reminiscent of homes found on antebellum plantations in the South. He passed the cast-iron figures of two Negro boys holding a splendidly carved wooden sign with the raised letters:

MAGNOLIA BLUFF

The sign had been there the previous March when Haynie and Gerhard Stein came looking for Horace J. Mooney and Grace Stringfellow. It was here that Haynie confirmed Grace Stringfellow to be Grace Mooney.

When Haynie and Gerhard had appeared at the door, Hoppy, the estate's caretaker, jumped to the conclusion that they were Pinkerton agents hunting down Rebel spies for the government.

"What took you so long?" Hoppy had exclaimed as he ushered them into the house. Haynie saw no need to clear up the man's confusion.

Hoppy explained that when the Mooneys were not there, he spent a few afternoons a week at the house, reading in front of the fire and avoiding his wife.

"She's become a real nag in her old age," he had said.

Smoke curled from the stone chimney, a signal that Hoppy was indeed inside.

Haynie rapped and the door opened a mere crack, allowing the man behind it to identify his visitor. Hoppy pulled the door open, his grin showing gaps between stained, uneven teeth.

"Jumpin' Jehovah," he exclaimed. "Haven't you fellas caught up with Mooney and his woman yet?"

Haynie laughed. "When did you start growing the chin whiskers?"

"Few months ago, when I found out how much it vexed the old woman."

Looking beyond his visitor, Hoppy scanned the veranda.

"Where's the other fella—the quiet one?"

"I'm alone," Haynie said as he came through the door. "We need to talk."

They sat in front of the snapping fire. Hoppy's lazy right eye wandered as he studied Haynie's face.

"What's goin' on?

"You heard of the state Oyster Navy?"

Hoppy nodded. "Yup. Read up on it in the newspapers. You know me—I like to keep up."

"One of the force's boats, the steamer *Emma Dunn*, is tied up down at your dock. We put in here so I could talk to you about Mooney and the woman. A crowd gathered so I told them to go aboard and look around. Wanted to see you without anyone taking notice. Let's keep this visit between ourselves."

Hoppy nodded. "Fine by me. You just along for the ride, or did you sign on as one of the crew?"

"I'm the captain."

Hoppy's cackle filled the room and he slapped a knee.

"The captain! If that don't beat all. Just up and left Pinkerton, did ya?"

"I was asked to be the deputy commander of the force. I couldn't say no."

"What brings ya back to Popes Creek? You sayin' that phony colonel's in the business of poachin' oysters?"

"He and Hollins are wanted for other crimes."

"Ain't surprised."

"Have Mooney and the woman been here recently?"

"Funny thing. Colonel Mooney—guess I can't call him that no more. How 'bout we call him 'the spy'. The spy and that fella Hollins showed up—maybe three weeks ago. Come in a buggy. The next day they come through town on their way out; the buggy loaded down to the axle.

The spy stopped at my place and paid up for six more months of caretakin'. 'Said for me to keep the place real nice as he might be sellin' it and wanted to get top dollar. 'Course I come up here straightaway. They cleaned out that room I showed you, the one with all the signal contraptions and Reb uniforms."

Hoppy flashed a grin. "I checked in the main bedroom. He even took that book of family tintypes you was lookin' through."

The grin disappeared, and he scratched a finger over his baldhead.

"He got snippy with me. Wanted to know what I done with a carpetbag was in his closet. Says it was 'most new and had red flowers sewed on it. Well I got testy right back and says that I didn't know nuthin' about it. If he took me fer a thief I'd give back his money and be done with 'em. That set him straight, and he mumbled that maybe the woman—the one he was passin' off as his sister," Hoppy cackled, "Sister, my ass. Anyhow, he says, maybe she packed it up without him knowin' it."

Haynie said nothing.

"Wait just a dern minute. You didn't make off with it, did ya?"

Haynie shrugged. "What would I want with a carpet bag? Besides, you were with me the whole time."

Hoppy wagged a finger. "Hold on. Right at the end, you told me to send in your pal, and I stayed out in the hall as a lookout. 'Member?"

"So I did. Anyway I'm sure Mooney found it when he got back to Virginia."

Hoppy studied his visitor for a moment. "Mebbe," he said.

Quickly Haynie asked, "What can you tell me about the other man, Hollins?"

"Not much to tell. The spy did most of the talkin'. Me and Hollins traded howdys."

"Anything else?"

Hoppy shook his head.

Haynie stood to leave. "In my new job I'm also interested in anything you can tell me about poachers in the Potomac."

"Well, folks are stewin' about oystermen from Virginny takin' out our oysters. My question to them is; how do they know where they is from? I never seed no boats flying Virginny flags, and I know folks don't sail up to a boat and ask the crew where they is from."

"Still, keep an eye out for oyster poachers. If anybody asks, that's why I was here."

Haynie stood and Hoppy followed suit.

At the door, Haynie said, "If you get any news about the spy, wire me at the state capital in Annapolis."

"Ya know them telegrams ain't free."

"You'll get paid," Haynie said.

"Hot damn. I'm working for the state," Hoppy chortled as the door closed.

10

Peace Officer Zack Bramble stepped into the galley. "Aye, there you be, Captain. Sorry to bother, but Officer Furniss has a drudger in his glass. Looks to be workin' at a legal depth, but he is mighty close to the line."

Haynie drained his coffee mug and stood. "Let's have a look."

At the wheelhouse, Devil Furniss passed the telescope to his captain. "Aye. She's a big one, sir."

Haynie adjusted the focus and quickly located the ship. "A two-masted bugeye. At least 50 feet."

He swept the glass across the surrounding sea. Deal Island loomed beyond the dredge boat; to starboard he made out the shoreline around the mouth of the Manokin River.

"Strange to find a drudger working alone."

Devil laughed. "Maybe that's why she's alone, sir; the rest of the fleet be workin' up the Manokin."

"Or, maybe he's heading for a shallow rock. Mister Barnes, as we close, bring her about so we can see the name on the stern."

Haynie returned the glass to Officer Furniss. "Let me know when you have a name," he said and turned to Bramble.

"Officer Bramble."

"Sir!"

Haynie handed him a key to the arms store. "We'll have a look at her catch. Assemble a crew, with weapons," he said, and headed back to the galley.

Within minutes, Bramble re-appeared gripping a musket in one hand.

"We're closing, sir. She be the *Davy Jones*." He shook his head. "Wonder how that crew likes sailing on a ship named after the graveyard of drowned sailors?"

Haynie followed Bramble into the wheelhouse. Smokey Barnes worked a corncob pipe to the corner of his mouth. "They're not runnin', sir," he announced through clenched teeth.

A telescope was no longer needed to see crewmen scurrying about the deck of the bugeye as they prepared to be boarded.

Haynie moved to the rail and, through cupped his hands, shouted, "Halloo to the *Davy Jones*. This is Captain McKenna of the Oyster Navy steamer *Emma Dunn*. Strike your jib. We're coming aboard for an inspection."

A bearded man, wearing a billed cap pulled low, appeared at the ship's rail. "Come ahead," he called, and turned away.

Haynie led the oyster force aboard the dredge boat. The two captains exchanged salutes and names then shook hands. They stood together as the oyster policemen fanned out across the ship.

The crew of the *Davy Jones* stood at attention before the mainmast.

"Captain Clary," Haynie said, "I've seen a good many dredge boats. Yours looks to be one of the fittest I've come across. The crew seems well-disciplined."

"Aye. I figured out a long time ago that I'm better off not cutting corners. Treat my crew better than most. Won't take on no man from shanghaiers; not worth the aggravation of keepin' the wretches they're peddling from jumping ship."

"Rare we see a dredger working alone. You make it a practice?"

Clary turned to Haynie. "Can't abide the way most drudgers carry on. There are those who think nothing of running tongers off a rock. Drown 'em like a stray cat if they can. So we work alone. Your men'll find no culls on this ship. Most drudge captains say 'Get it today, the hell with tomorrow'. Not me—I know we got to save some for next season and the next."

He waved toward the bow. "The *Davy Jones* is all I got to show for more'n 40 years at sea. It's my legacy, as you might say. For damn sure, I'm not gonna risk the state taking her away on account of havin' a few dollars worth of culls aboard. Foolishness, that."

Peace Officers Tydings and Dimitri approached from the ship's bow, grimly marching a black man between them. They halted in front of the captains.

The black man stood as tall as Haynie. Large ears drooped from a gleaming skull. Thick muscled hands dangled below knobby wrists. Empty eyes shifted between the captains.

"A stowaway or one of yours?" Haynie asked.

"He hired on at Crisfield a couple of weeks ago. Keeps to himself. Don't know much about him. Guess we're about to find out."

Dimitri tightened his grip on the man's arm while Tydings saluted the two captains. "Sir, we found him hiding under a bunk in the foc'sle. As he appears to be the only crewman not on deck, we brought him along 'til we can figure out what mischief he's been up to."

"Thank you, Peace Officer Tydings. Captain Clary."

Clary nodded. "Told me his name was Percy Overton. Good worker. Hasn't caused any trouble—that I know of."

Clary stepped toward the prisoner. "Overton. What possessed you to do that-a-way? Looks like you're hiding something."

The man stood mute.

"Dammit boy, I can't help ya if you don't speak up."

Haynie said. "Is Percy Overton your true name?"

When he got no answer, Haynie turned to Tydings. "Is our inspection completed?"

"Aye sir. Everything is in order." Tydings stepped back and resumed his grip on the man's free arm.

"Very well. Captain Clary, the state of Maryland appreciates your cooperation. I apologize for leaving you short a crewman, but he has left us no choice. We'll take him to the sheriff in Cambridge until we find out what he's been up to."

Dimitri and Tydings felt a tremor pass through the man's body.

Clary glared at the prisoner, his voice sharp. "Captain," he said, "you're welcome to him. Looks guilty as hell about something. He's certain to be trouble, and I don't want him on my ship."

Haynie stood at the rail, scanning the waters around Holland's Island now off the *Emma Dunn*'s port bow. Officer Dimitri approached him and saluted.

"Sir, the darkie says he needs to see you before we dock in Cambridge."

"So—he can talk."

"He won't say no more, but he was near begging when he spoke up. Close to blubbering."

"You and Officer Dimitri bring him to the galley."

After seating Overton at the table, the two officers stepped back, alert for trouble. Haynie nodded to Skillets, and the cook gave the black man a wide berth on his way out.

"Percy Overton. Is that your true name?"

Overton nodded and eyed the two men blocking his escape.

Haynie said, "I'm told you want to talk to me. If so, you are going to have to speak out. I've no mind to sit here and drag it out of you. If you came to fight, it'll be the three of us."

Overton lifted his head and sighed heavily. The man's lifeless eyes, reminded Haynie of corpses he had come across on the battlefield. Soldiers long dead, their eyes staring into nothing.

"Well, suh, I knows ya'll find out about me. I figure my only chance is for you to hear my side of it first." He tried to swallow and choked.

"You want coffee, or some water?"

"Yes sir, some water. If you be good enough to show—"

Haynie got up, filled a cup from the water pail, and sat it on the table.

Overton was stunned at being served by a white man. Maybe there was hope. His hands shook as he raised the cup. "Thank ya most kindly," he said, and drank noisily. He sat the cup on the table and wiped a sleeve across his mouth.

"I'd ask ya to kindly hear me out, before ya'll take to whuppin' on me."

"I'll listen as long as you don't lie to me. Regardless, no one on the *Emma Dunn* is going to whip you."

"Thank you suh, for that."

The man shuddered and then blurted, "They're gonna hang me if'n you make me go back to South Carolina."

Haynie was impassive.

"Here's the truth of it. One night—it was real late—the hounds started bayin'. I gets up and looks out the winda. Lordy, there's a bunch of 'em; just there by the porch, puttin' a torch to a big old wooden cross. They musta brung it with 'em. It weren't mine.

"I turns around to yell to my woman, but she and the babies was leavin' out the back. If you is wonder'n about that, we done already talked about what to do if they come for me, so there was nuthin' more to be said about it. She done the right thing.

"In the yard, the mens is all covered with bedsheets. They ain't making a sound."

Overton shuddered. "Quiet as a graveyard full of ghosts. When that cross gets to blazin', they turns around and heads for the front door. Now they is makin' a sound, like they is chanting something real low. The leader's swingin' a heavy rope with a big old noose hangin' from the end.

"Here's where it got real dark for ol' Percy. Any man could see they come to hang me. Only a damn fool would open his front door and ask how he could help 'em."

Overton shook his head vigorously. "No, suh. They wasn't there for directions to town. I keeped a loaded shotgun next to the front door. When that noose climbed on my porch, I grabbed up my gun and let go both barrels through the winder. That got their notice. They took to cursin' and hollerin' about how I'd killed one of 'em. I didn't wait no more. I lit out through the back, runnin' low 'til I got to a stand of trees.

"I looked back and nobody's a chasin' me. I couldn't believe it."

Overton paused to judge Haynie's reaction.

"I figure a man can't cover much ground with a bed sheet flappin' around his legs. They settled for puttin' a torch to my house, and dancin' around while it burned down."

Emotion edged into Overton's words as he relived the fear and rage of that night.

"My woman was hiding in the trees tryin' to keep the babies still. I tole her where to go to and, when she left out, I done run the other way. Come daylight they would be trackin' me with hounds and I had to git as far away as my legs could take me. I headed north."

He slumped back, defeated. When he spoke, his voice was again flat.

"After some days of hitchin' a ride when I could and walkin' the rest, I come into this here town of Crisfield. I heard that these erster boats stay out on the water for weeks. Sounded to me like a good place for to hide out. It was hard work, yes sir, real hard; but so is workin' in the fields. When the captain hired me on, I thought my luck had changed. Then ya'll come for me and here we is."

Overton shook his head. "Can't figure out—how did you all know where to find me?"

"We didn't come for you."

"What, suh?"

"We were there to inspect the *Davy Jones*. If you had been standing at attention with the others we wouldn't have noticed."

Overton cradled his head in both hands. "Lordy, Lordy. I was so scared when they said you was a comin', it got in my head that you was comin' for me. I knew you'd see the only black face in the crew so I hid it the best I could. Lordy, I done caught my ownself."

Haynie leaned forward, resisting an impulse to comfort the man. "From your story, I'd say you had a visit from the Ku Klux."

Overton nodded.

"You were not convicted by a jury, of any crime, in South Carolina?"

"If I was, nobody ever tole me."

"And the only reason you believe you killed one of them is because someone in the mob yelled it out?"

The man nodded.

"Well then, there's a good chance you didn't kill anybody."

Overton began to sob. "I didn't want to kill nobody, I swear it. For sure, they was there to hang me."

He wiped the back of one sleeve under his nose and looked up. "Can you help ole Percy, suh."

Haynie studied the man then he said, "I believe you shot a white man in South Carolina; for who would tell a lawman he was a killer if he wasn't one. Beyond that, I don't know."

Overton blinked. "What do ya mean suh?"

"Maybe it didn't happen like you're telling me. Maybe you shot him while you were robbing his house."

"Oh no suh! No suh!"

"Maybe he said something you didn't like: called you a nigger."

"No—"

"Or you were drunk and believe you killed him. You dreamed up this story while you were on the run."

Overton's shoulders sagged.

Haynie continued. "No way for me to know that. You seem desperate enough to gamble that I'd believe you and let you go. If it's as bad as you claim in South Carolina, you have nothing to lose."

Eventually Overton looked up. "Suh, do you believe that all of us is God's children?"

"Well, yes, I guess I do."

"Our skin comes in different colors." Overton pointed to his heart. "But He made us all the same on the inside."

Haynie nodded.

"No white man's gonna wait around while a mob is workin' up the courage to hang him. Why do folks expect a colored man to do any different?"

"That's a good argument for your defense."

"What you mean, defense, suh?"

"At your trial. Remember to tell it to your lawyer, just that way."

"Trial? They ain't gonna have no trial. That's why I'm beggin' ya'll. They was fixin' to hang me *before* I killed one of 'em; they ain't gonna wait for no trial."

Haynie shook his head. "A deputy U.S. Marshall will take you to South Carolina. The local sheriff'll protect you during the trial. There won't be a lynching."

"Mercy me!" Overton cradled his head in both hands. "No sheriff is gonna stop a gang of whites comin' to hang a nigger. If I made it into the courtroom, that jury will be white men; all friends or kin of the man I killed. You 'spect any one of 'em is gonna raise a hand for old Percy?"

"Your lawyer will see about that."

"Guess you never spent no time in South Carolina. Percy Overton will be the only darkie in the courtroom, if he lives to see it."

"Even if I believed your story, I couldn't let you go. "Could be you did other things they're after you for."

Overton glanced over his shoulder, and then turned back to Haynie. "How about this. You let me run outta here and jump over the rail. It's dead of winter, and I has to swim to shore in all my clothes. Doubtful I can make it; but it's a chance. If I has to go back to South Carolina," he shook his head, "I'm done for."

Haynie said, "I raised my hand to God to uphold the law. The law doesn't allow for a lawman in Maryland to decide about something that happened in South Carolina."

"Tell me, suh; is the law and the justice both the same thing?"

Haynie thought a moment. "I'm not sure," he said. "It seems to me that we can have law without having justice. But I don't believe we can have justice if we don't first follow the law."

Overton nodded. "For sure, in this country we is long on law and short on justice. And old Percy don't have time to wait around for justice to catch up."

"You maybe right, but some men deciding to ignore the law when it doesn't suit them, is what got you into this fix."

"Well, that is the end of ole Percy."

11

Dorchester County, Maryland
December 19, 1868

Nathan Jacoby paced the floor of the tiny Tobacco Stick post office in rapid steps. At the front window, he glanced up and down the dirt road, freckled with patches of old snow. It was 11:30 by the wall clock. The *Emma Dunn* would be waiting for him at Jenkins Creek at two o'clock, and he was anxious about being late.

Jacoby had been told that here he would meet a man done wrong by the Blanchards. The man, afraid for his life, insisted the meeting take place at this remote post office.

The stranger was already thirty minutes late, and Jacoby fretted over how much longer he could wait.

If he's scared maybe his nerve quit on him. Or, he never meant to come and is sitting by a warm fire having a good chuckle while I fret in this shanty.

Earlier Jacoby realized that it was pointless to wait at the window, as he did not know the man by sight. Nevertheless, with nothing else to do, he was back. Still no one appeared.

The postmaster watched Jacoby pacing.

"Looks like they're not coming," he said.

Jacoby turned from the window. "I hope I'm not bothering you. I won't wait much longer."

The postmaster laughed "Oh no, no. Just so's you make room for the noon rush."

Jacoby smiled at the thought of more than two people in the tiny room at the same time.

The door opened and a strapping young colored man gazed at him briefly then closed the door without entering.

Jacoby rushed outside to see the man striding toward a copse of fir trees about fifty yards to the rear of the post office. Trotting to keep up, Jacoby reached the trees seconds behind him and plunged ahead through the wall of branches. The two men were crowded into a small clearing of packed earth carpeted with brown needles.

The other man whirled on Jacoby. "What you 'spect to find in here?"

"Somebody who can help me. Is that you?"

"Mebbe. Who was it sent you way out here?"

Though the man was younger and much stronger, Jacoby did not feel threatened. *He's not had much experience talking hard to a white man.*

Jacoby replied, "A fellow I know over on Taylors Island."

"Name of?"

"Name of Benny Crème."

"This Crème a white man?"

"I expect you know he's about the same hue as yourself. He's the reason you're here."

The man called over his shoulder, "It's—"

"I heard." An older Negro man appeared through the trees from the other side of the clearing. A straw hat with a jagged brim was secured by a piece of cord knotted under his chin.

Jacoby felt the cold through his own pea jacket, yet the old man, wearing only a thin sweater over a faded flannel shirt, seemed not to notice. The younger man disappeared through the boughs.

"You want to talk about the Blanchard clan?" Jacoby asked.

"Depends."

"On what?"

The old man studied Jacoby. "I figure I'm stickin' my neck out—like a turkey at Thanksgivin'," he said, and drew a finger across his throat. "If those boys hear I've been talkin' to the law..."

"You come this far, why you holdin' back now?"

The old man shrugged. "You that—Oyster Navy—as they call it?"

Jacoby nodded.

"Guess I'd like to hear that it will be worth the trouble for me to talk to you."

"What are you aiming to get for your trouble?"

"Some justice. Sure didn't get any in their court."

"Sounds like they dragged you before old Orville T."

"Ya'll know about him?"

"Look here, Mister..."

"You can call me Roscoe."

"Is that your name?"

"It'll do for now."

Jacoby stood silent and the man calling himself Roscoe turned to leave.

"You're puttin' me in a bad place," Jacoby said.

The old man stopped.

Jacoby continued. "We're huntin' the Blanchards under the direct order of Commander Hunter Davidson himself. Some bigshots from Cambridge come personal to demand we do something about that bunch. I'm with Captain McKenna of the *Emma Dunn*. He's a good man, one of the best I've sailed with. He swore to get the Blanchards and I believe we will—if they don't get us first.

"I could promise you that everything will be all hunky and dory, but I don't know what's gonna happen down the road. Lord knows we could use your help getting them boys, but if you don't want to fight 'em, we'll keep on ahead as best we can. It's our sworn duty."

The old man's tone was sharp. "Oh, I'm gonna fight 'em all right," he said. "Only question is: Can I trust your crowd with my life, or do I go it alone? Who's gonna know about me if I throw in with you?"

Jacoby laughed. "It's likely Roscoe ain't yer real name. So it seems to me *nobody's* gonna know who you are, 'less you tell 'em."

"If it was to get to the Blanchards that an old darky is tellin' on 'em, it wouldn't take long for them to settle on me. Even if they wasn't sure, I 'spect they'd drown me for good measure. I believe I should talk to this Captain McKenna of yours."

"I expect he'd like to take your measure as well."

"The sooner the better."

Jacoby thought for a minute. "I can't make no promises on the spot. We got our orders and such. How about this: When I can get a time and day from the captain, I'll pass it on to Benny Crème. If I don't hear different, we'll meet right here."

"Me and the boy'll be here."

12

Bishop's Head
Dorchester County, Maryland
December 19, 1868

With some dread, Guy Blanchard brought his boat about and continued trailing the *Ville de Paris's* wake. They were in Hooper Straits, approaching an oyster rock off Bishop's Head point. A snow squall threatened off the stern.

After Justice Cromarte seized the *Miss Beulah* from Tubman, Marrok Blanchard took possession of the boat and rechristened it *Pluton.*

The evening before, Guy was named captain of the *Pluton* and toasted at the ritual dinner. During his toast, Marrok noted that the *Pluton* was the smallest *bateau* of the Blanchard fleet.

"But," he declared, "a Blanchard knows that it is not the size of the *bateau,* but the size of its captain's heart."

Guy donned his black beret and joined his brothers at the Captains Table.

Marrok Blanchard expected his sons to be replicas of himself, which, for the most part, they had become. His lessons had been hard ones, all with the same focus; a Blanchard need fear no man. When the boys were younger, he had recited to them countless tales of the exploits of Marrok's idol, Napoleon the 1st, Emperor of France.

Marrok preached that Bonaparte had been a short man who had achieved greatness because he possessed the heart of a lion and was merciless in his dealings with other men.

Benoit and Renard became eager disciples of these teachings, while Guy aspired to his mother's gentler nature. As children, the two older boys regularly fought over who would be the first to kill a tonger. Meanwhile, Guy had been cuffed about for his lack of interest in the ruthless ways required of a Blanchard man.

Up ahead, the *Ville de Paris* reached the shallower waters of Fishing Bay, Marrok intent on plundering a rich oyster bed. Guy, satisfied that his brothers were too busy to spy on him, tugged the accursed beret from his head shoving it deep into his coat pocket.

"Damn thing itches," he grumbled, scratching his scalp furiously with both hands.

Maryland law reserved shallow water oyster beds for tongers. Dredge boats like the *Ville de Paris* were restricted to deeper water where they could legally maneuver the massive iron-jawed cage through densely clustered mounds of oysters.

Marrok Blanchard did not intend to search the bay for a legal bed when one so rich was right there for the taking. This bountiful rock stretched for hundreds of yards upriver, with countless nuggets of the white gold shimmering just below the surface. Marrok believed that only a fool could expect a son of the French navy to ignore such a treasure.

"No one tells a Blanchard where he can sail," Marrok had said.

Guy's instructions were to sit far enough off the point that, with a glass, he could spot any boat sailing out of Hooper Straits, Tangier Sound or Monie Bay.

Any boat flying the state flag was likely the hated Oyster Navy. Guy was to fire three warning shots from his Spencer repeating rifle. If another dredge boat appeared, two warning shots would give the *Ville de Paris* time to prepare to repel the intruder. Marrok Blanchard had never shared a rock with anyone.

Tongers normally operated with one or two men in a log canoe, much smaller than the *Ville de Paris*, however Marrok considered any boat to be a threat. One shot from the Spencer would announce that a tonger approached.

About one year ago, along the far shore, where the Nanticoke and Wicomico rivers empty into Fishing Bay, two tonger canoes tried to stop a dredge boat from working a restricted bed. The much larger bugeye capsized both canoes. Two of the tongers drowned; the drudgers fled the area and remained unpunished.

Guy trimmed the *Pluton's* sail and watched the *Ville de Paris* shrinking toward the shoreline. Picking up his telescope he studied the emptiness of the water around him, pleased to find the snow squall moving to the north. The air was cold, and the day ahead would be numbingly tedious. Still, Guy preferred isolation to the clamor of his brothers competing for Marrok's attention. Opportunities for such solitude were rare. Now that he had his own boat, it was time to pursue his dream of fleeing his tyrannical father and malicious brothers.

While Benoit and Renard squabbled to win their father's favor, Guy feared that the day was nearing when he would be required to choose between his family and his soul. He could not stand idle while one of his kin killed a man over a few bushels of oysters. He need not pull the trigger to feel the terrible pain of another man's death at the hands of his own family.

When he was 16, Guy spoke to his mother about running away to join the United States Navy. She became so distraught that, after securing her promise not to mention it to his father, he abandoned the notion. This time he would leave, letting her know only after he was well away from Fox Creek.

Guy took his hand from the tiller and steadied the telescope. Eventually he located the topsail of the *Ville de Paris* nearing Bishop's Head point on a run out of Fishing Bay. Swinging the glass along the Somerset County shoreline, he made out a scow loaded with firewood. Likely coming out of the Wicomico River bound for Crisfield. South-southeast of his position, a tiny speck appeared coming from Tangier Sound. Unable to identify it, he finished his sweep and put the glass aside. In a few minutes he would look again, for now Guy resumed fretting over his need to flee his family.

I could never ask any woman to become my wife knowing she would have to live like Mama and the other two. 'Sides, if that Nellie don't leave me alone, there's gonna be trouble with Renard. Big trouble! I gotta get away from all of 'em.

I heard tell that the Underground Railroad, which helped the darkies escape slavery, was real active around these parts. Wonder if they're still out there? Would they help a white boy escape his own hell?

I feel real bad about holdin' that gun on those darky tongers. Good thing Papa didn't notice how much I was shakin'—I could never have brought myself to shoot them. Now I'm carryin' the guilt about Papa and that judge takin' this boat away from them.

They seemed decent enough folks. Same as stealing it was. I'd be pleased to give it back, if they would help me get free of this place. Why should they want to help me? I am a white man who stole their property. I did keep that patchwork sail they were using. Not store-bought; it looked to be made at home. Might mean something to 'em if I was to give it back.

Maybe I can figure some way to talk to them. What was their names? Seems the old man was name of Tubman. At the court, he said they hailed from Taylors Island. I'll have to figure a way to meet up with 'em.

Guy picked up the telescope and pointed it toward Tangier Sound. He was panicked to see a steamboat flying the Maryland state flag filling the lens.

Grabbing the rifle, he fired three shots into the air and pointed the *Pluton* towards Fox Creek.

13

Aboard Emma Dunn
Holland's Straits Chesapeake Bay
December 19, 1868

POW! POW! POW!

Haynie McKenna looked up from the charts spread before him.

"Officer Furniss!" he barked, "tell Officer Bramble to get a fix on those shots."

"Aye, Captain."

Devil Furniss hurried on deck, returning before Haynie had shrugged into his coat.

"Captain, the shootin' likely came from a single-mast log canoe off the port bow. Officer Bramble has a glass on him, but he's too far away to be sure it was him."

"Doubtful he was shootin' at us then."

Furniss nodded. "Aye. More'n likely a warning to some poachers over on Fishing Bay."

Officer Dimitri appeared in the cabin.

"Sir, Peace Officer Bramble reports the canoe is tacking into Hooper Straits. What are your orders?"

"Let's have a look," Haynie said and headed for the deck.

Bramble handed the telescope to his captain. "Sir, I doubt that we can overtake him before he's through the straits. No way to know where he's headed once he's through."

Haynie nodded and scanned the horizon.

"Those shots could just as easy come from hunters on one of the islands we're passing," he said. "They're not paying us to chase after a lone canoe. Besides, we got no time. Maintain a course for Cambridge; Officer Jacoby should be waiting for us."

When Nathan Jacoby was not waiting at the city dock, Haynie had Percy Overton brought on deck. With Overton shackled between them, Officers Dimitri and Tydings followed Haynie down the gangway. Once ashore, they struck out along Main Street for the county sheriff's office.

It was Commander Davidson's order that captains of the Oyster Navy were to make courtesy calls on the sheriff of every county with shoreline on the bay. This would give Haynie an opportunity to fulfill Davidson's order while sizing up Dorchester County's top lawman.

Inside the sheriff's office, Dimitri and Tydings arranged for Overton to be locked away in a cell, while Haynie located the man in charge.

"I'm Amos Tolley," the sheriff said. "We haven't heard much about your Oyster Navy, so if there's somethin' special we're supposed to call you fellas I don't know about it."

Tolley pointed to an empty chair beside his desk.

"What can I do for ya'?"

Haynie sat while he explained how the Oyster Navy came to lock up a colored man in Tolley's jail.

The sheriff nodded. "I'll check with the U.S. Marshal. We'll figure out what the boy did."

Haynie nodded. "As far as what you should call me, Haynie will do fine, Sheriff. I'm here to ask how the oyster police can help you."

Tolley stared.

"Hunter Davidson, our commander, wants you to know that we are ready to work together to stop the poaching and killings on Maryland's water."

Tolley shifted his gunbelt then tilted his chair back and folded his arms across his chest.

The sheriff was younger and more fit than Haynie had expected. He asked, "How long have you been the sheriff here?"

Tolley smiled. "Got the job last spring. Must be doing something right, was elected last month. Why?"

"I was wondering if you ever met up with a man name of Gastineau, used to be the sheriff over in Somerset."

"Didn't he get bushwhacked by that opium eater who killed those boys bein' held in one of those paddy shacks? Wait just a damn minute! McKenna! I thought I knew that name. You were the bailiff at Crisfield. The one who brought in that killer."

Tolley stood. "Let me shake your hand. Heard the whole town down there was real sorry when you left. I'd about made up my mind to try for the bailiff job when this opened up."

Haynie stood and shook the offered hand.

"It's a real honor to meet you, sir," Tolley said.

When they sat down again, Tolley asked, "Was it him, the opium eater? Was it him who killed your brother? Like we heard, back-shot him?"

Haynie nodded.

"Well, sir, this changes things. Got some hot coffee on the stove, what do ya say? Cold out there."

"Thanks. I drink mine the way it comes from the pot."

Tolley walked a few steps to a pot-bellied stove and filled two tin cups with coffee. Returning, he handed one to Haynie.

"Here ya go," he said and resumed his seat. "I believe I boil a right smart pot."

Haynie sipped from his cup and nodded in agreement. "Be hard to beat the pot Skillets our cook boils up, but this is tolerable."

Tolley was pleased.

Haynie sat forward, holding the cup with both hands. "What exactly is it that has changed since we sat down?"

"Sir?"

"You thawed out considerable after I said I had been the law in Crisfield."

"Well, we've not heard much about this Oyster Navy—as they're calling it— and what we did hear is not to some folks' liking."

Tolley hesitated.

Haynie drank his coffee and waited.

"Folks are saying that the only fellas gonna get a job with your outfit are some politician's lazy cousin, or a brother-in-law who can't get work any other way. Men as likely to cause trouble, as they are to stop it.

"Nobody believes that a bunch like that is going to stand up to the Blanchard boys and their kind. They expect you'll just go around makin' a big show out of botherin' some hard working tongers who won't put up any fight. Another thing: It's being said that the head of the oyster police was nothing but a clerk who takes his orders from the bigshots in Annapolis. But now, when I tell 'em that you're running the show, they'll take more notice."

"Why's that?"

"Well sir, you're a famous law man. At least the most famous we got in these parts. They got to take you fellas serious."

Haynie set his cup on a corner of the desk and faced the sheriff.

"First let me say that what you're hearing is all wrong. Hunter Davidson, our commander, was a brilliant naval officer during the war; and he is an inventor. No mere clerk—he is an experienced and capable leader of men. I am privileged to be his deputy."

Tolley's face flushed. "I—"

"It's true not every peace officer is an experienced lawman. But they're being trained, and each man is prepared to do whatever is necessary to bring law and order to the bay."

"Well, I—"

"We know we can't do it alone. We are going to need help from sheriffs and town constables all up and down the bay. Law and order's not comin' easy. It'll be a long fight."

The sheriff raised his hands in surrender.

"Maybe we heard wrong. Just the same, some folks got it in for ya down here. It's not just the Blanchards and their kind who'll fight ya."

Tolley waved an arm.

"The Choptank River is right out that front door. Our watermen are mostly honest folks trying to scratch out a mean living. Now they figure a bunch of landlubbers over in the state capital are sending you boys over to make it harder."

Tolley glanced around and edged closer. "I got a real problem here. If folks don't like what you're doin' and they see me as working with you, I'll likely have a fight of my own come next election. Same for other sheriffs, I expect."

Haynie nodded. "I didn't stand for sheriff in Somerset County 'cause I couldn't abide the politics, and now I'm right in the middle of it for every county around the bay. You may not wish to be seen working with us, but I don't want to hear that you're working against us."

"Can't say what you might hear, but the truth is, I'll not do anything to hurt you state boys. I'll help when I think I can."

Tolley lowered his voice.

"It occurs to me that I might be more use to you if folks believe I haven't thrown in with ya."

"You just might be right about that," Haynie said.

Tolley refilled their cups while Haynie talked.

"A minute ago, you said something about the Blanchards. What can you tell me about them?"

"The old man—Marrok—and his boys, cause trouble everywhere they go. And when they leave, folks are usually too scared to say anything. 'Course I can't do nothing about it if no one's going to speak up."

Haynie accepted the refill. "We'll have to figure a way to stop them," he said, "without folks looking wrong at you."

"I'd be obliged." Tolley shook his head. "They don't understand why I haven't done more. I know some of 'em think I'm in league with the Blanchards. Speakin' of being in league with them let me tell you about Orville T. Cromarte, our justice of the peace."

14

Annapolis, Maryland
December 19, 1868

Lila McKenna sat transfixed by the message she was hearing. Before tonight, she had been unaware of the woman who was now speaking so passionately about being denied the simple right to vote in a federal election.

Lila had been nonplussed when Wilma Winder excitedly announced that Sojourner Truth would speak at their next meeting. She almost asked who, or what, was Sojourner Truth? Now she was ashamed to admit that she had been unaware of the woman.

Truth, a former slave, had preached emancipation and women's rights for most of the last thirty years. She was concluding a variation of her "Ain't I a woman?" speech and Lila rose with the others, applauding fervently.

Past seventy, Truth leaned heavily on a wooden cane while accepting the adulation of a room full of white women. A colorful knit cap covered her skull, beneath which her face shone like polished leather. A gray shawl draped across stooped shoulders. Lila noticed that the woman's drab cotton hoop skirt hung shapeless from her waist.

No petticoats, Lila reasoned. *I suspect she refuses to wear them because they're so damn uncomfortable. Well, good for her. Wish I had her nerve.*

Lila resisted an impulse to join those fawning over the fiery suffragette and sought out Wilma Winder.

Her hostess stood apart from the group wearing a pleased look.

Elegant, was the word Lila had used recently in describing Wilma to Haynie.

"She's beautiful," Lila gushed. "Her features and complexion offer a hint of mixed blood. She's so striking that one forgets to ask who her husband is. She could easily be on a front plate of *Godey's*."

Haynie frowned.

Lila retrieved a copy of the latest issue from a nearby table and handed it to him. *"Godey's Lady's Book* is a fashionable monthly women's magazine,"* she said.

He quickly thumbed the pages.

"Looks expensive."

"Three dollars a year." Lila smiled. "But I think I'm worth it. It helps me fill the days while you are gone."

Wilma reached out and squeezed Lila's arm.

"So glad you could join us tonight. Isn't Sojourner Truth wonderful?"

Lila nodded. "It's hard to imagine what she must have endured in her lifetime."

Wilma watched the crowd engrossed in the former slave's every word. "I'm hoping to get Susan Anthony to speak to us."

Turning back to Lila she said, "It's sinful that men are the only real citizens of this country. Bein' born with that thing between their legs certainly has not made them any smarter than we are. It is my considered opinion that, if anything, it often causes them to behave more stupidly.

"It's been almost one hundred years since Abigail Adams politely asked her husband to remember the ladies when he helped frame our government. See what good that did us."

Wilma glanced toward Sojourner Truth. "She won't live to cast a vote for president, but at least she will die a free woman. Wonder how she feels about colored men voting when she cannot. No. It's time we stopped asking politely for what is rightfully ours, and started raising some hell."

Lila said, "If I'd thought about it before, I would have felt the same way. In Crisfield, there was no one to talk to about this. I am not very well-informed, but I know in my heart that we're right."

"You work with us and you will learn quickly," Wilma said. "I haven't had a chance to tell you how pleased I am—we all are—that you are with us. We need smart capable women to promote our cause."

"Thank you. I hope to become a worthy advocate for women's rights."

"Have you read an issue of *Godey's* yet?"

Lila smiled. "I enjoyed it very much. It really opened my eyes to what women can do."

"It's been around for years," Wilma said. "And though it is owned by a man, a woman, Sara Josephia Hale, is the publisher. She's one of us and encourages women to send in stories or articles. If it's well enough written *Godey's* will publish it."

Lila blushed. "This may sound silly, but I've long dreamed about writing stories. Especially now, with Haynie gone so much. Of course, it is just a dream. I haven't been able to bring myself to sit down and put pen to paper."

"Shame on you," Wilma scolded. "It's silly not to find out what you are capable of. Look at all the good Harriet Beecher Stowe did with her book. She had to start out some way. Her words rallied many folks against slavery; President Lincoln himself said 'she is the little lady who caused the war.' We need someone like that to stir our own pot."

"It's certainly something to think about."

"If I may ask," Wilma said, "what does your husband think about our movement?"

Lila was silent.

"I ask that because some men are threatened by the idea of women being their equals. We are naturally cautious about who knows our business. In this town, it can be a political liability for a man if it becomes known that his wife is active for women's rights. Not long ago the husband of one of our members became enraged after learning what she was doing. He twisted her arm until it snapped."

"Are you trying to scare me away?"

"You need to know what you're getting into."

"Haynie and I have never discussed women's rights; I doubt he's aware that we have them. But I cannot imagine him becoming violent toward me—over anything."

She smiled. "He has a lot on his mind right now, and I see nothing to be gained by bothering him with the details of my activities. I have the children and he knows that occasionally I keep company with a group of companionable ladies to help occupy me while he is away. That's enough—for now."

"My dear," Wilma said, "you'll be just fine."

15

Tobacco Stick
Dorchester County, Maryland
December 22, 1868

Tubman and Andrew shivered in the copse of fir trees behind the Tobacco Stick post office.

"Daddy, you gonna be all right with just those old canvas shoes? Snow doesn't look to stop anytime soon."

Tubman scanned the canopy of fir branches overhead.

"No snow getting' in here. We be all right. 'Sides it'll cover our tracks comin' into here."

"It'll be deeper when we leave; yer feet likely to freeze 'fore we gets home."

Andrew knew he would get no response. He had never heard his father complain about anything; not even white people.

"What if they don't show?"

Tubman shrugged. "Either way we still got a long walk in the snow."

Andrew brightened. "Maybe they'll come in a buggy and ride us home."

Tubman studied his son. "What you thinkin', boy? We sneak around, meetin' way out here in this grove and then go prancin' through town in a buggy with the state law a drivin' us like some dern parade. Go ahead on, I'll walk, thank you."

Andrew's ears burned, and he stared at the ground.

The boughs rustled and the state lawman they had previously met appeared in the clearing, followed by another white man. The second man was about thirty and big—big as Andrew.

The smaller lawman spoke up. "Roscoe, this here is Captain McKenna. He's the second in command of the whole Oyster Navy force." Jacoby shivered. "I hope you're not wastin' the captain's time."

Haynie offered his hand. "I don't see any horses or mules nearby, and if you know Benny Crème, it's likely you're from over on Taylors Island. I don't believe you walked all the way out here, through this snow, to waste our time."

Tubman shook his hand.

Haynie turned to Andrew. "Is this your son? Thanks for coming. We need your help to catch this Blanchard bunch. I can't say how it'll turn out, but I can tell you that no one will ever know from us that you helped. You have my word on it, and my word is good."

Tubman nodded as Haynie and Andrew shook hands.

"Why doesn't one of you tell us what you know about the Blanchards?" Haynie said.

Tubman replied, "Old man Blanchard—he's a little fella, but real mean. Anyhow, he done all the talking when they hauled us into court. He said they was helpin' out the Oyster Navy as you fellas is real short handed. That's why me and the boy was so skittish about meetin' with ya'll. Tell me if it's so."

Haynie frowned. "Blanchard was walking right along the edge of the truth," he said. "The law allows for a boat owner, or his captain, to bring lawbreakers before a proper judge. But no captain who does that is working for the oyster police."

"Them Blanchards took me and An—my boy here—before Judge Orville T. Cromarte. He didn't seem like no proper judge to me."

Jacoby nudged Haynie and grinned.

"I told you that was going on, 'member Captain?"

Haynie nodded. "Cromarte take your boat?"

"Yes sir."

"Does Blanchard have it now?"

Tubman shrugged. "No way to know. That old judge took everything we had. Said if we left town soon as we hit the door, he wouldn't put us in jail."

"What else can you tell us?"

"The Blanchards got'em a place somewhere along Fox Creek. They pretty much runs this side of the bay from the Choptank down to Tangier Sound. When they come for us, there was four of 'em, in two boats They was armed to the teeth; got a cannon on their big boat. How is it that the state lets a bunch like that to sail around threatenin' folks with cannon in the name of justice?"

"With your help, that's about to change," Haynie replied.

"I ain't an educated man," Tubman said, "but it seems such a law is gonna breed a bunch of rascals sailin' all over the bay trying to arrest one another. Some of 'em are gonna get shot for their trouble. What was them politicians thinkin'?"

Haynie smiled.

"Hell, if I can get me a leaky old rowboat and a shotgun for the boy, what's to keep us from rowing up to some tonger and tellin' him he's being arrested? That's how they done us."

"You're the wrong color," Jacoby said.

Tubman looked from Haynie to Jacoby.

Haynie nodded. "The law says only a white boat captain can make an arrest on the bay."

"That Blanchard fella said something about that, but I didn't pay him no mind." Tubman shrugged. "It ain't right."

"Doesn't have to be right," Haynie said. "It's the law."

"No use frettin' over it. What you need from us?"

The three men looked to Haynie.

"I'm going to say right out that bringing in the Blanchards won't be done quickly. I'm told they are poachers and marauders. "

Tubman and Andrew nodded in unison.

"If we can catch 'em working a rock the law says only tongers can work, that'd be a good start. Another thing, if you hear of them marauding anywhere get word to us, through Benny Crème. We'll head straight to the spot and talk to those folks. Maybe they'll tell us something that will show us it was the Blanchards."

Tubman spoke up. "If they is doin' things here in the county—on land—can you boys go after 'em, or do you have wait for the sheriff?"

"Our authority is restricted to the Chesapeake and rivers like the Choptank and Wicomico. Anywhere they could be poaching an oyster bed or marauding by boat. But that doesn't mean we won't help a county sheriff catch 'em if they're breaking the law on land."

Tubman and Andrew exchanged looks.

Haynie said, "If you have a problem with the local sheriff I need to know what it is. Now!"

Andrew spoke up. "Don't trust him."

"What'd he do?"

Andrew glared at Jacoby. "He's the wrong color."

"So are we," Haynie replied, "but you are here."

Tubman silenced his son with a look and then turned to Haynie. "White folks not the only ones to judge a man by his skin color."

He indicated Jacoby. "Only reason we's here is 'cause Benny Crème spoke up for that one."

Jacoby nodded. "Me and Benny grew up next door to one another; we was closer than brothers. Still are. His folks was free long before the war. Lots of nights I made sure I was over to his house come suppertime. My ma was...hell, she was drunk most days and Benny's ma fed me. When I come back from the fightin' Benny and her was runnin' that tavern on Taylors. They'd taken this old schoolhouse," Jacoby nodded at Tubman, "was a one-room school for them, and started this tavern. His ma does the cooking; Benny serves up drink and vittles and keeps the peace."

Jacoby turned to Haynie and smacked his lips.

"She still serves up the best catfish and cornbread I ever ate."

Tubman nodded. "We been knowin' Benny for a good while," he said. "I was tellin' him 'bout our run-in with the Blanchards, and he say I should talk to yer man here. Trustin' him and you is one thing, but trustin' the sheriff to know about us could be dangerous. We know that judge is crooked, it's not a stretch to believe the same of that sheriff."

"Did Sheriff Tolley do something wrong besides bein' born white?" Haynie asked. "If so, let's hear it."

Andrew said, "He's not done anything to stop the Blanchards. Seems like that should be enough right there."

"It might look bad, but it's hard to establish jurisdiction when crimes happen on the water."

Andrew scowled and exchanged looks with his father.

"On the water, it's real hard to tell where one county ends and another begins."

Tubman spoke up. "What difference does that make? Marauding is marauding. Poachin' is poachin'."

"It makes a legal difference, in court. If a sheriff can't be certain that what the Blanchards did happened in his county, he can't go after them."

It was clear that neither Andrew nor Tubman understood.

Haynie said, "That's why we're here. We only need to show that what they did took place in the state of Maryland. But, it's not something you need to worry about. I'll deal with the sheriff; no need for him to know about you two."

"It's fine that we're all learnin' to love one another," said Tubman, "but I haven't heard nuthin' about how we get our boat back. It'll be a grim winter without that boat."

"If we find that the Blanchards have your boat," Haynie answered. "Then we got to figure they're in cahoots with that judge. When we get the whole crowd, you'll get your boat back."

"Don't be too long about it; we need that boat to live," Tubman said.

Haynie nodded. "Let Benny Crème know when you got something to tell us, and he'll get a hold of Peace Officer Jacoby."

16

Fox Creek
Dorchester County, Maryland
December 22, 1868

Edith Blanchard sat erect, gloved hands folded tightly in her lap as Guy maneuvered the *Pluton* along Fox Creek.

"Relax, Mama. You won't enjoy the ride if you're so tense the whole while. If it's too cold we can go back."

Edith Blanchard shook her head and managed a smile.

"I'm fine," she said.

"We could wait 'til it gets warmer."

"It's not the weather. We won't be out long, but I need to talk to you without any chance he can hear us."

Guy saw the anguish on his mother's face and looked away.

She can't know that I've been thinking about leaving. Maybe she wants to warn me away from Nellie.

"If it's Nellie..."

"It isn't."

"Go ahead then."

"First off," Edith said, "you have to know that I only want what's best for you. You believe that, don't you?"

For the first time, Guy saw fear in her eyes. "Of course Mama."

"You must promise not to tell anyone—anyone—about this."

"I swear it."

She took a deep breath, "Son, do you love your father?"

He studied the creek ahead, trying to sort out a response. "I..."

"It's important that you tell me the truth. Don't say you do just to be saying it."

Guy thought some more before answering. "I never had to say this out loud so I hope it comes out right. I reckon the truth is I been afraid of him so long fear's the only thing I can feel. So if you are askin' yes or no do I feel love for him, then my answer is no."

Guy studied his mother for some sign of what she was thinking. Her pale features were set, her eyes impassive.

"Do you love your brothers?"

"Why are you asking these things?"

"Please just tell me, and then I'll explain."

The *Pluton* neared Duck Point and Guy tacked toward the shoreline.

"We don't want to reach open water so I'm going to anchor in the shallows. We'll be out of the wind."

Edith waited patiently while her son satisfied himself that the anchor would hold and sat down facing her.

Guy said, "You want me to tell you if I feel any love for Benoit and Renard."

"Yes."

"I don't like 'em much but they're my brothers. Papa has treated them about as bad as me so maybe they can't help bein' how they are. It's for sure I don't want to turn out like them."

He shrugged. "I guess if they needed me I would do what I could to help 'em. Does this mean I'm awful?"

Edith patted his hands. "No dear. You are a good sweet boy; a son I can be proud of."

Guy asked, "How do you feel about Papa and my brothers? Do you love them?"

"That's why you can't tell anyone we had this talk."

Guy waited.

"I've never told this to a soul. Lord knows I have ached to, but livin' like we do there was no one for me to talk to. Something has happened that makes me do it now."

Guy waited for her to sort through her thoughts.

"I want to start at the beginning." She took a deep breath. "I never felt any love for your father. I took up with him to get away from my own family—Daddy and my brothers. I have a sister; she's your aunt Wanda. Daddy was always hittin' us kids and he did bad things to both us girls. Naturally, my brothers took up with him and mostly treated us the same.

"Some months after I run off with Marrok, one of my brothers, Orville, he come to me and said Daddy told everybody that I was no longer family. He would kill any of 'em he caught with me. That's the last I heard from them—and that's why you boys never knew any of my kin."

Tears welled in the corners of her eyes and Guy reached out to comfort her.

Edith smiled. "I'll be fine, dear; that was a long time ago. But you see what I went and done. I run away from that hell and right into this one. Only this one's of my own making. I had nothing to do with creatin' the Corkin brood and couldn't do nothing to make it right; but I helped create you boys and, by God, I will do something to make this right."

"If it helps Mama, I can say that I do love you. That'll never change. I'm sorry you was treated so mean. Don't say no more."

Edith bowed her head and her body shook with quiet sobs. She pulled a square of cloth from her coat pocket and attended to her face. Eventually she lifted her head and forced a smile.

"I know you love me. I truly believe that you are the only Blanchard man who can love anything. Now I need to finish this.

"I never really felt any feelings about your father. I wasn't used to feeling anything, so I never minded it. Now, after what he's doing to you boys—my sons—I begun to hate him. As for Benoit and Renard, it don't feel like they're a part of me. Oh, they came from me, but I had no part in their names, or how they was raised. He snatched them right out of the birth bed and they been his ever since. I don't like them much, either, but—like you said—maybe they can't help it."

Edith shuddered and took another breath.

"Now this is why we had to talk. I know what you men were talkin' about night before last."

Guy sagged, the color drained from his face. "How?" he whispered.

"I have understood the French for a long time. Can't say that I can talk it 'cause I never had no one to talk it to, but I know what's being said. 'Course Marrok has no idea about it. You all was plottin' how to declare war on that Oyster Navy. I can't just sit by and see you boys get killed, or just as bad, killin' other men. All because Marrok Blanchard fancies himself some sort of kin to the France Navy."

"I feel sick Mama."

"Take some deep breaths."

Guy gulped in air, the color slowly returning to his cheeks. "Papa had to leave a good oyster bed when a navy boat showed itself and he swore they was never gonna run him off again,"

"And now," Edith said, "we got Louie to worry about. We have to do something before he ruins that little boy."

Guy said, "I'm real glad you know. I been just sick with worry; didn't know what to do. I couldn't say nothing to Benoit or Renard. Ever since I can recollect they been fightin' over which one will be the first to kill a tonger. Now they're fightin' over which one gets to kill one of those Oyster Navy fellas."

Tears rolled down Guy's face and he swiped at his nose with a coat sleeve. "Mama—I don't want to kill nobody."

"I know, sweetheart, I know."

Guy squared around to face his mother. "It's time for it all to come out. You recollect how you fussed when I told you I wanted to run off and join the Yankee navy. Well I been workin' up to running away, only I wasn't going to tell you 'til after I was gone. This boat, the *Pluton* as Papa has named it, was stole by us from an old darky and his boy. We took them to a grizzly ol' judge in Cambridge name of Orville T. Cromarte. You ever heard Papa speak of him?"

Edith wanted to say that she never heard anything but curses and insults from her husband. Instead, she shook her head.

"Papa and Benoit had seen the darkies building this boat and Papa decided he wanted it for me. One day we was out plunderin' and run acrossed 'em over to Crab Point. Me and Renard held our long guns on 'em while Papa says they're arrested and we take 'em up to Cambridge.

"The hate I saw in the young buck's eyes is something I never want to see again. Old Cromarte takes away their new boat—this boat—and somehow Papa ends up with it. It was then I knew I had to get away from him. If I stay around he'll expect me to shoot somebody, or just as bad, stand by and watch while one of them does it."

Guy paused to mimic his father's nasal tone.

"Blanchard means 'white and brave' in the French," he said with no hint of humor.

"Don't be afraid," Edith said. "Together we'll figure some way out of this."

Guy went on. "What we did to those coloreds wasn't right—it was just stealing straight out.

They built this boat with their own hands. That old sail was patched together, likely by that buck's Mama. I was gonna use this boat to get away from here, but now I see that I won't feel right until they get it back. Maybe then the look in the buck's eyes will leave me alone."

"Guy, look at me. We will do whatever it takes to free us from him. We're going to be all right."

Guy searched his mother's eyes. "Momma, are you sayin' we're gonna kill him?"

"We'll do what we have to."

17

**Chester River
Queen Anne's County, Maryland
January 4, 1869**

Queenstown appeared off the starboard bow as the *Emma Dunn* churned its way up the Chester River.

"Officer Jacoby, our reports have poachers up as far as Corsica Creek. If we haven't come upon any by then, we'll come about."

"Aye, Captain."

Jacoby indicated the cannon lashed to the deck at the bow railing.

"I have a feeling we'll get some more practice with that."

Haynie agreed. "The *Leila* is still not in service or it would be sitting on her deck."

Haynie eyed the ice chunks swirling past the bow.

"Sure hate to put a man into that water," he muttered.

The *Emma Dunn* rounded a bend and Jacoby pointed upriver.

"Looks like some drudgers working, Captain."

Haynie raised his glass and identified two dredge boats maneuvering over an oyster rock at the mouth of Tilghman Creek. Beyond them, the sails of twelve more boats were visible working the middle of the river.

"Mister Jacoby, unlock the magazine and have each officer report on deck, armed."

"Aye, sir," Jacoby replied and headed below.

Haynie poked his head inside the wheelhouse.

"Mister Noble, I know you didn't sign on for gunplay, but I need you at the wheel." He pointed through the window. "At least until we find out what we're facing up ahead."

"Aye, Captain. Figured I was too old for such adventures—guess I was wrong," Noble said, and steered the *Emma Dunn* toward the dredgers.

Haynie scanned the boats ahead. The crews, fully engaged in their work, seemed unaware of the approaching steamer.

When Jacoby returned, Haynie handed him the glass.

After a moment the mate said, "They be busy drudgers, sir. I wonder how close we can get before they see us."

"They'll know when we halloo them to lower their jibs."

Haynie retrieved the glass.

"Assemble the men at the bow rail, their muskets at the ready. Brief the crew and then halloo the captain of that first boat to strike his jib."

"Aye, sir," Jacoby said and left the wheelhouse.

Through the glass Haynie made out the name of the nearest boat—*Tangier*.

"Mister Noble," he said, "reduce power and prepare to stop the engines on my signal."

Haynie stepped out of the wheelhouse and crossed the deck. His officers stood at the bow, intent on the two dredge boats. Each man wore a sidearm and held a musket at the ready.

"They're payin' no mind, Captain. I know they can hear me," Jacoby called.

"It's the *Tangier*. Halloo the captain."

Jacoby approached the rail. "Halloo, captain of the *Tangier* strike yer jib for the Oyster Navy."

Haynie tensed. Very soon, he could have an answer to the question of how his men would act under fire.

"They're getting under way, sir."

Haynie joined Jacoby at the rail. "Halloo. Captain of the *Tangier*, this is Captain McKenna and peace officers of the Maryland Oyster Navy steamer, *Emma Dunn*. You are required by law to strike your jib and stand down while we come aboard for inspection."

"She's leaving, sir."

"Mate, have all peace officers stand by. On my order, they are to fire across the bow. If the *Tangier* does not heave to, reload and fire into the cabin. Post yourself at the cannon and wait for my order to fire into the rigging."

"Aye Aye, sir," Jacoby called and headed for the bow.

"Halloo, captain of the *Tangier*, if you do not heed this lawful order, we will fire on you with musket and cannon."

About 100 yards of icy water now separated the police steamer from the *Tangier*.

"Peace Officers," Haynie shouted, "you may fire on the *Tangier* as directed."

As one man, the men of the *Emma Dunn* raised their muskets and fired a warning volley, sending the crew of the dredge boat diving to the deck.

Hearing nothing from the *Tangier*, Haynie shouted, "Fire at the cabin!"

A hail of minie balls splintered the wooden cabin of the dredge boat.

As the echoes of the second volley subsided, a voice called out, "Halloo to the captain of the *Emma Dunn*, this is the captain of the *Tangier*. Stop your damn shootin', we're stayin' put."

"Cease firing," Haynie ordered, as the *Emma Dunn* closed on the *Tangier's* port bow.

"Officer Jacoby, take two men and board her. Proceed with your inspection, then anchor her and leave an armed man aboard. We're going for the other dredger."

"Aye, Captain."

The second dredge boat, a bugeye, was under way and headed for the Queenstown shore. At least 150 yards separated her from the *Emma Dunn*.

Back in the wheelhouse, Haynie asked, "Mister Noble, can we catch her before she reaches the creek?"

"Doubtful, Captain. I can't be runnin' at full speed too close in or we'll run aground. I'm gonna have to slow her down real soon."

Haynie shook his head. "We'll not catch her in time. Return to the *Tangier*."

Nathan Jacoby, now back on board the *Emma Dunn*, reported to his captain. "Found lots of culls, sir. I told the captain to anchor and stay there 'til we got back. I left Peace Officer Dimitri aboard. He didn't like it much, but there he is."

Through the glass, Haynie studied the remainder of the oyster fleet. "The rest turned tail. They're headed upriver."

Jacoby nodded. "Looks like ants scurryin' away from a stomped-on hill."

"We'll chase them for a while. Maybe one will be too slow to outrun us. Like a wolf picking off the runt of a deer herd."

Haynie scanned the water ahead with little hope. The winter evening closed rapidly as the dredge fleet scattered.

"Peace Officer Jacoby."

"Aye."

"Post a watch on the bow and have our lamps lit."

"Aye, sir."

The cold light of a new moon filtered through thin clouds chilling the air. Off the starboard side, lights from a few lamps sparkled from homes along the riverbank.

When Jacoby returned to the wheelhouse, Haynie asked, "The crew of the *Tangier* give you any trouble?"

Jacoby shook his head.

"If there was ever any fight in 'em, it was gone by the time we boarded."

Haynie returned to scanning the river ahead.

"Jesus!" he exclaimed and handed the telescope to the mate. "What do you make of that?"

Jacoby swept the glass across the breadth of the Chester River.

"Never seen anything like it, sir. At least ten dredge boats lashed together, headin' right for us. Each one showing red and green running lights. Looks like trouble."

Haynie took the telescope and scrutinized the approaching line of ships.

"Station the men amidships, on the starboard side. Take one man with you to the bow and prepare to fire the cannon on my command. If they refuse an order to lower, we'll fire across their bow with muskets."

"Hard for them to tell we're only firing warning shots at night."

"I have no other choice."

"They're getting mighty close, sir."

"Get the men in position."

"Aye Aye, sir."

Haynie's demand that the dredge boats haul in their sails was met with an eerie silence. The row of red and green lights glistened in the cold air as the line of ships glided closer. White sails billowed above deserted decks, creating the image of a ghostly armada bearing down.

From the wheelhouse, Haynie ordered, "Fire across their bow."

Suddenly heavily armed drudgers swarmed the decks of the oyster boats.

"Pour it on 'em boys," someone yelled and minie balls ripped the walls of the *Emma Dunn's* wheelhouse.

Haynie shouted, "Return fire!"

Turning to the ship's engineer, Haynie yelled, "Hard to port, Mister Noble! I want to run across the front of that line. Mind we don't get tangled with their bowsprits."

"Aye, sir."

The *Emma Dunn* began her turn. Minie balls smashed into the rigging and rang off her iron plating as flashes and smoke poured from the drudgers.

"Mister Noble, when we pass in front of the last boat, turn upriver. Once we get behind them we'll run their stern while I look for a spot to move at 'em."

A ball shattered a window, narrowly missing Noble. Haynie crouched low and motioned the helmsman to do the same.

Noble shook his head. "I don't know, Captain. It's real chancy steering her while trying not to get myself shot."

"We're almost to the end of their line," Haynie said.

The *Emma Dunn* crossed in front of the last dredger and the gunfire ceased.

Jacoby crawled into the wheelhouse, mindful of the shards of glass littering the deck.

"Everbody all right in here?"

"Near misses," Haynie said, and both men stood. "Anyone hit out there?"

"No sir. Good thing those boys are oyster poachers and not hunters."

"I believe they're waiting to see if we have had enough and are pulling out."

"Are we, sir?"

"We're not running from our first fight. Besides, the state wouldn't understand why we shot up all those expensive minie balls with nothing to show for our trouble. We're going to come in behind them and see if we can't take somebody with us when we leave."

Jacoby grinned. "Aye, sir."

"Going to try and split them. Pass the word. Likely we'll have to ram one of them if they won't yield."

The *Emma Dunn* passed to the rear of the line of dredge boats and the pilot began a sharp turn to starboard.

"Take her farther upriver before you make your turn, Mister Noble," said Haynie. "Let them think we're pulling out."

"Aye, sir." Noble made the correction.

"I want to be some distance off their stern when we turn to make our run behind them. Keep us out of range of their guns as long as possible."

As the *Emma Dunn* chugged upstream, Haynie went to the stern and scanned the line of dredge boats moving downstream into the night. Armed men, clustered at the stern of each boat shaking muskets in the air amid derisive shouts. "Sail away, Oyster Navy!" "Show us yer tail!"

Haynie moved among the crew, explaining what they should expect in the next few minutes. Satisfied that they were primed for the fight ahead he returned to the wheelhouse.

"Make your turn, Mister Noble. Be prepared for a second turn pointing us downstream on my order."

Noble nodded. "Aye, sir."

Through the telescope, Haynie selected his prey, the lights of a small pungy in the middle of the line.

"Now, Mister Noble!"

The pilot gave the wheel a sharp turn. The *Emma Dunn* responded; the bow came about and headed downstream in pursuit of the dredge boats. A headwind hampered the sailing fleet as the steam driven *Emma Dunn* closed behind them.

The oyster police boat had pulled within two hundred feet of its target when a cry of alarm arose from the decks of the dredge fleet.

"The bastards are back, boys! Let 'em have it!"

The *Emma Dunn* plowed forward. Musket balls pinged off the hull and splintered her wooden framework. A ball entered the wheelhouse through the shattered window, striking Smokey Noble.

"I'm shot, Captain!" Noble groaned and slumped to the deck.

Haynie grabbed the ship's wheel. "Officer Furnisss, I need you in here!" he shouted.

"I believe I'm dyin' Captain," Noble moaned. "Tell me it ain't so."

"I'll see to it as soon as I get someone to take the helm."

A hail of musket rounds peppered the *Emma Dunn* shattering the running lamps.

Devil Furniss appeared on hands and knees. "You want me at the wheel, sir?"

"Aye. Keep as low as you can. We'll be ramming that pungy just ahead."

"Aye, Captain."

Haynie knelt beside the wounded engineer and proceeded to cut through the right sleeve of his greatcoat, revealing a blood-soaked shirtsleeve.

"Lucky you're wearing that heavy coat. You'll mend. I'm going to cut off your other shirtsleeve and wrap the wound. You keep a hold on it to stop the bleeding."

Haynie finished dressing the wound and peered through the shattered window. They were no more than forty feet off the stern of the pungy. Musket balls continued to splatter around him.

He yelled, "Officer Jacoby! Fire that cannon into their rigging!"

From the bow of the *Emma Dunn* the cannon roared. The mast of the pungy splintered, sending sails and rigging crashing onto her deck.

Haynie turned to Furniss. "Ram her in the port quarter."

With the cannon's roar, the pungy's crew threw down their muskets and scrambled below deck, leaving behind one of their mates screaming, his legs pinned beneath a section of the fallen mast.

The *Emma Dunn's* hull ripped through the pungy's timbers with a grinding screech.

On the decks of the adjacent ships, men screamed curses as they feverishly hacked at the lines linking them to the stricken dredge boat.

"Damn boys, get 'er cut or we might go down with her!"

Crews, scurrying to free themselves from the next boat in line, abandoned their attack on the *Emma Dunn*.

"Back us out, Officer Furniss," Haynie ordered.

Through the broken window he shouted, "Officer Jacoby, reload that cannon and stand by."

Three men appeared on the pungy's deck showing empty hands. One of them yelled, "Don't shoot!"

The three drudgers leapt from the battered pungy onto the deck of the *Emma Dunn*.

"Peace officers hold your fire," Haynie ordered. In front of him, the three drudgers stood motionless, their hands raised.

"We surrender to ya, Captain!" one shouted. "We didn't mean no harm." He glanced at his comrades. "As for me, I'm done with drudgin'."

The others nodded in eager agreement.

Haynie looked them over and called out, "Peace Officer Tydings."

Tydings rushed forward without taking his eyes from the intruders, his musket pointed at their bellies.

"Search them for weapons, then secure 'em below."

As they turned away Haynie called after them, "What's the name of your boat? Who's the captain?"

The first man spoke up.

"The *Barbara Ann*. Captain Mahoney."

Haynie nodded and Tydings herded them toward the hatch.

With a grinding roar, the *Emma Dunn* shed the pungy, leaving a gaping hole in her hull.

Aboard the *Barbara Ann*, three men stood with their hands raised and empty.

"Help us, we're going down," one called out.

"Officer Furniss," Haynie ordered, "aim for that sloop to starboard."

To the men aboard the *Barbara Ann* he barked, "Stand as you are, we'll take you off shortly."

Gunfire erupted from the line of dredgers as the *Emma Dunn* closed on the sloop, *Hilda M.*

Haynie returned fire over the sill of the shattered wheelhouse window as Furniss steered for the sloop.

"Jacoby can't show himself enough to fire the cannon!" Haynie shouted. "Ram her."

The *Emma Dunn* struck the *Hilda M* amidships, cracking her hull from water line to deck. Musket fire peppered the police boat and the sloop clung stubbornly to the steamer's bow.

"We're hung up, sir!" Furniss yelled. "I can't get free of her."

"Ram her again with full force."

The *Emma Dunn* shuddered as her engines reversed, hesitated, then surged forward with a roar, snapping the sloop's timbers. The bow of the *Hilda M* pitched and the ship rolled on its side, hurling her screaming crew into the murky river. Bobbing in the icy water, the men clutched at the main mast, spewing curses at the police boat.

Abruptly gunfire ceased along the line of dredge boats. The river was suddenly silent, except for the cries of the men struggling alongside the capsized *Hilda M.*

Haynie holstered his revolver and ordered a cease-fire.

The remaining dredge boats began disappearing into the night, leaving it to the police boat to pull their comrades from the frigid river.

Haynie stepped out on deck.

"Peace Officer Jacoby, fish those men out of the water and get them below deck. We'll collect the others and lodge 'em all in jail tonight. Tomorrow we'll take the lot of 'em before the judge in Queenstown."

18

Queenstown, Maryland
January 5, 1869

Captain Mahoney and the crew of the *Barbara Ann* stood arrayed before the judge's bench. Some glared at Haynie and Jacoby, stationed at either end of their line. The rest shifted awkwardly, embarrassed by the ill-fitting clothing they had been given.

Behind them, officers of the Oyster Navy stood quietly, forming a barrier to escape. The Queen Anne's County sheriff and a deputy stood in front the judge's bench facing the prisoners.

Judge Bell peered down at the men lined up before him. A full head of gray hair and a thick mustache accented a fierce look.

"Which one of you is speaking for this here Oyster Navy?"

Haynie stepped forward.

"That would be me, Judge. Haynie McKenna, deputy commander to Hunter Davidson."

"Mister McKenna, I expect you can tell me just what the hell went on out in the Chester River last night."

"Yes sir."

Haynie nodded to the crew of the *Emma Dunn*.

"The men in that second row are all peace officers—"

"From what I hear there was nothing peaceful about it."

"—from the state oyster police boat the *Emma Dunn*. Our lawful orders are to sail Maryland waters alert for unlicensed oyster boats, poachers and watermen keeping culls. Last night we were patrolling the Chester River in response to reports of dredge fleets working there. Above Queenstown we encountered the *Tangier* and a fleet of about 12 dredge boats poaching on beds that, by law, are meant only for tongers."

Haynie returned the judge's hard look and continued.

"After a brief chase we were able to take the *Tangier* into custody. We continued upriver after the others and were met by a fleet of dredgers heading downstream. They were lashed together and spanned the width of the river showing red and green lights. The captains ignored a lawful order to strike their jibs and kept coming at us. We fired across their bow, as is proper by law, and the whole pack of them opened up on us. We spent the rest of the battle defending ourselves."

"You sunk one boat and rammed a big hole in another. Was that really necessary, Captain?"

"We were outgunned near ten fold, and they shot my pilot. We were fortunate it wasn't worse."

Haynie looked down the line of prisoners.

"They need to learn that we mean to enforce the law. If we had let them run us off, law and order on the bay would likely be done for. It's as simple as that."

"I was told you were bringing in three crews. This can't be all of them."

"No, Your Honor. The sheriff thought it would be better to bring in one crew at a time."

The judge pointed his gavel at the array of men in front of him.

"Who we got here?"

"Captain Mahoney and the crew of the *Barbara Ann*," Haynie said.

"Which one is Mahoney?"

The man standing beside Haynie looked up.

"That's me," he said.

The judge scowled.

"Mister Mahoney, and this goes for any of you who need to address the bench—that's me—you'll show proper respect for the court. You will address me as Your Honor, or Judge. As in, 'that's me, Your Honor.' We clear on that?"

Along the line, each man dropped his gaze.

"Yes, Your Honor," they murmured.

"Now then, Captain Mahoney, remove your cap and tell me what your take is on all this."

Mahoney yanked the knit wool cap from his head.

"Well, sir—Your Honor—we was just sailin' down the Chester, minding our own business, when this here big steamboat starts shootin' at us. 'Course we was forced to shoot back."

Haynie interrupted. "Your Honor—"

The judge silenced him with a gesture and directed his question to Mahoney. "Sir, didn't you see their signal, or hear their halloo to strike your jib?"

"Er—musta missed it," Mahoney said and resumed glaring at Haynie. "What with all the shootin' they was doin'."

"Is the *Barbara Ann* a dredge boat?

"Well—yes sir."

"Was the Barbara Ann part of a fleet of dredgers?"

Mahoney shrugged. "I—reckon..."

"What were you all doing that far from the bay?"

Mahoney scratched his head. "We was..."

"Don't tell me some story. It'll just make it worse for you. Were you dredging up there?"

Mahoney eyed his crew. "Well, er, um..."

Judge Bell rapped his gavel. "That's enough. One hundred dollar fine or ten days in jail for you; twenty-five dollars or two days for each crewman."

He looked at the sheriff. "Bring in the next batch."

"Excuse me, Your Honor," Haynie protested. "The state of Maryland wants to seize the boats we brought in. The *Barbara Ann*, if it can be salvaged, along with the *Tangier* and *Hilda M.* A fine, even a stiff one, seems too lenient. If you recall, one of my men was wounded in the gunfire. The state takes this as real serious."

The judge's face glowed red.

"You sink this man's boat—the only means he has to feed his family—and now, on the slim chance it can be salvaged, you want to take it away from him?"

"It's the law, Your Honor."

"It may be the law in Annapolis, but I am the law over here. As for shooting your pilot, you point out the man who did it and I'll deal with him."

"There's no way to know, Judge."

Bell jabbed his gavel toward Haynie. "Well," he growled, "I'm certainly not of a mind to punish the whole lot of 'em."

He rapped his gavel. "Bring in the next gang."

19

Annapolis, Maryland
January 7, 1869

Lila grabbed Haynie as he walked through the front door and held him as tight as she ever had. With her face buried in his chest she asked, "How many were killed?"

Haynie held her away from him and smiled.

"No one was killed. I'm sure it wasn't nearly as bad as you heard."

She released him while he hung his coat on the hook in the hallway, and then led him to his chair. Lila sat beside him and gripped his hand.

"It's been two nights," she said. "Where have you been? I've fretted the whole time. The children cried because they didn't know why I was crying. I didn't know what to tell them."

"We had to take the ones we caught to jail. The next morning we took them before the judge, which took up most of the day. After court, we went back up the Chester River to see about the dredge boat that was sunk, and have a look around. After we docked in Annapolis, I reported to Commander Davidson and came straight home."

"Tell me the truth. I believe you owe me that much. I heard some were shot. Was that wrong, too?"

"We winged a couple of drudgers. One on our side was nicked."

"This is the first real encounter you've had with them."

Haynie nodded.

"If you're going to be shooting it out every time you try to board one of those boats, I doubt you'll live to be at Ella May's birthday."

"Fortunately for us, they were mostly firing six-shooters and old smoothbore muzzle loaders. Fortunately for them, so were we."

"What does that mean?"

"Smoothbores don't have rifling, so they are not very accurate. General Grant said of smoothbore guns: 'You might fire at a man all day from 125 yards without him ever finding out.' A muzzleloader takes longer to reload, so a man gets off fewer shots. "

"What did the state give you to defend yourself with?"

"We have a few Springfield Model 1842s left over from the war. The state got them cheap from the national government. Some of the boys brought their own guns when they joined up. When the shooting starts and minie balls come a calling, a man can't get a good aim at where he's shooting."

"That's all the state will give you to defend yourself?"

Haynie shrugged.

Lila opened her mouth and Haynie kissed her on the forehead. Sniffing the air he said, "Smell's like supper's close. Hate to see it burned."

Lila laughed through her tears and squeezed his hand.

"Damn you," she said and rushed into the kitchen.

Lila put supper on the table while Haynie lay on the floor with the children squealing as they crawled over him.

With supper over and the children in bed, Haynie and Lila sat before the fire.

"That was a mighty fine supper, ma'am."

"I usually cook some extra, in hopes, I guess, that you'll come through the door."

"It looks like I'll be home for supper a couple more nights. Have to stay around to answer questions about the Chester River fracas."

"Good, you can practice your answers on me. I have some questions of my own."

Haynie yawned. "I'm not up to thinking about it tonight. You can ask me anything tomorrow. Instead I'd like to hear what you have been doing to pass the time while I'm away."

Lila wanted to say that she "passed the time" by taking care of his children. Instead, she talked about the women she had come to know from her weekly get-togethers at Wilma Winder's home.

"Some of the ladies I meet with, especially the older ones are not shy about having a glass or two of wine. It's gotten so we start every meeting with a toast."

It occurred to Haynie to inquire who was minding his children while she was away at these meetings, but he knew the children's welfare was always foremost in Lila's thoughts. Instead, he said, "Is it safe to ask what goes on at these meetings, besides drinking wine?"

"Mostly we chat about things that interest us." She laughed. "Like our husbands and children—the latest fashions. You know—lady things."

Haynie yawned and stretched. "Sounds boring. I see why the ladies are so eager to get to the wine."

"That's because you men lead lives which are much more exciting than ours. Our options for amusement are limited. Once in a while we take up a discussion of politics."

"You have no interest in politics; it must be awful for you."

"I'm learning. After all, you did bring me to the state capital."

She paused and watched his face. "Some of the ladies are upset about the Fourteenth Amendment to the Constitution."

"Why?"

"Do you know what it says?"

Haynie shrugged. "Mainly it says colored folks who are citizens can vote. Is that what has them upset?"

Lila shook her head. "The amendment does not say colored folks—only colored men. The ladies are not upset about who the amendment included; they're upset about who was excluded. All women."

"You keep saying *they*, yet you sound vexed. Are you upset too?"

"What do you think?"

20

Silas Wallis raised his glass. "To Captain McKenna, a true warrior. Well done," he said.

After tasting the wine, he held the glass up to the light.

"I cannot imagine a more beautiful white burgundy than this Montrachet. See how the light dances through the golden hue."

Haynie nodded and sipped from his glass.

Wallis appeared in better spirits than at their last meeting. He was clean-shaven, his suit pressed. "I want to say how proud I am of you," he said. "The newspapers are hailing you as a hero. Tell me, how accurate were they in the details?"

"Can't say. I don't read any papers. They seldom get it right."

"They said it was one hell of a battle, with lots of shooting and you sinking a couple of dredgers."

Haynie shrugged.

"While the reports herald your deeds, a *Sun* editorial complained that you overpowered the dredgers. It said the last thing the people want is more fighting. The paper also got in some licks at the legislature for creating a seagoing war machine."

As Colonel Wallis refilled his glass Haynie said, "Commander Davidson is being bombarded with demands for explanations. One delegate insisted that we account for every minie ball that we fired. He is threatening to deduct their cost from our budget. I was ordered to wait a couple of days before taking the *Emma Dunn* out, in the event there are more questions. Not exactly a hero's welcome."

"That's a bunch of political mumbo jumbo. Anarchy on the bay has to long been ignored. I am tellin' anyone who will listen that if they run scared they're going to lose the few good men we have. Moreover, if they drive out men like you and Davidson, who will take your place? An assortment of political hacks is who."

"I need to get back out there. With the *Emma Dunn* in port, and the *Leila* still not commissioned, the *Kent* is our sole presence on the water. Captain Pack is a good man but, like the rest of us, a bit overwhelmed by our responsibilities and lack of resources."

"Praise be that no one was killed. You had just the one wounded, so your crew is otherwise undisturbed?"

"One man left the ship in Chestertown and hasn't returned. Just as well, I would have fired him anyway."

"What for? Cowardice?"

"I suspect it, but it would be hard to prove. During the battle, a couple of drudgers jumped aboard the *Emma Dunn* and surrendered. I told Officer Tydings to take them below. After a couple of minutes Officer Stainbrook goes below and tells Tydings I sent him to watch the drudgers and Tydings was to go on deck. Nothing is said about this until the next morning, when we form up for court. By then Stainbrook is gone."

"He figured to stay below until the shooting was over then hightail it."

Haynie nodded. "We'll catch up with him later. Actually, I'm grateful to him. It gives me an opportunity to bring Gerhard Stein aboard. You met Gerhard didn't you?"

Wallis nodded. "He carried our luggage from the dock to your office when Sterling and I came to Crisfield for Landon. He insisted on carrying every piece himself. A giant of a man."

"Gerhard was a Prussian soldier who ran out of interesting wars in Europe so he joined ours. We went through most of the war together. Afterwards, he came home with me to Crisfield. He is the most loyal and fearless man I know. Helped me take that killer Rat alive."

Haynie drank some wine and said, "It seems to me that shooting it out on water is a whole lot different than on land. I expect if we had been on dry land, men on both sides would have thrown down their guns or fled. But when a man's only choice is to fight or jump into black icy water, he's more likely to stay and fight."

Wallis nodded.

"Or, hideout below deck," Haynie added.

Colonel Wallis glanced at the empty tables around them and leaned forward. "Recognizing that you have other responsibilities, I hope I won't be disappointed. Have you any news?"

"Seeing Mooney and Hollins pay for their crimes is never far from my thoughts. Fortunately there are a few quiet hours on the water when I can devote some time to them."

Wallis smiled broadly. "Excellent!" He refilled both glasses.

"Please continue," he said and offered his glass in another salute. "Here's to a painful end for them."

"Keep in mind that pain comes in many forms," Haynie replied.

"The more pain the better, where they are concerned."

Haynie sipped some wine and set his glass on the tablecloth.

"I visited Popes Creek and spoke to our friend Hoppy. He told me the same thing he wrote in his wire to you. Mooney and Hollins spent the night and stopped by to see him on their way out of town. They had a wagonload of belongings.

"Mooney told him that he was thinking about selling the place and paid Hoppy for six months to keep the grounds real nice. Before they left, he challenged Hoppy about what had happened to the cloth bag with the red flowers—the ransom bag. Hoppy came right back saying that he knew nothing about it. If Mooney was saying he stole it, he'd give Mooney back his money and be done with him. Mooney apologized and said Grace must have it, and they drove on."

Wallis blinked. "Is that important?"

"I think it is. Before this, if we confronted Mooney he could say he knew nothing about the ransom bag. Had no idea it was there and we could not prove otherwise. Now the sequence is: You gave that same bag to Hollins with $75,000 in ransom payment; I found it in Mooney's house, empty; and Mooney has claimed ownership."

"Yes, yes. I see. Should I tell the city police?"

Haynie shook his head. "Let's wait. It's not much by itself; however it could be a piece of the rope we can hang them with."

"Where is the rest of this rope?"

"We don't have it all yet; but it's out there. We just have to find it."

"If we don't find it soon, I have an alternate plan."

"What is that, sir?"

"You may have noticed that I'm taking more care with my appearance, and my mood is more affable since we last spoke. I feel more spirited than at any time since I buried my darling Abbie."

Haynie smiled. "Yes, more interested in life I would say."

"It was literally an overnight occurrence. Christmas night, actually. The hour was late, and I was sitting in the dark, brooding and feeling sorry for myself, as was my custom. Having been at the wine with some vigor, I was drowsy. I had been muttering a litany of requests to the Lord Almighty. Then, I experienced an epiphany that eased my pain. I went straight off to bed and slept like a babe. The next morning I proceeded to restore my appearance to the condition you see before you."

Haynie raised his glass. "That is indeed wonderful news, sir. May I ask the nature of your revelation?"

Wallis returned the salute. "Of course, my boy," he said. "I can remain patient for a while longer, however, if our quest fails I'm going to hunt Hollins down and challenge him to a duel. Then I'm going to kill him."

Stunned, Haynie stared across the table. "Are you joking, Colonel?"

"I'm deadly serious. I find nothing humorous about those rascals."

"But the Congress has passed a law forbidding dueling."

Wallis smiled. "We the people tend to pick and choose among the laws imposed on us by the National Congress. I choose to ignore this one. Who in Maryland, a state where dueling is still legal, is going to enforce such a law?"

"But, sir—"

"Are you familiar with the field near Bladensburg which has been rightly dubbed 'The Dark and Bloody Ground'?"

Haynie shook his head.

"Over fifty duels have been fought there, many after the federal law was passed. More than one gentleman of note met his end on that field, hence the name. Commodore Stephen Decatur; Daniel Key, son of the man who wrote The Star-Spangled Banner; and a couple of congressmen, to mention only a few."

"That must have been years ago."

Wallis drank some wine and looked at Haynie. "Admittedly," he said, "dueling is no longer the solution to disputes that it once was. Still, it can serve a useful purpose."

"What will you do if Hollins refuses the challenge?"

"I considered that. Being that he is from Virginia, I doubt that he has heard of the Ground. If all else fails I will lure him there under a pretext. Once he's on the field, it will be over for him."

"No. No. You cannot do this. Think of your good name—your legacy."

"The only way you can deter me is by bringing him to justice first. I would much prefer that he spend the rest of his days enduring the agony of prison, instead of rotting in the ground in ignorance."

"How long are you prepared to wait?"

"Only as long as I feel there is hope."

"Did you also consider that if Hollins dies, there is virtually no chance of bringing Mooney to justice?"

"Let's hope it doesn't come to that."

Haynie studied Wallis's face closely. "I want to make certain that you understand the full consequences of any such action. I am in sympathy with your hate for Hollins. He duped you into thinking he was your friend and then took your money and, in your eyes; he took your precious Abbie.

"As I see it, Mooney was the leader and therefore responsible for everything that went on. The Drumm brothers; the ones who shanghaied Landon causing Abbie's decline were in Mooney's employ. Very likely most of their dealings were with Gastineau. It's quite possible Hollins never saw them.

"Mooney hired Rat knowing the man was a killer. Hollins, acting on orders, merely escorted him to Somerset County for the meeting with Sheriff Gastineau. It was well after that when Rat shot Caleb. I hold Mooney, not Hollins, responsible for the killing of my brother, Horsey Towne and those boys in that shack. I'm certain that without Hollins there is no way to bring Mooney to justice."

Haynie paused, held Wallis's gaze before saying, "So that is the answer to your question—who in Maryland would enforce the federal law against dueling? It is I, sir."

21

Dorchester County, Maryland
January 9, 1869

Marrok Blanchard was unbending. "There's no other way," he growled. "This Oyster Navy has to be dealt with *tout de suite*; we cannot delay. They will only become stronger. We will make an example of their bravest officer, this *Capitaine* McKenna."

Blanchard gulped some wine, looked at his sons and laughed.

"It is too bad we cannot wait while he destroys more of those scum who foul the water that is rightfully ours. The time is right; today he is a hero in the newspapers." He shrugged. "Tomorrow, who knows? By acting now, his death will be on the front page of every newspaper in the region. We will assassinate him on his own boat and the others will say, 'If they can get to him, there, what chance do we have?' No other *capitaine* in this Oyster Navy will dare to venture into our waters."

Blanchard laughed again and drained his wine goblet.

Benoit was first to speak. "Papa, I also believe McKenna's death is necessary. Still, I must ask how can we do this? Only the four of us? Surely we will be discovered before we could even get aboard the navy steamer."

Marrok looked at Renard. "Your brother has little faith in us. 'Only the four of us' he says."

He turned his scorn to Benoit. "Four Blanchards are worth twenty others," he snarled.

Renard said, "It seems my brother does not share my faith in you Papa." He turned to Guy. "Perhaps Benoit should stay home with this one and the other women. I am certain you have a good plan. I pray that I will be the one you select to bury the knife."

Marrok turned to his youngest. "Guy, *mon fils*, what say you?"

Guy summoned the will to utter, "It must be done."

22

The door swung open. Andrew blocked the entrance, eyes narrowed his hands quickly became fists.

"What you here for, white boy? We got nothin' left to steal."

Guy, his voice barely audible, struggled to meet the man's eyes. "I came to say...I'm real sorry about what happened to your boat. I didn't want any part of it and I want your Papa to know that I'm gonna get it back to you."

He thrust a small parcel wrapped in brown paper toward Andrew.

"See," he said. "I brought back the sail that was on her. I figured your Mama might have sewed it."

Andrew glared.

Tubman appeared at the open door. "What is it, Andrew?"

"This 'un say he gonna see we gets our boat back."

"You got our boat?"

Guy swallowed hard. "Well—er—uh—Mister—Tubman, is it?"

"Tubman'll do. Now, if you have something to say to me, you're gonna have to come inside 'cause I'm closing this door against the cold."

Guy moved to step in, but Andrew filled the doorway. "This is my house," Andrew said before stepping back.

Guy nodded, removed his fur cap and squeezed his way inside. The three men were crowded into a tight room, which served as a kitchen and dining room. A low ceiling pressed in and Guy found himself struggling for breath.

The oppressive air was laden with smoke leaking from a pot-bellied stove in one corner. Grimy pieces of muslin over the windows fluttered occasionally as drafts of cold air crept between the logs. Four wooden chairs were drawn up to a small table. The furniture had been cobbled together from randomly collected boards. A piece of worn oilcloth served as a floor covering.

Tubman nodded toward the chairs.

"Might as well sit while you say your piece."

"Thank you," Guy said and laid the parcel on the table.

"You're a Blanchard, ain't ya?" Tubman asked.

Guy nodded.

"I recollect when ya'll come for us you was the only one not wearing one of them funny foreign hats. Why was that, I wonder?"

Guy resisted an urge to bolt from the house. "Papa gives them to us boys as a kind of reward. He didn't think I'd earned it—back then."

"You got one now?"

Guy nodded.

"You earn it by stealing our boat?"

"Not—exactly."

"How come you ain't wearin' it?"

"I hate it." Guy glanced at Andrew, desperate to remove the hatred in those eyes.

"I do have your boat, sir. How that came to be I couldn't say. I didn't ask for it, and I sure don't feel right having it. One evening, a few days after we took you and your son into court, Papa and my brother Benoit come home with it. Papa makes a big thing about the French Navy—always has. He named your boat *Pluton* after some French warship and gave her to me—along with the beret."

"Beret. That the name of that funny little hat?"

"Yes sir." Guy twisted his fur cap with both hands.

"Look, sir, I been feeling real bad about takin' your boat 'til finally I couldn't stand it no more. I wanted you to know I'm trying to think of a way to get it back to you without getting us all killed."

"Who do you mean—us all killed?" Tubman asked.

"I'm sorry to say, but my Papa is a real scoundrel. I hate him for what he has done to our family—and to yours. If he was to find out I gave the boat back to you, he would kill me himself. Or, have one of my brothers do it—a test killing for one of them. And killin' a couple of darkies wouldn't bother him one bit."

With a tone matching the malice in his eyes, Andrew growled, "Guess he would have no trouble believin' us darkies stole it back. Why don't you give it back and tell him that?"

Guy shook his head.

"He would be furious however I let it get away. It would amount to the same thing. After he finished with me, he and my brothers would come looking for you. It wouldn't matter to them how you got hold of the boat; they would kill you both. No—I got to think of somethin' else."

Tubman studied Guy's face and then said, "It's been more'n a month. So how come you just now decided you had to give us back our boat?"

"Well, I, I expected you would have it back before now." Guy shrugged. "But I haven't been able to figure out how to go about it."

Guy dared a quick glance at Andrew. "I hope you will rest easier knowin' that you're soon going to have it back."

Guy nudged the parcel across the table.

"I brought this here sail off of yer boat. You should have it."

Both men ignored the package.

"Look here, young fella," Tubman said, "maybe yer bein' straight and maybe you ain't. Don't know. But yer dead wrong if you think I feel all warm inside 'cause you say we're getting' our boat back. You know that my boy and me can't work without that boat. It's been more than a month now with nuthin' comin' in. It could be that we'll miss the whole oyster season."

"I'm real sorry, sir. But you must see I took a big risk just comin' here."

Tubman pointed to the nearly empty shelves of a homemade pantry.

"Look at them shelves. Most empty they are. You planning to bring us food while you're thinkin' on how to give us back our own damn boat? Well don't bother. Wouldn't take it if ya did."

Guy gripped the table and looked from father to son. Andrew's hate blazed hotter.

Guy swallowed hard. "I promise it won't be much longer. I won't let you starve."

Andrew pounded the table with a huge fist.

Tubman snorted. "Listen to yerself, boy; you ain't makin' no sense. You say ya been thinking on this for all this time and haven't come up with nuthin'; so how you 'spect to make me believe you can figure it out before we starve?"

Tears welled in Guy's eyes and he dug his fists into his face.

Oh God! I can't be cryin' in front of these men. What'll they think of me?

He gulped in air. "I don't know, I don't know." His voice quavered. "My Mama is a good woman. She's tried to help me but, the truth is we can't do it alone."

"What can't you do alone?" Tubman asked.

Guy's shoulders sagged.

"I expect ya'll have heard of the state Oyster Navy."

Tubman nodded.

His voice almost a whisper, Guy said, "Papa wants to kill the head man—a Captain McKenna."

Guy drew himself up, his voice suddenly stronger. "I won't be a party to killing any man, certainly not a state lawman. Me and Mama believe Papa's touched in his head. The only thing we can think to do is to—well—to kill him ourself. But we can't figure how to go about it so ever' body don't know it was us. You can see the fix we're in."

Tubman thought a minute. "You pay attention to what I'm gonna tell you," he said. "If you are sayin' the truth I believe we can get you some help."

23

Aboard Ville de Paris
Honga River
Dorchester County, Maryland
January 12, 1869

Marrok called Benoit to take the helm while Renard stood at the rail scanning the shoreline around Norman Cove.

Guy watched with dread as his father approached. Since docking the *Pluton* yesterday upon his return from Taylors Island, Guy had feared the moment when Marrok would challenge him to explain his absence. After hours of worry, he now wished that moment to be over. Still, his pounding heart almost eclipsed his father's question.

In French Marrok asked, "Where did you go yesterday in the *Pluton*? I might have needed you; yet you say nothing?"

How would he react to that question? Guy had thought of nothing else as he sailed home from Taylors Island. Heat rose in his neck, turning his ears hot.

Following the plan he had devised, Guy looked straight at his father and replied in French. "Sorry, Papa, but I must get better at tacking my new boat. I spent the day out on the Honga."

Studying his son's red ears, Marrok said, "The *soleil* must have been stronger out there, than here."

Marrok glared and Guy held his father's eyes, convinced that all would be lost if he wavered. Should he falter at any time before he and his mother finished their desperate scheme, she would rush to protect him and both of them would be doomed.

A relentless pounding filled Guy's ears, making his father's words barely distinguishable.

"No," Marrok was saying, "Only a *petite amie* could make a young man's ears red in January. Tell me, *mon fils,* does your mother know about this girl?"

Guy's mind churned. *What was he saying? A girlfriend? Why didn't I think of that?*

Marrok pointed to Benoit standing at the helm and began a mock scolding. "*Mon fils,*" he said, "do not repeat the mistake made by your oldest brother and bring home an *infirme* strumpet."

Guy recovered to answer, "No, *mon pere* Momma does not know about *ma petite ami.* No one does."

Marrok stepped closer, fixing Guy with a menacing look.

"Do you expect me to believe that you did no tell your mother when you took her out in the *Pluton*?"

It took all the courage Guy could summon to return Marrok's gaze. "It was not the time..."

"*Capitaine! Capitaine!*" Renard yelled. "Come quickly."

Before turning away, Marrok snarled, "It would not be wise for you and that woman to keep secrets from me."

At the rail, Marrok took the glass and focused on the shoreline where Renard pointed.

"What is it *Capitaine*? Have you seen such a thing before?"

A shaken Guy, grateful for the distraction, joined them at the rail. His father might think it strange if he hung back, showing no interest in Renard's discovery.

Marrok watched a lone waterman pole a tiny boat along the marshy shore. A large iron pipe, extending well beyond the bow of the craft, was pointed in the direction of the marshy shore.

"It looks like he's toting a huge shotgun," Renard exclaimed.

"Benoit," Marrok shouted, "get us as close to that punt as you can."

Renard grew more excited. "What is it, Papa? What is it?"

"That little boat is a punt. That big gun looks to be about twelve feet long and likely weighs more'n a hundred pounds. It's lashed down tight to the boat. About the only thing the punt is good for is toting that gun around. That's why they call it a punt gun."

"What do they shoot with it?"

Marrok handed the glass back to Renard and made a large circle with thumb and forefinger.

"Most punt guns have a two inch diameter barrel and are loaded with about a pound of shot or nails, either'll do. See where the gun is aimed, just above the water line. A hunter gets the punt pointed at a flock of ducks or geese floatin' on the water and he fires the gun. Boom, she goes, and as the birds fly away, he drops 40 or 50 with one shot."

"Wow!" Renard exclaimed.

Marrok retrieved the glass and held it steady on the punt as the *Ville de Paris* closed.

"Boys. I been wantin' one of them for a while now. Remember, when we sail out of a morning, I say that we're going to the store, we just don't know yet what we're coming home with. Well, today we're going to the store for a punt gun."

"What if he lets go at us with that gun?" Renard asked. "It'll likely sink us."

Marrok scoffed. "Renard, you sometimes give me pause," he said. "He'd have to get that thing turned clear around 'fore he could line up on us. That's why you boys are going to be lookin' right down yer muskets when we hallo him. He'll be dead before he could get that pole in the water. Get your guns and stand at the rail."

The hunter, his back to the *Ville de Paris*, was intent on maneuvering his boat precisely in line with a flock of ducks floating close to shore.

Renard and Guy stood at the rail, their muskets trained on the punt.

Marrok called, "Ahoy in the punt, stand easy for the Oyster Navy."

Guy, taken aback by his father's words, resisted an urge to throw down his weapon.

The hunter whirled to see the bugeye sitting some 60 feet behind him. Instinctively, he reached for his shotgun then withdrew at the sight of muskets pointed at him.

Suddenly, the shore vibrated as hundreds of waterfowl took flight heading south, away from this threat.

The hunter shook his fist at the disappearing flock. "Damn, there goes today, flying away."

He turned to face the *Ville de Paris*. "See what you done. There was no call for that."

"You might want to change your tune," Marrok warned. "I'm a peaceful man by nature and right now I'm of a mind to let you off easy. You keep yapping and that could change right quick."

"What's that mean, let me off. If you're the state navy, how come you ain't flying the state flag? And—"

"Hush up," Marrok snapped. "I said I was ready to believe that you don't know punting is against the law. The law says we must seize any illegal guns we come across. So, I'm willing to seize your rig right here and let you go without taking you into court."

"What the—since when?"

"I'm trying real hard to do you a kindness. I'm offering to save you a hundred dollars or more and likely some days in jail. You're starting to sound ungrateful."

Filled with despair, the hunter held his hands out, palms up and said nothing.

Marrok nodded. "That's more like it. Here's what you do. You pole that punt out here and throw us your line. Then you hand up that shotgun, stock first, all the time you holdin' the barrel."

The hunter, shaking his head and cursing under his breath, picked up the pole and pushed the punt toward the bugeye.

After giving up the line and his shotgun, the hunter started to ask just how the Oyster Navy expected he was going to get to shore.

Marrok stopped him with a raised hand. "There's nowhere along here that this boat can get any closer to land. So, I'm thinking you should leave those heavy boots in the punt. Be easier for you to walk to shore without 'em."

"What in the hell! Walk to shore? It's too deep out here for any man to walk to shore. And, it's January, I'll catch my death in that water."

"What kind of waterman are you? This won't be the first time you've been in cold water. With them boots off, you can easy swim a few yards to the shallow water. Then you walk. You keep moving and you'll stay warm enough."

Marrok scanned the woods. "How far to your house?"

"It's dern near 4 miles down that a way." He pointed south toward Bishops Head, "Can't you tow me down a ways? It'd be better for me."

Marrok shook his head. "Like to help ya, but the Oyster Navy keeps a tight schedule and we're headed north. Look at it this way, all that walkin' will help keep you warm after your swim."

The hunter dared a last hard look and sat down to remove his boots. With that done, he stood, stepped to the stern of the punt and turned to face the men on the deck of the *Ville de Paris*.

He shook his fist and stepped off into the icy water.

Renard turned to his father, "Papa is it really illegal to have those big guns?"

Marrok shrugged. "Don't really matter, does it."

As the sails on the *Ville de Paris* billowed, Guy watched the hunter struggling toward shallow water. He heard his father chortle.

"Look at that punt gun, ain't she a beaut boys? Going to the store can be great fun."

24

Taylors Island
January 19, 1869

Guy stepped into Benny's tavern and was greeted by the smell of fish frying in cornmeal and butter. He brushed the snow from his coat while his eyes adjusted to the dim interior. Vestiges remained of the one-room school it had been. Heat radiated from an iron chunk stove in the center of the room.

Guy had spent a few years in such a schoolhouse and, for a moment, he was overcome by memories.

Being in school meant hours and days he did not have to spend defending himself from his brothers, and fearing his father.

Guy looked back at the door and visions of noon recess surfaced. He was always the first out of the door and the last back inside. He did not want to miss a minute of the games; Annie Over—at which he excelled—or Bug in the Gully, at which he did not.

Beyond the stove sat a massive wooden desk.

Must have been the teacher's desk.

Behind the desk, a colored man ignored Guy and scrawled the day's menu across a chalkboard.

Walls had been erected in the far corner forming a small kitchen, the source of the tantalizing aroma.

Tubman sat at a table along the sidewall, clutching a small glass of whiskey. He gave a quick nod as Guy approached.

Benny Crème glanced at Tubman, and returned to the chalkboard.

"You have any trouble findin' it?" Tubman asked.

"A little," Guy said and sat down.

"You fancy a drink of whiskey against the chill?"

Guy shook his head and looked around. "Your son with you?"

"Nothin' to be gained by him coming. 'Sides, he don't like bein' around you."

Guy unfolded his hands and picked at a finger.

"I guess I don't blame him. Is it just me, or is it all white folks?"

"Andrew don't like no white folks. You he hates."

"I never seen so much hate in a man's eyes before. I'm gonna try my best to make it go away."

Tubman took a drink and looked at Guy. "You decide if you'd be willin' to go with me to meet up with that Oyster Navy man I tole you about?"

"I want to sure enough. I told Mama and she was, well, she was relieved. She said that it was likely the only way we would get it done. Thing is we got to be careful of Papa."

Guy related Marrok's warning about keeping secrets, and Tubman nodded.

"You're right to be worried. Sometimes a body can work up such a hate he gets in a rush to see the other person done in and forgets all about bein' careful. How'd you get away to come here?"

"Mama sent me for some stores. Flour, bacon and such; wine for him. He thinks I'm seein' some girl so I believe we're okay for a couple more trips. I figure one trip to meet the policeman and one to get Papa killed.

25

Fifty or sixty women were crowded into the Winders's parlor. Lila McKenna was thankful that Wilma had reserved a front-row chair for her. Every seat was filled, and women stood two deep along the walls. Though the wind was howling outside, the press of bodies in the room dictated that Wilma shut down the coal stove.

Susan B. Anthony had been speaking for about three quarters of an hour. Lila wished she had thought to bring writing materials to record the ideas she was hearing.

What had she said about the Union? Something like, "It was we the people; not we, the white male citizens; nor we, the male citizens; but we, the whole people who formed the Union." How memorable.

I think my favorite is, "Men their rights and nothing more; women their rights and nothing less." Very succinct.

She is a wonderfully inspired woman, clearly doing the Lord's work. Still I feel sorry for her. Her appearance—that severe black dress and hair in a tight bun, those rimless spectacles— tells me that she is very unhappy. Mostly it shows in her face. The thin mouth turned down at the corners as if she has never smiled. And her eyes. No hint of passion. Anger certainly, but no hint of passion spawned by love.

Anthony was saying, "Educated white women would be better voters than ignorant black men or immigrant men."

Her piercing eyes darted about the room as her voice reached a crescendo.

"How can you not be all on fire? I really believe I shall explode if some of you young women do not wake up your voice in protest. Do come into the living present and work to save us from any more barbaric male governments."

As was her custom, Lila waited while her hostess bade everyone goodnight. Eventually Wilma approached, lighting a cigarette.

"What did you think of her?" she asked.

Lila's eyes followed the trail of smoke escaping from Wilma's mouth, the woman's words lost amid the haze.

Wilma laughed. "Am I the first woman you ever saw smoking a cigarette?"

Lila made a face and nodded.

"You don't approve."

"I'm so sorry. No, it is not that. I was just imagining how they must taste."

"Does your husband smoke?"

Lila shook her head.

"I just took it up," Wilma said, "largely for spite. It is acceptable for a man to smoke, but forbidden to a 'lady.' Then, maybe I am not a lady. In any event, I find it relaxing after a stressful time, such as tonight. I don't believe you heard me—I asked what you thought of Susan Anthony."

Lila drew her attention from the cigarette. "Her words were very inspirational. Of course I agree with her completely; but I wonder..."

"What is it?"

"I hope you won't think ill of me."

Wilma blew smoke away from Lila. "Of course not," she said. "Please go on."

"From what I know of the women who have spoken to us, this, this crusade—if you will—is their entire reason for being. It seems particularly true of the most ardent ones, Sojourner Truth and Susan Anthony. Am I wrong?"

"I would not disagree with that."

"It made me wonder if it's possible for a woman to love a man and, indeed, have a family with him; and still be able to put forth the energy needed to work alongside such women."

Wilma stepped to a nearby table and crushed out her cigarette.

"I'm sorry if I've upset you," Lila said. "I shouldn't have said anything."

Wilma returned smiling. "You didn't upset me. Actually, I have had the same thoughts, and the answer is; I do not know. I have decided to do what I can, and if that is not enough for me, I will try to do more. I think you'll know when the time comes that you must make a choice."

Lila sighed. "You're right—of course. I was hoping for an easy answer to a difficult problem and, like most things in life, there isn't one."

Wilma lit another cigarette and offered one to Lila.

Lila shook her head. "Not yet anyway."

"Have you given any more thought to writing something for *Godey's*?"

"Oh yes, thank you. That is what I wanted to tell you before I was sidetracked. I took it to heart when you said, 'Shame on me for not even trying.' "

Lila took a deep breath. "I sent a piece to them," she said. "So— we'll see."

Clearly disappointed, Wilma managed a weak smile. "That's very exciting, but I was hoping I would get to read it."

"I didn't want to bore you. If they print it, we will read it together. Here, at one of the meetings, if you like. If they don't print this, maybe I'll try something else."

"What did you write about?"

"It's a story about one of the strongest women I've ever met, my husband's mother, Lettie McKenna. Living next door to her was a bit awkward. It was clear she didn't think highly of me and we had our clashes with her over Young Tench. In spite of our differences, I admire her for leaving Smith Island and her struggle to raise her two boys after her husband was murdered. She—well never mind. I'll save that for you to read if they publish it."

"What name did you use?"

"I made up names for her and the boys."

"I meant, what name did you give when you sent it in?"

"My own. I am certainly not ashamed of what I am doing and I will not hide behind another name. Besides, no one who knows me is going to see it, except for you and the others here."

26

Aboard Emma Dunn
Eastern Shore of Maryland
January 26, 1869

In turn, each of *Emma Dunn's* crew shook hands with the man introduced by Captain McKenna as the ship's new assistant engineer.

"Gentlemen," Haynie said, "this is Gerhard Stein. He is coming aboard to help Smokey Noble while his arm mends. He fought in the Prussian army and beside me in our war. You can count on him if we get in a tight place."

The new man was even larger than the captain and carried with him the assurance of a man unafraid.

Zack Bramble grabbed Stein's hand.

"Peace Officer Bramble. Glad to have you aboard. We was in a tight scratch the other night. Sure could'a used ya."

Stein smiled and nodded as he shook each hand. Afterward he followed Haynie into the wheelhouse.

Smokey Noble waited at the ship's wheel anticipating orders to get under way. His right arm still in a sling, he extended his left hand to his new assistant.

Haynie said, "Mister Noble, this is the help I promised you. For a while, I was not sure if you would return. We're all glad you did."

"Thank ya, Captain. The wife is upset with me. She said I would rather go off and get myself killed than sit home with her."

Noble chuckled. "When I didn't deny it she threatened to head into town and find herself a new man. But, I just couldn't let you fellas down. Not after what we went through on the Chester."

"The whole crew is glad you're back. Show Gerhard what you need done. His English is getting better. He's a quick study and he never tires. Get us under way with a heading to Cambridge."

"Aye, sir."

Haynie laid a hand on Gerhard's shoulder. "You all set *mein freund*?"

"*Ja.*"

Emma Dunn docked at Town Point on the Little Choptank River. Nathan Jacoby appeared from the leeward side of the wharf building where he had taken shelter from the biting wind. He tied off the lines thrown to him and hurried aboard.

Jacoby shivered as he entered the galley. "Hope you got lots of hot coffee."

Skillets scoffed. "It's the dead of winter, Mate. Have you ever been in my galley when the coffee wasn't hot?"

Still wearing his greatcoat, Jacoby carried a mug of steaming coffee to the table. He stirred in sugar and drank as he waited for the captain.

Haynie stuck his head in the galley. "Mister Jacoby," he said, "I hope you have something good to report."

"Sir, you ain't gonna believe it."

Without waiting for a signal from his captain, the cook put on his coat and hoisted a burlap bag. "I'm goin' below for some stores Captain."

Haynie nodded and brought a mug of coffee to the table.

"Am I going to need something stronger than coffee for this?"

Jacoby grinned. "Benny Crème got word to me that Roscoe wanted to meet. Too damn cold for that grove at Tobacco Stick. Benny told me on the sly that the old man's true name is Tubman; that boy of his is Andrew. 'Course when we met, I didn't let on that I knew his real name. He was alone, left the boy home. Not sure why. I figure the boy for a hothead and maybe the old man don't want him knowin' everything that's going on."

"To be safe," Haynie said, "we'll keep calling him Roscoe."

"Aye, sir. What are we gonna call his boy? Doesn't make good sense to call one by a false name and the other by his real one."

"Let's make it easy on ourselves. Old Roscoe and Young Roscoe."

"Aye. Old Roscoe told me that one day he opened his front door and there stood one of the Blanchard clan."

"Alone?"

"Alone. It was Guy, the youngest. He'd come to tell them not to fret about their boat because he was going to give it back."

"So the Blanchards did get it. With Roscoe getting his boat back he won't be so anxious to help—"

"Oh no, sir. That's not how it went. Listen to this. The Blanchard boy—"

"Guy."

"Aye, Guy. He blurts out that he can't give the boat up yet or his daddy will kill him."

"Kill his own son? That's pretty strong."

"That's what he told Roscoe."

"Doesn't make sense. Why come all the way over there to tell them about something that he can't do because it will get him killed."

Jacoby got up and went to the stove. "Want yours warmed up captain."

Haynie held out his mug. "Thank you."

Jacoby continued with his story as he poured coffee. "I figure the old man reads folks pretty good, especially a young white boy. Benny says Roscoe can read a man's face as easy as some can read a newspaper. They stopped playin' cards with him a long time ago."

The mate returned the steaming mugs to the table. "Roscoe said the boy talked about how the look of hate in Young Roscoe's eyes kept haunting him 'til he had trouble sleepin'. He owned up to feelin' real guilty because it was the same as if his kin had stole that boat, and he aimed to give it back to them."

"Well, mate, you were right when you said I wasn't going to believe it. Sounds like one of two things—the Blanchards are layin' a trap for them, or someone is layin' one for us."

Over the brim of his mug Jacoby said, "There's more. Roscoe had trouble with the story so he says to the boy, 'You come over here and tell us to be patient; that we're going to get our boat back—and that's it. You can't say when, or how, it's gonna get done. Makes no sense. By now the buck—Young Roscoe—is burnin' holes through the white boy with his eyes. He yells out, that he and the old man will up and steal it back and be done with it."

"Can't really blame them."

"Guy says he wouldn't hear of it. If they stole it Marrok would kill him—for lettin' it get away—and then come after both of them. So now they're stumped again."

Haynie shook his head. "Why did Guy go there with all this talk of killing? I'm going to give your boat back, except, if I do, we'll all get killed? If he's not setting a trap, it could be all talk. He's hoping they'll forgive him because he's really trying to do the right thing."

"Roscoe didn't buy it either and called him on it. Guy holds back for a minute then blubbers that the only way out is—to kill his father. Admits he and his mother have been trying to think of ways to do it so's no one would know it was them; but couldn't come up with nothing."

"He came over there to ask them to help with killing his father? Why now? There must be something else."

Jacoby nodded. "He didn't ask for their help, but there is something else. Something big. The boy blurts out that Marrok and the two brothers are anxious to kill tongers. He says he wants no part of it, but is scared he'll be forced into it. Finally, he fesses up that Marrok has a hate on for us, the Oyster Navy. Says the old man means to drive us out of *his* water. Now their plotting to kill an Oyster Navy man on his own boat—and soon."

"Any idea who they want to kill?"

"The hero of Chester River. You!"

"They are figuring to come aboard the *Emma Dunn* and kill the captain, easy as that?"

"That's what he told 'em.

Haynie drank some coffee. "Mate, it sounds like we need to get ready for company," he said.

27

The justice of the peace hooked his thumbs through the straps on his bib overalls and faced the irate men before him.

"I'm the justice of the peace in these parts and I come straight from milkin'," he said without apology. "The name's Henry Stevens. What the hell is all this?"

The county sheriff gave up trying to work his gun belt up over his sagging belly and took the corncob pipe from his mouth.

"Well, Henry—"

"Not here, Elroy! Dammit!"

"Sorry—Judge. It seems we had a visit from that state navy we've heard about." He nodded at Haynie. "That one says he's a Captain McKinny. His gang brought in all these other fellas here."

The sheriff waved a hand at the ten men huddled between Haynie and Devil Furniss.

"McKinny here said his gang come upon this crowd drudging oysters in the Potomac. Seems they are citizens of the Commonwealth of Virginia."

Obviously pleased with his account of the events, Elroy returned the pipe to his mouth.

The judge limped to a nearby table and eased himself into a scarred wooden swivel chair.

"Sorry there's not seats for everyone. We'll make this as quick as we can."

Once settled he scanned those before him, letting his eyes rest on Haynie.

"Captain—McKinny, is it?"

"It's McKenna, your honor."

"McKenna then. I guess my first question is: were these men in Maryland or Virginia when you come upon them?"

One of the prisoners edged forward, shifted a cud of tobacco to his cheek. "We was in Virginny, Judge," he declared.

"They were in Maryland," Haynie replied.

"He's a-lyin' Judge. We was so close to Virginny I could a spit on the bank."

With that, he faced toward a corner of the room, tilted his head back and expelled a stream of brown juice almost twenty feet into the far corner of the room.

"That close we was."

The judge followed the brown arch with admiration. "Damn!" he said and dug into his own pocket.

After gnawing a sizable chew from a plug of tobacco, he turned to Haynie. "Hell of a shot. Was his boat that close to Virginia?"

"Can't say—but it doesn't matter. The Potomac River to the south bank, at low tide, is in Maryland."

The drudger bristled. "The hell. I seen a map with the state line drawed right down the middle of the river."

The judge shook his head and looked to the sheriff.

"Elroy, you ever hear of such a thing?"

Elroy removed his hat and scratched at a bald spot at the back of his head.

"Nope. And I don't believe it, 'cause I don't have a boat."

"Elroy, what the hell you talkin' about?"

"Were it true, I'd have to tend to every soul who fell in and drowned himself or shot himself duck hunting. The county didn't give me no boat when I took the job. Seems to me if the county stretched across the river they'd of give me a boat."

The judge nodded. "I'll be damned if you ain't making some sense, Elroy. What do you have to say about that, Mister McKenna?"

"Well, Judge, I've seen that same map and all I can say is, whoever drew it was wrong. As for Elroy here, I expect he had better get himself a boat. The state of Maryland wants its laws enforced to the south bank of the Potomac."

Judge Stevens turned to one of the drudgers. "Where's your home?"

"King George County in Virginia."

"You ain't all off the same boat, are ya?"

The drudger shook his head.

"Speak up when you're in my court. What's yer name?"

"It's Hurley, Judge. I'm the captain of the one boat."

Another drudger stepped forward.

"The name's Barnes; the other boat's mine."

The judge spat a stream of brown juice at his feet and looked at Hurley. "Not even going to try and come near to your shot."

He chewed in silence for a while then pointed to Haynie, "Here's the thing: I have to think that this Oyster Navy man knows what he's talkin' about. But that don't really matter: I hate drudgers, and drudging in the Potomac River is wrong. Here's what we're gonna do—I'm fining you captains one hundred dollars each, and your boats now belong to Mister McKenna, there. As for your crews, they're gonna be stayin' with the sheriff here for ten days. You're not gonna need 'em anyways."

Haynie and Devil Furniss approached the *Emma Dunn*. On deck, Nathan Jacoby stood alongside a man wearing a Stetson hat and a fringed buckskin jacket, a pearl handled revolver holstered at his side.

"Captain McKenna," Jacoby said, "this here is Captain James Sewell of the Virginia Oyster Navy."

Sewell looked to be about forty with the weathered face of a seafarer. His hands stayed in his coat pockets, and Haynie nodded a greeting.

"Captain Sewell. Welcome aboard the *Emma Dunn*. How can we help you?"

"Captain McKenna, can we talk in your cabin?"

Haynie led the visitor aft to the galley. He entered first and motioned for Skillets to leave.

"Hot coffee, Captain?" Haynie asked.

"Thank you, no. I do not smoke or chew, no coffee or spirits. It is my own idea, not the doing of any church. If I may, I'll sit while you serve yourself."

Haynie returned to the table with a steaming mug and sat down. He crossed his legs, drank his coffee and waited.

Sewell laced his fingers on top of the table.

"I always like to know who I'm dealing with, and I expect the other person feels the same—especially in this business. As for myself, I served honorably in the Confederate Naval Forces, reaching the rank of captain. I had the pleasure of serving with Hunter Davidson. As fine an officer as I have come across. After the war, I was pleased to accept a command position in the Virginia navy."

Sewell sat back. "And you, sir?"

"I wore the blue and got my exercise marching back and forth across Maryland and Virginia. Didn't like it much. Never thought of the men I killed as my enemy and certainly not evil. It was an unlikely war. One where soldiers could have switched uniforms and no one would take notice. Both sides the same race, talked to the same God, and, with the exception of some men from Alabama I ran across, we spoke the same language. I figured they were just as scared as I was and, like me, would have been happy to throw down their guns and go home to their families."

Haynie shrugged, "But we all stayed on and killed one another."

Sewell sat back and studied the other man before offering his hand.

"My apology for staring, Captain, but a philosopher was the last thing I expected to find in the Maryland Oyster Navy."

As they shook hands Sewell said, "I never told this to anyone before, but I chose the navy hopin' I wouldn't have to see men dying close-up."

Sewell slapped the holstered revolver at his side.

"What we're doing now is quite different. The men we're facing have a choice and, if they choose to fight the law, they're going to pay."

He waved a hand toward the Potomac.

"They aren't fighting for a cause, or out of fear; they fight us out of their own greed."

Haynie nodded. "That's how I see it," he said. "I'm determined to beat them. What brings you aboard the *Emma Dunn*?"

"I'm the captain of the steamer *Shenandoah*. She's tied up over yonder."

Haynie nodded. "I noticed her. Fine looking vessel."

"I'm one for keeping my boat trim and my crew hard. We did it that-away in the recent war and, the way I see it, this here is a war."

Haynie nodded again.

"We heard you boys had brought in some drudgers and I was asked to see what it was about. Are they Virginians?"

"Two crews. Said they hailed from King George County. Claimed to believe they were in the Virginia half of the river. None of them seemed to know that the Maryland line starts at the southern shore; neither did the judge or sheriff."

"What happened?"

"Judge said that he hates drudgers. Took their boats and fined the captains one hundred dollars each. The crews got ten days in jail."

"Whew. He's tough. Reckon the captains would rather be doing the ten days."

Sewell shifted in his seat. "There's something else I'd like to discuss with you."

Haynie waited.

"Most everybody in the Virginia navy knows the Potomac belongs to Maryland, but nobody's gonna say it out loud. They're still hoping some court will rule that at least half of it is in Virginia. Up to now, we've had free run along the whole river. Who was going to say anything? But now that Maryland has its own navy we need to figure out what to do about the river."

"I'm not sure there is anything to discuss. You can't enforce Maryland laws, same as I can't enforce Virginia's. Besides, we each got plenty of work in our own waters."

"That's fer damn sure. Why, the Rappahannock alone is a full time job for one vessel. None of us wants to work the Potomac. But we have a couple of creeks running out of there that, from time to time, require our attention. The only way we can get to them is from the Potomac. Our commander wants the state of Maryland to know that we'll only use the Potomac as a road, so to speak, to get where we need to go. None of our boats will be conducting business on the big river."

Haynie drank some coffee and made a face.

"Cold. I'll just get some warm."

Returning to his chair, Haynie said, "I'll tell Commander Davidson when I get to Annapolis. I doubt there'll be a problem."

"Thank you captain," Sewell said and stood to leave.

"Before you go," Haynie said, "I could use your help with some other business in Virginia."

Sewell nodded.

"This will take some telling. You may want to sit back down."

28

Southey Hollins stepped into the Henley House and was jarred to see a stranger seated at a table with Horace J. Mooney.

Henley House was a one-story tavern with a Dutch roof over gray weatherboard siding, dating back to the late 17th century. Walk-in fireplaces crackled at either end of the long room. Mooney and the stranger had taken a remote table along the rear wall.

When Robert E. Lee surrendered his Army of Northern Virginia, Horace J. Mooney and Grace Stringfellow were well established in Maryland society. They cursed Lee for giving in to the Yankees and swore that the cause of Southern rebellion was not dead.

Mooney recruited Hollins, a former comrade, into their rag-tag corps. Hollins was given the rank of major and ordered to Maryland to raise funds to finance their rebellion. By whatever means necessary.

Hollins insinuated himself into the life of Silas Wallis, becoming an agent for Wallis & Sons Merchant Traders. He accepted Wallis's money under the pretext of being influential in Virginia shipping circles.

The shanghaiing of young men for sale to renegade oyster boat captains also turned a profit for their cause. The rebel group hired thugs who prowled the waterfronts of towns and villages bordering the Chesapeake Bay, preying on recent immigrants and other lone males. Occasionally the son of a wealthy family was caught in their snare. If Mooney and Hollins learned of their victim's prominence before he was sold to a drudge boat captain, they connived to extract a substantial ransom from the family.

When Silas Wallis learned that his son, Landon, had been kidnapped, he naively turned to Hollins for help. Hollins alerted Mooney to the opportunity and was instructed to send a ransom note demanding $50,000.

Hollins quickly realized that this was a rare chance for him. In no other instance, had he been so close to the source of the payment. Preying on Wallis's despair, Hollins increased the demand to $75,000 and boldly volunteered to deliver the payment himself.

At the appointed time, Hollins walked out of Wallis & Sons carrying a colorful carpetbag stuffed with $75,000 in cash. Once certain that no one was watching, he hurried to his own living quarters, took out $25,000 for himself and stashed the bag. After an appropriate interval, Hollins returned to the office of Wallis & Sons and collapsed into a chair.

"There was two of 'em," he gasped. "Ugly brutes, I feared they would kill me on the spot."

"You are a brave man, Southey," Wallis said. "What you have done for this family will not be forgotten."

Hollins had remained close to the distraught family selectively offering advice meant to thwart any rescue. His efforts at diversion grew bolder after Silas Wallis hired Haynie McKenna to head up a search of Somerset County for his son.

When Landon Wallis escaped from the oyster dredge boat *Fish Hawk* and returned home, Hollins abruptly departed from Baltimore, citing the press of business in Virginia. He proceeded directly to the house at Popes Creek, where he delivered the remaining $50,000 to Horace Mooney and a greedy Grace Stringfellow.

Possession of such a sum seemed to ignite Grace's passions. Her emotional turbulence became wholly unpredictable. Mood swings transported her from deep depression to intense agitation.

At a Baltimore social event, Grace physically attacked her hostess. Another evening, after swigging champagne from the bottle, she cursed all Yankees and warned those present that, Robert E. Lee be damned, the South was not dead. Soon after this outburst, Mooney took her home to Staunton, Virginia.

Since that time, Hollins lived in dread that Mooney would somehow discover his perfidy in increasing the ransom amount and holding out the $25,000 for himself. Any mention of the ransom money brought him to the edge of panic.

Hollins reminded himself repeatedly that Mooney and Grace could not know of his treachery; still, why press his luck? Grace's vile outbursts, often directed at him, offered Hollins a convenient excuse and he had avoided the couple for months.

Several weeks ago Hollins had unhappily agreed to accompany Mooney to Magnolia Bluff. His finances were painfully depleted and he had hoped to learn details of the couple's current money making scheme. It quickly became evident that there was nothing to be gained by this foolhardy venture into Maryland. Mooney spent the trip lamenting Grace's deteriorating condition, while Hollins searched over his shoulder for imaginary pursuers.

Very recently, after returning home from several unproductive weeks in Norfolk, Hollins had received a note from Mooney asking him to meet.

Approaching the table, Southey Hollins fretted over Mooney's reasons for insisting that they meet in this remote village on the banks of the Rappahannock River.

Certainly, they have ceased that foolishness about renewing the war; yet, they are up to something. He can't know about the $25,000. Still...And who is this stranger? He could be anyone behind that swooping handlebar.

Hollins absently rubbed a finger across his clean upper lip.

God, did I look like that when I had my handlebar? Between the bush under his nose and the shiny hair, he resembles a stage villain at the opera house. One thing—if they somehow learned about the money, they won't kill me until they can get their hands on the $25,000. Unless, they figure that it is gone, which it is.

Horace does not have the grit to kill me. He would bring someone else to do it—like this fellow. Grace, on the other hand, would kill me herself with delight...

Both men stood as Hollins neared the table. Mooney's head of black hair showed streaks of gray at the temples.

"Southey, my good friend, it has been too long," Mooney said. "Please shake hands with Simon Berrien."

"Mister Berrien."

"No formalities, Southey. Since we'll be working together please call me, Simon."

Hollins glanced at Mooney.

"Working together? This is the first I'm hearing about this."

Mooney motioned them to take a seat. "Not surprising," he said. "You've been hard to locate."

"I need to earn a living." *No need for him to know where I was.* "It has been lean."

"That's about to change," Mooney said and signaled the proprietor.

Hollins glanced toward the door. "Is Grace with you?"

Mooney shook his head. "I'm afraid the poor dear's mind is failing her. She's confined to the house in Staunton."

After ordering three whiskeys, Mooney rubbed his hands and looked at both men.

"We have a great deal to discuss, so let's get to it. I apologize for the extended delay, but I have been occupied with Grace. Her dementia—for that is what it is—has transformed her. A stranger now inhabits her shell, but there are still moments when she rails against Lincoln and begs me not to surrender in shame as did Lee. I believe that our setbacks in Maryland contributed to her condition. When I can report to her that we have renewed the offensive, she will rally."

Shaken, Hollins said, "You can't intend to continue with—"

Mooney waved him away with a laugh.

"Our little insurrection? No, no. What a man tells his wife often has little semblance to the truth. If you had ever married you would know that. The war business was Grace's doing. I admit I enjoyed being the head of an army, even one consisting of rabble. Every now and again, I will put on my colonel's uniform and wear it around the house. It seems to brighten her."

Hollins glanced at Simon Berrien for a reaction. Berrien had taken a tin from his coat pocket and busied himself applying wax to the points of his mustache.

Mooney said, "We're going to be getting our hands on some Yankee money. It will be for a good cause; you can count on that. "

Hollins smiled and swigged his drink. He had always believed that Grace served as her husband's spine; prodding him to act in ways, she, as a woman, could not.

Let's see what we have in store now that Horace Mooney is in charge.

Aloud Hollins said, "It's a relief to hear this. I was never comfortable with that war business. I am in need of funds and was growing concerned that you and Grace had forsaken me. What do you have in mind?"

Mooney turned to Berrien. "Simon, please."

Berrien capped the tin and carefully returned it to his coat pocket.

"Well, sir," he began, "I was the pastor of the Redemption Church of America in Mecklenburg County, Virginia. The war was real hard on my congregation. Yankees came through and burned anything they could set a flame to, even our little house of God. We tried every way we could think of to raise money to rebuild, but they left us with so little. Then the carpetbaggers swarmed over us, like the carrion eaters they are, and picked us clean. Well—I am loathe to admit—we all just gave up."

Berrien took a long drink of whiskey; Mooney gazed at the snapping fire.

"Funny thing," Berrien continued, "Before the war there wasn't a person in Mecklenburg County who had ever seen a Yankee. Now the damn carpetbaggers are running the place. They left me no choice but to abandon my brethren in search of generous souls not so devastated by the war and this wretched Reconstruction."

Hollins opened his mouth to speak, but Mooney interjected, "Wait, there is more."

Berrien continued. "Hard as these years have been on whites, they have taken a worse toll on darkies. We can never atone for all of their suffering—but we must try. With the help of the good Christian people of Maryland, I am determined to rebuild my church. A church where all will be welcome—black and white worshiping together."

With a dramatic flourish Berrien added, "My dream is to see that coloreds have a school to go to. If this dream is denied, I fear that a tidal wave of these wretched souls will sweep across Maryland devastating everything in its path. Amen."

Simon Berrien sat back and twirled his mustache.

"I have one question," Hollins said.

Mooney nodded. "Yes?"

"Is there one word of truth in any of that?"

29

Dorchester County, Maryland
February 11, 1869

Rivulets of sweat trickled beneath Guy Blanchard's shirt, and he wished that Tubman had chosen a table farther from the glowing chunk stove. Across the room, Benny Crème sat behind the big desk, a scarred Colt revolver and a tin cashbox set before him. The gun butt mere inches from Benny's hand.

Guy's discomfort stemmed more from his anxiety over meeting this Captain McKenna of the Oyster Navy—the man his father had sworn to murder—than the heat radiating from the stove.

In the days following Marrok's warning against keeping secrets, Guy sensed that he was being closely watched by his brothers. Were they acting on orders from their father, or merely following their own desire to catch him doing something that they would delight in reporting? In either case, this could well be his last trip to get stores without one of them for company.

The door opened, admitting a gust of cold wind and Guy was relieved to see another dark face not one of his brothers or the oyster policemen.

Customers came and went, without a glance toward the only white face in the room. Being with Tubman, Guy was invisible to the others.

"Sit easy," the old man said. "They'll show."

Guy nodded but kept an eye on the door.

The door opened and a bandy-legged white man entered trailed by a much bigger man.

Oh God! That must be McKenna. He's twice as big as Papa.

The men stopped at the desk while the smaller one spoke to Benny Crème. The tall one's gaze drifted over Guy with a nod to Tubman.

The two men came to the table and sat down and the short one looked at Guy. "This the Blanchard boy?" he asked.

Tubman nodded and waited for Guy to speak.

Benny Crème appeared, set mugs of steaming coffee in front of the newcomers and left.

Guy swallowed. "I'm Guy Blanchard. I don't know what all Tubman here has told ya, but you should know at the start—I'll do what I have to do for me and Mama, but I'm scared."

Tubman's expression did not change at the mention of his own name.

Guy continued. "I'm scared of getting' caught talkin' with you all. And I'm scared that if you folks can't stop Papa I'm gonna have to kill somebody. I'm afraid…"

Haynie interrupted. "I'm Captain McKenna of the state oyster police force. This is Peace Officer Jacoby."

Guy tried to hold McKenna's gaze but failed.

"I know," he said. "You're the one Papa wants to kill."

"Look at me," McKenna ordered. "You can stop being afraid. You are not in this alone. From here on you are under the protection of the state of Maryland. We will stop your father. He is not going to kill me, and you won't have to kill anyone. You have my word on that—and my word is good."

Tubman gave a slight nod and tasted the whiskey warming in his glass.

"You need to listen real good to what I'm telling you," Haynie said with a nod at Tubman. "This man's name is Roscoe and that's how you will call him. No one is to know his real name. If you don't understand why it needs to be that way, I'll explain it to you."

"But Papa—"

Haynie glared.

"Yes sir. I understand—it's Roscoe."

"For the same reason, you'll be known to us as Caleb. That was my brother's name. You put me in mind of him and I know he would not mind. I'm told that your mother knows what you're doing."

Guy nodded.

"She's been real anxious for us to get this done."

"Does she know about this meeting?"

"Yes. If it wasn't for her—"

"Can't be helped. Make sure she doesn't let it slip to anyone."

"You don't have to worry, mister. She's just as scared of him as me."

"It's better if she doesn't know anything else."

Guy hesitated, and then said, "I need to tell her when we'll be rid of him."

"No".

"She frets 'cause it's taking so long. I gotta tell her something."

"Marrok Blanchard maybe your problem, but he is not the Oyster Navy's only problem. We have other duties to attend to. We're going to do this right and legal, that will take some time."

"You expect me to just wake up some mornin' knowin' that's the day he's gonna die, and not say nuthin' to her?"

"Listen to me," Haynie said. "You're the only one here talking about Marrok Blanchard dying. If you and your mother are expecting the Maryland oyster police to shoot your father because he's been mean to you, you're thinkin' wrong. What we are going to do is arrest him for crimes he has committed. "

A trace of a smile crossed Tubman's lips.

Haynie continued, "You'll tell us as much as you can today. If you can't get away again, that'll have to do."

Guy persisted. "I'll tell you everything I can think of but I got to know something ahead—you know, to get ready. I'm sticking my neck way out just being here. It's only right for you to tell me your plan. How else am I gonna know the day?"

Haynie studied the boy. "Your father will tell you," he said.

30

**Fishing Bay
February 24, 1869**

Guy Blanchard stood at the bow of the *Ville de Paris* as it approached the mouth of Tedious Creek. Pine trees clustered along the shoreline at Bishop's Head Point shielding the bugeye from the blustery winds churning up the Chesapeake Bay.

Marrok was at the helm. Benoit and Renard, armed with muskets, fiercely guarded each rail.

It had been thirteen days since Guy met with Captain McKenna and the growing dread was a weight pulling at his chest.

When Guy returned from the meeting at Benny Crème's, his father and brothers stood waiting at the dock. They watched in silence as he toted the stores, in three trips, into the main house.

It bothered him little that they did not offer to help; he just wished them gone. Their eyes never left him and his mouth was drier each time he passed in front of them. The dread grew heavier and he prayed they could not recognize his panic.

Guy had prepared an explanation for his anguish. Unable to bear their silence any longer, he halted in front of them and blurted out in French, "I had a terrible fight with my girlfriend. There, you happy now?"

Marrok laughed. "*Mon fils,*" he said and nodded to Guy's brothers. "You are learning what we three already know. Women are God's afterthought. A necessary evil for men to endure."

"I don't think it's funny. It is time for me to marry and I believe she is the one."

"It is just as well. There will be plenty of time for your love making after we have dealt with this McKenna. Now, we will make our plans and, from now on, the women will fetch our stores."

"But Papa, I must see her again to explain. I have to let her know that I'm sorry for the awful things I said."

Guy's brothers rolled their eyes and Marrok scoffed.

"You are not ready for a woman," he said. "A Blanchard never tells a woman he is sorry. It shows weakness. Have you forgotten what the name Blanchard means? 'White and brave' in the French."

This morning Marrok had gathered his sons on the deck of the *Ville de Paris* and announced, "Today *mon fils* we will sail aboard our flagship, the *Ville de Paris*. With this wind, the open waters will not be hospitable. It is likely even the wretched tongers will not be out, but, if they show their sails, we will win the day."

Guy stood next to the Blakely rifle, with no defense against his father and brothers. How could he refuse an order to fire on another boat? Panic stuck in his throat.

What good is Captain McKenna's word if I have to fire the cannon?

"Ahoy!" Benoit shouted. He pointed at tongers working from two log canoes in the shelter of Tedious Creek.

"Aye," Marrok said and nosed the *Ville de Paris* toward the creek's mouth.

"Renard, hoist the flag."

Guy watched as Renard raised the Maryland state flag over the *Ville de Paris*. With the flag secured, Renard rushed to join his brothers beside the cannon.

It was Guy's salvation that his brothers were so engrossed in brandishing their guns, and working up their rage at the tongers that they failed to notice his shaking hands.

The tongers worked about one hundred and fifty feet up creek as the *Ville de Paris* settled in across the creek's mouth.

"Halloo tongers!" Marrok shouted. "This is Captain McKenna and officers of the oyster police. You are in restricted waters. Leave now and no more will be said about it."

One of the tongers shouted, "The hell you say! This here is Tedious Creek."

Benoit pointed his gun at the tonger's head. "You calling Captain McKenna a liar?" he hollered.

Undaunted, the tonger shouted back, "How do we know you're the oyster police?"

Marrok pointed at the state flag. "If that flag don't satisfy ya, I'll have some of my officers come aboard and we'll haul the lot of ya into the judge at Cambridge."

Renard joined Benoit and raised his musket as the tongers talked animatedly among themselves.

"If ya can't make up your mind," Marrok shouted, "maybe a shot from this here cannon will convince ya!"

One of the tongers held up his hands in surrender.

"We give. Move your damn boat so's we can get out into Fishing Bay and we'll leave. I still can't figure what we was doin' wrong."

Marrok yelled to be heard aboard the canoes, said, "Officers of the Oyster Navy stand down. We're gonna let these fella go—this time."

With the tongers gone, Renard lowered the state flag.

Benoit stomped across the deck. "Why did you let them go Papa? It was my chance to kill a tonger." He whirled on Guy. "And find out if our brother here is the man he is supposed to be."

Renard nodded in agreement.

"Patience *mon fils*," Marrok replied. "You must learn to pick your battles. We could not let them remain here while we work in Fishing Bay. The open water is too rough to take them up to Cambridge." He waved a hand. "Those canoes were too small for our needs; but most important for our plan—those men are free to tell how badly they were treated by McKenna and the Oyster Navy."

Marrok looked at Guy. "As for your brother, he is a Blanchard. He will do what he is told, or his mother will be very sad."

31

Annapolis Maryland
March 9, 1869

Lila McKenna closed her copy of *Godey's Lady's Book* and accepted the polite applause of the women seated before her. Though the gathering did not equal the numbers who came to hear Sojourner Truth or Susan Anthony, Lila was gratified that these women had braved a sudden March squall to attend her reading.

Wilma Winder was the first to grab Lila's hand.

"That was a wonderful story, Lila. Your mother-in-law must be an exceptional woman. Your writing is fresh and exciting. I'm sure this is just the start."

Others made brief comments or smiled and nodded as they hurried by on their way to the table laden with wine and cakes.

Lila, the last one to the table, poured some wine. Raising her glass, she said to Wilma, "I could have used this before. This was my first attempt at speaking before others. But that was obvious."

"Once you got into it you were fine. Your passion about your subject was evident."

"Cora Clemson didn't seem to care for it. She and Lucy Buck sat like monuments."

"Actually, I'm surprised they were here. Cora has failed in her efforts to get *Godey's* to print any of her stories—if one can call them that. Closer to gibberish from what I have seen. I am certain she was livid and, as you have seen, Lucy trails after her like a small child waiting for permission to speak. Whatever Lucy says, you can be certain Cora said it first."

Lila sat her wineglass on the table. "I'm glad that's over with," she said. "It's been a lot of worry."

Wilma lit a cigarette and blew smoke through her nose.

"What do you mean—over with? This is just the beginning."

"What do *you* mean? Beginning of what?"

"I keep forgetting how naïve you are dear. Unless I'm very much mistaken, you will be hearing from others in the women's movement. Women of the stature of Susan Anthony and Sarah Hale will soon be making demands for more. What was your husband's reaction to your story about his mother?"

Lila gave a nervous laugh. "He doesn't subscribe to *Godey's*."

"He hasn't seen the story? Hasn't seen your name in print?"

Lila shook her head.

"Are you accustomed to keeping things from him?"

"Uh no."

"He will eventually learn of your new found fame. It should come from you."

"Fame?"

Wilma nodded. "I believe that is what awaits you."

Lila thrilled at the magnificence of the dining room in Walton's City Hotel as Haynie poured wine for each of them.

"What a wonderful surprise," she said.

"Who knows how long we will be in Annapolis?" he said. "We need to take advantage of the finer things while we may. You deserve an evening away from children to mind and meals to cook."

He raised his glass. "Here's to you."

"Thank you, sir. This is all very flattering."

Haynie noticed the server hovering and waved him away. Turning to Lila, he said, "We have precious little time to talk, anymore."

"I know. When you were the bailiff at Crisfield we talked, at least some, every day. I knew everything you were involved in; now I know almost nothing."

Haynie nodded. "The little time I am home is taken up with the children. I feel terribly detached from your life."

"But..."

"It can't be helped—for now. I can't leave the force just as we're getting our sea legs."

"I know you need to be out there. I just wish it were not so violent. Marylanders killing one another; Marylanders and Virginians killing each other. It's almost as if the war hasn't ended."

"Some would say it's God's will."

"It would be much easier to accept if I could believe that."

Lila drank some wine. "You must have come upon some memorable souls," she said. "Entertain me with stories about some of them."

"That's easily done. Let's order our meal before we forget what was posted on the bill of fare."

After ordering dinner, Haynie topped off their wine glasses. "I've told you some about Nathan Jacoby, first mate on the *Emma Dunn*, and how much I have come to rely on his counsel."

Lila nodded.

"I believe you would enjoy hearing about a colored man over in Dorchester County named Tubman."

Startled, Lila said, "Tubman?" Is he kin to Harriet Tubman?"

Haynie shrugged. "Who is Harriet Tubman?"

"She's a famous Negro emancipator from Dorchester County. We learned about her at one of the ladies meetings I told you about. It is all very exciting. Before the war, she risked her life to free hundreds of slaves. She was what they called a conductor on the Underground Railroad. Then she joined the Union army and fought Rebs."

"Tubman and I haven't gotten around to discussing our family lineage. With both of them hailing from Dorchester County, I would deem it likely they are some kind of kin. Whether they are shirttail relations or kissin' cousins, I can't say, but it sounds like they share the same streak."

"What does that mean?"

"The Tubman I know seems to possess a pretty strong opinion about right and wrong. He's for making wrongs, right."

"Any wrongs in particular?"

"He and his son built a log canoe for tonging. It was their livelihood. The Blanchards I told you about, came along and just took it away from them."

"That's awful. Isn't there something you can do...oh, you are. That's how you know of him."

Haynie smiled over the rim of his wineglass.

Lila said, "An independent waterman—who built his own boat to tong oysters—does it brings to mind your father's struggles?"

They were silent as the server set their meal in front of them and hurried away to another table.

Lila forked a small piece of sea bass and looked across the table. "I was surprised when you ordered fried oysters. I wouldn't think you would want to be reminded of oysters when you are off of the bay."

"On the contrary, knowing how much turmoil is involved in getting them to the table makes them all the more savory. And, to answer your question, I don't relate Tubman's troubles to Tench's. I am determined that this will end differently."

Haynie related what he knew of Tubman's encounter with Marrok Blanchard. When he finished, Haynie said, "I believe it's your turn."

Lila looked at him.

"To tell me about your activities. It sounds like more goes on at your ladies' meetings than just idle gossip."

"Captain McKenna, you should know better than to think that I would be content to sit around listening to idle gossip. We discuss important people and events. It's been wonderful for me."

"Such as?"

"Such as the Fourteenth Amendment—and people like Harriet Tubman."

Lila felt terrible about deceiving her husband. She would tell him about her story appearing in *Godey's* in due time. *For now, a little white lie.*

Aloud she said, "What's more, I've been thinking about doing some writing."

"Letters? To whom?"

"Not letters. Maybe an essay—or a story."

"What would you write about?"

Lila put down her fork and dabbed her lips with a napkin. "Interesting people; people who have done heroic things."

"Like Harriet Tubman?"

"Yes exactly. Maybe some day I could talk to this Mister Tubman—or, I could make up my own heroes."

"It's just Tubman."

"What?"

"He objects to being called mister."

"Is Tubman his given name or his surname?"

Haynie shrugged. "I don't know."

"Would you ask if he is related to Harriet Tubman? For me?"

"It's not the right time. Maybe someday, after we finish with the Blanchards."

32

Fox Creek
Dorchester County, Maryland
March 10, 1869

Nathan Jacoby deftly guided the single-mast log canoe along the Asquith Neck shoreline and into Fox Creek.

Haynie McKenna lay flat across the culling board, scanning the water ahead with a glass. Gerhard Stein sat stiffly in the bow a large-bore musket across his knees.

"Mister Jacoby, keep as tight to the shore as our draft will allow. Don't want to be seen if we can help it."

"Aye, sir. You expect we can find the spot from what the lad told us?"

"If we can't, I need to know it now not later."

"You think old Marrok would send the boy out to lie to us?"

"I wouldn't put anything past him; but I believe the boy was as scared as he looked. Still, I'll feel a lot better if we find their stash where he said. It would say a lot about whose side he is on."

Haynie pointed ahead. "The place we're looking for should be just around that point."

Jacoby tacked along the wooded strip of land and into a sheltered cove while Haynie studied the opposite shoreline.

If Guy was telling the truth, the Blanchard family compound was just across Fox Creek, obscured behind that row of pines.

The canoe rounded the point. "This looks like the spot," Haynie said.

"Aye, sir."

Haynie handed the telescope to Gerhard and pointed across the creek. "Keep the glass on those pines. If a boat sails out of there, call out."

"*Ja.*"

Turning back to Jacoby he said, "We'll soon know. Hold her steady while I work these tongs. If Gerhard calls out, get us the hell away from here. It's likely we'll be outgunned."

Haynie lowered the tongs into the trove of oysters shimmering below the surface. He worked the jaws together and then lifted the tongs over the side releasing the catch onto the culling board.

Gerhard's eyes did not move from the tree line. Being distracted, even for a moment, was not a consideration.

Jacoby said, "What do you think, Captain? Them oysters could have growed there."

Haynie grabbed up some oysters in each hand and closely examined the shells.

"Looks to me like they were recently moved." He fished an oyster knife from his coat pocket. "Maybe this will tell us," he said.

Jacoby watched as Haynie selected a large oyster from the catch and deftly pried the shell apart.

"See if I got this straight," Jacoby said. "The Blanchards poach a rock in, say, Fishing Bay or the Honga River. Then they bring their booty here, close to home, and stash 'em for later when oysters will fetch a better price."

Haynie nodded and slurped down the fresh oyster. "Looks like Guy was telling the truth. This oyster was recently in a saltwater bed. Another day or two and the salt will be filtered out."

Jacoby grinned. "Good to see a man enjoying his work, Captain. Ya know a couple more pulls on them tongs and we'd have enough for tonight's supper."

Haynie picked up the tongs. "Keep her steady, Mister Jacoby."

33

Dorchester County, Maryland
March 11, 1869

With the *Emma Dunn* tied up to the wharf at Town Point, the crew hurriedly assembled amidships, anticipating some hours of shore leave.

Jacoby would join the others for a glass of beer then move on alone to Benny Crème's tavern.

Haynie refused Gerhard Stein's request to accompany him ashore.

"I'm sorry but I don't want people to see us together just now. One day I may need you to do something where others can't know you work with me. Do you understand?"

"*Ja,*" Gerhard said and returned to the galley.

In Cambridge, Haynie accepted Sheriff Tolley's offer of coffee and set the mug on a corner of the sheriff's desk.

"What brings you around?" Tolley asked. "Thought maybe you forgot about us."

"I've not forgotten. It's a big bay, and Dorchester County is not the only place with villains."

"So are you here for my coffee or the Blanchards?"

"Both are worth the trip, but today it's mostly about the Blanchards and Judge Cromarte. You heard anything?"

Tolley settled into the chair and lifted his mug.

"Well, sir, since we spoke I been payin' more mind to that bunch. Blanchard has a place over along Fox Creek."

Tolley paused and Haynie nodded.

"You knew that?"

Haynie, still uncertain where Tolley's loyalty lay, would not reveal his meeting with Guy Blanchard. He said, "We heard some talk, but I want to know what you found."

Tolley beamed. "I found Marrok's place."

"That'd take some doing, from what I hear. You go by land or water?"

"It took a right smart of doing. I went on horseback, alone. Didn't want to chance word getting back to Marrok that the law was interested in his antics."

Haynie nodded.

"An old progger pointed me in the right direction, and I picked up a faint trail they must use when they go out by land. I 'spect they mostly travel the water. Real hard to track a man over water."

Haynie smiled. "What'd you find?"

"I got close enough to see a couple of buildings—houses, I reckon—through the trees. You'd never see 'em in the summertime until you was right on them. I had a feelin' I was close, so I got down and was walkin' my horse real slow tryin' to keep to that trail. Right as I spot the houses, four big dogs come yappin' through the trees. Well, I'd seen enough so I hightailed it. I wish I could'a got closer."

Tolley shrugged. "But it couldn't be helped."

Haynie nodded.

"Good to know though, huh Captain McKenna."

"It's very good. Saves us a lot of work."

Tolley smiled.

The sheriff's brief description of the Blanchard compound matched with what Guy had told them.

It helps to know that both the boy and the sheriff are telling the same story.

Aloud Haynie said, "Anything about Cromarte?"

"Talked to a fella who'd be happy to empty both barrels of birdshot into Orville T.'s backside. He says Cromate keeps a pungy over near Jacktown on the Choptank. He believes the old goat got the boat from Blanchard, in some shady deal."

"I wouldn't think a man of Cromarte's age would be sailing around on such as a pungy."

"The man believes Cromarte keeps it anchored; might be he lives aboard. He's heard the old goat sits on the deck in the nice weather and drinks juleps."

Haynie, lost in thought, stared past Tolley.

Eventually the sheriff said, "What are you thinking, Captain?"

"I have an idea how we can go after Blanchard *and* Cromarte. When the time is right I will ask you to get a message to Cromarte, but you cannot let him know it is coming from me. Can you do that?"

"Sorry, but I don't see what you're getting at. What sort of message?"

"I'll want the judge to know where the *Emma Dunn* is going to be anchored on a particular night. Maybe you could tell it to somebody else, where Cromarte could overhear it."

Tolley scratched his head. "I must admit, I'm flummoxed. For one thing," he said, rapping on the table, "Cromarte is about as deaf as this table. Got an ear horn but won't use it anywhere folks can see. The only thing he could overhear is cannon fire."

Haynie understood how difficult it would be to make the sheriff understand his plan without revealing that he had direct knowledge of Marrok's intention to storm the *Emma Dunn*.

He said, "If Cromarte is in league with Blanchard, he'll get word to him about what we are doing."

Tolley hesitated wanting to be certain he was not missing anything.

"Likely you're right about that; but even if Cromarte does pass it along, I can't see how that helps us."

"Cromarte and Marrok have an arrangement. The judge uses his power to seize the boats, and then gets money to pass them on to Marrok. Cromarte will do whatever is needed to protect this arrangement, so it follows that he will tell Marrok anything he hears about our movements.

"For my plan to work, Marrok must learn the whereabouts of the *Emma Dunn*. If we can show he was tipped off by Cromarte, we can arrest both of them."

Tolley shrugged. "Okay. Still seems peculiar. I have a deputy works over in Cromarte's court. He's as close to the old bastard as anyone; he'll tell him."

"When we're ready."

Tolley gave Haynie a puzzled look.

"It's bait," Haynie said. "We hope Marrok will take it."

34

Horace Mooney and Southey Hollins were seated at a round wooden table in the front room of a one-story log house on the banks of the Rappahannock River. A map of Virginia was spread out between them.

"I was fortunate to find this place," Mooney said. He traced the routes with an index finger as he spoke.

"Just out this front door, the Rappahannock runs straight to the Chesapeake. The main road through town gives us a good land route to King George County. From there, it is just a short boat ride across the Potomac to the house at Popes Creek. Yet we are off the beaten path. Who would look for us here?"

Hollins, following Mooney's appraisal intently, looked up.

"That's my question. Who *would* be looking for us?"

"If we are smart—no one. It was a mistake to involve ourselves with that laudanum-crazed killer and those depraved Yankee prison guards. I admit that. That is history now. If Simon plays his part, we won't have to strong-arm anyone for their money; they'll be happy to give it to us."

"What about the kinfolk of those boys the Drumm brothers shanghaied? Any of them could cause trouble."

"That's the least of our worries," Mooney answered. "Look here, the boys who lived to get back home just want to let it rest. The ones that didn't, well their folks have the boat captains to blame. And the way I heard it, the boys that died in that paddy shack had no kin to fret about them."

"But—"

"You're stewin' over nothing. The only ones that saw your face were the Drumm brothers and the sheriff over in Somerset County. They're all dead."

Hollins shook his head. "One of the Drumms didn't drown with his brothers. He's out there somewhere."

"Each Drumm was stupider than the next, but none of them was so dumb as to just walk in and start talkin' to the law. Even if the last one was to tell everything he knows—which is not much—who's going to believe him?"

Hollins said nothing.

"Now what? Mooney asked. "You don't believe what I'm saying?"

"It's the Wallis boy's father and that McKenna, the rube he hired to search for his son. They could be trouble."

"No reason they should. You stayed with that family until the boy got home. You did nothing wrong that Wallis can tell. We were careful; there is nothing to tie us together. And even if they suspect something they got no evidence."

Hollins stared out the window.

"This is why Berrien's not here," Mooney said. "I figured we'd need to talk about this and it's better if he doesn't know any of the details. I'm not saying anything to him about those days and I don't reckon you will."

"Never said a word to anybody—and never will. I still have nightmares."

"That's history. Soon you'll be too busy counting your money to think about anything else. "

Hollins shifted in his chair and looked at Mooney. "I'm guessing you feel this Berrien fellow can be trusted with whatever you got planned."

Mooney nodded.

"Where did you run across him?"

"Providence sent him to us."

"You're beginning to talk like him."

Mooney smiled. "Actually, he's beginning to talk like me."

Hollins gave him a look.

"The man you know as Simon Berrien is a stage actor. A troupe came into Staunton, gave a couple of shows and then folded up. He and I got acquainted. He says Simon Berrien is his real name, but I have my doubts. Anyhow, we talked and our discussion came round to needing an easy way to make some money. We came up with this plan."

"That's all you know about him?"

"I know he's a damn good actor. I write the part and he plays it. That story you heard the other day was the opening scene. Every word penned by yours truly."

Mooney slapped the tabletop. "We're going to put on the damnedest theatrical performance ever given north of the Potomac. The state of Maryland will be our stage and the audience will be shouting *bravo* and begging for more."

"That's all you know about him?"

"Damn it, Southey, why do you keep saying that?"

"Lot of those actors join a traveling show because they're running from something."

Mooney shrugged. "What would be the point of asking? If he has something to hide, he would just lie about it. If he were wanted in Maryland, he wouldn't be so eager to open our show up there. This is our big chance, Southey. After Maryland, who knows, we might just take our act to New York. Bigger audience—more money."

35

Magnolia Bluff
Popes Creek Maryland
March 17, 1869

Hoppy opened the front door, admitting the two men standing before him.

Southey Hollins smiled as he stepped inside. "Mister Hopkins, I see by the cheery fire that you were expecting us. My name is Hollins. You may recall we met some weeks ago when I was here with Colonel Mooney. This is Doctor Berrien; I believe the colonel mentioned him in his wire."

"Howdy."

Berrien offered a slight nod. "Fetch my grips from the buggy."

Hoppy struggled the three large leather bags into the vestibule. He took a breath and straightened. "Where's your gear, Mister Hollins? Not that I'm looking for more baggage to tote around."

"I'm not staying. I must get back across the river. Doctor Berrien has rented Magnolia Bluff from the colonel and most of his staff will be arriving tomorrow. Oh—Colonel Mooney wanted me to thank you for your work here. As the doctor has his own staff, your services are no longer required."

Berrien stopped at the bottom of the sweeping stairway and faced the caretaker.

"Be so good as to bring those grips up to the master bedroom."

Hoppy grunted then turned and walked out of the house closing the door behind him.

Baltimore Towne
March 20, 1869

Wallis & Sons Merchant Traders was housed in a two-story structure in the Fell's Point area of Baltimore Towne. Just across Thames Street, the company's wharfs crowded the harbor.

On the second floor, Silas Wallis occupied a massive captain's desk adjacent to the wall of single hung windows stretching across the building front. Three wooden chairs and a small leather settee faced the desk. The rest of the cavernous room stood empty, reminiscent of a deserted warehouse.

Landon Wallis sat in the chair at his father's right hand; Haynie McKenna was settled onto the settee.

The elder Wallis drummed his fingers while Miss Hazlett finished pouring coffee.

"Nice to see you again, Miss Hazlett," Haynie said.

The girl blushed. "Thank you, sir."

Landon dismissed her with a nod and she wheeled the wooden cart from the room.

Colonel Wallis stirred sugar into his coffee. "I apologize for requiring you to make the trip here," he said, "but I could not travel to Annapolis just now."

"This actually worked out well," Haynie responded. "Commander Davidson was pleased when I mentioned my need to come here. He asked me to inquire of Sanner & Company the reason for the latest delay in delivery of the *Leila*. He is so disgusted with them he doubts he could hold his temper."

"Good. Good. Landon has an interest in this, so he is sitting in."

Silas Wallis unfolded a telegram. "This is a report from Hopkins at Popes Creek. My intermediary brought it to me straightaway."

"Hollins showed at the house yesterday. Only stuck around long enough to get a fellow he called Doctor Simon Berrien in the front door. Then Hollins 'lit out' as Hoppy so colorfully put it. It seems this Berrien fellow has rented the place from Mooney."

Wallis peered over the page. "Before he left, Hollins fired our man. He said this Doctor Berrien would be using his own staff. Damn shame. Just when they are very likely stirring something up, Hopkins is no use to us. Do you think they figured out he was spying on them?"

Haynie shook his head. "I doubt it. They're up to something and don't want an outsider around."

He set his coffee cup on the low table in front of him. "It's possible Hoppy can still help us, if you're willing to continue paying him."

"Of course, if you think it to be worthwhile."

Haynie said, "No doubt this is a setback. Most likely Mooney and Hollins are not going to be spending much time on this side of the river. I have no doubt Berrien is in league with them, but we cannot touch him until we know what his game is. Hoppy may be able to help us figure out what's going on."

"How can he do that?" Landon asked.

"Someone's going leave that house and come into town to the post office or pick up provisions. They will say something to somebody. Hoppy can ask around; maybe we can figure out their scheme. Whatever it is, Berrien is going to try and get his hands on somebody else's money. To do that he will be leaving Popes Creek or folks will be coming to the house. If we're watching, I have no doubt we'll learn something."

Silas Wallis nodded.

Landon looked at his father. "There must be something I can do," he said. "I went through several kinds of hell because of those men."

The elder Wallis turned his gaze across Thames Street to an ocean-going schooner disgorging bags of Brazilian coffee into a Wallis and Sons warehouse.

"I have an idea," Haynie offered.

Silas looked across his desk. "All right, let's hear it."

"You will send Hoppy a message and thank him for his help. With both sources of his money being cut off he'll be pretty desperate. In a few days, Landon and I will show up at Popes Creek. I will introduce Landon as one of my men who will stick around to help him keep a close watch on Magnolia Bluff. I can't pay him with state money, but Landon will pass your funds to him and Hoppy will believe it is coming from the state."

Landon moved to the edge of his chair, eagerly awaiting his father's reaction.

"Are you suggesting that Landon should live there?" Silas asked.

"That sounds more permanent than I had in mind. If they are plotting something, as we believe, things may begin to develop fast. We will need someone there—someone reliable who knows the whole story—to keep us informed. Likely he can find a room in the area for a few weeks."

"They killed my mother!" Landon blurted out.

Silas studied his son. "There will be some strict rules about your activities. If it becomes threatening you're coming straight back."

Colonel Wallis turned his gaze on Haynie. "Sir, I will hold you responsible for my son's well-being."

36

Harris Creek
Talbot County, Maryland
March 20, 1869

The *Ville de Paris* tacked into Harris Creek from the Choptank River. Marrok Blanchard had the helm, his three sons standing rigid before him.

"*Mes fils,* I have a surprise for you. Today is the day you have waited for. Before we leave these waters, one of you will have killed his first tonger."

Benoit blurted out, "Which one of us will you choose, *mon pere?* I am the oldest. It is my birthright."

Guy's head swirled at Marrok's words. The ship's rigging swayed and he gripped the musket at his side for support.

Renard was saying, "No one has been more faithful to you than I, sir. The *honneur* should be determined by who has worked the hardest, not the oldest. The privilege is mine."

Marrok studied his older sons briefly before turning to Guy.

"You look sick, *mon fil.* Something that does not agree with you?"

Benoit scoffed. "He lives in fear."

Guy drew himself to attention and glared at his older brother. "Fear? I have no fear. I, too, am a Blanchard."

Facing his father, he said, "When it my turn to be so honored, I will not fail you."

"I expect nothing less from any son of mine."

Marrok surveyed the water ahead. "We will find our prey up there. Each of you will load your musket and await my orders. If there is only one tonger in the area, we will look further."

"*Pourquoi, mon pere?*" Benoit and Renard asked in unison.

"You must keep our mission always in mind. Our plan is to kill a captain of the Maryland Oyster Navy. Preferably the one named McKenna, but any of them will serve our purpose.

My plan calls for us to attack while the ship is at anchor, during the night. It has been our bad fortune that none of their fleet have anchored overnight in these waters. The last time we met tongers we let them go to spread the word about their terrible treatment by Captain McKenna and his men. Nothing happened. No Oyster Navy boat came. It seems that to get their attention, we must raise the stakes. We require a witness to a killing committed by a crew of an Oyster Navy ship. We need two tonger canoes. One of them will run away and spread the news."

Benoit and Renard began loading their weapons.

"That is brilliant, *mon pere*," Benoit said.

"*Oui, oui,*" echoed Renard.

Guy's heart raced, his mouth dry, as he tamped a minie ball into his musket.

"Papa, do I have time to go the cabin?"

"*Pourquoi?*" Marrok questioned.

Benoit and Renard jeered their brother as they hoisted their muskets and took aim at the shoreline.

Guy said, "I must confess my mouth is dry. I need some water."

"You must hurry. Return to your post immediately."

Guy gripped his musket as he hurried across the deck. Inside the cabin, he ladled a dipper of water from the bucket and took a mouthful. Watchful of the cabin door, he tilted the dipper and dribbled the remainder down the barrel of his musket.

"Ahoy!" Marrok shouted. "All Oyster Navy men to their posts!"

Guy left the cabin and immediately saw two canoes off the port bow. Determined that no tonger would be shot today, he ran to the rail and wedged himself between his brothers.

Benoit shouldered Guy into Renard. "Get out of my way," Benoit said. "Go cover your ears while I kill my first tonger."

Renard braced himself and shoved back, squeezing Guy away from the rail.

"You have no business here," Renard snarled. "Go drink some water and leave the killing to us."

Guy cleaved his way between his brothers, grabbing the rail with one hand, clutching his musket with the other.

Less than two hundred yards separated the *Ville de Paris* and the log canoes. The bugeye closed on the smaller boats as their sails filled and they got underway.

"Damn you, Renard," Benoit yelled as the two brothers struggled to keep Guy from the rail. "They must have seen the Maryland flag and are a runnin' 'cause they don't have no license. You were too quick hoisting that flag. If we can't catch 'em before they get into one of those little creeks...you're gonna pay if I miss my chance to kill a tonger."

Marrok cursed in French as he maneuvered the boat in pursuit.

"Stop it, damn you, stop it! Your squabbling will ruin our plan. Guy, pick out a man in the closest canoe and shoot him."

"*Mon, pere,*" Benoit protested. "It is my right."

"Silence! You and Renard behave like small children. If you cause us to miss this chance, I'll peel the hide from both of you."

To Guy he said, "Make me proud, *mon fil.*"

Guy, stunned that his father had selected him, struggled against his brothers while assessing his dilemma.

I can shoot no one with wet powder. It will be hard to convince Papa and those two that I was blameless when no one gets killed. Still, that is better than if I am forced to stop one of them from doing the killing. There must be some way....

Gripping his musket with both hands Guy swung his arms wildly smashing each brother in the head with an elbow.

"Give me some room," he shrieked.

As Guy had hoped, Benoit retaliated with a sharp elbow to his ribs and Renard shoved him away from the rail.

Guy staggered back lost his balance and fell heavily to the deck. As he went down, he judged that the two canoes were now within musket range.

"God Damn you both!" Marrok screamed. "Renard come and take the wheel. Now!"

Still clutching his musket, Guy struggled to his feet and lurched to the rail where Benoit was taking aim at the nearest canoe.

"No," Guy cried. "It is for me to do." He lowered his shoulder and rammed Benoit in the middle of his back jamming him against the rail. To save himself from toppling overboard Benoit grabbed the rail with both hands and his musket fell away into the water.

Benoit, face twisted with rage, grabbed at Guy's musket.

"You little bastard," he choked as he struggled for the gun. "It is my birthright. I demand you give me your musket. I must be the first Blanchard to kill a tonger."

Guy resisted mightily as his brother tugged at the weapon with all his strength. Suddenly, Guy released his grip and Benoit staggered back against the railing and pitched over the side carrying Guy's musket with him.

The canoes were fleeing into a small creek when Marrok struck Guy with a closed fist driving him to the deck. Leaving his youngest clutching his head, Marrok ran to the bow to find Benoit grabbing at the hull.

Marrok picked up a coil of rope, tied one end to the rail and dropped the remainder over the side.

"If you are smart you will swim for shore," he shouted.

Edith Blanchard slipped through the door to the pump house and closed it behind her.

She spoke quickly. "For God's sake tell me what happened. Your father glares and says nothing. Benoit can barely walk. Renard vomits and moans. Your face is swollen and turns all colors."

Guy worked the pump with one hand as he splashed the cold water over his face with the other.

"He wanted us to kill a tonger. Benoit went crazy when papa picked me to do the killing. We fought and I pushed him overboard. Papa flew into a rage and got to me first. He thrashed me, then, while he waited for Benoit to climb back aboard, he knocked Renard down and kicked at him with his boot. "

"He wanted you to kill a stranger for no reason?"

Guy winced as the cold well water stung his face. "Papa has a Maryland flag which we hoist over the *Ville de Paris*. Other boats are to believe that the Oyster Navy is full of outlaws who kill innocent watermen. It is his plan to kill a tonger and people will believe it was the Oyster Navy. He is certain that the real navy will have to send a boat here to answer charges about the killing, that is when we will board the navy boat and kill the captain. In the past, he has prayed they will send McKenna; but now anyone will do."

37

Popes Creek, Maryland
March 23, 1869

"Throw me a line and I'll tie you off," Haynie called as Jimmy Hopkins poled his skiff toward the dock.

"How they biting?"

Hopkins hoisted a rope, displaying a stringer of largemouth bass. A wide grin split his face, revealing dark gums and stained teeth worn to stumps.

"What d'ya think?"

"Look good enough to eat."

Hopkins cast a lazy eye over the village waterfront. "Where's your big boat?"

"Didn't want to cause a fuss again, so we came over from Port Tobacco by buggy."

"Who's that with ya? Kinda young to be an Oyster Navy man."

"We call him Lucky."

Landon offered a hand. "Nice to meet you, sir," he said.

Hopkins grunted. "Hoppy'll do just fine," he said and handed up the stringer of fish.

Once on the dock, Hoppy tied the stringer to a piling and eased his catch back into the river. "They'll keep better in there while we talk. I reckon ya'll didn't come all the way from Port Tobacky to see my catch."

Hoppy took a seat on a nearby empty crate.

"Sorry I can't offer any better. If you didn't hear, I got run off up at the spy's place."

Haynie and Landon each upended a crate and sat.

Hoppy studied Landon closely with his good eye. "What's Mister Lucky's story? He wouldn't be a hearin' what we got to say about the spy 'less he had a stake in it, now would he?"

Haynie laughed. "Got to get up pretty early to get anything past you."

Hoppy said, "And I get up before dawn." He tilted his head toward Magnolia Bluff. "Guess you heard about this fella, Berrien, takin' over up there."

"A little. Wanted to get your take on it."

"First off, I wish ya luck if you're still after the spy and that Hollins fella. I don't figure them to come around anymore. As for the new one, Berrien—he calls himself Doctor Berrien, doctor my ass. Lots of strange doin's up there. He was only here two or three days when a wagon comes through town packed to the gills with darkies and their trappings. They all goes inside the big house and damned if they ain't been there ever since. I swear if Berrien ain't the only white man in the place."

Hoppy looked from Landon to Haynie. "I figure they got to be his slaves, but that's supposed to be done with, ain't it?"

"It is," Haynie said.

"Well, there ya are. You can get him for that."

Haynie shook his head. "It's not that simple. With Reconstruction going on, a man who was a slave is now called a freedman. The law says that if they want to work they must sign a labor contract with someone—who is always a white man—and they are bound to him. They can't quit him to take a better job even if one was to come along. It's likely Berrien got them to sign such a paper."

"How's that different than the way it was before the fighting?"

"A lot of folks are asking that question."

"You still gonna want for me to keep an eye on the place?"

"Can you get a good look at what's happening up there?"

Hoppy cackled and slapped a knee. "You betcha. If you remember, there's a thick stand of pines along the road just at the top of the hill."

Haynie nodded and Hoppy cackled again. "Well, I can get myself in amongst them pine trees and a fella would have to be standin' next to me to know I was there. Got a straight look to the front verandy with my good eye. I can know all their comings and goings."

"What was the strange doin's you mentioned?"

Hoppy heaved a weary sigh and shrugged. "Oh, I doubt it's much. Besides, now that the spy ain't payin' me, I really can't waste my time up there. I got to rustle up a job of work that pays cash money."

He touched the fish line with the toe of a boot. "Won't be this lucky ever' day. So I got to find me something to keep food on the table. I don't require much; but the missus, she's an eater."

He waved his hand toward the few buildings in the town. "Trouble is, not much work here abouts, and I'm too old to go traipsin' over the countryside a-lookin'."

Landon looked sharply at Haynie and said, "But—"

"What if," Haynie interrupted, "you were to be paid for your time? Could you keep an eye on the place, then?"

Hoppy cackled. "Sure enough. You sayin' the state's gonna pay me to be a secret agent?"

"We'll figure out something. But you've got to play this tight to the vest. Don't know who you can trust around here."

Hoppy glanced at Landon. "You ain't told me Mister Lucky's part in all this."

"I'll get to that, but first I want to hear what's been going on up there."

Hoppy stared out over the river and grunted. "I'm trying to recollect it all. First off you 'member that sign for Magnolia Bluff settin' in the front lawn?"

Haynie nodded.

"Gone. The first thing. See, that's what makes me believe the spy and the woman ain't comin' back. They made a issue out of their place bein' called Magnolia Bluff. Claimed it was really part of Virginny itself."

Hoppy shook his head. "Berrien comes along and puts up another sign, painted on old wood, not fine chiseled like the first one. Looks like it was did by a small child."

"What does it read?"

"Big as life it says 'Southern Cross School for Coloreds.'"

"Anybody from the school come down the hill into town?"

Hoppy chortled. "Two of 'em come right past my lookout—close as from me to you and never knew I was there."

"What did they do in town?"

"They took a passel of mailings to the post office for sending out."

"And?"

Hoppy leaned in, motioning Haynie and Landon closer. "Don't say nuthin', but me and Clarence at the post office, we're tight. After the darkies leave, I waltzes in just as careless as you please, and seeing the stack of mailings, I says, 'Looks like you been snowed under.'"

Hoppy looked at each man and cackled. "See, the mailings was all white; pretty good, huh?"

Both men smiled.

"What did Clarence say?" Haynie asked.

"He laughed and said, 'Take a look at this,' pointin' to the mailings. So I hustled over and took me a look. They was mostly being sent up to Annapolis and Baltimore Towne, to Colonel This and The Honorable That. All comin' from the school name on the sign. Well me and Clarence was thinkin' the same thing, they must be from that Berrien fella, 'cause it wouldn't do for coloreds to be sending mailings to such folks as these."

Hoppy paused and shook a bony finger in the air, "'Sides, their kind don't know letter writin' anyhow."

"This could be important," Haynie said, "do you remember any of the names?"

Hoppy studied hard on the question, finally saying, "'Fraid not. Don't believe that Berrien fellow has spent a lot of time writing to folks. Real hard to make out the peoples names."

Haynie straightened. "Good work."

"So, you think this Berrien is up to no good?"

Haynie nodded.

"Ya reckon mebbe the spy and that fella, Hollins, got a hand in this?"

"It wouldn't surprise me."

Hoppy looked at Landon. "I'm still waitin' to hear what Mister Lucky is all about."

Haynie said, "He needs to rent a room in Popes Creek."

"For how long?"

"Hard to say. Maybe a month or two."

"He here about the goings on up at the spy's house?"

Haynie nodded.

"If you was already planning for him to stay here, what you need me for?"

"I need you to watch the place. Being local, you can get around without worrying folks. Whatever you find out, you tell Lucky and he will get the news to me. We need you to keep in touch with Clarence and talk with anybody else who might know something."

Hoppy cast his good eye toward Landon. "He the boss of me?"

"No."

"That'll do." Hoppy thought for a minute, before saying, "I don't know of an extra bed in town. We got the two beds—if I was to go back to sleepin' with the old woman, he could have the other one." A big grin spread across his face. "If we do 'er thataway, I'd have to charge ya extra; but, if the lad would bunk with her, there'd be no charge."

Landon, a stricken look on his face, stared at Haynie.

Hoppy laughed. "Oh, she won't bother you none. But, I gotta tell ya, she snores like a boar hog."

Haynie laughed along with Hoppy while Landon managed a weak grin.

"I believe Lucky should have his own bed," Haynie said. "You might as well get the money, as anyone."

"That part'll go to the missus," Hoppy said. "Make her happy and keep her nose out of my doings." Then he frowned at Landon. "Going to have to tell folks a story about him."

"He's a surveyor for the state." Haynie said. "He'll carry around some charts and maps."

Hoppy grinned. "Damn," he said.

"Why don't you carry those fish on up to the house and tell her company is coming. Lucky'll be along directly."

Hoppy cackled as he collected his fish and headed for home.

With Hoppy gone, Landon said, "I don't know about all this. What if his missus doesn't want me in the house? What happens if he gets caught up there? Would they kill him? Oh mercy."

Haynie smiled and placed a hand on the boy's shoulder. "It'll be up to you to figure it out. You wanted a chance to prove yourself. You know what they say—if you can't run with the big dogs, don't get off the porch."

Landon smiled.

"It's not like the army," Haynie said. "You can leave anytime you want."

Landon balled his fists. "I'm staying. Those men killed my mother."

38

The crew of the *Shenandoah* stood at attention as Haynie McKenna came aboard. Captain Sewell returned his salute then stepped forward to shake hands.

"Welcome aboard, Captain," he said. He then turned and called, "Mister Crocker, dismiss the crew."

Sewell led the way to his cabin. "I recall that you drink coffee. I can have a pot brought in."

"Thanks, but I've had my fill for today."

Sewell motioned to a chair while he unbuckled his gun belt and laid the rig on a small table.

Once seated, Sewell said, "I trust you have some news about our ships using the Potomac."

Haynie nodded. "There is considerable anxiety over the fact that Virginia has not been re-admitted to the Union. Someone questioned whether Virginia is, in fact, a foreign nation. Can the state of Maryland enter into a binding agreement with the commonwealth at this time?"

Sewell removed his Stetson and vigorously scratched his head with one hand. "Re-admission is likely just a few months away. We're just looking for a short-term answer."

"Good, because that's all this is. If your use of the river is strictly as a roadway from one place to another, the Maryland Oyster Navy will not interfere. If some other body questions your activity—like one of our southern counties—let me know and we'll see about it."

"That should work. Thank you, Captain."

"Of course. Now, were you able to find out anything about Mooney and Hollins?"

"Very little. From what I could learn, Mooney spent the last several years in Maryland and only returned to Virginia a few months ago. As for Hollins, he was a headquarters staff officer and nobody seems to know of him before the war. Not even certain he was from Virginia. No word of either of them doing anything underhanded in our state."

Haynie rubbed his chin. "Seems strange," he said.

"What does?"

"It's certain that they have been involved in kidnappings, shanghaiing and killings. Seems like they would have left some sort of trail before coming to Maryland."

"Don't rely too much on that. Many county court houses were burned during the war, along with all their records. Same for newspapers. Have to be real lucky to run across someone who knows something about any of them, but I'll keep looking."

"I thank you for that. We're going to keep after them. Here is another name for you: Simon Berrien. He has moved into Mooney's place at Popes Creek. It looks like he's their front man for some new scheme."

Sewell said, "I'll do what I can, but it's near hopeless."

The *Emma Dunn* steamed north around Smith Island into Kedge's Strait. Another Oyster Navy ship stood anchored at the mouth of Black Cove. The *Kent,* a side-wheel steamer, was one-third longer than the *Emma Dunn* with twice the tonnage.

Haynie, as Deputy Commander of the Oyster Navy, had chosen the *Emma Dunn*. He reasoned that the smaller craft could get in and out of places the *Kent* could not.

The *Emma Dunn* anchored, and Haynie watched from the port rail as a dory was lowered from the *Kent*. Moments later, the *Kent's* captain boarded, paused to salute the colors and headed toward Haynie.

"Permission to come aboard, sir."

Haynie laughed. "Permission granted," he said and the two men warmly shook hands.

"Captain Billy Pack, welcome to the *Emma Dunn*."

Haynie led his guest to the galley, where he poured coffee for both of them.

Pack said, "I was surprised when I got my orders to meet up with you over here. Odd they would have both of us in the same waters. Only leaves the *Leila* to be everywhere else. What's up?"

Haynie glanced at the ship's cook. "Skillets, take a turn around the deck. The air will do you a world of good."

When they were alone, Haynie said, "There's a rogue drudger running out of Fox Creek, up in Dorchester County, name of Marrok Blanchard. Sails around flying the state flag and claiming to be Oyster Navy. He and his boys make a big show out of running tongers off a rock. Mostly the oystermen are legal and they get mad as hell thinking the state law is running them off a good rock. Others he hauls into a crooked judge in Cambridge. After a sham court session, Blanchard ends-up with the tonger's boat and anything else he has taken a fancy to.

"What's your plan?"

Haynie eyed Pack. "We know for a fact this Blanchard crew is plotting to kill me."

Billy Pack threw up a hand. "Whoa!" he said. "That's bodacious. How could you know that for certain?"

"Blanchard fancies the eastern bay his own private ocean and intends to run the law out. Figures that if he can kill the captain of the Chester River battle everyone else will be afraid to come back. Moreover, he means to do it right here, aboard the *Emma Dunn*."

"How do we know this?"

"The Blanchards have churned the water real good. Word gets around."

Pack shrugged and, as it was his old friend talking, decided not to question the explanation.

Haynie went on. "Commander Davidson didn't want to get into it until the *Leila* was in service and, as you know, that was long delayed. We have the go ahead to set a trap for them."

Pack shook his head. "Haynie, my friend, you must forgive me. I'm having trouble with all this. I guess you are not going to tell me how it was you came upon this singular information. But, as it's you, I'll let that slide. Let's say this Blanchard does aim to see you killed aboard your own ship. It's hard to understand how he could imagine carrying out such a plot. Could be whiskey talking."

Haynie shrugged. "We're about to find out."

Emma Dunn docked at Town Point and Haynie waited patiently for Gerhard Stein to return with Sheriff Tolley. Haynie deemed it best that he not make another appearance in the sheriff's office. Some folks in Cambridge could think that their sheriff was a little too friendly with the state oyster police.

Stein and Tolley approached the pier and Haynie waved them aboard.

"Thanks for coming, Sheriff," Haynie said. "If you'll follow me to the galley you'll get a chance to rate your coffee with that boiled by our cook."

Skillets hovered over the visitor until satisfied that his coffee was appreciated before leaving the galley.

Haynie said, "I hope you understand why I sent Gerhard for you."

Tolley nodded. "It was a good idea. Our citizens are getting real stirred up. Lotsa talk about you boys threatening to shoot tongers and running them off a legal rock. A while back, I heard you took a fella's punt gun away from him and made him swim ashore.

"More and more tongers are grousing about bein' run off their beds by a drudge boat flying the state flag. Some are saying it's no more than legalized poaching. They figure you boys are letting them find the good beds, then you run 'em off and help yourselves to the white gold."

"What do you think?"

"Got to be Marrok Blanchard. No one else with the sand to do it."

Haynie nodded. "The Blanchards have been running loose for too long; time to put an end to it. You ready?"

"I've been waitin' for this."

"I need you to pass the word to Cromarte that the *Emma Dunn* will be anchored off Bishop's Head for the next two nights."

"I'll let my deputy hear it and—"

"That won't do. I thought more about that and the word has got to come direct from you to Cromarte."

Tolley shrugged. "I don't see—"

"When we accuse Cromarte, he can deny it. He will likely say that the deputy must have told someone else and it was them who spilled it to Blanchard. If it comes down to it, you can swear Cromarte is the only person you told it to.

"This is where you not being too friendly with us can pay off. *What the hell are those state boys up too, Judge? Next, they'll be trying to take over the whole damn county.*

"He'll believe you."

39

**Bishop's Head
Dorchester County, Maryland
April 6, 1869**

Marrok Blanchard steadied the telescope on the node of a sweet gum tree. The *Emma Dunn* rocked at anchor about one hundred fifty yards off Bishop's Head. Thick clouds obscured the moon, making the ship's silhouette barely visible against the treeline.

Benoit and Renard sat nearby perched on a fallen log.

Guy remained with the *Pluton* in a small cove a few yards through the forest.

Before leaving Fox Creek, Marrok had ordered his sons to wear their berets. Waving his own cap, Marrok had said, *"When doing battle, a warrior must be known to his enemy by a badge of honor. This is the badge of honor for Blanchard men."*

"Why are we waiting, Papa?" Benoit asked. "What if those men who sailed off should come back?"

Renard grumbled. "Why didn't we bring anything to eat?"

"Stop your sniveling," Marrok growled. "Bring food! This ain't no damn picnic. Renard, get up here and take the watch. You pay mind to that steamboat. There'll be time for supper after we take care of business here."

Renard focused the glass. "I can't see anything. It is too dark."

"You cannot see the outline of that big ship?"

"Yes. But—"

"The lamp in the captain's cabin?"

"Yes."

"Keep the damn glass there and report any movement. Is that so hard?"

"No Papa."

Marrok walked to Benoit and stood over him. "*Mon fils*," he said, "you must learn patience and planning when preparing for battle. You complained because we came while it was still light. That is why we saw the dinghy taking the crew ashore and we know there cannot be more than one or two aboard. Very important information."

Marrok pointed through the trees. "No one as big as this Captain McKenna was in the small boat. Is it not so that he must remain aboard?"

"*Oui,* Papa."

"Also very important."

Benoit asked, "How is it that you know his stature?"

"From the judge, a very important man. His friend, the sheriff, also hates these state navy men. He was quick to tell the judge everything. Never forget that the judge is our good friend; always treat him with respect."

Guy appeared through the trees. "Is he the one who told you where we would find this McKenna?"

"Yes—that too. See how he helps us." Marrok looked at Guy. "Why have you left your post?"

"It is late. I was afraid there was trouble."

Marrok laid a hand on Guy's shoulder. "Don't be impatient. This is to be our great battle. It will return control of these waters to the Blanchard family fleet. After tonight, this Oyster Navy will plague us no more."

In the darkness, someone snorted.

Marrok stepped toward the log. "You doubt me, Benoit?"

"Not you Papa, you are a lion. But we would have a better chance if the one standing next to you had stayed home with the other women."

Marrok sensed Guy preparing to lunge at Benoit and thrust a hand against his chest. "Stop it! Fools! We must be united in the face of our enemies; not like mainlanders, where brothers kill brothers."

Marrok turned toward the sweet gum tree. "Renard, any movement out there?"

"No Papa."

"Come, bring the glass and join us—it is time."

Renard made his way to the log. Marrok forbid a campfire or lantern light leaving them to pick their way carefully through the thick woods.

The four Blanchard men stood in a tight group. Each armed with a musket or shotgun, a revolver and a hunting knife. At Marrok's order, they made certain that their weapons were loaded.

"Are there any questions, *mes fils?*"

Renard spoke up. "Papa, what are we to do if the dory returns with the crew?"

"The judge said the ship will be anchored for two nights. The dory will not return before morning. Follow me."

Marrok led them along the path back to the *Pluton*. Once onboard, Guy cast off and joined Renard on the starboard side of the boat, while Marrok and Benoit manned the port side. Each man dipped a paddle in the water propelling the canoe silently across the cove. It was his plan that the *Pluton* would ease quietly against the *Emma Dunn*. He and Benoit would be the first aboard, with Renard next. Guy was to secure the *Pluton* to the steamboat and follow immediately.

With the *Emma Dunn* looming just ahead, Guy dug his paddle deep, propelling the *Pluton* hard into the steamer's hull.

Marrok swore and gripped the police boat's rail with one strong arm. As the *Pluton* settled against the bigger boat, Marrok vaulted onto the steamer's deck, with Benoit close behind.

Renard hesitated. "You bastard," he cursed, and then scrambled aboard the police boat.

Marrok quickly led the way aft. As they neared the ship's cabin, Benoit pushed ahead. He cocked his shotgun and the sharp click echoed in the stillness.

"I will make you proud, Papa," he said and shoved his way into the cabin.

Gunfire flashed and exploded inside the small room. Simultaneously four peace officers burst from a portside hatchway. The leader shouting, "Give it up."

Marrok, standing behind Renard, threw his musket to the deck and slowly raised his hands. As the officers approached, Marrok grabbed his son by the shoulders and shoved him into their midst. While the lawmen grappled with Renard, Marrok darted around the cabin, ran to the starboard rail and leapt over the side into the black water.

As soon as Renard left the *Pluton,* Guy pushed off from the *Emma Dunn* and ran to the bow. He jerked the hated beret from his head and flung it into the water. Grabbing a paddle, he dug furiously in an effort to distance himself from the scene. Gunfire erupted behind him and Guy dug even deeper, striving for the jut of land ahead.

Haynie rushed from the cabin, revolver in hand, Gerhard close behind. Devil Furniss was thrashing about the deck, struggling to hold down one of the intruders.

"Gerhard, help him."

"*Ja.*"

Gunfire echoed from both rails, and Haynie ran to the starboard side. Bryce Tydings was firing at a shadowy figure fleeing in a small boat toward land.

Haynie shouted, "Cease fire, Officer Tydings."

"But, sir, one's getting away."

"We'll find him. Follow me."

"Aye, sir."

At the port rail, Jacoby was firing into the water.

"What is it, mate?"

"One of them jumped in right here, sir. I was hoping to get lucky, but I don't think I hit him."

Haynie nodded. "Let's go see what we caught in our trap."

Amidships, Gerhard straddled the remaining intruder while Devil Furniss bound his hands.

Haynie motioned for Jacoby to follow him into the cabin. There, Officer Bramble held a lamp over the lifeless body of Benoit Blanchard.

Haynie nudged the carcass with the toe of his boot. "Too young— must be one of the sons. Like many a day at sea—the big one got away."

40

Taylors Island
Dorchester County, Maryland
April 8, 1869

Guy Blanchard tied off the *Pluton* at a dock on Slaughter Creek. The sunshine and warm spring breeze did nothing to stir him from the funk that had possessed him since the attack on the *Emma Dunn*, two nights ago. Before that night, whenever he thought about this moment, he was always jubilant: He imagined Tubman's face breaking into a wide grin when he saw his boat tied to his dock. The hate in Andrew's eyes would vanish. Now, as he trudged along the path, he felt nothing.

He shuddered as he rapped on Tubman's door. It was flung open by Andrew who stood before him, eyes blazing.

"I need to see your father. You gonna let me in?"

Andrew glowered.

"Glare all you want," Guy yelled, "you don't worry me anymore because I no longer give a damn."

From inside the house, Tubman's voice was barely audible. "You let him in."

Guy followed Andrew through the empty kitchen into a dusky little room. Tubman sat in a makeshift chair cut from an old tobacco hogshead, a ragged shawl draped over him. Guy was jolted by the change in the old man's appearance. Only moments before, he had thought it impossible to feel any lower.

Tubman was a skeleton encased in pallid leather. Bony fingers held the shawl close. A racking cough shook his frame, and he spit into a cloth held close to his mouth.

Behind Guy, Andrew growled, "Come to see what you done?"

Tubman lifted his head. "Andrew—please—don't," he whispered. Slowly he nodded for Guy to proceed.

Guy's voice faltered, "Sir—I brought your boat back." He turned to Andrew. "Just like I promised. It's tied to the dock on Slaughter's Creek."

Unable to face what his family had done to this man, he looked away. "When I leave, it'll still be there. Yes sir, it will," he added.

Tubman managed a feeble smile then laid his head back and closed his eyes.

Guy started. "Is he—?"

"Not yet. If ya'll are waitin' for a thank you, ya might as well go ahead on out that door."

Guy stared for another minute then turned away. "I'm very sorry. What happened to him?"

Andrew motioned Guy outside and closed the door behind them.

"He can't hear us out here. The good Lord willin', this is the last time I'll have to look at your ugly white face, so I'm gonna tell ya. You done brought our boat back, yes sir. 'Cept it's too late. It's too late for him and it's likely too late for my mama. Theys both in a bad way."

Andrew's hands clenched into fists and he choked as he spoke. "You 'member them table and chairs in that kitchen when you was here in the winter?"

Guy stood his ground and nodded.

"Daddy made them with his own hands; just like we did that boat. Thanks to your family, we had to sell it off piece by each to get us through the season. What we couldn't sell got burned in the stove for to try and stay warm. You recollect there was a big ole wooden pantry in the kitchen?"

"Uh huh."

"Did us no good standin' empty, so it went into the fire."

Andrew indicated the house. "As for him, a bowl of warm water with a onion or turnip floatin' on top—when we could get it—ain't enough to keep away the sickness. Not when you're old and shiverin' all the time with the cold."

Guy, determined not to quaver, stepped into Andrew's glare, his own fists clenched.

"The good Lord willin', this the last time I'll have to look at your ugly black face, so you're gonna listen to what I have to say."

Andrew leaned forward on the balls of his feet, fists cocked at his side.

Guy flinched at the movement, then continued, determined to say his piece. "I've said it before, but this is the last time; I'm sorry about your father and what we did to your family. You should know that there are some good Blanchards, a few of us, anyhow. Did you know I was helpin' the Oyster Navy to stop my family from doin' bad?"

Andrew gave no sign.

Guy nodded toward the house. "That man in there knows. It was him took me to meet up with McKenna. It was then I told them about Papa's plan to kill him. The other night us Blanchards attacked their ship, the *Emma Dunn*. I did the only thing I could think of to let them know we was there; I bumped the *Pluton* hard into their boat. They was waiting 'cause of me. Afterwards, I snuck home and mamma told me my oldest brother, Benoit, got killed that night and my other brother, Renard, is sittin' in jail. My Papa jumped off the deck into the black water.

"I made off in my—in your boat—with them shootin' at me. They didn't hit nothin' important."

Guy waited. Getting no response, he continued, "I hid out all night and didn't go home 'til well after sunup. Papa had come there during the night, stole Louie, that's Benoit's boy, from his bed and left out with him in Benoit's own boat, the *Saint-Esprit*. He left his big boat tied to our pier. Guess he figured it was too much boat for just him and Louie—who's only four—to handle. My Mama is real scared about Louie."

Guy took a breath and finished. "I'm not telling you this to hear a thank you. I know one ain't coming. I'm tellin' you 'cause you need to be real careful. If Papa sees the *Pluton*—that's your boat—no tellin' what he'll do; but he'll do something—bad, real bad. Oh—he took his big ole punt gun with him. If that don't scare you, it should. One shot from that thing would sink the *Plu*-your canoe."

Andrew stared straight ahead giving no sign he had heard a word Guy had spoken.

"You understand me?" Guy asked.

"You had your say." Andrew turned and walked into the house, closing the door behind him.

Guy stared after him, then turned and headed into the woods in the direction of Benny Crème's tavern.

I'm sorry about it, but I can't do no more—and the look in those eyes is done haunting me.

41

Annapolis, Maryland
April 8, 1869

Lila McKenna wore a light jacket and reveled in her freedom from the heavy winter coat as she walked the few blocks to Wilma Winder's home. She regretted not having time to savor the blossoms that lined her path, but she was determined to have a moment alone with Wilma.

Lila found her standing on the veranda enjoying a cigarette.

"How brazen!" Lila called. "Smoking in public."

Wilma shrugged. "I'm a real hussy."

Lila climbed the steps and stood beside her. "Does it really soothe the nerves, as I have heard?"

Wilma nodded. "I find that it helps when I'm feeling frayed. I'm certain you know that feeling, especially after that awful affair on the *Emma Dunn*."

"If you are referring to that battle on the Chester River, I found wine to be a comfort. Wouldn't do to make a habit of it though."

"I'm talking about two nights ago, across the bay, at Bishop's Head."

Lila gasped and covered her mouth, "Oh my! What has happened now?"

Wilma crushed out her cigarette and guided Lila inside to a chair.

"Sit here. I'll pour us a glass."

"Is he—?"

"I'm sorry," Wilma called from the next room, "I assumed you had heard. From what I know, your husband was not injured."

Lila covered her eyes with one hand and accepted the wineglass with the other.

Wilma sat nearby. "It's fortunate that you were early. You have a chance to collect yourself before the others arrive. No doubt you will receive a sympathetic pat from some."

Lila gripped the glass tightly in both hands and got it to her lips. "Please, what do you know?"

"Remember," Wilma cautioned, "this at least fourth-hand. The story is that the *Emma Dunn* was anchored for the night when some armed men crawled aboard, intent on killing the captain."

"Haynie."

Wilma nodded. "It seems he and his men were waiting for them and killed one. Another one's in jail and two escaped. I was told that no Oyster Navy men were hurt."

"Damn him. I live in fear knowing that he is out there being shot at. I have to hear about it like this, and still, I don't really know what happened."

"The others will be here shortly. Did you get a chance to talk to him about our rights conference in June?"

Lila, her fear mixed with anger, drained her glass. "I merely told him that it sounded like a wonderful opportunity for those who would attend, but it was not the time to discuss my going. Am I less deserving of an exciting life than he is? He believes it is his calling to bring justice to the bay. I, too, have a calling—justice for women." She looked into Wilma's face. "I have never seen New York and I am determined to go with you."

Wilma stood. "That's wonderful news. They are coming up the walk we'll finish this later."

Cora Clemson introduced Doctor Simon Berrien in glowing terms and took her place in the first row.

Berrien, never shy on stage, enjoyed his place at the center of a female audience. His wardrobe was carefully chosen to give the impression of a proud gentleman, once of means, now struggling vainly to overcome the tragedies of war. For this performance, the actor had chosen a faded gray tweed sack coat and worn fawn-colored trousers. A pointed black bow tie failed to conceal the frayed edges of a shawl cut shirt collar. His hair was fashionably oiled; his mustache waxed to a stiletto point.

Berrien, applying his most seductive gaze, evaluated the women seated before him. It was his practice to establish contact with one or two in each audience, who he deemed worthy of additional attention. He noticed two likely prospects before turning his attention to a smitten Cora Clemson.

"First, let me thank the lovely Missus Clemson for inviting me to meet with your wonderful group."

He paused allowing Cora to revel in a smattering of polite applause then said, "You see before you a man tormented. Tormented by his own failure and its terrible consequences.

"My church, the Redemption Church of America in Mecklenburg County, Virginia, admitted coloreds before the war. We did not just admit them, we welcomed them with our arms wide and smiles on our faces. "

Berrien hung his head and accepted the applause.

"It was no more than good Christian folks should do, and I can honestly say that the coloreds in my flock felt true Christian love. During the long years of the recent conflict, those poor souls struggled mightily just to survive. After months of living mostly on broken promises, they came to look upon me with distrust and loathing. Soon they reviled me with curses and shouts of 'devil' and 'scalawag,' before turning their faces away."

A murmur spread across the room.

"Their hatred of me was terrible, but, worst of all they had lost faith in their God for which I accept the blame."

Gazing about the room, he said, "I thank the good Lord that he spared this lovely home and you genteel folk from such outrages."

Berrien straightened. "I will not upset you ladies by describing the horrors committed by these once gentle souls. It is sufficient that you know they despaired enough to burn down our church, loot stores and sack homes,."

In a quiet voice, he added, "Oh, the unspeakable things a few tormented bucks did to white women."

Cries of anguish erupted among the women.

Berrien shuddered and gestured to the south. "All of that and much worse, just a few miles from where you are sitting."

Several hands flew to mouths but failed to stifle the gasps and moans.

"Yes, many of them were quite vicious. Through it all I managed to scrape together some funds and started a school for a few freedmen and their children. I taught some basic reading and writing and the wonderful lessons found in the Bible. But, in the end, this did not stop them from attacking me and wrecking the school."

A mixture of "Oh no!" and "Praise be!" filtered across the room.

"I had no choice but to flee with as many students as I could bring with me. The closest sanctuary was across the Potomac River here in Maryland."

The gathering responded with knowing looks and nodding heads.

"God has surely smiled on you in all of His glory. He has spared you and your loved ones the ravages of war that were visited on thousands of us."

He pointed dramatically. "Just over there, through the grace of God, I have re-established my school on the Maryland shore. It sits high on a hill, a beacon of hope for the wretched. A shining light for all who wish to learn, and to experience God's love."

Berrien silenced the applause with a raised hand.

"I have yet to earn their approval, or yours. I pray that I may rebuild my school and my church. And, with God's help, I will restore their faith in me and in themselves. If I fail them, I also fail you. I shudder to think of the consequences of such a failure, for all of us. The restless hordes will descend upon us like the plague, in their desperate search of a better life. If that happens, I beg you to show them some kindness. Turn the other cheek, for they have suffered mightily."

Lucy Buck, half rising from her chair cried, "Isn't there something we can do?"

Wilma whispered to Lila, "So nice of Cora to give Lucy a line."

Berrien was saying, "That's very kind of you, Missus Buck"—Lucy reddened at the mention of her name "—I'm fearful that the need is too great—"

Cora joined Lucy on her feet. "Please tell us what to do," she pleaded. Others nodded encouragement.

Berrien feigned surprise. "I am indeed overwhelmed by your willingness to help these poor souls who have suffered so much. Please let me have a moment to consider this gracious outpouring."

He struck a pose with one hand to his mouth and gazed beyond the women.

Cora and Lucy sat down.

After a moment of study, Berrien clasped both hands behind his back, his look sweeping the group.

"This may be something," he said. "Please bear with me for it has just come to mind.

Through my work with freedmen, I have been in close contact with the national government's Freedmen's Bureau. You may know that the bureau has helped thousands of coloreds across the South since the war. Unfortunately, it is a small agency easily overwhelmed with demands for medicine, clothing, food and education.

"In addition to seeing to these needs, it is the bureau's responsibility to distribute confiscated and abandoned land to freedmen—'40 acres and a mule'—as the saying goes."

Berrien lowered his voice and assumed a conspiratorial look. "My contacts in the Abandoned Lands section tell me that, only a fraction of the thousands of acres held by the national government, have been distributed. And," he leaned forward, "I'm told that it is very likely the government will shut down the Freedman's Bureau in a matter of weeks. If that comes to pass, thousands of acres will remain unclaimed."

Berrien maintained an aura of intrigue. "A fine Christian gentleman of my acquaintance, who toils in the Abandoned Lands section, recently remarked on his frustration at being able to do so little to help those who need so much."

Cora raised a timid hand. "Pardon me, Doctor Berrien, but are you saying that the government has had trouble giving away this land?"

"Unfortunately, the land is not entirely free. There are title fees, which, though nominal, are beyond the means of many freedmen. That fact, and a strangling government bureaucracy, has served to stifle the efforts of my dear comrade and his associates. A good Christian, he is searching for a way to provide as much land as possible to deserving freedmen in the short time left. In a few weeks, the bureau will shut down and this land will likely remain unclaimed for years to come. Or, worse, be gobbled up by a few greedy politicians for pennies an acre."

Cora jumped to her feet, her body a quiver with excitement. "I've had the most wonderful idea. Why couldn't the women of this club take title to some of this land? We are looking for worthy causes to support. This certainly qualifies. In turn, we would donate it to your church; you could distribute these precious acres among your flock."

She paused and looked around for reaction to her words. "Maybe then they would stop hating you."

From his acting repertoire, Simon Berrien summoned a look of humbled surprise. His voice trembled with emotion. "I—I don't know what to say. For the first time in my life, I am truly speechless."

Berrien covered his face and turned away. His shoulders quivered slightly and it was moments before he was able to compose himself. He turned to face the group and paused, allowing anticipation to build, before delivering his next line.

"What a wonderful idea. I don't know what the Freedman's Bureau will say about this, however it is clearly the work of a Divine Providence. My Christian brother and I will find a way. We will not let man's rules obstruct the Lord's work. Together, we shall make this noble offering come to pass. Amen."

"Amen," the ladies intoned.

42

Annapolis, Maryland
April 8, 1869

"Missus Bishop, I'm home!" Lila called as she closed the front door.

Haynie appeared in the doorway to the parlor. "I asked her to take the children home with her for the night."

"Oh! What did she think of that?"

"I can only imagine, given the twinkle in her eye. We need to talk without any distractions."

"We certainly do," she said, and followed him into the parlor. "I came from Wilma Winder's. She told me about those men who tried to kill you."

Haynie stopped. "I'm sorry you heard about it that way. I had hoped to get to you first."

Lila sighed and slumped into her chair, Haynie claimed his rocker.

Lila said, "I haven't been sleeping well. Nerves, I guess. Forgive me if I close my eyes while you tell me what happened."

"It can wait if you like."

She gave him a hard look, then rested her head on the back of the chair and closed her eyes.

"Well," he said, "Marrok Blanchard—"

"Yes, Marrok. What kind of name is that?"

"French. He fancies himself as some sort of descendant from French naval heroes. He's had the run of the Eastern Shore for years.

He and his three boys sail about terrorizing tongers; taking their boats—"

"They're the ones who took that colored man's boat." She opened her eyes, "Tubman."

Haynie nodded. "Blanchard has tried his best to rile folks against us. He and his boys attacked watermen, flying the state flag, heavily armed with cannon and long guns. Marrok proclaimed he was Captain McKenna of the Oyster Navy, threatened the tongers and drove them off of their beds."

Lila nodded to signal that she understood.

"Blanchard got it in his head that if he snuck aboard one of our boats and killed the captain, the oyster police would be scared away from his part of the bay."

"Would any old captain do, or was he after the famous Captain McKenna of the Chester River battle?"

"Hard to say," Haynie said. "There was talk that he was aiming for me."

She watched him for a moment before closing her eyes again. "Some talk? Go on."

"*Emma Dunn* was anchored for the night. Blanchard and two of his boys crept aboard and stormed the cabin. I was fortunate they didn't get a shot at me."

"I want to make certain I have this right," Lila said, "when I tell it to the ladies. There you are, sound asleep in your bed, when these three killers break in; but before they can fire a shot you kill them all. Is that what happened?"

"Only one of them was killed, Benoit—Marrok's oldest."

"So you shot the first one to come in and the other two ran away."

"That's not how it was."

"Sorry. Guess I'm tired. What did I miss?"

Haynie shrugged. "Like I said, the first one through the door was killed—"

"By you?"

"Or Gerhard. Could've been Jacoby. We were all shooting."

Lila opened an eye. "The three of you bunk in the one cabin?"

Haynie shook his head.

"Okay. The three of you are sitting around talking. I'm surprised the Blanchards didn't see your light, or hear your voices."

"It was quiet."

Lila raised her head. "So you are sitting around in silence and shoot the first person who comes into your cabin? Doesn't that worry your crew?"

Haynie said nothing.

"What happened to the other two—Marrok and the other son?"

"The shooting brought the crew out. Marrok pushed his other son into them and escaped over the side. We have that son, Renard, in jail."

"You said this Marrok had three sons; where was the third one?"

"He escaped in their boat."

"Seems strange these three were stupid enough to come aboard knowing there'd be a full crew of oyster police on board."

"They might have thought the crew was ashore."

"What would give them that idea?"

"Earlier I met up with Billy Pack and took his crew on board. It is likely the Blanchards were watching the *Emma Dunn* for a while. If so, they saw Pack's crew rowing ashore."

"So! You knew they were coming and were ready for them. Why didn't you just admit you put yourself out as bait to catch these men."

Haynie shrugged. "I didn't want to upset you."

"Jesus! Is it any wonder I have trouble sleeping?"

When there was no comment, she asked, "How did you know they were coming?"

"I'm sorry. I can't tell you."

"Was it the colored man, Tubman, who told you?"

Haynie looked away.

"So it has come to that. I am no longer a partner in that part of your life. It must be lonely for you."

Haynie looked at her. "This is not the same as being the bailiff in Crisfield. It is no longer just the two of us to think about. Others lives are at risk and, like it or not, it is my responsibility to see that they are still breathing when this is over. It gets real scary when they are all looking at me, waiting for an answer. But, I signed up for it and I'm steering the best course I can."

"And I'm trying my best to deal with that." Lila reached over, touched his arm and said. "The truth is, they're damn lucky to have you at the helm."

She stood and turned toward the kitchen. "Now, I'm going to fix some supper. Are you hungry?"

Haynie nodded and closed his eyes.

Revived by the meal, and her resolve not to waver, Lila settled into one end of the sofa her legs tucked under her.

"Before you begin," Haynie said, "I am surprised at how calmly you took the news of the attack on *Emma Dunn*."

"After Chester River, I gave a lot of thought to how I should cope with the dangers of your work. It solves nothing if I rant and sob every time you come home. It is, after all, something you feel deeply about. A calling you might say. However, it does upset me to learn that you have no qualms about setting yourself out as bait. Like a chicken neck in a blue crab trap."

Haynie shrugged.

"My question is: What is it you would have me do to keep from going mad, day after day while you serve as bait to lure the likes of Marrok Blanchard into your trap?"

"I don't know. Whatever it is that women do, I guess." He glanced around. "The house. The children. Visiting with Wilma and the others."

"That doesn't sound very interesting, does it? Certainly not exciting."

"No, I suppose not."

"Would you agree that your life is interesting?"

"Yes—I guess it is."

"Often exciting."

"Well..."

"But, beyond those things—you are challenged by what you do."

Lila did not wait for an answer. "So, we agree that your life is interesting, exciting and, above all, it challenges you. And, you must admit, except when waiting to hear if you are dead or alive, my life is none of those things."

She waited.

Haynie sat back and tapped a finger against his lips. Eventually he said, "You speak as if we have a say in it, but we don't. Your lot in life was decided a long time before either of us was born.

"Women stay at home while men go out to work. It has been so since Adam and Eve. Our children need their mother here and I need to know that you are with them. I can't do my work if I have to worry because you decide to leave the children and gallivant off to—New York."

"Because I am a woman, I cannot have a calling?"

"Well, I guess you can, but within reason."

Lila leveled a look. "World history would be quite different today if you had been there to say no to Joan of Arc, or Molly Pitcher, or Harriet Beecher Stowe."

"I don't know about Molly Pitcher," Haynie replied. "As for Joan of Arc, she did not have a husband and two young children. Harriet Beecher Stowe wrote *Uncle Tom's Cabin* at home."

"For the record, Molly Pitcher was a hero of the American Revolution. She fought beside her husband at the Battle of Monmouth. I do not know where her children were. Like Harriet Beecher Stowe, I have been doing my writing at home."

"What kind of writing? You haven't said anything to me."

"Actually, I did. I told you I was thinking of writing and you said 'Letters? To who?'"

Haynie shrugged.

"I wrote a story which I sent to *Godey's* magazine, and they printed it."

"What did you write about? Nothing…"

"Nothing of interest ever happens to me—is that what you were going to say?"

"I meant—"

"Maybe I wrote about the adventures of Haynie McKenna."

Haynie rose from his chair. "This isn't getting us anywhere."

Lila pulled an envelope from her jacket pocket and held it out to him.

"This will tell you what you need to know."

"What's is it?"

"A letter from your mother. Please read it."

43

Dorchester County, Maryland
April 10, 1869

Guy Blanchard, his mother sitting next to him, glanced around the dinning room,

She patted his hand. "It's all right, dear. The girls are outside gutting the fish for supper."

They both eyed the empty chairs grouped at the far end of the table. Guy needed to assure himself that his father was not seated there on his throne.

Edith was most troubled by the absence of her grandson, Louie. Marrok, twisted by his hatred of the Oyster Navy, was in no state of mind to care for a small boy. His attack on the *Emma Dunn* satisfied her that he was a madman. Except for the absence of Louie, the array of empty chairs did not bother her.

The afternoon following the Blanchard's attack on the *Emma Dunn*, Sheriff Tolley and a deputy had come to the house looking for Marrok and Guy. Edith met them at the treeline.

After telling her that Benoit had been shot dead and Renard was in jail, Tolley pulled a wet black beret from a saddlebag.

"This was found floating near the state boat at first light. We believe it is Marrok's."

He waited, but Edith displayed no emotion.

"They didn't find Marrok's body so we figure he made it to shore."

"He ain't dead—yet," She said.

Tally shifted his eyes away from Edith while he scanned the grounds.

"Is he here?"

"He was. Took some dry clothes—and my grandson—then left out, hours ago."

Tolley reached into his bag and produced a second water soaked beret.

"This one was floating near where someone fled in a log canoe. We figure it was your youngest, Guy."

Edith answered with a fierce look.

"No body to go with this cap either. Is he here?"

Edith shook her head.

"It is better if you tell us where they are."

"I would, Sheriff—I know it's my duty—but I got no idea." She waved an arm toward the Chesapeake Bay.

"They could be anywhere out there; but they'll not be together. You tell that Oyster Navy captain not to shoot my boy—that goes for you, too. He's won't hurt anyone."

"I'll tell him. Guess you wouldn't mind if we had to shoot old Marrok."

"There you do what you have to do." She shook a finger at Tolley. "When you do find him, see that Louie's not hurt."

"Yes, ma'am."

Edith turned away and climbed the steps to the main house. *Marie, won't miss getting slapped around by Benoit. That bastard Marrok turned Louie against her by shouting out 'l' infirme,' and laughing every time they saw her. If ever a man deserves killin', it's him. Well, the lawmen had their chance and they missed him.*

She hefted the shotgun she carried. *I'll not miss if it comes my turn.*

Still patting Guy's hand, Edith said, "How come that sheriff is looking for you?"

"Captain McKenna said it was better he didn't tell no one about me, not even the sheriff. When he talks about me, he calls me Caleb. That was his brother's name. Caleb got murdered so he don't need it anymore. Anyhow, I gotta act like I'm running, 'til they catch Papa. On the chance he ain't figured out it was me who told, it wouldn't do for him to come around here one night and find me sleepin' peaceful in my own bed."

Edith tightened her grip on his hand. "You be careful until he's caught. He was here again last night, so he knows that both the

Souverain and the *Pluton* are gone. He'll wonder what use you have for two boats and might suspicion that you gave the little one back to the coloreds. Even if he don't figure out it was you who told McKenna about the attack, giving that boat back to them darkies will get him mad enough to hunt you down."

"He was here again last night? What was he after?"

Edith shrugged. "I lock myself in when I go to bed. It was late when I heard him moving around. At first I thought it was that sheriff or McKenna a-huntin' him, but the dogs didn't say nuthin' so I knowed it was him. I had a basket of new-washed clothes sittin' in the washhouse. He'd rummaged through it and took some for him and the boy."

Guy nodded toward the window. "What're you going to do about those two?"

"What do you mean?"

"Well, it won't take much attention from Papa for either one of them to tell what they know. About me bein' here, the sheriff comin' by, stuff that he don't need to be hearing."

"Don't sell either of them short," Edith said. "Mary—she don't answer to 'Marie' no more—is frantic on account of Marrok just up and took Louie from her. She'll shoot him herself, if she gets a chance. As for Nelly, she's real scared Renard'll get out of jail and give her a beatin'. I told her to run while she can. She said she would, if she can go with you."

"No! No! You gotta tell her no! I can't have a girl tagging along. It's gonna take all I can do to stay clear of Papa until Captain McKenna gets him."

Edith let go of Guy's hands. "We'll fix some supper right quick, then you have to skedaddle. You keep a sharp eye out for him."

Guy nodded.

She indicated his musket standing in the corner. "If you see him you start shooting. Don't, for one minute, fret about doing wrong. There is no wrong when it comes to him."

"What about you, Mama?"

"Don't you worry about me, I got the hounds. Nights I sleep with the shotgun, and it's never far away durin' daylight."

44

Crab Point
Dorchester County, Maryland
April 10, 1869

Marrok studied the tonger through his telescope and he was livid.

"Guy, that little bastard, gave my boat back to the darkies. And the buck has the nerve to be tonging in the same place we caught them last time. I told that judge you can't believe any of 'em. Now, some more folks have to die."

Louie looked up at his grandfather, then went back to stabbing a stick into a mound of dirt on the ship's deck.

After bringing his grandson aboard the *Saint-Esprit*, Marrok anchored in a sheltered cove where Hooper's Island is at its narrowest. Just aft of the anchorage, a break in the land formed a natural channel into the Chesapeake. Too shallow for a steamship, such as the *Emma Dunn*, to navigate, it offered a quick escape for the *Saint-Esprit*.

Their first day on the water, Louie had cried most of the morning. In the beginning, Marrok chided the boy to be still. When that failed, he followed with threats and promises, again with no success.

When Louie cried for his mother, Marrok stumped around the deck with an exaggerated limp, calling out *"l'infirme, l'infirme"* and roaring heartily. The boy began to sob.

In desperation, Marrok took Louie ashore and filled an empty wooden keg with dirt. He then cut a small branch from a willow tree and returned to the *Saint-Esprit*. Back aboard, Marrok sat his screaming grandson on the deck, amidships, and dumped the dirt in a pile beside him. He placed the willow branch in Louie's hand and said, *"Voila! Mon petit fils.* You play while I take us to wonderful places."

Marrok lowered the glass and said aloud, "The young buck works alone. It will be easier with only one, but both will have to pay. That is for another day."

He lifted Louie in his arms and pointed at the small boat bobbing on the waves. *"Mon petit fils,"* he said, "Soon your uncle will be out of the *bastille*. Then the Blanchard fleet will defeat this enemy in a great naval battle."

He kissed the boy on the forehead and sat him on the dirt pile. "Blanchard means white and brave in the French."

Marrok brought the *Saint-Esprit* about and headed back to the cove.

"There is much to do, *Mon petit fils*," he said. "But first I must free your uncle Renard."

He watched the sea ahead while Louie cried and flung fistfuls of dirt across the deck.

45

Aboard Hangman
Choptank River
Cambridge, Maryland
April 11, 1869

Marrok Blanchard took a drink of the mint julep handed him by Judge Cromarte. He made a face and spit it over the side.

"Damn, Orville! That's nasty—too sweet."

Cromarte nodded and smiled. "Glad you like it."

"You old goat!" Marrok shouted. "We go through this every time. I don't know if you're just forgetful, or you're funnin' with me."

Marrok believed that the old man was not as deaf as he wanted people to believe. "The old bastard hears what he wants to hear," he had told Benoit, "and turns away from the rest."

A large brass ear trumpet lay on the deck between them. Marrok picked it up. "Stick this in your ear; there's nobody else out here to see ya with it."

He glanced at Louie curled under a blanket asleep on the deck. "Except him."

Cromarte cupped a hand behind one ear. "Speak up. This breeze's taking your words before they get to me."

"I said put this in your ear. I got serious business to discuss and I want to know you're hearing what I'm sayin'."

The judge took the cumbersome device and fit it into his right ear.

"I ain't holdin' this contraption all day. It soon gets heavy."

Marrok looked around the cluttered deck and yelled into the ear trumpet.

"Jesus, Orville, you live in a damn pig wallow."

Cromarte snorted.

"Don't it bother you?"

"Nope." The old man waved his hand at the wooded shoreline. "Got no neighbors to fuss about it and you're the only one ever comes aboard. When it gets too ripe in the summer heat, I pitch the garbage overboard until it's tolerable again. The blue crabs seem to like it."

Cromarte indicated Louie with a tilt of his head. "How is it you come to have him along?"

"He's all I got left," Marrok said, "I wasn't leavin' him with those women; they'd ruin him for damn sure. He stays with me. Those state bastards killed Benoit, my oldest; and my youngest, Guy, will be dead soon as I catch up with him. The middle boy, Renard, is in your jail—for the time being."

Cromarte watched the sleeping boy. "How'd you get him to sleep through the day like that?"

"A generous dose of paregoric in some sweet syrup."

Cromarte drank noisily from his julep. "What's got you in a mind to kill your youngest?"

"He's a traitor to the Blanchard name. The night we went after McKenna, he run our boat into the police steamer—bang; and then lit out at the first sign of trouble. If that weren't enough, he went right over and give my boat away to the darkies. No, it won't do to have him usin' the Blanchard name—means 'white and brave' in the French. He's got a killing comin'."

Cromarte supported the ear trumpet by resting his right elbow on the chair's arm and waited.

"Never mind him," Marook shouted. "I want to know what it'll take to get Renard out of that jail."

Cromarte shook his head.

"Don't shake yer damn head at me."

"What you're askin' for can't be done."

"How's that? You're a damn judge. Give out an order to let him go."

"Not that simple. You really stunk the place up this time. Did you believe you could try for a captain of the Oyster Navy without anyone taking notice?"

Marrok snapped, "Them damn bastards declared war on the Blanchard family when they invaded the Chester River. Sure as you're sittin' there, the Choptank is next; then the Honga and Fishing Bay. All Blanchard water. I have to fight 'em."

Cromarte snorted. "The whole state is watchin' us—even beyond. Reporters from as far away as Richmond and Philadelphia are settin' up to learn all about the family of pirates who stormed the Oyster Navy boat. Yes sir, two things for certain when this is over: you're gonna be famous, and you're gonna be dead."

"I can't stop 'em from makin' me famous, but I can stop 'em from makin' me dead. Now what do I have to do to get my boy out of yer jail?"

Cromarte bent forward and chortled until seized with a coughing spasm. When able, he sat back, took a drink of mint julep, and wiped the tears from his eyes.

Finally, he said, "You may hear better than me, but you don't listen. Ever' body's watching over the court proceedings. The state can't let this slide. That'd be the end of their Oyster Navy—right there."

Marrok leaned back and slapped a knee. "I knew it. That was my plan from the very start. To run 'em out of here."

"There's talk of the state attorney general sending over a special lawyer for the trial. Maybe a judge from over there, to stop the likes of me from letting you boys go free."

"Then, damnit, we got to get it done right away."

Cromarte shifted his arm for more support. "If—it could be done," he said, "it would cost ya."

Marrok glared. "You think I don't know that? I can't show my face to anybody 'cept you, but don't think you can hold me up. I won't stand for it."

"I'm not the judge for your boy—Robinson is. I can sidle up to him, but he's not as disposed to such things as I am. Even if he was so inclined, he couldn't chance it right in the courtroom with ever body watchin'."

"I don't need to hear about how it can't be done."

"The only way I can see to do it is maybe get somebody to leave a cell door open in the middle of the night."

"A deputy sheriff? I guess you got one in mind."

Cromarte nodded. "There's a fella who hangs around my court; brings in them birds from the jail and takes 'em back. That kind of a thing."

"What makes you think he'll throw in with us?"

"Which one of 'em doesn't need cash money? He'll do it if yer willing to pay."

Marrok looked hard at him. "Just so we understand one another; if I pay you the money and Renard don't get free—" He ran a finger across his throat. "We'll see how the blue crabs like you. I expect you know that no one would miss you, ya old bastard."

46

Popes Creek, Maryland
April 14, 1869

"When are they coming, Simon?" Horace Mooney asked.

"A week tomorrow."

"I know you'll put on a good show for 'em with the school, but are they ready to invest in the land?"

Not wishing to be overheard by those in the house, the two men strolled across the estate's expansive lawn to the bluff overlooking the Potomac River. They stood watching the swirling water churning downstream to the Chesapeake Bay.

Berrien chortled. "They'll come through. You could see the fright on their faces turn to greed when I told 'em about the land."

Mooney nodded. "The line about the hordes sweeping across the Potomac is intended to frighten."

"I was going easy, like you said, but I'll crank it up if they need more scarin'."

"I reckon that your friend Cora did her part. Can we count on her to hold up?"

Berrien tugged at one end of his handlebar and winked. "I've had many a woman get all spoony over me, but she's got to be the worst. Too bad, though. I had my eye on a handsome woman in the first row. I could tell she is smitten; I just have to figure out how to reel her in."

"Watch yourself. The last thing we need is for this Cora to get jealous and turn around on us."

"The secret to handlin' them—the married ones—is to keep 'em dreaming about what they're missing. A little competition can make them more willing to please. She'd be afraid I'll leave taking her dreams with me."

"I reckon you've run across her kind before, travellin' with that stage show."

Berrien, as if suddenly reminded of something, withdrew a can of mustache wax from a pocket and pinched a glob between his thumb and forefinger.

"There's a few like her in every town," he said and began working the ends of his mustache. "They get of an age; they got a husband who pays 'em no attention once he's rolled off—until the next time. They're sick of getting no thank you's after doin' for him and the kids, morning to night; and tomorrow's always gonna be as dreary as yesterday."

Berrien struck a pose. "Now along comes the handsome stranger who gives them something to dream about and—if all goes well— something to remember. By the time this stranger is headed to the next town she's all warm and smiley."

Berrien abandoned the pose. "Instead of being irate, any husband should be pleased the stranger came along and took on the job. Now, the stranger is gone and the husband's got a happy wife without havin' to do any of the work. He may even find her more interesting the next time he rolls on."

"It's gratifying to see a man so taken with his work."

Berrien closed the can and winked again. "I've got to have an understudy in case Cora disappoints."

Mooney asked, "Have your niggers learned their parts? It's real important that they hold up their end. Those women must have no doubts they're going to get something for their money."

47

Kent Island
Queen Anne's County, Maryland
April 16, 1869

Haynie McKenna was surprised to see Landon Wallis standing next to his father in the shadow of a gnarled white oak tree.

"Landon, I didn't expect you'd be here," he said, shaking hands with the father and son.

"He came direct from Popes Creek with news," said Silas Wallis. "We figured you should hear it first hand."

With a nod, Haynie indicated the *Emma Dunn* tied up at a nearby pier.

"Glad you could meet here," he said. "We're headed straight for the Honga River. There's a scoundrel down there raising every kind of hell with us. I'm under orders to scour those waters until we catch him."

Landon fidgeted and Haynie put a hand on the boy's shoulder. "What's got you so jumpy, lad?"

"Well, sir, it's pretty big news."

"Let's hear it."

"You remember Hoppy told us about that stand of pines where he could watch the house without being seen?"

Haynie nodded.

"Yesterday he got himself settled in there, just before two white men came out of the house and walked straight across the lawn.

Looked like they was headed right for him. Old Hoppy, he starts getting real worried. Trying to figure if he could sneak out the backside of the stand without them seeing him when they stop to talk, not a dozen feet from him. It was Berrien and the other one—the spy."

Landon laughed in spite of himself. "Hoppy said he didn't dare move, or hardly breathe—scared they would find him. He was still shakin' when he was tellin' me. It seems like Berrien had met up with some women who he is scheming to get money from. He was telling the spy that the women were comin' to the house to look things over. The spy asks if Berrien thinks his niggers was ready, and did he think the women would invest in some land or other."

"It sounds like some sort of confidence game," Haynie said. "Get the women to believing that Berrien is helpin' the coloreds, and that he needs money to keep going."

"They talked about some woman named Cora." Landon's face reddened and he dropped his gaze. "Guess this Miss Cora has got real friendly with that Berrien—and her a married woman."

"Wonder what land they were talking about investing in?" Silas asked.

"Oh, there's something else, sir. The spy told Berrien these women needed to see that he was turning out happy niggers. Hoppy didn't hear about where the women are from. He's keeping a close watch on the place, 'til I get back."

"I believe I know who the women are," Haynie said. "But, there is more than one Cora in the state, so we need to be certain. Whoever it is they will most likely be coming by steamboat. Get word to Hoppy to check on the boats coming in and get the name of the one that brings them in. That should tell us something."

Silas said. "We'll get a wire sent as soon as we can. What then?"

"You can get word to me through Sheriff Tolley in Cambridge. I'll check with him as regular as I can."

Haynie turned and headed toward the *Emma Dunn*. He had gone a few steps when he stopped and turned back.

"Good work, Landon," he said, and then addressed Silas. "We'll soon have the rope we need."

48

Captain Haynie McKenna and First Mate Nathan Jacoby sat at a table in the *Emma Dunn*'s galley. Nearby, Gerhard Stein stood with his back to the bulkhead, braced for any trouble. To the crew, Stein was a ghost moving silently about the ship, materializing wherever their captain appeared.

After seeing Stein at work during the Blanchard's attack, Jacoby fully appreciated the man's worth to Haynie and the entire crew.

"Sure glad he's on our side, Captain," Jacoby said.

"I've said the same thing many times, Mate."

Haynie swirled the cold dregs in the bottom of his coffee cup and pushed it away.

"Mister Jacoby," he said, "What's your take on what Benny Crème told you?"

"Aye, sir. Appears young Guy Blanchard had ideas of skedaddlin', but he seems to be stayin' put to look after Tubman, long as the old man's alive."

"Does he know Marrok's looking for him?"

"He believes it. His ma told him that if Marrok finds out about Guy giving the boat back to Tubman, that's the end of it right there."

Haynie said, "He's got to be afraid, yet, he's stickin' around to do right by old Tubman. The boy's got more sand than I figured him for."

Jacoby nodded. "Here's something else. On one of his night visits home, Marrok snatched up his grandson—son of the one we killed—and took him away."

Jacoby's words sparked the memory of Haynie's mother and the Reverend Muse spiriting Young Tench from his bed and taking him to be baptized in the icy Annemessex River. Muse had convinced the boy's grandmother that Haynie and Lila were negligent about saving his soul. It occurred to Haynie that Marrok also believed he was saving his grandson. The notion inflamed him.

Jacoby eyed him. "Sir?" he said.

Haynie waved a hand. "It's nothing, Mate. We need to tell Sheriff Tolley that Guy is on our side."

"Aye, sir. If Marrok is already after him—."

"No point in keeping Tolley in the dark."

Jacoby nodded. "And, if the judge should give bail to the other one—Renard. Likely, he'd hook up with his pa."

"He would, but the attorney general won't allow bail. He's sending over one of his top men to get Renard tried and convicted—along with Marrok, when we catch him. The state cannot let them get away with stormin' aboard a state vessel. They once hung pirates for doing that, and the same fate is in store for those two."

"What's next for us, Captain?"

"We're heading for Cambridge. Gerhard and I'll go see Tolley, tell him about Guy, and have him take us to the Blanchard place. If Guy's mother wants Marrok dead, she'll likely help us find him. Meantime, you head for Benny Crème's place and get hold of Guy. We need to know how he's holdin' up in all this. When we get Marrok and Renard into court, Guy's gonna have to sit in that chair and tell on both of 'em."

Jacoby nodded. "Hadn't thought about that."

"He probably hasn't either—and don't say anything about it—to him or Benny."

"Aye, sir."

"When you catch up to Guy, bring him back with you. I want him aboard the *Emma Dunn*—until we catch Marrok."

Sheriff Tolley stood in the midst of a group of ten heavily armed men, inside the Dorchester County Sheriff's office. Each rested a long gun on one hip and listened intently to Tolley.

Unwilling to intrude, Haynie and Gerhard waited out of earshot. Within minutes, the men turned and, grim-faced, headed toward the door, ignoring the two men as they passed.

"Sheriff," Haynie called, "I see you're busy, but there's something I need to talk to you about."

Tolley, deep in thought, jerked around at Haynie's voice.

"Commander McKenna, I didn't realize you were there. I suppose you do want to speak to me." Tolley glanced at Gerhard. "You state boys sure don't waste any time do ya?"

Haynie shrugged. "What's all the fuss?"

Tolley dragged over two chairs. "Let's sit while we talk. Guess ya'll don't know what happened, so that isn't why you've come."

Gerhard ignored the seat and stood, back to the wall, and watched.

"It must be bad," Haynie said. "Looked like a huntin' posse stormin' out of here."

"It's real bad. Renard Blanchard broke jail durin' the night. Those men been out huntin' him since first light. They're going back out again and—soon as you get through with me—I'm headin' for the Blanchard place."

Haynie studied the sheriff, "How'd he get loose?"

"God, how I been dreadin' this. Well, sir, nights when there is someone in a cell, I have a deputy sleep in the office. Last night— about two o'clock—someone started raisin' a ruckus at the end of Main Street. It woke up my deputy, Roy Ochs. He heard a couple of shots, strapped on his six-gun and headed out to see about it. By the time he got to the end of Main Street, a couple of fellas in their nightshirts was standing around cussin' about being woked up said they hadn't seen anything. Roy checked some of the stores and walked on back. First thing in the door he heads for the cells; Blanchard's door was standing open—he was gone."

Haynie worked his jaw and said nothing.

Tolley continued. "Somethin' like that happens, makes a man jumpy. When I see you here, I figure you somehow heard about it and come to raise hell with me."

"You got any idea how he got loose?"

Tolley shook his head. "It wasn't Ochs. Known Roy a long time; it wasn't him. There sure enough was a ruckus on Main Street and Roy did run up there. Those two fellas in their nightshirts told me that. No sir, somebody else done this. Most likely Marrok."

Haynie leaned close to Tolley. The brim of his hat inches from the sheriff's head.

Tolley squirmed in his chair. "Yes sir," he said, "Marrok Blanchard is crazy enough to walk right into that jail and unlock

Renard's cell door.

Tolley eased back, seeking some escape from Haynie's dark look. "Anybody knows him will tell you; that's Marrok, yes sir."

"Seems to me he'd have to be mighty quick."

"What do you mean?"

"Hard to understand how Marrok could raise that ruckus at the end of Main Street then run past your man to the jail without anyone seein' him."

Tolley looked puzzled.

"Has Marrok ever been inside your jail?"

"Not as I know of. Why?"

"Say he was able to sneak past your deputy and make it to the jail without anyone seeing him. He'd have to get hold of the key and hunt for Renard's cell. Then they both get out before Ochs can get back." Haynie straightened. "Seems like a pretty tall order, even for Marrok Blanchard."

"You're sayin' it was two of 'em—one who knew the jailhouse." Tolley shook his head. "It's hard to believe Ochs would get hooked up with the likes of the Blanchards. That means he was waiting for the ruckus and, soon as he heard the shooting, jumped up and opened the cell door before he ran up there?"

"That's one way."

Tolley looked up. "No sir. It didn't happen like that."

"How do you know?"

"The two men who got woke up said how quick Roy got there. He ran up as they come through the door. From where he was sleepin' it would take a few minutes to go back to the cell and open the door; then for him to run up there."

"If Ochs was the man, he could've opened the door anytime. Renard could have been runnin' long before the ruckus even started."

"If it was that a way—and Renard was long gone—why bother with the ruckus?"

"To give the deputy an excuse for leaving the jail."

"Oh, yeah."

Tolley slumped in his chair. "Roy's the last one I would think to do something like this. There's one or two others I'd have in line considerable ahead of him."

"Either of them work around Cromarte?"

"Why, yes—."

"Let's start with him."

"That'd be Bunky Hill. His folks named him Bunker, after the battle, but everybody calls him Bunky."

Haynie sat back. "What do you know about him?"

"A few months ago, his pappy dragged him in here and begged me to take him on. 'Said it would be real easy for Bunky to be on either side of the law, and I would be savin' the boy from eternal hell if I'd keep him on the right side."

Tolley hung his head. "Now that I say it out loud, it don't sound like a real good reason for hirin' a lawman."

Haynie said, "Must be more to why you doubt him."

Tolley shrugged. "I wish I could say there was, but it's mostly how I feel. It is odd how he took up with Cromarte and how the old man seem to take to him."

"If Cromarte asked Bunky to do something, would he do it?"

"Seems like he would. He'd think that if a judge asked him to do something, it would be right for him to do it."

"We'll deal with this later. I want to go with you to the Blanchard place."

Tolley nodded.

"First, there's something you need to know about Guy Blanchard."

49

Guy Blanchard seated himself at a rear table in Benny Crème's tavern, his back to the wall. From this vantage point, he could see anyone entering through the open front door. The chunk stove was cold, and a spring breeze refreshed the room.

Drawn there by a feeling of security, Guy had occupied the same chair almost daily since the attack on the Oyster Navy ship. Though his was the only white face in the room, he was now accepted and the others took no notice as he came and went.

The first night he had faltered at the doorway.

What if Benny hates me for what we did to his friend? What'll I do if Andrew comes in? Still, I don't have anywhere else to go. It's the one place I'm sure Marrok will not show himself.

Guy breathed in, squared his shoulders and strode directly to the same chair in which he now sat.

Four colored men seated at the counter had swung around and followed him with hard looks as he passed.

Benny Crème appeared at the table. "You alone?" he asked.

Guy nodded. "Is that all right?"

Benny shrugged.

"I'd like to get some supper," Guy said. "But, could we talk first?"

Benny slid into a chair and the four men at the bar turned away.

"First thing is, I want you to know that I'm as sorry as I can be about what my family did to your friend Tubman."

Benny gave a slight nod.

"How's he getting along? I'd like to go to visit."

Before Benny responded, Guy added, "I brought their boat back, but his boy, Andrew, still hates me."

"The old man is alive," Benny said.

"He's not going to get better, is he?" Guy asked his voice aquiver.

"Hard to say. They don't come any tougher than that man."

"Then there's some hope?"

"There's always hope. You know, havin' the boat back, Andrew'll be out tongin' the rest of the season."

"You saying it would be okay for me to visit Tubman when Andrew's out on the water?"

"Up to you."

Guy picked at his fingers. "I don't know. Tubman likely hates me as much as the boy does. Be my luck to show up and send him into a fit that would finish him. Then Andrew'd be another one a-huntin' me."

Benny stood. "You want something while we talk?"

"Maybe a sarsaparilla."

Benny returned with two jars of sarsaparilla and sat down. "There's something you should know about Tubman," he said and took a drink. "He's a rare thing. Not just for a colored man, but for a human being. As far as I know, he never held any malice toward another person. He certainly never hated a white man just for being white; same way he don't hate you just for being a Blanchard. To him, a white man can't help bein' white and you can't help bein' a Blanchard."

"I don't mean no disrespect, Mister Crème—"

"Benny."

"Yes sir, Benny. Hard for me to see how it never bothered him, all the things whites must of done to him, and now what Papa and my brothers done. And me bein' both white and a Blanchard—well—"

"I didn't say it don't bother him. It bothers him a lot, but he takes the trouble to look at each man separate from the man before. A white man do him wrong and Tubman was ready for that man the next time. Still, he was always respectful to any other white man right up 'til that particular one gave him a reason not to. As for you, he knew right off you wasn't like yer kin."

"He told you that?"

Benny nodded.

"Then—he doesn't hate me."

"That's what I been tellin' you."

Guy drank from the jar and began to moan as he rocked back and forth.

"Mercy me. Mercy me."

"You gettin' sick?"

"I believe I am. Sick inside. Sick, because I don't know what to do and I got no one to turn to."

Benny took a drink and waited.

Guy looked up. "Please tell me, what should I do?"

"I don't mix into other folks' business. Some like to be told what to do, so that if things go south on 'em they can blame someone else for telling 'em wrong. Best I can do is to listen while you talk, 'til you figure somethin' out."

"I see—well—okay—here's my fix." Guy lowered his voice. "You hear about the gang of pirates tryin' for the captain of that Oyster Navy steamboat?"

Benny had responded with a slight dip of his head.

"That was Papa and my brothers. I was with them, but I wasn't—if you know what I mean."

Benny gave no sign.

Guy glanced toward the men at the counter and leaned over the table. "I told the oyster police we was comin'. Remember when Tubman and I met them, right here?"

Benny Crème folded his arms.

Guy went on. "Nobody's supposed to know about that—"

"If nobody's to know, then why you tellin' me?"

"You and Tubman are close. I figured he told you—"

"Well sir, you don't know Tubman. He didn't tell me. If he had, then I already knows it; and if he didn't, he had a reason. Either way, you don't need to be telling that to me, or anyone else. Gonna get yerself killed."

Guy hung his head and swallowed hard. "See, that's why I need somebody—to tell me about such things as that."

Benny looked up as more regulars wandered in. "I'm real sorry about your troubles, but I have to see after these folks. What else you got to say?"

"I'm sorry. I'm sorry. I'll hurry along. Even if Papa don't know about me telling, he'll nail my hide to an outhouse door for giving Tubman back his boat. And Captain McKenna—the big one that was here—didn't tell no one about me helpin', so the sheriff's a-huntin' me. Him, or a deputy, is likely to shoot me on sight and ask afterwards. I got nowhere to go, so I come in here to ask you: is that Underground Railroad you all used, still runnin'—and how could I go about getting' onboard?"

Benny shook his head and started to speak, but Guy said, "If Papa finds out I gave back the boat, he will go after Tubman and Andrew. With Andrew gone all day, old Tubman is helpless. Now, I'm thinking I need to stay around and watch out for him."

Benny stood. "I'm gonna bring you some of Mama Crème's catfish and cornbread. You think about this while you eat, and we'll talk some more after those folks have left out."

"Thank you. Thank you."

Benny paused, "One thing you should be thinkin'on: If it comes to it, you got the grit to shoot your own daddy?"

Two weeks had passed since Guy's talk with Benny Crème. Since then, Guy had discarded all thoughts of fleeing and settled into a routine. Nights he slept in Benny's tavern. Each morning he headed down to Tubman's house, carrying with him some cornbread and fish or fried chicken left from the night before. He followed a faint trail and approached the house with caution. Circling the area, he assured himself that Andrew was on the water and Marrok was not lurking nearby.

The first morning Guy had found Tubman in the same chair, a thin blanket covering his bony frame. To his relief, Tubman accepted the food without objection. Thereafter Guy spent each morning caring for Tubman and talking about oystering and the strife on the Chesapeake. The 'Missus,' as Tubman referred to his wife, remained in the home's only other room with the door closed. Guy worried that she would tell Andrew about his visits, but he could do nothing about that.

In the late mornings, Guy left the house before Andrew was due back and scoured the nearby woods for signs of trouble. Later in the day, when he saw Andrew's boat tied up at the dock, he made his way back to Benny's.

Now, waiting for Benny to bring out his supper, Guy mulled over something that caught his attention earlier in the day. Passing through a small clearing, some two hundred yards from Tubman's house, he happened upon a pile of dirt. Clearly, it was not put there by nature. Someone had heaped the dirt for God only knows what reason.

Guy had settled on his haunches for a closer look. He studied the mound for several minutes, unable to account for the several holes punched into the dirt. Eventually, he stood and walked away shaking his head.

Benny placed Guy's supper on the table. "How's the old man?" he asked.

"Some times he seems stronger; then he fades. But at least there is hope."

Benny smiled.

"And," Guy said, "You were right. It is better that I figured out for myself what I should do."

50

Fox Creek
Dorchester County, Maryland
April 17, 1869

Sheriff Tolley led the way through a woods thick with budding trees. Haynie, rigid in a borrowed saddle, eyed the trees on the left side of the trail as his mare plodded along behind Tolley's mount. Next in line, Gerhard Stein studied the area on the right hand side. A deputy, named Cecil, sat uneasy on the trailing horse.

Before leaving Cambridge, Haynie left orders with the watch officer on the *Emma Dunn*.

"When Peace Officer Jacoby returns, tell him to get under way and make for Fox Creek. I want you anchored just off the point across from the Blanchard compound. You are to chase down any boat that comes busting out of there and hold the crew. If I wave you over, send the dinghy to pick us up."

"Aye, sir."

Tolley stopped abruptly and leaned back in his saddle, motioning Haynie closer. In a low voice he said, "We're getting real close. The hounds should come busting out here anytime. When they do, we need to go charging in."

Haynie nodded and passed the message to Gerhard and they moved forward.

Moments later, Tolley said, "Those dogs should be out here yappin' at us by now. Wonder what that means."

Within five minutes, Tolley halted, swung down from the saddle and gestured to his right.

Haynie dismounted then unholstered his Navy Colt revolver and held it at his side. Leading his horse by the reins, he moved forward, keeping pace with Tolley.

Just as they emerged from the treeline Deputy Cecil's horse whinnied. Inside the house, the dogs erupted with snarls and deep baying.

"Gerhard," Haynie ordered. "You and Deputy Cecil stay back here."

"*Ja.*"

Haynie rushed after Tolley and, rounding the corner, found the sheriff rigid at the end of a double-barreled shotgun held by Edith Blanchard.

"I'm glad it's you, Sheriff," she said and lowered her weapon. "We're pretty jumpy around here."

She looked over Tolley's shoulder. "That the Oyster Navy man— McKenna—with ya?"

Haynie stepped forward. "Haynie McKenna, ma'am. Sorry if we upset you, but we're looking for Marrok and Renard."

The look on the woman's face told Haynie what he needed to know. She had not known of Renard's escape.

Edith gasped. "Oh, Lordy!" she said, and looked at Tolley. "Whatever possessed you to let him loose?"

"He broke jail during the night," Haynie said. "We figure him and Marrok to be running together."

Haynie holstered his weapon and stepped to the corner of the house.

"Gerhard," he said, "we're going to talk to Missus Blanchard. You and Deputy Cecil keep a sharp eye on the woods."

"*Ja.*"

When he turned back, Tolley was saying, "—we figured to meet up with your dogs comin' in."

"I keep 'em in to warn me—and so Marrok can't get at 'em."

"Get at 'em?"

"If he comes inside the house, and gets mean, they'll go after him—and he knows it. Runnin' loose they'll go right up to him, and he'll kill 'em so's they can't be of no use to me."

Haynie removed his black slouch hat and said, "We want you to know that we're not hunting Guy. The sheriff knows he was meeting with me and warned us that Marrok was planning to storm the *Emma Dunn*."

Edith nodded.

"It's best if Guy would stay aboard one of our boats, until we find those two. Do you know where he's holed up?"

Edith was trembling. "Guy's got no chance against the two of them. Marrok's got a taste for killin', and Renard's itching to prove he's the same."

She looked up to the sky. "Oh Lord, what have I done to be punished so?"

"Can you tell us where to look for them?"

Edith rested the shotgun on one hip. "Marrok'll be aboard his own boat and only come ashore when he must."

She thought some more. "You know about the *Hangman*?"

Haynie looked to Tolley who nodded. Tolley said, "Remember me telling you about Cromarte livin' on a boat. That was the name, *Hangman*."

Edith spoke out. "I heard Marrok and the boys talking about it one night at the table. Marrok roared when he told 'em the name that judge give it—*Hangman* he said. He tried to get Cromarte to use the French—*executeur*—but the old judge wouldn't hear of it. He said no one around here would know what it meant. I expect Marrok would meet with him on that boat. For damn sure he ain't gonna go into the court house." Edith snorted. "Unless you all drag him in."

Edith gave each man a hard look and shook the shotgun at them. "I'm tellin' both of you to remember Marrok's got Louie with him. You may be lawmen but if any harm comes to that little boy, you'll have me to deal with."

Haynie nodded. "You women going to be all right—out here all alone?"

Edith held the shotgun at arms length. "Long as I get the first shot," she said. "No tellin' what Nellie'll do when she learns Renard is loose. I reckon she's better off here, with me to look out for her."

Edith shrugged. "But she might up and run off."

"If Guy comes around," Haynie said, "you tell him to get himself up to Benny Crème's and wait there 'til we come for him. Then get word to the sheriff in town."

"Anything else?"

Haynie looked beyond her to the *Ville de Paris,* tied up in front of the house.

"Any arms, besides the cannon, on that boat?"

"Can't say. Never set foot onboard. 'No women allowed.'"

"Guy told us Marrok has a punt gun. I don't see it."

"It was gone when he took the *Saint-Espirit*. Must be towing it behind."

Haynie said, "We'll need to take any guns aboard the *Ville de Paris*.

She shook the shotgun again. "This is all I need. You take the rest, so him and Renard don't get 'em."

"An Oyster Navy boat is anchored in Fox Creek. I'm going to have a crew come in here in a dinghy and take that cannon, and any other arms."

Edith nodded. "As long as yer talkin' about arms and such, you should know that, after Marrok was here the other night, I found his crossbow was gone from its place on the wall."

She shuddered. "Nasty thing, that."

Sheriff Tolley and Deputy Cecil disappeared into the woods, leading the extra horses as Haynie and Gerhard Stein boarded the *Ville de Paris*.

On the main deck, Haynie stopped. "Gerhard," he said, "Stand watch here while I have a look around."

He touched his cheekbone with one finger; his other arm swept the ship from bow to stern. "Watch everywhere—the woods and the water."

Gerhard nodded.

"When the others get here, halloo them aboard."

"*Ja.*"

Haynie headed for the main cabin. His officers could handle the search for arms; he was interested in what he could learn about Marrok Blanchard.

In the cabin, he eyed a large camphorwood sea chest sitting at the foot of the bunk bed. The dovetail joints and thin brass straps were delicately crafted, the Beckett handles finely twisted.

Had Marrok made the chest? *More likely, he stole it from the poor beggar who did the work.*

The chest was locked and, unable to find a key, Haynie pried open the top.

A shame, but it can't be helped.

The drawer, containing an assortment of button, needles, pins and thread, was of little use.

He dug through clothing, shirts and pants wadded together, and an oilcloth slicker. Beneath them he found a Spencer carbine and a Star Army percussion revolver wrapped in a gray wool blanket. These he laid on the bunk.

At the bottom of the chest lay a black, leather bound ledger book.

Peace Officer Devil Furniss appeared in the cabin. "We're here, sir."

Haynie looked up. "Good. We're takin' that cannon at the bow and any other arms you can find on this boat. Scrub her down good, fore and aft."

He nodded toward the bunk. "You can start with those. And send Officer Jacoby in here."

Furniss looked at his captain.

"What is it, Devil? Where's Jacoby?"

"That's just it, Captain. We ain't seen him. We waited a good while, but when he didn't come back to the ship, I figured we'd better get under way. You know, in case you needed us."

Haynie struggled to keep the alarm from his voice.

"You did the right thing, Officer," he said and managed a smile. "Let's get this done and get back up there. We can't leave Mister Jacoby waiting."

51

Popes Creek Maryland
April 17, 1869

Horace Mooney stood at the road's edge and watched as Southey Hollins struggled up the hill. A few steps to Mooney's left a sheer bluff fell away to the Potomac River. Overhead puffy high clouds scudded across the sky.

"You made good time getting here," Mooney laughed, "until you got to the bottom of this hill."

Hollins stopped and gasped for air.

"That's the ticket, Southey. Act like you're winded in case they're watching from the house. We need a few minutes to talk before we go on in."

Hollins bent over with hands on both knees. "I'm not acting," he wheezed. "Next time, if there is one, you send a buggy to meet me at the dock."

"Of course. Sorry, but Simon's off somewhere with it. Come and enjoy the view of the Old Dominion state just there, while you catch your breath."

Hollins stepped around a grove of fir trees and sucked air in.

"I've seen Virginia and the river before. Now what's this all about?"

"I have a role for you in our stage play."

"A role?"

"You will have a featured part as Simon's good Christian friend; an official from the Freedmen's Bureau.

Hollins straightened. "I'm not an actor. I can't fool folks into believing I'm a government official?"

"There's no one else I can trust."

"Do you expect me to play this part in Washington City?"

Mooney shook his head and pointed at the ground. "Right here in Popes Creek."

"I despise being in Maryland. You know that."

Mooney dismissed the objection with a wave of the hand. "It's a one time appearance. A brief walk-on to convince any potential investors that the Freedmen's Bureau has thousands of acres of land, available for a small initial investment."

Hollins studied the frothy rapids far below. "Why can't you do it?"

"The reasons are several my friend. Here in Popes Creek, I am closely associated with our previous military maneuvers, as Colonel Mooney, while you are unknown. I am not asking you to appear in Annapolis or Baltimore. Surely there's nothing here to worry you."

"What about that village idiot, Hopkins? He's seen me."

"You worry too much. He is a rube and, if you recall, I did not mention your position. He'd believe you were the president, if I said so."

Hollins clasped his hands behind his back and studied the ground as he worked a small hole with the toe of a boot. "Berrien must know another out of work actor, someone who would be better in the role."

"Simon is not one to make lasting friendships. Besides, if two actors get together they might decide to take over our production and carry on without us."

Mooney laid a hand on Hollins's shoulder. "I need you, Southey. Some of the women are reluctant to invest and are in need of additional assurance. Don't let me down. As ye reap, so ye must sew."

"What the hell does that mean?"

"It means if you want to drink you must carry your share of the water."

Hollins stared. "Where will you be while I'm risking my neck over here?"

Mooney removed his hand. "I am dismayed to have to prove myself to you; after all we've been through. It was always our plan that Maryland would be our first stop, a mere dress rehearsal if you will. I have scheduled visits to Pennsylvania and New Jersey, to identify lucrative arenas for our little troupe. From there, it is on to New York and, maybe, Boston.

"In any case you will only be required for a brief appearance here. As I said, a mere rehearsal. By the time we leave Maryland, you'll believe you are a government official."

"You say nobody knows me here; but those women are from Annapolis. One of them might recognize me."

"Do not fail me, Southey. You could quickly become dispensable."

Hoppy was furious. "That Hollins fellow called me the village idiot, and the spy say's I'm a rube. I don't know what it means, but it ain't nice. It was all I could do to keep from bustin' outta those trees and showin' them what fer.

He looked at Landon. "You be sure ta tell McKenna how I was standin' right next to them two. Heard every word of it and they had nary a idea that I was around. If I'd a said boo, they'd a jumped outta their skin and right into the river."

Landon, uncomfortable at Hoppy's outburst, watched as Nanny Hopkins labored to settle herself into a chair across the supper table. She ignored her husband's antics.

He's likely been bragging to her the whole time.

Nanny bowed her head, and said a short, private grace. When she finished she looked at her husband.

"I said some words for you. If you ain't careful, you'll be the one in that river. They find you spyin' in them trees, one of 'em'll reach in and grab you by that scrawny neck and throw you off that bluff like a twig."

"They ain't gonna see me," Hoppy said and wagged his knife toward her. "And I ain't no spy."

"I don't know what else you'd call it—hidin' amongst the trees and listenin' to folks' private talk."

"What of it? They're up to no good. Have been since the first day."

Hoppy jabbed a finger at himself. "'Sides, I'm a working for the Oyster Navy of the state of Maryland."

"Well, it ain't right to be pokin' yer nose into other folks' business."

Hoppy turned to Landon. "Be sure and tell 'em how that fellow, Holland, don't want to be in Maryland. He's ascared of something over here."

"I won't forget."

Early the next morning, Landon rode to Port Tobacco and wired his father with the details of Hoppy's report. Within an hour, he received a reply.

Landon.

Excellent report. I'll see that Mister Hopkins receives an ample reward for his good work.

Inform me immediately should Hollins return to Popes Creek. Exercise caution.

Your Father.

52

Crab Point
April 17, 1869

Marrok held his glass on a solitary tonger working just off Crab Point.

"Well looky here," he said. "I believe they're back poaching our rock, in our boat."

Renard stood at the helm of the *Saint-Esprit*. "I can't make them out, Papa," he said.

Marrok pointed toward the shoreline just south of Crab Point. "That's your heading. I'll know quick enough if it's them."

A brisk breeze pushed them along and very soon, Marrok, his voice aquiver with anger, called, "It's him damn his black hide. The young one—working alone. I told Cromarte they was liars, that they'd be back."

"Are we going to get our boat back, Papa?"

Marrok lowered his glass and shook his head. "Don't want the damn thing. It's cursed. Your traitor brother saw to that. 'Sides it's too small for the two of us. We'll find us a better one."

"We just gonna leave him be?"

"Never! We have to show ever body the price you pay for insulting a Blanchard. *Mon fils*, get ready, you're going to fight your first naval battle."

Marrok returned the glass to his eye. "He's working the other side of the boat, with his back to us. Soon as we get in range, I'll take the helm you get yourself into the punt. Work quietly while you get that thing pointed at him, it's already chock full of death. When I give the command, you fire it just like I showed you."

"*Oui,* Papa! *Oui*! I will not fail you."

Silently, the *Saint-Esprit* closed on Andrew as he intently worked the oyster tongs. When Marrok judged them to be in range, he brought the sloop about until the trailing punt was in line with the target.

As Renard positioned the huge gun, he thought of Benoit and smiled.

I doubt you went to heaven, but, if you did, I hope you can see that it's me who is about to win the Blanchard's first naval battle. The first one to kill a tonger.

Renard, satisfied that the punt was aimed at the log canoe, signaled that he was ready.

At the top of his voice, Marrok shouted, "*Marins* of the Blanchard fleet, fire your *canons*!"

Andrew turned an instant before the punt roared propelling a black cloud of nails and shot directly at him. Instinctively he threw himself over the port side as the charge shredded the starboard side splintering the mast.

Renard shaded his eyes and looked to the *Saint-Esprit's* helm. "Did I make you proud Papa?"

Marrok studied the carnage through his glass. "*Oui, mon-fils!* Come up and see for yourself. The enemy ship is sinking; all hands appear to be lost."

Renard clamored aboard the *Saint-Esprit* and eagerly focused the glass. He scanned the water around the canoe as it disappeared beneath the surface. "Did I kill him? I don't see him anywhere."

He lowered the glass and glanced at his father. "It would have been my first tonger."

Marrok laughed. "Did you expect a trophy? Perhaps to take his ears. Do not fret. No man can survive a direct blast from a punt gun and we have no time to search for the carcass. Set a course for Taylors Island, your brother and that old darkie will be dead by sunrise tomorrow."

53

Taylors Island
Dorchester County, Maryland
April 17, 1869

While Tubman ate some soup, a restless Guy Blanchard decided to explore the surrounding woods.

Tubman paused and watched the white boy grab his musket and head for the door.

"I won't be long," Guy said, closing the door behind him.

He held the gun in front of him with both hands at the ready. About fifty yards into the trees he turned to his right and began a wide circle of the house.

Mama must be near mad with worry—unless, oh God! Unless he's already killed her. I gotta sneak back there to make sure she's okay. Ain't that awful—I got to sneak into my own house.

The woods were dense with emerging foliage. Guy moved cautiously crouching every few feet to scan the area below the tree limbs for signs of movement. It was eerily quiet. No singing birds or chirping insects.

Wonder why old Tubman don't have a dog or two. Maybe I'll bring one of our hounds with me when I do get home.

Guy had covered about three-quarters of the circle when he recalled the odd pile of dirt he had come across.

Let's see, it was over there. Reckon I'll have me another look. See if I can make something of it.

About 150 feet deeper into the woods, he squatted down to scan the area ahead when a six-point buck emerged from a nearby thicket. Upwind from Guy, the deer stiffened and eyed his surroundings.

I know he can't smell me. Wonder if I dare to take a shot? Papa is most likely on the bay. That would be some good eating for Tubman and his missus. I could cut some steaks for Benny Crème. Pay him back for all his kindness. Lord knows where I'd be without him.

Slowly Guy brought the musket to his shoulder, and sighted down the barrel. Suddenly, the deer jerked forward, cried out, stumbled and collapsed heavily to the ground.

Startled, Guy lowered his musket.

The deer quivered, and lay still; the bolt from a crossbow protruding from its chest.

That thing. It looks like one of Papa's—

Someone came crashing through the thicket behind the deer.

"It is this way, Renard."

Guy clamped a hand over his mouth. *Renard? Papa? Oh, God!*

Unwilling to turn his back on them, Guy crawled backwards until he reached the nearest cover, a winterberry bush. Peering around the bush, he saw his father and brother kneeling beside the deer. Once they were intent on dressing out their kill, he crept away. When his movement was screened from their view, he stood and dashed toward the house.

Guy burst through the door and rushed to Tubman's chair.

Shaking with fright he hissed, "They're here! We must get out of here! Now!"

Tubman stirred. "Who's here?"

"Papa and Renard! I don't know how my brother got out of jail, but they're together."

Tubman closed his eyes. "Andrew will be home by and by, he'll see to 'em."

"There's no time!"

Guy was determined that Tubman would survive the Blanchard family.

"They've been here before so they gotta know where the house is. They could come any minute and I can't protect you from two of 'em."

He turned and called through the closed door to the next room. "Missus you must come out and help me with him."

The door cracked open and Tubman's wife hesitated in the shadows.

Guy struggled to get Tubman out of the chair. "We need to get out of here. Now! I'll get you both hidden near Slaughter Creek while I bring down my boat. We'll get you folks aboard and head up to Benny Crème's. It'll be safe there."

"What about Andrew?" Tubman asked. "He won't know where we gone."

"I'll see about Andrew. If he was to come home and found I didn't do all I could for you, he'd have my hide."

Tubman chuckled and threw aside his blanket. "'Spect he would."

54

Dorchester County, Maryland
April 17, 1869

Haynie McKenna gazed through the porthole of his cabin as the *Emma Dunn* plowed through choppy water.

Where the hell is Jacoby? What would he do if he showed up and the Emma Dunn *was gone? Go to the sheriff's office, or go to Benny Crème's? Benny's'll be our first stop. If he's not there, I'll send a man over land to the sheriff while we try to figure out where to look.*

The heavily timbered shoreline of Taylors Island loomed off the starboard rail. Haynie dug his hand into a jacket pocket and absently fingered a piece of paper. It was the letter from his mother. "Please read it," Lila had pleaded when she handed it to him.

Turning the envelope over, he saw that it was addressed to Lila McKenna. It occurred to him that seeing the writing in his mother's hand evoked no feelings.

I can't bother with this now.

He jammed the letter deep into his pocket and turned back to the porthole.

The *Emma Dunn* anchored in the Little Choptank River at the mouth of Slaughter Creek. The crew assembled amidships waiting impatiently to hear from their captain.

Haynie strode across the deck stopping in front of them.

"I'm taking Gerhard and Officer Bramble ashore with me. Officer Furniss will serve as the mate until Mister Jacoby returns. He's likely on the island here, or at the sheriff's office in Cambridge. But, on the chance that we have to start a search, be ready: There are only a few hours to sundown."

Two black men sat at the counter, dipping chunks of fresh warm bread into bowls of muskrat stew. They looked up at the sight of three armed white men coming through the door, but quickly lost interest when Benny shook hands with the men.

"Benny, we need to talk," Haynie said.

"What's wrong?"

"We're trying to catch up with Nathan. The *Emma Dunn* had to leave before he returned to the ship. I want him to know we're here."

A troubled look crossed Benny's face. "He came in, early, lookin' for that Guy Blanchard. I told him that the boy'd left out for Tubman's place. He's been going there ever' day, dead set on saving the old man."

Haynie nodded.

"Nathan asked me how to find the house. I told him and he left out the door. I figured they would be back by now."

"How far is Tubman's?"

"About half of an hour on foot. There's some white folk's houses along Slaughter Creek, but his place is straight through the woods."

After receiving directions to Tubman's house, Haynie turned to Zach Bramble.

"Peace Officer Bramble, get back to the ship and bring the crew down here. Tell Officer Furniss to break out the arms for each man and leave one man aboard as a watch. I want Furniss here. If we're not back when you arrive, get directions from Benny and head for Tubman's."

Bramble stood. "Aye, sir. Who should I send to see the sheriff?"

Benny looked up. "Don't waste yer time with that. Nathan wouldn't leave Taylors without he saw me. No sir, he's still on the island."

Bramble waited for a sign. Haynie nodded and the officer started for the door.

Haynie glanced at the men eating at the bar and called out, "Officer Bramble. Don't come chargin' in here, all bristlin' weapons. Leave them outside, under guard."

"Aye, sir," Bramble called over his shoulder.

Haynie picked up the trail and Gerhard followed him into the woods. "I've got to keep my eyes on this trail, *mein Freund*," Haynie said. "You watch for trouble."

"*Ja.*"

The trail between Benny Crème's and the Tubman house had become well trampled.

Likely, from Guy's daily travels. Easy for us to follow. Means it's also easy for Marrok.

Haynie cursed under his breath. *Damn! Guy said Marrok came to Tubman's to look at the boat. He'd have no trouble finding the place—'Spect we're getting close.*

The trailed snaked between two oak trees and Haynie stopped abruptly. "Oh, no!" he cried. "Oh God! No!"

Just ahead, at the edge of the trail, Nathan Jacoby's lifeless form was impaled on the trunk of a gum tree; the bolt from a crossbow embedded in his back between the shoulder blades.

Haynie stared at the sight, his mind racing. With a shudder, he turned to find Gerhard crouched low, scanning the forest around them.

"Help me get him down."

Gerhard completed his sweep of the area before laying his musket at the base of the tree.

They worked the body backward, along the shaft, ignoring the blood draining from the wound as he came free of the shaft. Carefully they lowered Nathan to the ground.

"*Was is?*" Gerhard asked. "Not arrow."

Haynie unsheathed a hunting knife and dug into the tree bark surrounding the buried bolt head.

"It's a kind of arrow used with a crossbow, called a bolt. That son-of-a-bitch, Marrok, has a crossbow. I need to see if this is one of his bolts. It may take a while. Keep watch."

"*Ja.*"

55

Sheriff Tolley sat a tin cup of hot coffee in front of an unseeing Haynie McKenna. Without comment, he laid a sealed envelope addressed to 'Commander McKenna' next to the cup.

"I believe you take your coffee straight from the pot, Captain."

Tolley sat at his desk and waited. Gerhard Stein stood nearby, his back to the wall. Watching—everything.

Eventually Tolley said, "Your mate is being well taken care of by our undertaker, Mister Cross." After a moment, he added, "Is there anything else I can do?"

Haynie turned slowly toward the sheriff, his face empty.

"Is there anything else I can do, Captain?" Tolley repeated.

His voice a whisper, Haynie replied, "Nathan Jacoby was a good man, a damn good man. But most of all, he was my friend. I'm trying to understand if he was killed because I did something wrong. If I had done things different, would he still be alive?"

"It doesn't do any good to think like that," Tolley replied. "We need to concentrate on catchin' Marrok and his boy."

Haynie flared. "I'm responsible for the men on the *Emma Dunn*! I've got to know." He nodded to Gerhard. "Last year he was shot because of me; just luck he wasn't killed."

Haynie grimaced at the memory. "He and I had taken my brother's killer, Rat—that's what he called himself: Rat. We had him roped and laid out on the floor of the general store. The long gun he shot Caleb with, a .72 caliber Prussian musket was just a couple of steps away, leaning against the counter. Gerhard stood over him while I went for the gun. Rat always wore a buffalo hide for a coat and, someway, he worked a hand under the hide to where he hid a Sharp's pepperbox."

Haynie paused and slowly shook his head. "I wanted so bad to get my hands on the gun that killed my brother—I forgot about Rat having the little gun." He looked at Gerhard. "Thank God, the one shot he got off only took Gerhard in the arm."

Gerhard grunted.

Turning back to the sheriff, Haynie added, "Before you say anything—I was wrong on two counts. That pepperbox belonged to the town bailiff. We knew his killer took it and, by then, we knew Rat was the man. Any lawman—even one as green as I was—knows to check a desperado for a knife or gun. But, I was so furious about him killin' my brother I wasn't thinkin' straight.

"I can't be wrong again—too many folks expecting me to be right. When I saw Jacoby with that bolt through his back I thought, 'what have I done'?"

Tolley chose his words carefully. "You will do what you gotta to make your own peace. Nothin' I say can fix that. But me and my deputies won't be sittin' around waitin' for you to figure it out. Jacoby was a state law officer killed in my county. I'm going to be out lookin' for the Blanchards as hard as I can. Are you comin' along—or will you still be sittin' here when I get back?"

Haynie nodded. "You're right," he said. "We won't catch that bastard sittin' here."

Tolley said, ".72 caliber. Don't often run across a gun like that. Doubt that I've ever seen one. I 'spect you got it at home."

"Rat died in my jail cell." He caught Tolley's look and shook his head. "No. He was near dead with rabies when we took him. Once he was gone, I took a hacksaw to the rifle and buried the pieces in the box with him. That gun had killed my brother and some other good folks. I swore it wasn't going to kill anyone else."

Tolley shrugged and said. "What was your man, Jacoby, doing so deep in the woods?"

"Nathan was close to a colored named Benny Crème. You know him?"

Tolley nodded. "Everybody around here knows Benny and his ma. They opened up on Taylors during the war. Still hard feelin's back then—what with a lot of folks in Maryland ownin' slaves. It would be trouble for a white man to show in there. But she set out a real tasty plate, so I'd go around back and tap on the door. Benny would hand me a plate and I'd sit out there and eat it."

Tolley shook his head. "I know it wasn't right, but—."

Haynie broke in. "Benny and Nathan were real close so we knew Guy Blanchard had been hiding out there. Since Renard and Marrok are hunting Guy, I wanted the boy to stay on the *Emma Dunn* until we catch them. Nathan went over there to bring Guy aboard. When Crème told him that Guy was at Tubman's, seeing to the old man, Nathan set off to collect the boy. That bastard shot him in the back with a crossbow. I don't intend to show them any mercy."

Haynie held out his hand and Gerhard handed him the bolt. "I figure this goes with the crossbow Missus Blanchard told us about. I'd like to see if she can say for sure."

Tolley balanced the iron shaft on one palm and fingered the pointed tip with the other.

"Ugly thing. Still, you have to admire the work. A smith who knows his craft forged this."

"It's an assassin's weapon. Quiet. A few Reb snipers used them in the war."

Tolley laid the bolt on his desk. "What's become of Tubman and the Blanchard boy?"

"Before we brought Nathan back, my officers searched around Tubman's place. A blanket thrown off a chair and some stew left in the bottom of a dish make it look like they left in a hurry.

I doubt Marrok would've killed them and then hauled their carcasses off. He'd have left them for us to find." His voice trailed off. "Like he did Nathan."

"So you figure them to be alive."

"Unless Blanchard came across them in the woods. There was a bloody carcass about two hundred yards the other side of the house. A fresh-killed deer."

Tolley said, "I'd sure appreciate it if you and your men can help with the search. It's a big county, and I'm a man short."

"I thought we could split up the work," Haynie said. "We'll go back to Taylors and give it a good scrubbin', if you like, while you head for Fox Creek."

Tolley agreed.

"One thing," Haynie said. "Did you know that Marrok has a punt gun?"

"So that's what happened to it."

"What do you mean?"

"Well," Tolley said, "sometime back a fella stops me on the street and proceeds to tell me about a neighbor of his. 'Said the neighbor was out market hunting with a punt when the Oyster Navy sails up. The navy boat captain said the punt gun was illegal and he was going to claim it for the state. Forced the man to leave a 12-foot punt gun and swim to shore. It was January, he near froze before he got home. I told the fella to have his neighbor come in and see me about it. Never heard anymore until you just mentioned it. Guess he figured a county sheriff would be of no use as it was the state took his gun."

Haynie nodded. "A minute ago you said something about being a man short," he said. "How'd that come about?"

"I told you about Bunky Hill. Remember?"

"The one ahead of Deputy Ochs on your list of fellas in Renard's escape."

"That's him. He's not showed up for work since a day or two after the Blanchard boy broke jail. Heard he's been makin' the rounds of the taverns. Stayin' pretty drunk. Reckon his pap will give up on him now."

"Who's buying his drinks?"

Tolley shrugged. "Don't know. Guess he is. Come to think of it, one of the boys said Bunky's bought drinks for the whole place a time or two. You think it means something?"

"It seems like Bunky is spending pretty free. How would he come to have that kind of money?"

Tolley thought a minute. "Are you thinking he took cash money to let Blanchard loose? "

"Could be someone offered him money to unlock a cell door and look the other way. And he took it."

While the sheriff pondered the prospect that his deputy had been corrupted, Haynie picked up the envelope lying next to the cup of cold coffee.

"What now," he grumbled. Anger flared as he read the message.

Annapolis, Maryland
April 18, 1869

Captain McKenna:

I share in your grief and anger over the tragic killing of Peace Officer Jacoby.

However, a dire situation requires the presence of the *Emma Dunn,* and its crew, at the mouth of the Little Annemessex River.

There you will find several dredge boats at anchor with their crews still aboard. They consist, for the most part, of German immigrants who have been terribly abused. Reports say that the poor devils suffer from a variety of severe injuries sustained during floggings administered by their captains and first mates.

Captain Pack was dispatched however before he arrived the dredge captains and mates fled, abandoning their boats and stranding the beleaguered crews.

The Germans are terrified and ready to fight anyone who approaches them. One man, though seriously injured, jumped overboard in a panic and, refusing aid, was drowned.

Captain Pack is proceeding after the villainous captains, who are said to be headed for the Potomac River. Likely aiming to disappear into the Commonwealth of Virginia.

No one has been able to communicate with the crews; requiring the immediate presence of Gerhard Stein, to act as a translator. A local doctor is standing by to treat the injured once the crews understand that he is there to aid them. After receiving treatment, the German crewmen will be taken aboard the *Emma Dunn* and transported directly to Baltimore, there to be released to the care of the German-American Society.

There can be no delay. Word of this has spread and the society is inflamed over this matter. I am besieged with angry demands.

Please be aware that the *Leila* is not available for duty. The governor and several ranking members of the General Assembly have taken her for a tour of the bay. She will be so occupied for the next several days.

Proceed at once to the Little Annemessex.

Hunter Davidson, Commander

Haynie stared at the paper in his hand.

"Bad news?" Tolley asked.

Haynie folded the telegram, shoved it into his pocket and looked at the sheriff.

"Let's go find Bunky Hill."

They located Bunky Hill in the Town Tavern on Water Street, sitting alone and staring deeply into a mug of beer gone flat. The sound of men approaching penetrated his mood and he swung his head around. Rheumy eyes blinked above a matted beard.

Bunky forced his eyes to focus on the intruders. "Whatcha lookin' at?" he snarled.

Tolley moved to respond, but Haynie cut him short.

"Goddamit, I said whatcha lookin' at?"

A bartender watched from down the bar as he ran a towel over a row of whiskey glasses.

Tolley nodded. "Burt, how long's he been here?"

"Well sir, he was sittin' on that very stool yesterday when I come in, and he was there today when I come back." Burt wrinkled his nose. "Nobody will sit within six stools of him, unless he is buying. Be obliged if you would take him out of here."

Bunky turned away from his tormentors and faced the massive mirror spanning the wall over the bar. Reflected eyes darted between the images of the two men standing behind him.

"Not right! Don't speak civil to a man when he asks a civil question. Not right!"

Bunky, hands shaking raised his glass in a futile effort to get a drink without spilling any.

Haynie held Bunky's mirrored gaze and bent down, his mouth close to the deputy's ear. Speaking softly he said, "The man you let escape from jail the other night has already killed a man."

Bunky felt the law officer's hot breath on his neck, and his eyes filled with fear; his voice quavered with false bravado.

"The hell you talkin' about?"

"Not just any man," Haynie breathed, "a sworn peace officer of the Maryland Oyster Navy. His name was Nathan Jacoby. He came from around here, did you know him?"

Bunky's chin dropped to his chest.

Haynie's voice rose. "Did you know him?" he barked.

In spite of the beer, Bunky's throat was parched; his neck pounded, filling his ears. Unable to speak, he shook his head.

"Officer Jacoby was one of my men. The first one to be killed while on duty with the Oyster Navy."

Bunky raised his eyes to the mirror, trying to take the measure of his troubles. "I didn't have nuthin' to do with that," he said.

Haynie's tone was hard. "It looks to me like you got two choices. You can pull out that gun you're wearin'—right now—and I'll kill you where you sit; or I'll drag you off that stool, haul you out to an oak tree, and hang you before sundown. Now choose one."

With pleading eyes, Bunky looked to Tolley. Tears ran, quickly streaking his grimy face. Grasping his glass in two trembling hands, he tried to raise it to his mouth. The mug wobbled, spilling beer over his chin and soaking the bib of his overalls. He returned the glass to the countertop and wiped a crusty sleeve across his face.

"I swear to the Almighty I didn't know they was going to do anyone that-a-way."

He turned away from the mirror and looked directly at Tolley. "The judge said I would be helpin' an innocent boy get home to his mama," he blubbered.

Bunky rubbed his eyes and wiped at the mucus streaming from his nose. "I swear the judge told me the boy was innocent."

"Judge Cromarte?" Tolley asked.

Bunky, seeing a chance to shift the blame, nodded. "It was him. I was just doin' what the judge told me to."

"How much did he pay you to open the cell door?" Haynie growled.

"What?"

"Goddam you! How much money did the judge pay you?"

Bunky looked from one man to the other then, dropped his eyes. "Two hunnert of dollars."

Tolley snapped. "Was it your idea to start that ruckus to get Ochs to the other end of town?"

"No, Sheriff, I swear it weren't. They said all I had to do was open the cell when Ochs run out of the jail."

"They? Who was with the judge?"

"A mean looking little fella. The judge said he were the boy's pa."

Haynie took the revolver out of Bunky's holster and handed it to Tolley.

"I'll go back with you to lock him up. The *Emma Dunn* has been ordered to Crisfield. We'll be gone two days, maybe three. Peace Officers Furniss and Bramble will stay on Taylors. I want them to find Guy Blanchard and Tubman. I'd appreciate it if you would show that bolt to Missus Blanchard when you go out there. Maybe she can say for sure it was Marrok's."

Sheriff Tolley stood facing the judge's bench, his right hand gripping the arm of his former deputy, Bunker Hill. Word of Hill's arrest had spread across town, and beyond, as if wind-borne. The courtroom was filling with townsfolk anxious to share their version of the facts with their neighbor.

Nob Hill, Bunky's father, ambled to the front row of the courtroom and elbowed himself into a seat. Pulling off a grimy cap, he stared straight ahead ignoring the looks from those around him.

Tolley stationed Deputy Ochs at the railing that served as a barrier between spectators and the court. Ochs surveyed the gallery for any signs of trouble, with specific orders to be carried out if Marrok or Renard Blanchard dared to show himself.

Ochs left his post and approached Tolley. "Cromarte's here," he whispered, indicating the row of men standing at the rear of the gallery.

The prisoner turned his head and Tolley abruptly jerked him back. "Face the bench." To Ochs he said, "Keep an eye on Cromarte and let me know if he talks to anyone."

Ochs nodded and returned to his post.

Judge Robinson entered the room and strode to the bench. Deputy Ochs ordered the spectators to stand, glaring at those slow to respond.

"Be seated," the judge said, rapping his gavel for quiet.

Tolley summarized the facts of the case against Bunky. He spoke rapidly, his voice muted, with only an occasional word reaching the spectators.

Nob Hill lumbered to his feet and called out, "You call this a trial? I can't hear nothin' that you all are sayin' about my boy!"

Deputy Ochs moved quickly, inserting himself between Nob Hill and the court.

The judge banged his gavel twice before saying, "Be seated, sir, or you'll be joining the defendant in a jail cell. This is not a trial." He pointed his gavel at Bunky. "It's a hearing so I can decide if Mister Hill here should stay in jail until his trial, or can have bail set. Now sit down."

The elder Hill grumbled and sat down.

The judge grunted as Tolley described Judge Cromarte's role in the jailbreak.

Leaning forward, Robinson shielded his mouth with one hand. "Does Cromarte know Hill here has told on him?"

"No sir."

The judge scanned the courtroom. "I wondered why he was back there. He couldn't hear anything if he was standing next to you."

"Maybe not, but he knows what's going on."

The judge looked at Bunky. "Did you hear what the sheriff said about you?"

Bunky nodded.

"Speak up."

"Yes, Yer Honor."

"Is that what you told him?"

Bunky raised his eyes. "It's hard for me to recollect it all. I had been drinkin' steady for a couple—"

"Don't get me mad. I'm the one's going to decide how long you stay in jail. So, I'll ask you once more: is that what you told the sheriff?"

"Yes, Yer Honor."

Judge Robinson glared down at Bunky. "When you opened that cell door, you let loose a passel of woe onto this town. A state lawman is already dead by the Blanchards' hand. Others are likely to follow."

Bunky's body shook and he began to cry. With his free hand, he covered his face. "I'm sorry!" he bawled. "I'm terrible sorry!"

The judge gazed over the courtroom. In a loud voice he said, "I find there is sufficient evidence to hold Mister Hill on the charges brought. No bail. Court is adjourned."

Tolley turned and glimpsed Cromarte disappearing through a side door.

56

Taylors Island
Dorchester County, Maryland
April 18, 1869

"All quiet," Devil Furniss called as he and Guy Blanchard came through the front door of Benny Crème's tavern. The regular customers no longer paid any attention to the armed white men making their way toward the back wall.

There, Peace Officer Zach Bramble sat in a wooden chair tilted back on two legs, a musket across his lap.

To Bramble's left, two tables had been shoved together, creating a make shift bed for Tubman. The old man napped under a thin blanket, his wife patting his hand as she dozed in a chair.

Guy reached the table and stood waiting for the old man to stir.

Tubman's wife squeezed her husband's hand, and he opened his eyes.

Guy leaned over, and speaking softly, said, "We didn't see nothing outside. The Oyster Navy man says Captain McKenna and his crew will be here soon as they can."

Guy nodded in the direction of the two state lawmen. "When he gets here we'll get you aboard their boat. You'll be more comfortable there. Meantime we'll keep watch. I swear nothing is gonna happen to you tonight."

Tubman moved his head slowly from side to side.

Guy leaned over the old man. "What is it?" he asked.

Tubman's eyes fluttered open. "Not...going..."

Guy straightened and looked to Benny Crème seated behind the old desk.

"He says he's not going," Guy said. "Why won't he go?"

Crème shrugged. "Ask him."

"You gotta go," Guy said. "It's not safe with Papa and Renard huntin' us."

Tubman moaned and his wife held a cup of water to his lips.

She said, "It took 'most everything he had to get this far. Maybe after he rests some."

"Not...going...without...Andrew," Tubman gasped, and closed his eyes.

Benny Crème stood and motioned the others to the middle of the room, away from Tubman.

Wherever he went, Benny gripped the .36 caliber revolver in his right hand. "He means it," said Benny. "He won't move 'til he sees his boy. And don't think you can lie to him, just because he's in a bad way. If he can't see the lie in yer face, he'll hear it in your words."

Devil Furniss asked, "You got any idea about what happened to Andrew?"

Benny shook his head and looked at Guy.

"I always checked to make certain Andrew was out in the boat, before I'd go in the house. I'd ask Tubman, where was Andrew? Every day the same answer, 'he's out oysterin'. Up 'til the last day of oyster season, then he'd say, 'My boy's out fishin' today.'"

Guy lowered his voice. "Knowin' how vexed Andrew was about missing the best months fer oysters, I believe he's been poachin'; and the old man knows it."

"Still," Benny said, "that doesn't answer for Andrew not comin' home to see to his father."

The four men were quiet for a couple of minutes then Devil said, "If he's poachin' oysters, maybe he got took in by one of our boats."

"Or by a bounty hunter—like Papa."

"He could of been run over by a dredge boat poachin' in the same water," offered Zach Bramble.

"It's gonna be dark in a couple of hours," Benny said. "So what you 'spect to do about Andrew?"

Devil Furniss spoke. "What would Andrew do if he was to get home and find them gone?"

"Not much else he could do, but to come up here a lookin' for 'em."

"That's what I'm thinking. If Andrew can't make it here on his own, it won't do to split our forces overnight to go out huntin' him.

When Captain McKenna and the boys get here we'll figure out what to do."

Devil glanced toward Tubman and murmured, "'Sides, who's gonna stop us if we decide to pick him up and cart him aboard the *Emma Dunn?*"

Benny snorted. "Old Tubman himself," he said.

"How's he gonna do that?"

"He'll give up and you'll be carrying a dead man."

The tavern had been quiet for hours. Benny slouched uneasily in his chair behind the big desk. The sounds of rhythmic breathing reached him through the gloom, causing him to wonder if anyone else was awake. A candle and match lay atop the desk, next to the heavy revolver. Each of these would be essential if Tubman needed to be carried out back to the privy.

Tubman's wife pillowed her head on rough hands at the edge of his table. Guy had taken the chair at the foot of Tubman's bed, his musket propped against the wall.

Peace Officers Furniss and Bramble occupied chairs on either side of the front door, their forms faintly visible in the pale light of a new moon leaking through the front windows. Benny hoped the lawmen were not sound sleepers.

A heavy thud stirred Benny, and he grabbed up the revolver. Something had hit the outside rear wall, just above Tubman's bed. Shortly, another thud.

"What the hell was that?" Guy rasped.

"Don't know," Benny hissed. "But somethin' ain't right."

"You all right back there?" Furniss called.

"So far," Guy said.

Bramble was already poised at one of the windows.

"See anything?" Benny called.

"Something's moving among the trees. Can't make it out. Could be a deer."

Furniss was at the door, his musket raised. "We'll check around back," he said. "You fellas watch the door. We'll give a holler before comin' through." Then he and Bramble were gone.

Tubman cried out. "Andrew?"

Guy left his chair and stood next to the old man. "It's all right. Go on back to sleep."

Tubman's wife lifted her head and resumed patting her husband's arm.

A faint patch of moonlight lay across the floor where the front door stood open.

Again, the rear wall was struck. The sound lower this time, about chest high on a man standing erect.

Guy, heart pounding, dove to the floor, dragging his musket as he crawled under the nearest table. From there, he made out Benny's silhouette sitting ramrod straight behind his desk.

Guy's panic ebbed and reason returned. *No one screamed, so it's likely nobody outside was hurt. What made that racket? Hope those lawmen don't wander off very far.*

Guy focused on the moonlit doorway. Suddenly, a shadowy form blurred the light. Guy's heart clogged his throat, choking off a cry.

The form vanished, restoring the patch of light, and Guy glimpsed a dark shape just inside the door.

Did I really see something? Maybe it was one of the lawmen and he forgot to call out.

The dim outline of a head bobbed up and down, briefly framed in the watery light filtering into the room. The shape appeared closer.

The hammering in Guy's ears became a roar; he tipped a table over with a crash and crawled behind it.

It's moving'! One of the lawman wouldn't do that. Is it Papa? No—more like him to send Renard.

Through the pounding in his head, Guy heard the faint scrape of leather on the wooden floor.

"I'm comin' for ya—you traitor."

Oh God! It is Renard!

"Papa wants you dead, and that table ain't gonna save ya. Don't expect no rescue from them state fellas; Papa's got them chasing their tail. Stand up and face me like a man; let's get you done."

Guy wiped sweaty palms across his shirtfront and clutched his musket as the voice came closer.

"While I'm here I'm gonna kill any niggers you got with ya. Think about that while yer dyin'."

Guy looked up to see the muzzle of Renard's double barreled shotgun inches above his face; then two rapid fire explosions filled the room. Renard pitched forward sprawling heavily over the up turned table. One lifeless arm falling across Guy's shoulder.

"Guess you didn't see me over here," said Benny Crème.

Guy scrambled to his feet and stumbled back against the wall. "My brother was going to kill me!" he cried.

Marrok crouched behind a sourwood tree, eyes probing the dark as he listened for movement. Minutes ago, he heard two rapid shots followed immediately by the sound of two men moving away through the brush. They had been closer than he realized, and he cursed himself for his own carelessness. Now he was poised to make certain they were not sneaking back to take him by surprise.

I'll sit tight for another few minutes before heading back to the boat. Sounds like Renard got his nigger-lovin' brother, and the nigger. Didn't hear no one shootin' back. I told him it would be easier than sinkin' that boat with the punt gun.

It's a real shame, too. I had figured Guy for the smartest of the lot, and maybe he was, but he quit his family to take up with those coloreds. Where the other two was hard inside, he was soft; but I figured, being a Blanchard, he would turn out all right. Reckon I should've known something bad would come from that woman. He spent too much time with her.

Something moved to his left, and Marrok took aim with his crossbow. A doe and her fawn appeared, and then crashed away through the underbrush.

Yer lucky I don't have time to fool with ya, he thought and lowered his weapon.

When he felt it was safe, Marrok picked his way through the trees, moving south toward Saint Johns Creek where the *Saint-Esprit* lay at anchor.

Soon as Renard gets back, we'll head over to Dunnocks. Be holed up in our cove before daylight.

Aboard the *Saint-Esprit*, Marrok stood at the helm, searching the creek banks for Renard, and any pursuers. The crowns of mature pumpkin ash and swamp black gum trees canopied the creek. As Marrok watched, tree trunks took form in the gray light, their shadows dissolving with the approaching dawn.

Marrok glanced at his grandson sleeping atop a burlap bag stuffed with dry grass and leaves that they had collected in the woods.

It takes a heap of that paregoric to keep him quiet for so long. Soon as we run that Oyster Navy out of these waters, me and Renard can give him proper teachin'. He can't learn to be a Blanchard man sleepin' all the time.

Damn Renard! Where is that boy? Can't wait much longer. This here creek is too narrow to get around a boat comin' upstream. I'd be trapped for sure.

Birds warbled nearby. Marrok made out the sad call of the mourning dove and, the strident, nasal call of a blue jay. Upstream, a doe made an appearance at the creek's edge, taking her first drink of the day.

That's real good. Them jays'll raise some hell if them damn bastards try and sneak up on me. That's it! Renard ain't comin' here. He's a leadin' them straight away from me.

Marrok busied himself with hauling in the anchor and getting under way.

He's a good boy. Thinkin' like that to protect his commander. Soon as he finishes with them two lawmen, he'll make his way down to Dunnocks.

57

The crew of the *Emma Dunn* stood silently at the starboard rail, awed by the eerie spectacle ahead. A tangle of sloops, pungys and bugeyes bobbed at anchor. Many showed peeling paint and crusted hulls, their decks in disarray. Sails drooped from mast to deck, amid tangled lines. The dredge boats seemed a fleet of derelict ships. Frightened and haggard men huddled together staring warily from every deck.

Skillets stood with Haynie. "Jesus H. Christ," he muttered. "They look worse'n the Johnny Rebs I saw at the Yankee prison over to Point Lookout."

Haynie nodded. "Poor devils are half starved."

After The *Emma Dunn* tied off at the town pier, Doc Ward and a group of townsfolk led by Councilman George Noch greeted Haynie. Noch, resplendent in a bowler hat and vested suit, was the town official who had asked Haynie to replace the murdered town bailiff, Horsey Towne.

"Haynie McKenna, thank God it's you," Doc Ward said as they shook hands.

"Amen to that," said Noch. "It's good to see you, McKenna. Sorry it's under such circumstances."

Haynie shook Noch's hand and nodded toward the drudge fleet.

"What the hell happened out there? I got a brief cable. It didn't say much."

Noch, usually eager to be the center of attention, deferred to Doc Ward.

"Damndest thing," Ward said. "Three mornings ago the town woke up to find a fleet of drudgers set up right out there in the Little A. Local folks, 'specially the tongers, got right put out about it. 'Course it was worth a tonger's life to try to leave the docks, but a couple of 'em stood here shakin their fists and cussin' a streak. The drudgers paid 'em no mind. By evening a crowd gathered to help with the fist shakin' and the cussin' when a real ruckus broke out on that sloop over there."

Haynie followed where Doc pointed, and nodded.

"I didn't see it myself, but two fellas was goin' at it. One had what looked to be a belaying pin; he began yelling in American and took to whaling on the other fella who jabbered back in German. The one with the belayin' pin—likely the captain, who else would try it? He kept hitting away at the other one. A third fella jumped into the fracas, got whacked for his trouble, and fell back. The captain gives the German fella a final smack and shoves him overboard. Seems he was unconscious when he hit the water and he drowned. By and by, his corpse floated over here to the dock. That's when somebody headed for the Western Union and cabled Annapolis.

"To pass the time waiting for you boys, some of our folks gathered chunks of wood and piles of rocks on the wharf. Which they took to heaving at the nearest drudgers, all the time yellin' that you boys had been sent for. It wasn't long and all the drudge captains piled into one boat and, by the time your Captain Pack sailed in, they had skedaddled leaving what you see out there."

Noch added, "We fished the one out of the river but nobody could get near those fellas on the boats. Somehow Pack figured the captains, and their mates, was headed for the Potomac. He got some warrants signed and lit out after 'em."

"Where's your bailiff?" Haynie asked.

"He's laid up with the ague," Doc replied. "I just came from there."

Noch nodded at Gerhard. "Glad you brought him, maybe he can get the German fellas to listen to reason."

Again, he shook Haynie's hand. "I'll leave this in your capable hands. Don't forget what I said when you left here. You did a lot for this town, and, if I can ever do anything for you, just ask."

Haynie, Gerhard and Doc Ward stood in the bow of a dinghy for the short ride to the first boat at anchor; a sloop named *Nelly B.*

On her deck, three crewmen fiercely guarded the rail, ready to fight anyone attempting to board. All were young, no more than boys, each with dirty blonde hair and a scraggly beard. Their eyes glistened with fear and hate.

Each was armed, after a fashion. The one in the middle, the obvious leader, gripped a culling hammer in his right hand. A well-placed blow from its forged iron spike could penetrate a man's skull or rip the hide from his face. The boy to his left hefted a six-foot length of jagged wooden pole, broken off from one of the ship's spars. The other lad loosely held a length of rope with a lump of iron tied at one end. As the dinghy edged to the sloop's rail, he began to swing the rope over his head in warning.

"*Sprechen Sie Englisch?*" Gerhard asked.

The German crewmen, clearly surprised, glanced at one another. "*Nein,*" the leader responded.

"*Haben Sie kiene Angst. Wir sind Freunde.*"

Gerhard turned to Doc Ward. "I tell those not to be afraid. We are friends."

During the months they served together in the Union Army, Haynie had worked to teach Gerhard the English language; in return, Gerhard helped him learn basic German. While Haynie understood what was being said, he was not going to risk a misunderstanding by trying to speak to these distraught boys in their native tongue.

Behind the three, other wretches stood watch over two comrades writhing on the deck. The dinghy carrying Haynie and Gerhard bumped the dredge boat and cries of pain were heard.

Gerhard pointed to Doc Ward, telling the dredge crew to drop their weapons. Only then would the doctor come aboard to help them.

"*Gut! Gut!*" the leader cried and passed the word to the others. After an agitated exchange among the crew, the leader pointed to Haynie. He asked Gerhard if men with guns, were going to take them to another dredge boat and more abuse.

Gerhard, standing in the bow of the dinghy, held several minutes of intense conversation with the drudge crew.

Abruptly, the leader barked, "*Waffen ablegen!*" and his culling hammer clattered to the deck. The others followed his lead and then raised their hands and stepped back from the two men moaning on the deck.

"*Bitte, helfen!*" their leader pleaded.
Haynie nodded. "*Wir helfen,*" he said.

58

Annapolis, Maryland
April 20, 1869

Haynie McKenna fidgeted in his chair as he waited for Commander Hunter Davidson to return. He was struck with the notion that the commander of the Maryland Oyster Navy deserved a more spacious office than this cramped room. The desk and a small worktable spilled over with books and documents. Additional mounds of papers were stacked about the floor.

Davidson was currently immersed in the drafting of a report on the health of the Chesapeake Bay oyster industry. In addition, he was routinely bombarded with nuisance questions from the General Assembly and anyone titillated by the excitement and reckless danger of the Oyster Navy.

Haynie smiled at the thought that this might have been his own office. A year ago, Colonel Silas Wallis put forth Haynie's name during the state's search for a commander of the new oyster force.

Though not eager for the post, a curious Haynie had traveled from Crisfield to Annapolis to meet with three distinguished members of the state governing board.

Sitting here, he reflected on how fortunate he was to have been denied the post. A job for which, he readily admitted, he was ill-suited.

I hope I can hang on as long as he is in charge. I would not last the week with one of those political namby pamby's running things.

Commander Davidson rushed in, carrying a sheaf of papers that he deposited on top of the nearest stack. "Sorry to keep you waiting, Captain."

Davidson closed the door, hung his frock jacket on a wall peg and adjusted his waistcoat.

Once settled behind the desk, he looked across at Haynie.

"Now then, let's hear your take on that dredger mess in Crisfield."

"Yes sir. After Doc Ward patched up the injured, we took thirty-two men off five boats and carried them directly to Fort McHenry. There, they were turned over to representatives of the German American Society, as ordered."

Davidson nodded. "What kind of shape were they in?"

"Two were taken to a hospital; the others were in better shape, but every man had been beaten and starved. Any civilized man would be outraged at their condition. It turns my stomach to think that these poor devils came to America looking for freedom and opportunity. Instead they endured slavery, starvation and torture."

"I understood one of them drowned trying to escape."

"One man was killed by his own captain. Beaten and thrown overboard to drown. This kind of cruelty is apparently commonplace with some dredge captains and it is occurring right under our noses. We need to add this to the list of crimes our officers should be alert for."

Davidson nodded. "What do you have in mind?"

"Our officers must be vigilant for victims of beatings and starvation during routine inspections. Inflicting such pain is, after all, a violation of existing law. We would be derelict in our duty if we cited a captain for being unlicensed or having culls aboard, while ignoring men who have been beaten and starved. These drudge captains need to learn they are not God and must obey the laws of man, even while at sea."

"Yes, yes. Such an order should require checking cabins and below decks for injured crewmen."

"Yes sir. And our men should look for all kinds of mistreatment. This is especially true if immigrants are aboard. Our officers must not leave a ship until they are satisfied no one aboard is being abused."

Commander Davidson swept one arm over his desk. "As you can see, I'm swamped. If this office were a ship, it would be sinking. I'd like you to draft such an order to be published. We'll go over it the next time you're in town."

"Aye, sir."

Davidson leaned forward and rested his hands on a stack of papers. "I received a short cable from Sheriff Tolley reporting some sort of ruckus at Benny Crème's. "It was sparse but I take it that Renard Blanchard was the only one killed."

He looked at Haynie. "It sounds like the sheriff is waiting for you to return and tell him what to do. What the hell happened over there, Captain?"

Haynie described finding Nathan Jacoby's body and Renard Blanchard's escape from jail. "Protecting Guy and the Tubmans from Marrok is critical. With him still loose, Renard's death doesn't change anything."

"How certain are you that the bolt that killed Mister Jacoby came from Blanchard's crossbow?"

"I have no doubts. I expect Missus Blanchard will confirm it."

Davidson sighed, "Please understand; I had no choice but to order you to Crisfield. I would not have sent you if I had another option. I expect you will want to return promptly to Dorchester County."

Haynie nodded and rose to leave. "With your permission, the *Emma Dunn* will sail tomorrow at first light."

Davidson nodded and Haynie added, "I know that you could not prevent it; but, what was so dire that those politicians needed to take the *Leila* out of service during such a critical time?"

Davidson slowly shook his head, before meeting Haynie's gaze. "I still find it hard to believe. The chairman of the Senate Finance Committee approached me and asked—actually demanded—that I drop whatever I was doing and take him and his nephew for a ride on a real Oyster Navy ship. Seems he'd promised the boy such a ride. At first, I thought he was joking; then I recalled what a humorless man he is. I said no. Perhaps my tone was somewhat impatient. Not a man to be denied, he organized a tour of the bay for certain legislators and invited the governor along."

Davidson shrugged. "I was given a note from the governor's office instructing me to have the crew of the *Leila* ready—along with ample provisions which, by the way, are coming out of our budget—at eight the following morning. They sailed just before word came in about the German crews. They're still out."

"Is the nephew aboard?"

"Yes, of course."

"Jesus!"

"Daddy's home! Daddy's home!" Young Tench screamed as Haynie came through the front door. The boy ran to his father laughing, his arms out stretched.

Haynie scooped the child up with one arm.

"Hug my neck!" he ordered with a mock sternness.

Ella May screeched, pulled herself upright and waddled across the room. After two steps, she wobbled and sat down heavily in the middle of the floor.

Lila came in and lifted her shrieking daughter into her arms. "Just so you know," she said, "I'm as glad to see you as they are, but I decided against jumping into your arms. I can shriek though, if you like."

Haynie laughed and bent to kiss both of his girls. "I'll be happy with a kiss."

Ella May, though quieted by the kiss, fussed as she stretched her chubby arms toward him.

Haynie gave Young Tench another hug and lowered him to the floor, quickly replacing him with Ella May. Laughing, she patted her father's face with both hands.

Haynie and Ella May followed Lila into the kitchen with Young Tench trailing along, a firm grip on the hem of his father's coat.

"Hope it's not too late to get my name in the supper pot," Haynie said.

"I think I can find enough for you. I was just getting ready to put a beef loaf in the oven."

"With real beef?"

She shook her head. "I chopped up a venison roast, and you won't notice the difference. And, in honor of your appearance, I'm going to make your favorite dessert, poor man's pudding."

Haynie smacked his lips. "Maybe someday, we'll be able to afford rich man's pudding."

"I doubt it would taste any better."

Haynie sat in the kitchen, a child perched on each knee. "I'm sorry, but I don't have a lot of time. I'll be leaving early in the morning."

"I would be shocked if it were any other way."

He kissed each of his children on top of the said and said, "There are some things I need to tell you, but that should wait for later."

Lila looked at him and nodded.

He smiled. "So I'll take your report first."

Lila turned back to her meal preparation. "Did you read your mother's letter?"

"No time."

Lila sighed deeply. Not wishing a heated discussion in front of the children, she changed the topic. "Wilma and some of the others took a boat ride to a place you're familiar with."

"Popes Creek. You didn't go?"

"No. And, I'd have thought you'd guess Crisfield."

Haynie bounced a knee under each child and said, "Simon Berrien is not in Crisfield."

Lila whirled around, knocking over a bowl, sending several eggs splattering to the floor.

"Damnit," she muttered. Grabbing a towel, she began sopping up the stream of yellow and white oozing from the broken shells. "Keep them up there until I get rid of this mess."

Haynie clutched both children now struggling to wiggle free and join their mother on the floor.

"The important thing is: Do you have enough eggs left for my pudding?"

Lila nodded.

"Tell me about Simon Berrien," he said.

"After supper. I can't even imagine how you know about him, but one thing is certain; it can't bode well."

Seated in the parlor after dinner, Lila described, in detail, Simon Berrien's appearance at Wilma Winder's home. When she had finished she asked, "He's not a reverend trying to help colored folks, is he?"

"No. You didn't give him any money, did you?"

"We each made a donation," she said firmly, "I gave just enough to save face. Cora Clemson brought Berrien to us; she is clearly smitten with him. She and Lucy Buck gushed over him the whole day. Wilma is going to be gleeful when she hears this."

Haynie's voice bore a hard edge. "You cannot say a word to anyone about this. Not to anyone." He waited then added, "Tell me you understand. No matter how much you admire Wilma, you cannot tell her."

Lila studied his face. "It's not by accident that he's in Popes Creek, is it? He's in league with that Reb colonel who had Caleb killed."

Haynie nodded. "And now we're going to get them."

59

The *Emma Dunn* cleared the mouth of the Severn River turning south toward Dorchester County.

Captain Haynie McKenna carried his morning coffee on deck to witness the emergence of this day. A warm breeze stirred, unraveling the fabric of a thin fog. The wooded shoreline of Kent Island loomed off the port bow; sea gulls wheeled and dove at the steamer, impatient for a meal.

Haynie desperately sought time to apply some reason to the tumult surrounding Jacoby's killing and Renard Blanchard's escape from jail.

Gerhard Stein, sensing his friend's need to be alone, watched dutifully from the galley.

The *Emma Dunn* would soon make port near Cambridge. It would be foolish to formulate a plan of attack until Sheriff Tolley could bring him up to date. One thing for certain, he would not leave the county again, until Marrok Blanchard was dead or in a secure jail.

There was no doubt in Haynie's mind that the man deserved killing, but *revenge is not punishment*. He believed Marrok should face a judge in a court of law, so the people can see that law and order have come to the bay. Still, it is doubtful Marrok could be taken alive.

At their meeting yesterday, Haynie had asked Commander Davidson for additional men.

"It'll be a real set-back for us if we can't keep our word to protect folks who are willing to stand up to the likes of the Blanchards."

Davidson had assigned two sworn officers, Parmalee and Carter, who had not sailed with the *Leila*.

"I'm sorry, but there's no one else available."

It also nagged at Haynie that, until Marrok was in jail, he could not pursue Hollins and Mooney. *As soon as this is over, I need to devise a scheme to lure Mooney and Hollins back to Maryland.*

As if these torments were not burden enough, visions of Percy Overton frequently intruded upon his thoughts. This particular agony usually appeared late at night, as he struggled to clear his mind for sleep. Of late, it came more frequently, and more violently.

A lone black man swaying gently from a tree limb and there was no one to cut him down. A Negro woman clutching two babies running for their lives as pursuers bore down on thundering horses.

Haynie shook his head. *I can't think about that now.*

Emma Dunn berthed at Town Point and a somber crew assembled amidships. Haynie's gaze moved over them, issuing an individual challenge to each one.

"Every man here is a sworn officer of the law. Each of you knew Nathan Jacoby. He is the first peace officer of the Maryland Oyster Navy killed while doing his duty. Nathan was shot in the back by the man we are hunting, Marrok Blanchard."

Haynie swallowed hard, struggling to keep the rage and grief from his voice.

"None of us will leave this county until he is caught. We will split into two search parties. Officer Furniss will head up one party; Officers Dimitri and Tydings, along with Officer Parmalee from the *Leila*, will go with him. Gerhard and Peace Officer Carter will come with me. I want him alive, but don't hesitate to shoot. It's damn certain he won't."

Smokey Noble appeared on deck carrying a .36 caliber Colt revolver. The sling was gone from his arm and Noble flexed his right hand to demonstrate his recovery. "Captain," he said, "Mister Jacoby was my friend and I want to be a part of this hunt."

"And so you shall, Mister Noble. Join us."

Noble crossed the deck and merged with the sworn officers.

Haynie said, "The *Emma Dunn* will be our headquarters and message center, manned by Mister Noble." He looked at the ship's pilot. "I'm afraid I'm going to have to ask that you handle this alone for a time."

Noble beamed. "Aye, sir."

"As soon as we know the current situation, we'll send someone back to be with you."

"Not necessary, sir. I can handle it."

"I believe you can. But Marrok stormed the ship once and would not hesitate to try it again—especially if he thought you were alone. Besides, if we don't catch up to him right away, we'll need another man here to relay messages between search parties."

Haynie paused. "Any questions, so far? Good. Officer Dimitri—"

"Sir!"

"Draw your weapons and ammunition from the arms locker, along with two days worth of provisions. You'll be heading to Benny Crème's place to join up with Officer Furniss. I'm going into town and talk to the sheriff; then strike out for the Blanchard place or join you for a search of Taylors Island, which ever seems most likely."

Haynie focused again on the engineer. "If we find the Blanchard is aboard a ship, we'll hustle back here and get under way. You'll need to ready."

Noble nodded. "Aye, sir."

When the oyster policemen walked into his office, Sheriff Tolley rushed to grab Haynie's hand. "McKenna. I'm glad you're back. You got my cable."

Haynie nodded.

"Sit while I fill you in."

Gerhard and Peace Officer Carter stood nearby.

Tolley said, "A couple of nights ago the Blanchards attacked Benny's place. They shot a couple of bolts into the back wall and the commotion drew your men outside. Renard snuck in and was fixin' to shoot his brother until Benny Crème shot him dead. Marrok stayed outside leadin' your men deeper into the woods. They come a runnin' when they heard the shootin' and Marrok slipped away."

"Guy and Tubman okay?"

"Last I heard. Might be a problem for Crème, though."

"How's that?"

"He killed a white man."

"Sounds like he saved Guy's hide. Who's going to raise a fuss? Not Renard's mother."

"Still—"

"Did you show that bolt to Missus Blanchard?"

"Yes sir. She says it was with Marrok's crossbow. He had them special made by a smithy on Tilghman."

Haynie nodded. "My men still at Benny's?"

Tolley shrugged. "Hard to say. One of them came along with Guy when he brought his brother's body in. Guy said he was heading home to tell his mother about Renard. I reckon your man was going with him."

"Anything else?"

"We got one less thing to worry about."

"That's welcome. What is it?"

"Cromarte. Judge Robinson was real pleased to issue a warrant for the old bugger. Near gleeful, you might say. I took a deputy out to the *Hangman* and found him sittin' on deck next to an empty corn likker jug. Dead as an old crab."

"What killed him?"

"Doc thinks it was the corn likker—white lightning. It can strike without warning. Doc says steady drinking from that jug would likely do in an old sot like Cromarte."

"Likely the easiest way out for everyone—especially him."

Haynie stood. "How long ago did they leave here for Fox Creek?"

"Two hours. Maybe a little more."

"We're going to try and catch up to Guy there. You coming?"

"Lord knows I'm itching to, but I got a shooting trial startin' this afternoon. Judge Robinson wants me to stay in town."

"You have a posse out?"

Tolley shook his head. "They looked everywhere we could think of. Anyhow, most of them had to get back to their work."

Haynie nodded. "The *Emma Dunn* is at Town Point; we'll be underway for Fox Creek as soon as I get aboard. Another crew of officers is headed for Benny's."

Tolley nodded. "I'll join up with you as soon as I can," he said.

When the *Emma Dunn*, anchored at the mouth to Fox Creek, Haynie and Gerhard boarded the dinghy; Peace Officer Carter remained aboard with Smokey Noble .

Haynie had said, "With Renard dead, Marrok will likely be alone. He could come from any direction; if he shows up by water don't let him get that punt aimed."

Haynie and Gerhard maneuvered the dinghy into the basin of the Blanchard compound. About 40 feet in front of Marrok's house, they stilled their oars and Haynie called out. "Missus Blanchard. It's

Captain McKenna, Maryland Oyster Navy. Show yourself—we need to talk. If we don't see you outside, alone, I'll figure you're being held and we'll be required to use force against the house."

Shrill baying announced four long-eared hounds as they charged around the corner of the house. Edith Blanchard appeared, adjusting her skirts with one hand, and dragging the shotgun with the other.

"Hounds shut up!"

She peered out at Haynie. "Sakes alive, what's the rush? It's a sad thing when a body can't get a few minutes of solace in the privy. Let me put these hounds inside and then you come ashore."

Gerhard remained in the dinghy; musket pointed at the woods, as Haynie climbed out and approached Edith.

Hat in hand, he said, "My apologies for disturbing you, Missus Blanchard. We're trying to catch up with Guy."

"That all?"

"Yes ma'am."

"I was hoping you came with news about Marrok."

"We're still looking for him. Sorry about Renard."

"I'm sorry, too. The boy never had a chance with Marrok for a father. As for Guy," she motioned to the back of the house, "he went down the trail about an hour ago."

"Alone?"

"No. There was a nice young man with him—one of yours, I believe. He promised your men would take care of the only son I got left. I begged Guy to stay with me and the girls, but he was anxious about that colored man, Tubman. In case you're a-wonderin' about why a son would leave his mama and run off to help a stranger, it's because Guy feels real guilty about what Blanchard men done to that family."

When Haynie said nothing, she added, "He's a good boy."

"Yes, ma'am, I can see that. You should be proud."

Edith shrugged and looked up to the sky. "At least, when I go up, I can tell Saint Peter that I saved one."

She grinned and pushed the shotgun out in front of her. "If I have to shoot that bastard, Marrok, then I'll likely be headed the other way along with him. That'll be my hell."

"There's a lot of men searching for him," Haynie said. "We'll find him soon."

She shook the gun with both hands, "I'm ready, if he dares to show his face around here."

"Have you thought of any place we might look, since we last talked?"

"Good thing you said somethin'. Guy told me, if I was to see you before he did I should tell you about Dunnocks Island. You know of it?"

Haynie shook his head.

"It lies twixt Taylors and Meekins Neck. Guy remembered being there with Marrok a time or two. No one lives there anymore. Just an old rundown planter's house and bunches of birds—herons, egrets and such. Marrok took the boys there and showed 'em the house. Said they was taking the place over and when the Blanchard navy ruled these waters; he was gonna call it Elba. You know about that Frenchman Napoleon being sent to Elba Island?"

Haynie nodded. "Did Guy say anything else?"

"Said to tell you the gut leading into Dunnocks from the bay is real tricky. Marrok was real proud of himself about that. He bragged that, if anyone did make it through the gut, the herons would sound the alarm for him. If you are going in by boat you might should find a waterman who knows it, to take you in."

"Thank you, ma'am. We'll head back to Benny Crème's. I want to make certain Guy is there."

"Captain McKenna."

"Ma'am?"

"Next time you come here, I expect you'll be bringin' Louie home to me."

60

Taylors Island
Dorchester County, Maryland
April 21, 1869

Haynie stood at the edge of a clearing about 60 feet from the front
door to Benny Crème's place. He and Gerhard studied the tavern
while the others watched the woods behind them.

The midday sun reflected sharply off the two front windows,
making it impossible to glimpse any movement inside. The door
remained closed. No one had entered or left the building since they
arrived.

Haynie motioned the officers to his side. "I'll halloo Benny Crème.
If we get a friendly answer, we'll move single-file, at double time,
across the clearing and in the door. That is when Marrok will attack if
he's out there. He'd like to pick us off one at a time with that
crossbow. Keep a sharp eye as we move."

"Aye, sir."

"Halloo in the tavern. This is Captain McKenna and a troop of
peace officers of the state Oyster Navy."

The thud of a door bolt being thrown echoed across the clearing,
and the door cracked open. "This is Devil Furniss, Captain. Come
ahead."

Haynie was the first to move, when he reached the tavern, he
gave a nod and ducked inside. Gerhard moved to the side of the door,
positioning himself to watch their backtrail until the last officer was
across the clearing.

When Gerhard was inside Devil slammed the door shut and slid the bolt home. Then he resumed his post at a front window.

Haynie shook hands with Benny and Guy, and looked over at Tubman. "How's he doing?"

"About the same," Benny said.

"We need to get him aboard the *Emma Dunn*."

In a low voice, Guy said, "He won't go without his boy. Have you heard anything about Andrew?"

Haynie shook his head.

"But, it's been four nights."

Haynie moved beside Tubman. "It's Captain McKenna, sir. I'm here with a troop of state law officers. Heard you had some excitement last night."

Tubman opened his eyes and moved his head only slightly.

"We're going to get you aboard our steamer—the *Emma Dunn*—where you can rest without a lot of ruckus. We'll be leaving soon."

Tubman coughed. "Not—going—without—Andrew."

Haynie rested a hand on Tubman's shoulder. "Tomorrow the *Emma Dunn* is heading for the lower Honga River to search for your son. It would be a big help if you were aboard to point out where we should be looking. You want to be there when we find him, don't you?

Tubman nodded.

"Rest easy," Haynie said and moved away to rejoin Crème and the others.

"That was pretty slick," Benny said. "Hard to put anything over on him."

"I don't believe I did," Haynie smiled. "I expect to be on the Honga looking for his son. First, we need to make a stop at Dunnocks Island. Do you know the gut into Dunnocks?"

Crème nodded. "I hunted it some. It's only a few acres across; was an old covered log bridge connected it to the mainland. Before the war, the family grew tobacco there. Something happened durin' the war years; they just picked up and left."

Crème shrugged. "Don't know why. They abandoned the place and burned the bridge behind 'em. Nothin' there now but a shell of the old house and flocks of birds."

"From the charts," Haynie said, "it looks doubtful we could get the *Emma Dunn* in there."

Crème signaled agreement.

"Could you guide a dinghy through the gut?"

"I 'spect I could. The bottom don't figure to have changed much in two years. Why would you think Andrew's there?"

Haynie looked to Guy Blanchard. "It is likely where we'll find Marrok."

Benny tightened his grip on the revolver in his hand. "I'll get you in there."

Shortly after midnight, the *Emma Dunn* anchored just off shore, where Dunnocks Slough joins the Chesapeake Bay. In the galley, Skillets tended to the Tubmans who had settled onto two cots.

The sworn officers crowded into the captain's cabin to plan their assault on Marrok Blanchard's hideout. Haynie and Devil Furniss stood on either side of Benny Crème studying a map of the waterways circling the tiny island.

Haynie said, "We're pretty sure that he's running a twenty foot sloop called the *Saint-Esprit*. Could he get a boat of that size through the gut?"

Benny ran a finger over the map, stopping just short of the island.

"There's a small cove about here; doesn't show up on this map. He can't get much closer in a boat that size, and that's the best spot to hide any boat. It's only a few strokes to the island in a canoe."

Devil said, "We need to know if he's stayin' aboard the sloop, or goes across to that old house."

Haynie placed an index finger on the map and made a circle around the small island. "The streams that make Dunnocks an island look to be real narrow. Seems a man standing in the treeline on the mainland could easy see across to the old house."

Benny nodded and Haynie continued. "We'll send out a scouting party at first light. If the *Saint-Esprit* is anchored there, Marrok'll be nearby. If there's a canoe pulled up close to the house, that's where we'll likely find him."

The crew murmured their understanding.

"One more thing. In addition to the crossbow, its likely Marrok is pulling a punt gun behind the sloop. Keep a sharp eye for it."

Haynie looked at Guy. "Anything else we should know about the place?

"He's got a hideout that we dug along the stream bank. I can show you."

Skillets poked his head in the cabin. "Sorry, captain. I'm having the devil's own time with that Tubman fella. He keeps fightin' to get up. Says he's got to look for Andrew."

"I'll be right along." To the crew Haynie said, "Get some sleep; we'll be turning out before dawn."

61

Dunnocks Island
April 22, 1869

Benny Crème crouched in the bow of the dinghy, silently directing its path through the gut. Peace Officers Tydings and Furniss hunkered over the oars alert for his signal. A mist clung to everything, and they strained to make out Benny's gestures through the gloom. Aft, Haynie shared a bench seat with a sullen Guy Blanchard. Gerhard sat alone at the stern. Haynie had ordered Guy to leave his musket aboard the *Emma Dunn*.

"How can I defend myself? Papa sent Renard in to kill me. If he sees me alive, I'll be the first one in his sights."

"You mind what I say and he won't get a chance at you," Haynie responded. "Sworn peace officers will do any shooting if it comes to that."

Benny motioned frantically. Tydings dipped his oar and the small boat veered sharply to the right. Benny immediately pointed ahead and the oarsmen resumed a steady course.

The mist that slowed their progress served as a curtain concealing them from detection by anyone on Dunnocks. After sunrise, the shroud would quickly evaporate revealing their movements to the host of great blue herons populating the island. The jarring call from hundreds of the great birds would alert anyone in the vicinity to their presence.

Suddenly, Benny thrust out a hand. The officers dipped their oars deep and the dinghy stopped. Reaching ahead, Benny grabbed hold of a taut anchor rope and pulled them alongside the starboard bow of the *Saint-Esprit*. Silently and methodically, they maneuvered the dinghy along the hull until they reached the stern. They continued along the port side circling the boat until they returned to the anchor rope. No punt or canoe was found.

Benny held the *Saint-Esprit's* anchor rope while the others crowded to the bow of the dinghy. Gerhard kept a vigil at the stern.

Speaking softly Haynie said, "No small boats means Marrok is likely on the island. Since we did not find the punt gun, he probably has it with him. "

Turning to Guy, he said, "As he's on the run, do you think he would have scuttled the punt?"

Guy shook his head. "He loves that gun. It's with him."

Haynie indicated the sloop. "We need to board her and disable the rudder so he can't run if he should slip by us. Guy and Officer Furniss will go aboard with me; Officer Tydings, you stay here with Benny. Gerhard, will keep watch at the stern. Everyone keep a sharp eye that Marrok doesn't sneak in on us through this fog."

"Aye, sir," Tydings said. He and Benny steadied the dinghy while the others silently boarded the sloop.

The three men in the dinghy watched and listened, hearing only the rhythmic lapping of the water against the two boats.

Devil Furniss, the first of the boarding party to appear at the rail, handed his musket to Benny. Once back in the dingy, he turned and accepted a stack of folded canvas from Haynie. With the canvas stowed, Haynie and Guy reboarded the dinghy.

"That's all of his sail," Haynie said, "and the rudder's disabled."

The mist thinned in a stiffening breeze, revealing stands of alder and elm trees crowding the mainland shore.

In a low voice, Devil said, "It's starting to clear."

Within minutes, they were able to discern that the *Saint-Esprit* was anchored in the small cove Benny had described. Dunnocks Island, still obscured in fog, would be about 50 yards beyond.

Haynie pointed to the mainland shore. "Get us over there. Devil and Gerhard will come with me. We'll work our way through the trees to a spot just across from the east end of the island. When the fog lifts, we should be able to see the house. Guy, you come with us."

Turning to Benny and Tydings, he said, "You two get out to the *Emma Dunn* and bring back the cavalry."

He pointed at the *Saint-Esprit.* "When you return, make shore here, across from his boat, then fan out and work your way across the island. We'll be situated on the other side as you approach. When you get within a hundred yards of the house, fire two shots in the air so we'll know you're in position, and keep moving in. Officer Tydings."

"Sir!"

"Marrok won't know what we did to his boat, so he may try for it. Post two good men between it and the house. They're not to move until he's caught."

"Aye, sir."

Haynie gripped Benny Crème's shoulder.

"Mister Crème, thank you for your service. We wouldn't have gotten here without your help. When you go back, I'm going to ask you to stay aboard the *Emma Dunn.*"

Benny grabbed the handle of the revolver wedged in his belt.

"No, sir. I got my gun and I showed I ain't afraid to use it."

"I'm sorry—"

"Nathan Jacoby was my best friend all the years we was growin' up. He was little, but his heart was big. More'n once he saved me from a lickin' from other white boys."

Benny glanced at Guy and continued, "I can't rest until that Marrok Blanchard is as cold as Nathan."

Guy looked away.

Haynie said, "You don't have to kill Marrok to do your best for your friend. Peace Officer Jacoby was a good man. He trusted me to get the job done and I'm asking you to trust me. I need your help to protect your other friend, Tubman."

Benny frowned.

"When Peace Officer Tydings returns with the other officers, Mister Noble will be the only one left aboard ship. If Marrok should slip around us, the *Emma Dunn* sits just off shore. Easy run in a canoe. If he gets aboard her again, Smokey would be no match for him. I really need you there."

The morning became leaden gray as the fog hovered in the treetops. Haynie and Gerhard lay behind a sweet pepperbush the outline of a frame house visible through the trees just across Punch Island Creek. On the island, hundreds of blue heron crowded the water's edge.

Guy sat with his back to a maple tree and peered into the surrounding woods. Devil Furniss had moved off to scout the area downstream for a hidden canoe and any evidence of a path leading to the island.

Just across the creek, the ugly barrel of a punt gun pointed in their direction.

Haynie sighted a small red glow flickering between the tree limbs. He nudged Gerhard who nodded. This light, the glowing end of a cigarette, appeared in a second floor window.

62

Dunnocks Island
Dorchester County, Maryland
April 22, 1869

Several years before the war, Dunnocks Island was cleared to make way for the planting of tobacco. In doing so, the planter spared a small grove of chestnut trees, on the east side of the island. Among these trees, he had built his home.

Early in the war, the plantation had been abruptly abandoned and the resulting neglect was obvious. The outer walls of the house were largely overgrown with ivy and sumac vines. Mud plaster had shriveled and fallen away from between the logs, leaving gaps through which small vermin scurried.

The first floor was divided into three rooms. Each contained a fieldstone walk-in fireplace, black with soot and cold from disuse. Bird feathers and ragged twig nests littered the entire downstairs. In the middle-room sat two slat-back chairs and a wooden table, each crusted with a hardened shell of bird droppings.

In the back room, a crude wooden ladder provided access to the second floor. At the top of the ladder waited a vast empty room. Marrok concluded that it had served as a sleeping area for the planter's slaves. Still, he decided that he and Louie would sleep up there when they were ashore.

The first time in the house Louie eagerly scaled the ladder and, once on the second floor, struggled to help his grandfather pull it into the room.

Marrok told him, "*Mon petite fils*, this is a magic stairway to our secret fort. Nothing can touch us once we are hidden in here."

At each end of the room, just below the peaked roof, double windows provided a secure place to watch for intruders.

Marrok sat by one of the windows smoking a cigarette while he watched for Renard. He dragged deeply and studied the glowing ash as it dimmed.

This is the last day I'm gonna wait for that boy. Something must a happened. Damn bastards.

Marrok looked at Louie asleep at his feet. *Now it's just me and him.*

Louie cried out and scratched his arms furiously in his sleep.

Marrok sighed. *I told him to stay away from the ivy, but he don't listen. I've rubbed on the rhubarb and the honeysuckle, but nothing seems to help.*

He cries most all the time now and don't eat hardly nothing. Fool boy throws whatever vittles I give him on the ground. Can't figure a Blanchard who won't eat jerky or bacon. No sense tryin' to give him greens, I hate 'em myself. He's got so he don't mind anything I tell him, and sets off howlin' 'til I have to give him a good swat. He keeps that up he'll bring the law right to us.

He sure don't act like a Blanchard. With that hussy for a mother, there's a real good chance he ain't one; but he might be all I got now. Wonder if Renard killed his traitor brother. I heard two shots; he could've got him. If he didn't, then I'll have to do it myself.

Soon as I get that done, the boy and me will head out on the Saint Esprit. I figure to sail south 'til I find a spot we can hole up in while I teach him the ways of Blanchard men.

The mainland shore was now visible just across Punch Island Creek. Below the window, hundreds of birds jostled one another, vying for space at the water's edge.

Marrok looked down at Louie. "Blanchard means white and brave in the French," he said softly.

Abruptly, great herons and snowy egrets erupted in a flurry of flapping wings and a cacophony of sounds. The jarring *raaannk, raaannk* call from hundreds of herons and the grating *rrrow* of the egrets filled the air as squadrons of birds took flight.

About time Renard was gettin' here.

Marrok leaned across the windowsill and searched up and downstream.

"I don't see Renard. It must be them damn bastards."

63

Dunnocks Island
Dorchester County, Maryland
April 22, 1869

Haynie, intent on the punt gun sitting across the creek, almost missed the movement at the second-floor window.

"There!"

Gerhard followed where Haynie pointed and nodded.

"That ruckus must have put him on guard."

"*Ja.*"

"The others should be here soon; then we can move in."

Haynie kept his binoculars trained on the windows and called to Guy. "He just stuck his head out of the upstairs window."

"It's been more'n three days," Guy answered. I doubt he's still expectin' Renard."

"Where is that secret lair you were talking about?"

"It would be easier to talk if I could come around to that side of the tree."

"Come ahead, but lay flat and keep a sharp eye to our back."

Guy scooted around the maple tree and lay facing into the woods, his feet resting on the creek bank. He said, "His hideout is beyond the house. You can't see it through the trees. He had us boys dig a slit trench into the creek bank and cover it with a brush pile. He crawls in there and pulls the brush over top of him and you ain't gonna know he's there. He can set that crossbow among the brush and hit a man comin' across the creek, or out of the house. For practice, us boys killed a deer and strung it up by the back door. Papa never missed.

"Usin' the crossbow, you don't hear gunfire, so the first anybody knows about it is when the shot person cries out, if he can. Papa figures anybody who came along with the man he shot will figure the bolt come from the woods across the creek and go chargin' over there."

Haynie retuned his attention to the punt. "I'm keeping my eyes fixed on that gun. Gerhard, you watch for him leaving the house."

"Ja."

"Guy, don't take your eyes off of those woods behind us. If he figures it was us who spooked those birds, he'll likely be on the move."

"I'm watching real good," said, Guy. "He can get to that lair I told you about, without us seeing him from here. I 'spect that's what he'll do."

"Maybe. Hard to tell about him."

With the departure of the raucous birds, the woods grew quiet and the three waited, each straining for sounds or motion.

Out of the corner of his eye, Guy glimpsed movement just through the trees. He leapt to his feet and darted from behind the tree.

"No Papa! No!"

A startled Marrok swung his crossbow and fired. The bolt thudded into the tree inches from Guy's head.

Haynie rolled to his right and fired at Marrok disappearing among the trees.

Gerhard rolled the other way, shooting as he moved.

Haynie sprang to his feet and rushed past Guy with Gerhard close behind.

To Guy he said, "Get behind us and keep up," and plunged into the woods. They followed the sounds of Marrok crashing through the underbrush ahead.

"He'll have trouble reloading that crossbow as he runs," Haynie said. "When he stops, we need to take cover."

On they pressed, guided by an occasional glimpse of Marrok darting among the trees.

The thrashing sound shifted direction and Haynie spotted a dark form moving to their right. He motioned those behind him and altered course.

"He might double back. Gerhard, try to get between him and the house."

"*Ja*".

Gerhard moved away at a right angle, running parallel to the sounds.

Guy stayed on Haynie's heels. "I could catch him if you let me go ahead," he called.

Abruptly, the thrashing stopped. Haynie and Guy ducked behind a thick oak tree and waited. It was suddenly eerily quiet. Nothing moved.

Haynie unholstered his revolver and, gripping the barrel, passed it over his shoulder.

"Don't use this unless I go down."

"Yes, sir. I really don't want to shoot Papa. But, if we don't do it, Mama will have to."

"We're gonna take him alive if we can. I'm going to halloo him to come out. If he comes toward us you are not to shoot."

"It ain't in his nature to give up."

"Do you understand?"

"Yes sir."

As he reloaded his musket, Haynie called out, "Marrok Blanchard! This is Captain McKenna and a passel of officers from the Maryland oyster police. We have come to bring you in for the killing of Peace Officer Nathan Jacoby, here in Dorchester County."

Marrok replied immediately, his voice strong.

He's real close, Haynie thought.

"So it is you, McKenna. You're the one going to pay up, for killin' my oldest boy. Now I see ya got that traitor with ya, so I guess you bastards got Renard. He dead too?"

When there was no reply, Marrok said, "That's what I figured."

Gerhard was concealed behind a nearby chestnut tree. Haynie motioned him to circle around behind Marrok. Gerhard nodded and slid away.

When Marrok spoke again he was moving to Haynie's right, in Gerhard's direction.

"Thing is, McKenna, I judged I could sneak up on ya while you was watching my big gun. I had it right too 'cept I got spooked when that damn boy jumped out from behind the tree. Otherwise, you'd be dead as my sons. Still, you need to watch your back, for that one's a sneak and a liar. I seen alley cats more loyal than him. He betrayed his own kin in favor of a nigger; he'll do you no different."

Haynie whispered, "Gerhard will soon be behind him. Get ready to move—and stay close," When there was no response, he looked over his shoulder. Guy was gone.

Damn it! "Listen up, Marrok, you can't get away—"

"Don't want to—"

"—You're surrounded."

Marrok laughed. "It sure didn't sound like no passel of men crashing through the woods behind me. Sounded more like just three of ya; only two if you don't count that traitor. Two of ya can't surround Marrok Blanchard. Blanchard means 'white and brave', in the French.

"That's some gun ain't it? Me and Renard had us a hum-dinger of a naval battle. Sunk the enemy with all hands lost."

"What the hell are you talking about? Did you murder that colored boy, Andrew?"

"Naval battle! Lost at sea!"

Haynie peered around the trunk of the oak and glimpsed the terrain. About 100 feet ahead, the ground cut away.

Could be a gully or stream bank. Likely, Marrok is moving around below the cut bank. Can't worry about Guy now; he's on his own. There, Gerhard's moving in. Need to keep Marrok's attention on me.

A bolt thudded into the tree, just missing Haynie's jaw. "What the hell!" he muttered, jerking his head back. Keeping an eye on the cut, Haynie crouched low and darted forward to the safety of a thick maple, while Marrok reloaded.

From behind the tree, Haynie called, "This is your last chance, Marrok, give it up and you'll live to see tomorrow."

"Mebbe it's your last chance, McKenna. You ever think of that?"

Haynie was no more than 25 feet from the cut. The foliage between was sparse, offering little cover. To his left, he spotted Guy stretched prone along the cut bank, Haynie's revolver clutched in his right hand.

On Haynie's right, Gerhard crept along atop the cut's far bank, well behind Marrok's likely position.

Ahead, Haynie saw the crossbow edging forward over the lip of the cut about six feet to his left.

Marrok, gripping the weapon in his left hand, supported it with his left arm resting on the ground. Now, his head and shoulders appeared as he sought his target.

Haynie stepped from behind the tree, his raised musket pointing at Marrok's head.

"Marrok!" he called.

Blanchard swung the crossbow toward the voice and Haynie fired.

Gerhard standing behind Marrok shot into the cut.

As the minie balls struck him, Marrok's body twisted violently causing the bolt to discharge harmlessly into the treetops.

Haynie was the first to reach the prone figure. He flung the crossbow aside and felt for a pulse.

He looked up as Gerhard ran to him. "He's done for."

"*Ja.*"

Guy stood and moved slowly along the bank toward them, awed by his father's twisted form.

His face was ashen and his hand shook as he handed the revolver to Haynie.

"I couldn't do it," he said.

Haynie holstered the gun. "We better go find that little boy."

64

Annapolis, Maryland
April 24, 1869

Haynie walked through his front door and stopped, his hand gripping the knob.

"Mother? What are you—?"

Lila appeared behind her mother-in-law. "If you had read her letter, you would have known she was coming."

His face was mottled with anger and embarrassment. He had not seen his mother in more than a year and her physical appearance was startling.

During those months, on the rare occasions that he had given thought to her, he invariably recalled a younger, stronger Lettie McKenna. Before him, now, stood an old woman wearing a shawl over stooped shoulders, her gray hair tied back in a tight bun. A flicker of a smile crossed her lips.

"Don't you have anything you want to say?" Lila asked.

Young Tench flew passed his mother, calling, "Daddy! Daddy!" Ella May waddled behind her brother, struggling to keep up.

Haynie scooped Young Tench from the floor. "There's a lot I would like to say," he replied. "But it would not be wise."

He stepped toward his daughter, picked her up with one hand and, with a child cradled in each arm, walked passed the two women into the living room.

Lila followed on his heels while Lettie stood in the entryway, wringing her hands.

Lila laid a hand on his arm, "I know your mind has been filled with catching that awful man, but you can't expect us to abandon our lives until you have time for us."

Haynie kissed each child on the top of the head. "Would you ask her to mind them while we talk?"

When she returned, Lila found Haynie seated in his chair, rocking gently, eyes closed.

"Before we start on Lettie," she began, "are you finished with that Blanchard family?"

"The little that is left of them, yes. The way it ended is troublesome though."

"How so?"

"We were given no choice; we had to kill three of them. Marrok Blanchard was a real bastard, but I wanted him alive. With him and Renard dead there will be no public trial to expose the extent of his depravity. People need to know the price he paid, not just for killing Nathan Jacoby, but for choosing the life he led. A long prison term, or a public hanging, would serve notice that the laws of the state of Maryland are being enforced on the Chesapeake Bay. As it is, newspapers will quickly lose interest. People will learn little of the anguish he caused, and that will be quickly forgotten."

Lila hesitated, and then asked, "What will become of the Blanchard family? And the colored man, Tubman—did he survive?"

"Gerhard and I went with Sheriff Tolley to take the two living Blanchard men home."

A brief smile appeared as Haynie said, "Edith Blanchard's as tough as they come, but she couldn't keep the tears back when she saw her grandson."

Haynie looked away and swallowed.

Lila put a hand on his arm. "What?"

"She was crying mostly because of how bad off the boy was. For one thing, he was covered with poison sumac. Marrok kept him drugged most of the time, and he was so thin. Looked to be nearly starved.

"When Tolley asked her what she wanted done with Marrok and Renard's remains, she said, 'Whatever you need to do to get them on their way to hell. They can rot in your tomato patch for all I care.'"

Haynie shook his head. "I wonder about Guy. He tried so hard not to be like his father and brothers; I wonder if he has what it takes to get by. He's vowed to take care of Tubman 'til his own boy, Andrew, comes back. He could be in for a long stay."

"What happened to Andrew?"

"Nobody knows—for certain. We took the *Emma Dunn* down the Honga, around Crab Point and into Fishing Bay. Looked anyplace old Tubman could think of; no sign of Andrew or his boat."

"Did Marrok kill him?"

Haynie shrugged. "When you don't know what happened, anything is possible. At the end—there in the woods—Marrok bragged about using that punt gun on some boat. A 'naval battle' he called it. Said he and Renard 'sunk the enemy boat with all hands lost.' "

"What is a punt gun?"

Haynie described the gun and explained how deadly it could be.

"We didn't see a sign of Andrew's boat, or his body."

"Would you find if it had sunk?"

"It's doubtful. The size of the *Emma Dunn* prevented us from getting near the shallow water where Andrew would have been tonging. If the mast was snapped off, his boat could be laying on the bottom and we wouldn't have seen any evidence of it."

"Sheriff Tolley's going to send some men in a skiff to search the shallows along there..."

Lila said, "Anything else, before I start?"

He closed his eyes and renewed a gentle rocking. "Isn't that enough?"

Lila shifted in her chair. "What I—"

"Wait," Haynie said. "I'm too exhausted to fight. I doubt I could put a sensible argument together, even if I came up with one. Just tell me why she's here after all this time."

A relieved Lila said, "You have asked how I was spending my days while you were gone. I told you about attending meetings of a women's group and doing some writing. Do you remember?"

"Vaguely."

"I mentioned my plan to do some writing and you replied— 'Letters, to whom?'"

Haynie shrugged.

Lila sighed. "A few months ago, a story I wrote appeared in *Godey's*, the magazine for women."

Haynie stopped rocking and stared.

"Good! You are listening. Your mother was the main character — with a different name, of course. It was the story of a brave and determined woman, left a widow with two boys to raise.

"I never dreamed that anyone I know would read it; much less recognize that it was Lettie and you boys. But her friend, Miss Maude..." She waited for Haynie's nod before continuing. "... figured out that it was Lettie and showed her the story. That's why your mother wrote that letter to me."

"Is that why she's here, because you wrote a story about her?"

"Not entirely. She confessed that she had held me in little regard all of these years; in large part because she believed I felt the same toward her. What I wrote about her changed her mind."

"And that's—"

"Stop interrupting! Miss Maude died quite suddenly soon after showing Lettie the story. It made your mother realize that if her grandchildren were to remember her, she could wait no longer to see them. She's been here two days and we have talked the whole time. She wanted to set things right between the two of us, and become re-acquainted with the children. We both agreed that my trip to New York would be the perfect time for her to get to know them."

Lila watched for a reaction. "It will also give the two of you a chance to talk."

Haynie sat up. "You're leaving the children with her so that you can go with Wilma Winder to that women's meeting in New York?"

"Any reason why I shouldn't?"

"What if she is still under Muse's spell."

"We spoke of that. She assured me that she has come to accept the fact that he is a charlatan. If you are still worried, spend some time here—with the three of them. Talk to her."

When Haynie said nothing, she continued.

"The meeting in New York will be historic. Millions of citizens of this country are being denied the right to vote, for God's sake. If our movement falters, your daughter, and likely your granddaughter, will remain second-class citizens.

"*Godey's* has asked me to write about what I see and hear while we are there. It is a chance for me to make a difference. For years, I have supported your struggle against injustice; you owe me the same consideration."

Lila cried out and sat bolt upright.

"What is it?"

Excitement filled her voice. "I just realized how I can help you. By telling the Blanchard story."

Haynie frowned. "I..."

"I will write a story for *Godey's*, telling all about Marook Blanchard's awful crimes and what he did to his own family. People will have to take notice if it's in *Godey's*."

"That's a nice idea, but why would a woman's magazine print a story about such a man?"

"I'll tell it from Edith Blanchard's point of view. How she survived in spite of him. The tragedy of losing two sons."

Lila rushed from the room, returning shortly with paper and pencil.

Haynie watched as she wrote furiously for a moment. She stopped and looked over at him. "This is very exciting," she said and returned to the paper. "I'll want to talk to Edith Blanchard. Get her to say what it was like, living with that awful man. In her own words."

Still writing, she added, "It's important that I talk to Tubman. Hear how he feels about what Marrok Blanchard did to his family. We can only pray that his son will be home by then."

Lila glanced up. "If not, that'll be part of the story. Oh, I hope he can tell me about Harriet Tubman. That could be grist for another story."

Haynie sighed. "If you tell this story don't make me out to be some kind of hero."

She nodded. "This will be about those families. I can write about the Oyster Navy's role in bringing him down without mentioning you by name."

Eventually, Lila set her writing aside and asked, "Where were we?"

Haynie resigned to the inevitable, shook his head. "I was just about to ask: when do you leave for New York?"

"Next week."

"So soon."

He resumed rocking and said, "There's something I need to do before you leave and I'll need your help."

65

April 27, 1869
Annapolis, Maryland

"Thank you for meeting with me on such short notice."

Lila sat with Cora Clemson in a corner of Wilma Winder's parlor, their knees almost touching. Wilma watched from a distance, smoke curling from a cigarette held loosely in her hand.

Cora nodded. "Wilma said it was urgent. That none of the others could know. Naturally, I came at once."

Poor Cora, Lila thought. *I almost feel sorry for her.*

The woman was short and plump, her outfits gaudy. Today, she wore a red satin dress with wide pagoda sleeves. Ringlets of brown hair hung below a buckram bonnet adorned with cascading velvet and ribbon ties.

She's loath to admit her age; and her outfits always cry out to be noticed.

Lila smiled. "I haven't had the opportunity to thank you for introducing us to your Simon Berrien."

Cora flushed at the depiction of Berrien as 'hers'. "His cause is so worthy," she said, "I just wish I could be of more help."

Lila reached out and patted her hand. "That's why I wanted to see you right away. I'm so sorry that my husband and I couldn't take advantage of his wonderful offering. And for Doctor Berrien to know such high government officials—well, I never. You must be so proud."

Cora's face grew redder and she looked away.

Lila smiled. "But I'm very happy to say that I have someone who has agreed to invest in much of the acreage available through your Simon."

Cora squeezed Lila's hands. "That is wonderful news. Simon—Doctor Berrien has been somewhat frustrated because he has not been of more help to his friend. This will certainly cheer him; I can't wait to take him the news."

Lila drew back. "There is one necessary consideration—."

"Oh my! What is it?"

"The benefactor is a dear man—my Uncle George—but he is cautious. Overly so, some would say."

Lila laughed. "He says that is how he has kept his money. Uncle insists that he meet Mister Berrien's friend from the Freedmen's Bureau, to verify the acreage."

Lila leaned in and lowered her voice. "He doesn't trust the government. He is concerned about what he terms 'bureaucratic chaos' in these times. He is worried there may be some difficulty in obtaining clear title to the land."

Cora waved a hand. "You mean Mister Hollins. That should be no problem. Simon told me, privately, that Mister Hollins will do whatever is asked of him."

"Good. Good," Lila said. "I know it's short notice, but it must be done this Saturday. Uncle is sailing for Europe on Tuesday. Can it be arranged?"

Cora nodded. "I'm certain of it. I will leave straightaway—to tell Simon." She smiled. "He will see that Mister Hollins is there to meet your Uncle George. Don't you worry."

"Oh, one more thing. I prefer that my name not be mentioned. I will accompany Uncle George to Popes Creek, but I deserve no credit. It would be wrong to detract from the magnificent effort you are making on Doctor Berrien's behalf."

Lila squeezed her hand. "You've worked so hard."

Cora smiled. "As you wish."

66

Southern Cross School for Coloreds
Popes Creek, Maryland
May 1, 1869

Simon Berrien and Cora Clemson smiled broadly as the buggy bearing Lila McKenna and a distinguished gentleman drew up to the veranda.

Lila, her hair tucked under a blue bonnet, wore a plain gray skirt with a dark blue Zouave jacket over a high-necked white blouse. The gentleman wore a vested suit and bowler hat.

Berrien rushed to them and offered his hand. "How wonderful to see you again, ma'am," he drawled as Lila descended from the buggy. "I recall seeing you in the front row for my talk."

She looked into his face and smiled. "It's been far too long, Doctor Berrien."

"Please, Simon to my friends. I certainly hope that I can count you among them, missus..."

"McKenna. Please call me Lila, Simon."

She turned to her companion. "Let me present George Noch, of Crisfield. Uncle George, this is Simon Berrien, the wonderful man I've been telling you about."

The men shook hands and Berrien, with Cora Clemson at his side, led his guests into the house.

Standing in the foyer, Noch twirled his bowler on one finger. "Thank you very much for agreeing to meet with me so quickly. I hope you have not been inconvenienced."

"Not at all. You will require some refreshment after your journey."

A colored boy and girl stood in the doorway leading to the parlor. Their mood was somber and both gazed at the floor. The children were similarly dressed; the boy in sharply pressed tan pants and a long-sleeved white shirt. The girl wore a tan skirt and newly ironed white blouse. Both were well scrubbed, with hair carefully combed and oiled.

Cora jostled her way next to Berrien. "How adorable they are. What a wonderful job you have done, Simon."

Berrien nodded. "They are here today as a reward for doing so well in lessons."

Indicating the girl, he said, "This is Rebecca; her basket name was Aboto. Rebecca, these are the guests we have been expecting."

The girl curtseyed briefly; her eyes remained downcast.

Berrien turned to the boy. "And this is Thomas."

Thomas bowed stiffly and waited.

"Please bring our guests some sweet tea."

The children turned and marched away.

"They are very smart," Simon said, "and I'm so pleased to be able to help prepare them for a better life. Shall we sit?"

As they moved into the parlor, Cora pressed close to Berrien, determined to claim a seat beside him.

George Noch took the chair indicated by his host.

"Please don't think me rude," Noch said. "I can think of nothing more pleasant than spending a social afternoon in such elegant surroundings, however, I am pressed for time. It is imperative that we conclude our business as soon as possible. If the gentleman from the Freedmen's Bureau is available, I would like to proceed."

Berrien frowned, "I am sorry to hear that. I have a fine dinner planned." He glanced at Lila. "I had hoped you might stay the night."

Quickly turning to Noch, he said, "Mister Hollins is not here at present. However, he is due any moment. Clifford is waiting at the dock and will carry him directly here. ...There—I believe I hear the whistle announcing the boat's arrival."

Cora, desperate to be included, nodded her head. "I heard it, too!" she exclaimed.

Lila stood. "Please excuse me," she said and turned to leave the room.

Both men stood. "Cora," Berrien said, "please show Missus McKenna out to the necessaries. It wouldn't do to have her get into theirs by mistake."

Lila waved Cora away. "Thank you. For now, I want to retrieve something from the buggy. I'll only be a minute."

Berrien started toward the door. "Please, allow me—"

Noch lay a firm hand on Berrien's arm. "Do not trouble yourself, sir," he said. "I wish to get on with our discussion."

Berrien hesitated, and then reluctantly returned to his chair as Lila swept from the room.

At the top of the bluff, concealed in the copse of fir trees, Haynie held the binoculars on Lila as she descended the veranda steps to the buggy.

She withdrew a bright-red parasol from under the buggy seat, and then proceeded to hold it parallel to the ground for several seconds. She glanced toward the trees before climbing the steps to the veranda.

"Patience, Silas," Haynie said. "She's telling us Hollins is not in the house, but will be arriving shortly."

Silas Wallis nodded and patted his coat pocket.

"What about Mooney?" he asked.

"There's been no mention of him, and she dared not ask. That is why Captain Stewart is here. If we can get Hollins to tell on Mooney—"

"Then I'll have him arrested in Virginia," Stewart said over Wallis's shoulder.

Wallis nodded. "Landon and that fellow Hopkins are vexed at being left down below," he said.

Haynie kept his glass on the house. "Can't be helped," he said. "There's not enough room in here for everyone. Captain Stewart and Gerhard are needed with us."

Stewart reached out, tapped Haynie on the shoulder, and put a finger to his lips. In the quiet, the creaking wheels of an approaching wagon were heard. Within moments, Southey Hollins, seated in a horse-drawn wagon, passed within 6 feet of where they were standing.

Silas Wallis plunged a hand into his coat pocket and gripped his revolver.

Haynie caught the movement out of the corner of an eye. Grabbing Wallis's right forearm, he held it tightly. After the wagon turned down the lane to the house, he pulled Wallis's hand from the coat and took the revolver.

"No, Colonel. They will be all ours by nightfall."

Southey Hollins pulled the pocket watch from his vest and noted the time.

That boat leaves in one hour. I'll say my piece and be back aboard. I'm not spending one minute longer than necessary in this state. Berrien can finish this business by himself.

"We're here, Mister Southey."

Hollins returned his watch to its pocket, gathered the leather pouch from the seat and stepped down. On the ground, he turned to the wagon driver and fixed him with a hard look. "What is your name again, boy?"

"It's Clifford, sir."

"I must be back at the dock within the hour, Clifford. Be damn certain you are sitting right here when I come out of that front door, or I'll personally peel your black hide."

Hollins turned and marched up the steps and crossed the veranda.

Berrien was waiting at the front door. "He's in the parlor. I see you have the documents."

"Let's get on with it," Hollins hissed. "I will be on that boat when it leaves."

Berrien, smiling broadly, led Hollins into the parlor. "Mister Noch, may I present Mister Southey Hollins of the Freedmen's Bureau."

Noch stood and the two men shook hands.

"Southey is an official in the Bureau's Abandoned Lands section. We met through my work with their Refugee Department. As you may imagine he is extremely busy these days and his time with us is short."

Hollins sat, perched on the edge of his chair, poised to dart from the room.

Noch smiled. "Of course. Thank you for making time for me, and my apologies for any inconvenience."

"Nonsense," Berrien said. "It's all part of his job." He took the pouch from Hollins. "These are the necessary documents for your consideration."

Berrien held the case out to Noch. "I trust you brought a certified financial instrument to complete our transaction."

Noch smiled and patted his jacket pocket as he took the pouch. "Mister Hollins," he said, "how long have you been with the Freedmen's Bureau?"

"From the start."

"And you have the authority to transact such business for the national government?"

Hollins nodded. "The government has thousands of acres of land lying fallow," he recited. "It is my responsibility to see that this land becomes productive as quickly as possible."

Hollins pulled out his watch. "I'm very sorry, but I have to return to the dock."

Berrien gave him a hard look.

"I must get back to Washington City. I'm certain these documents will satisfy any questions you may have."

Lila and Cora appeared at the doorway and the three men rose to their feet.

"No, please," Lila said, "we do not wish to intrude on your business."

Berrien moved quickly to Lila's side. "This lovely lady is Mister Noch's niece. Missus McKenna, may I introduce Mister Southey Hollins of the Freedmen's Bureau."

Hollins gaped, his face drained of color. "McKenna?" he stammered. "McKenna—from Crisfield, Maryland?"

Lila offered a hand. "Mister Hollins. I've heard so much about you."

Hollins shoved his way past the two women and broke from the room. He flung open the front door and charged onto the veranda; stopping abruptly at the sight of four men blocking his way.

What the bejesus! It's McKenna and Wallis! I'm caught!

Behind the line of men, Clifford was perched on the wagon seat holding the reins and smiling broadly.

"It's me, Clifford. Here I is, suh, just like you tole' me."

Hollins, anchored in place, could not move. Haynie and Stewart each grabbed him by an arm, jerked him around, and marched him back into the house. Hollins's boots barely touching the floor.

Berrien rushed forward in protest. "See here!" he shouted, "What is the meaning of this? Who are you people? Clifford, fetch the shotgun! Immediately!"

Haynie nodded at Berrien. "Gerhard, take him into another room and sit on him until I get there."

"*Ja,*" Gerhard said, and shouldered a sputtering Berrien from the room.

Cora cried out and ran after them.

Lila stood fascinated by the scene before her.

Haynie looked at her. "Try and get Cora to go home with you. For her own good."

He turned to Noch. "George, thank you. As soon as I get Hollins settled down, I'll take that leather case. I would appreciate it if you would see Lila and Cora home."

Noch followed Haynie and Stewart as they muscled Hollins into the parlor.

"I must admit," Noch said, "As we neared this place I experienced an agitation which I assumed was fear. However, once our charade commenced, I discovered it wasn't alarm I was feeling, merely stage fright. As I got into the role I rather enjoyed it."

Haynie pushed Hollins deep into a chair.

Noch smiled. "It would appear that I played my part rather well," he said passing the leather pouch to Haynie.

67

Popes Creek, Maryland
May 1, 1869

Following fits of screaming and crying, Cora Clemson reluctantly consented to leave with Lila and George Noch.

"She only agreed to come to get me away from her man," Lila explained.

Haynie pushed a chair beside Hollins's seat and sat down. Silas Wallis planted himself beside the doorway, arms folded across his chest.

Hollins was a terrified man without the strength to stand. His fingers clawed into the chair arms, thrusting his body deeper into the seat to escape Haynie's hulking presence. Breath came to him in short gasps; bulging eyes darted around the room.

Leaning close, Haynie spoke softly. "It is clear that you realize how much trouble you are in. In case you have forgotten me, I am Haynie McKenna of the state oyster police. You are the bastard responsible for the murder of my younger brother, Caleb McKenna, among others."

Haynie tilted his head toward Wallis. "You know Colonel Silas Wallis, the man who befriended you. You are responsible for the kidnapping of his son, the theft of his money and the death of his wife."

Hollins cringed.

"You have a lot to answer for, Mister Hollins."

With a shake of his head, Hollins denied everything.

Haynie's words grew sharper. "Captain Sewell of the Virginia authorities is talking to the Negroes being kept here, as they are citizens of that state. When I'm finished with you, we'll see what Simon Berrien has to say about all this."

Hollins rasped. "You have no proof—of anything."

Haynie produced the leather pouch. "It won't be difficult to show that the documents you brought here are fraudulent. And your claim of employment with the national government's Freedmen's Bureau is a lie."

He set the pouch on the floor next to his chair.

"Simon Berrien will quickly realize that we are not interested in him and his small-time confidence game. I expect he will act surprised and shocked. Likely, he will say that he had no idea you were not the government official you claimed to be. He will say he was taken in by you and then construct a story to fit that lie. That's what I would do in his place."

Haynie put his mouth to Hollins's ear. "Very soon you will be going to prison—alone," he whispered.

"Prison!" Hollins gasped.

"Or worse, the gallows. Mooney will run away leaving you to swing alone. "

A panicky Hollins squirmed in his chair.

Haynie straightened and said, "What do you think Horace Mooney is going to say when we speak to him? I doubt he will admit sharing the $75,000 dollars in ransom which *you* demanded of, and received from, Colonel Wallis."

Hollins breath came in short gasps, his fingers digging deeper into the chair fabric. "No! No! No!" he cried.

"It looks to me like you are the only one with dirty hands in each of these schemes. You brought that assassin, Rat, into Somerset County and left him there to kill five people. Five murders that you will pay for. I'm afraid you are done for. Unless..."

Hollins gulped. "Unless—what?"

"Unless you can show that you were acting on Mooney's orders."

Hollins opened his mouth to speak and then stopped.

Haynie pressed forward. "How much of the ransom money did Mooney get? Maybe you kept all of it."

Hollins looked from Haynie to Wallis and his resistance collapsed.

"It was all her idea. For the rebellion, they said."

"By 'her', you mean Mooney's wife, Grace."

Hollins nodded.

"How much of the $75,000 did you keep for yourself?"

Hollins stared straight ahead.

"You'd better tell us the truth. Mooney's going to say you took it all and we'll have no choice but to—"

Hollins's head dropped to his chest. "$25, 000," he mumbled."

Haynie looked at Wallis and nodded. *We're going to get what we need.*

Hollins raised his head. "How's this going to help me?"

"You show us that Mooney and Grace were running the show. That they are the ones who hired Rat and told him what to do; they'll be the ones standing trial for murder, not you."

"It was them who killed that man she married, Stringfellow," Hollins blurted. "I had nothing to do with that."

"How do you know they killed the old man? The authorities called it an accident. They believe he fell overboard during a drunken turn around the deck."

"Mooney bragged to me about it. Any backbone he's got comes from Grace, so he's trying to make out to be more dangerous than he really is. Grace got the old guy drunk—which wasn't real hard, from what I hear. She took him out on the deck for some air; Mooney showed up and the two of them pitched the old sot over the side.

"Mooney crowed about how she dragged him straightaway to her bed and was like a wild woman. He says her antics were heated by the idea that old Stringfellow was drowning as they romped in his bed."

Hollins sagged back. "You won't get them." He released the chair and pointed a finger toward his head. "She's dotty, and he's crafty enough to put it all on her, if it comes down to that."

"Who gave you your orders? Mooney or Grace?"

"Mooney—of course. We were supposed to be a military unit; trying to raise money to continue the rebellion. No woman can issue military orders to a man. No doubt she let him have what for when they were alone, but she never said anything to the rest of us."

"How'd you first meet Jeremy Coates, the killer who called himself, Rat?"

Hollins glanced around. "It was right here in this room. Someone sent him—Rat—to Mooney after the war. Rat claimed he was a sharpshooter with Quantrill, out in Missouri. When he showed up here, and Mooney learned he grew up on the Eastern Shore—notice I didn't say 'raised up'; nobody raised him—Mooney told me to take him over to Somerset County. I took him to Gastineau—the sheriff— and left him. Had nothing more to do with him."

Haynie leaned in. "You took him to meet Sheriff Gastineau."

Hollins nodded.

"Rat knew you as Mister Brown, and Gastineau as Mister Green."

"What? How'd you know those names?"

"Rat told me everything before he died."

"That man was pure evil." Hollins slowly shook his head. "I would never figure him to talk."

Hollins straightened a stricken look on his face. "What the hell did you do to him, to make him spill?"

Haynie gave Hollins a minute to think about what might have befallen Rat to make him talk. If a hired assassin could not withstand Haynie's tactics, what chance did a man like Hollins have?

"Rat said it was you who gave the order to kill my brother."

"No sir! If it was anyone, it was Gastineau. But I believe that crazy bastard did all those killings on his own."

"The bailiff in Crisfield, Squire Towne."

"It was Rat. I didn't know about any of them until they were done."

"Gastineau."

"Dammit, I been telling you, Rat did them on his own. He was there, in Crisfield, when you and the bailiff were leading the Drumm brothers off to jail. I know he liked killing—any excuse would do. His mind was not right from all the laudanum. He figured that if those two stayed in jail they would tell about him. He just up and killed the bailiff and broke the Drumms out."

"Why didn't he just kill the Drumms and be done with it?"

Hollins shrugged. "I'm surprised he didn't. He was a lazy sort, likely afraid he'd have to take up their load. If anyone gave him orders, it was Gastineau—he had the same rank as me major. It was him who gave Rat all his orders. Guess they had a falling out and Rat did him in."

Haynie pressed. "Rat took a money belt off of Gastineau after he killed him. It had a wad of money in it that Rat said should be his. He believed it to be payment for killing Squire Towne and my brother." Haynie met Hollins's eyes. "And money for killing me; which, as we know, he never earned."

Hollins was rigid; his eyes searched wildly around the room.

Haynie snarled. "Rat said it was you gave the order to have me killed."

"That's a damn lie, and I can prove it."

"Let's hear it."

Hollins glanced at Silas Wallis. "Those killings all happened within a few days; all the while I was staying close to him on account of his boy being shanghaied. No way for me to issue any orders, or even know about them 'til they was done."

He turned back to Haynie. "Look here," he pleaded, "It makes no sense for us to give Rat an order to kill those boys in the paddy shack. They were worth nothing to us dead. And, here's another thing, Gastineau refused to take orders from me—only from Mooney. If any of those killings was ordered, it came from Mooney to Gastineau. Anything like that was between them. If I'd known back then there was killings, I'd a left 'em for sure."

Hollins sagged deeper into the chair. "It all makes a good story; but it's me against the two of them—Mooney and his crazy wife. There's no way to prove that I even knew those two. I was afraid to keep copies of any wires we sent. I burned 'em."

Haynie let Hollins sweat some before saying, "That's not exactly right. We have some papers and a tintype, showing that at least some of what you're saying is the truth. The tintype shows a group of you in your Reb uniforms. You and Gastineau are standing on either side of Mooney who is wearing the uniform of a cavalry colonel. It looks like the gathering of a regimental staff. Grace is not in the picture."

Hollins brightened. "I forgot about tintypes. There are more, somewhere. He loved to have his picture taken in that uniform."

"And we have the ransom note you wrote along with the carpet bag that you carried the ransom money in."

Hollins sagged. "That only digs me in deeper. How's that gonna help get Mooney?"

"It shows what you're saying is true—we got the carpet bag from this house."

Haynie pointed up. "It was upstairs, in the closet of their bedroom."

"But—"

"Do you remember when you and Mooney came here a few months back?"

Hollins nodded.

"Mooney asked the caretaker what had become of the bag. Mister Hopkins will testify that Mooney claimed the bag was his."

"I warned him we should stay out of Maryland." Hollins glanced at Haynie. "The damn fool had you figured for a rube. Guess he's in for a surprise."

Captain Stewart appeared in the doorway, and Haynie waved him into the room.

"Captain Stewart, this is Mister Hollins. He has given an interesting account of the activities of Horace J. Mooney of Virginia. Later today, I'll go to the county judge here and get the necessary warrants. Among them will be one for Mooney's arrest."

Stewart nodded. "It'll be my pleasure to go collect him. The darkies all want to go home to Virginia. Berrien and Mooney threatened them and whipped them to make certain they played their part in this fraud. Despite what it says on the sign out front, there is no school here. And we already know that there never was a Redemption Church of America in Mecklenburg County."

Haynie nodded. "If you'll ask Gerhard to come in and sit with Hollins, I'll join you in with Berrien. We'll see what he has to say about Mooney and this one."

68

Annapolis, Maryland
June 3, 1869

Hunter Davidson looked across his desk. "Any chance you will reconsider?"

"I'm sorry, sir," Haynie replied, "but no."

"The service can't afford to lose such a fine officer." Davidson studied Haynie for his reaction as he said, "Are you aware that the grand jury down in Talbot County is gunning for me?"

Haynie nodded. "There's been some talk. Dereliction of duty. You, for God's sake."

"I don't set much store in it. Some watermen hollering that the Oyster Navy is not protecting them from poachers. Still, if it comes to that, and I leave, you would be in line to sit behind this desk."

"I have thought of that and to be honest, sir, that is the main reason I have decided to leave at this time."

Stunned, Davidson rocked back in his chair, his mind churning. "Well—I—I'm flummoxed, Captain. Are you saying that you have no wish to succeed me?"

"None."

Davidson gestured with his hands, the palms turned up. "Would you please explain that. I'm at a loss..."

"There was some talk about the Talbot County fuss, a while ago. I took little notice of it, but of late, it has been getting louder. It got me to thinking some more about the politics we have to deal with. If the politicians can come after you, a man who has given so much to this state, what chance would I have in that chair?"

Davidson opened his mouth to speak, but was cut off.

"There is no way I could survive the politics of your job, and the man who replaces you is most likely to be beholden to someone else. If I leave now, maybe you will have a say in naming the man who replaces me."

"Is that all of it?"

"Sir?"

"Nothing more behind you leaving?"

Haynie shook his head. "Why?"

Davidson leaned forward. "The sheriff down at Popes Creek is raising some hell about the Oyster Navy stirring up trouble down there. He is bitter because we arrested some folks on charges that have nothing to do with watermen, or the water. I'm certain you have heard the talk."

Haynie shifted in his chair. "Yes sir."

"There are some who say the *Emma Dunn* and her crew should have been plying the bay, not tied up to a wharf, miles from it. A few of my friends are concerned that your actions in Popes Creek gives more weight to the Talbot County charges. Is that what's behind this?"

"I'm afraid that what happened at Popes Creek could hurt you, and I'm sorry for that."

"Still, you believe it was the right thing."

"Yes sir. It is something that had to be done and I saw no other way to do it."

"I agree that it needed doing. You did a hell of a job snaring those scoundrels. A lawman cannot hesitate to do what's right because he might hurt somebody's feelings. Is it likely that sheriff would have rounded up that gang if you'd left it up to him?"

Haynie shook his head. "Not likely, sir."

"Damn unlikely, from what I hear. What has become of that bunch of crooks? Are they all in jail?"

"Captain Stewart found Horace Mooney in Staunton. The Commonwealth of Virginia is getting ready to send him back here. Hollins was right about the woman. Stewart says she's crazy as a coot. As for Mooney, he claimed that all the killings came from lawful orders he received during wartime. His story is that his wife, Grace, was a Reb spy whose orders came from high up in the Confederate government. With a straight face, he said that Robert E. Lee's surrender at Appomattox was just a trick to fool the Yankees while the Rebs regrouped on the sly under Mooney's command. That is where it sets, for now. He'll have to change his story when he gets up here and finds out that Hollins will get in the chair and say it was him, not Grace Stringfellow, giving all the orders."

"What about that fellow Berrien?"

"He only hooked up with Mooney and Hollins a few months ago. Wasn't around for the killings. He was quick to point a finger at Mooney as the boss of the confidence game they were running in Popes Creek."

"Instead of whining about it, that sheriff should be thankful you stepped in. He was in real deep water and didn't know it."

Both men lapsed into a thoughtful silence. Eventually Davidson said, "Sometime ago I was shown a magazine story written by Missus McKenna. It was quite well done. You must be very proud of her."

"I am. Though, I must admit it took some prodding before I figured that out."

"It was also mentioned that Missus McKenna recently traveled to New York for a women's rights convention."

Haynie nodded.

"I wouldn't have guessed that you were so liberal in your thinking."

"Neither would I, sir." Haynie shrugged. "Things might be different if I had been home more. But, she's a strong woman so maybe not."

"I hope that Missus McKenna's liberation doesn't cause you any grief. Many men take offense at such activity. Men of importance."

"I doubt that will be a concern where I am headed."

Davidson waited.

"Do you recall Percy Overton, the colored man we found hiding on a drudger—the *Davy Jones*—last winter?"

"I recollect that he was wanted for shooting a white man. I believe you were troubled about sending him back to South Carolina."

"I've done a lot of tossing and turning since that day. It haunts me. If I had the courage to look into it, I'm afraid I would find that, just as he told me, he was strung up without ever setting foot in a courtroom."

"Has that got you to thinking of reading for the law, then? Help others like him in court?"

Haynie shook his head. "I already tried that. Can you see me sitting in a court room all day?"

Davidson laughed.

"Coloreds are getting hung, or beaten, or run off without ever getting to court. A lawyer can't help with that. Overton said something that has stuck with me—about this country being long on law and short on justice. And he's right. When men who swore to keep the law straight, twist it around to use as a club against other folks, justice is an illusion."

"You're speaking now, of the South, where many county sheriffs believe their duty is to the Ku Klux. To help keep the coloreds in their place."

Haynie said, "Not all twisted lawmen are from below the Mason-Dixon line."

"True. However, that seems to be where the most despicable of them are to be found. As you likely know, the Ku Klux got its start in Pulaski, Tennessee, around the time it became clear the war was lost. I guess groups of men galloping around; terrorizing the countryside made them feel like the war was not over.

"General Forrest was the first Grand Wizard and even he got so fed up with the lawlessness. A few months back he ordered the Ku Klux to disband in Tennessee."

Haynie nodded. "It was a noble effort on his part, but I doubt states, such as Mississippi and South Carolina, are going to pay attention to what he says. Hiding under bedsheets and terrifying helpless folks, appeals to a certain kind of man. I keep trying to imagine what it must be like to live your life frightened that at any moment a gang may show up at your door with a noose to hang you in front of your wife and children. Jesus."

"Well sir, how do you see yourself helping the Percy Overtons of this nation?"

"I believe it's time to get off the water. I expect to join up with the U.S. Marshals."

Suggested Reading

Two non-fiction books are recommended for those interested in exploring the history of these times.

The Oyster Wars of The Chesapeake Bay—John Wennersten.

Maryland's Oyster Navy *The First Fifty Years*—Norman H. Plummer

Museums of Interest

Chesapeake Bay Maritime Museum—213 N. Talbot St., St. Michaels, MD 21663
(410) 745-2916 www.cbmm.org

Richardson Maritime Museum—401 High St., Cambridge, MD 21613
(410) 221-1871

Ruark Boat Works—Maryland Avenue & Hayward St., Cambridge, MD
Affiliated with Richardson Museum.

Private Bay Restoration Organizations

Oyster Recovery Partnership—www.oysterrecovery.org

Chesapeake Bay Foundation *Save The Bay*—www.cbf.org

CPSIA information can be obtained at www.ICGtesting.com
Printed in the USA
BVOW080116210912

301001BV00001B/6/P

9 781450 726351